Staying the COURSE

BETTE PRATT

WestBow Press books may be ordered through booksellers or by contacting:

WestBow Press
A Division of Thomas Nelson & Zondervan
1663 Liberty Drive
Bloomington, IN 47403
www.westbowpress.com
844-714-3454

ISBN: 978-1-6642-0772-1 (sc)
ISBN: 978-1-6642-0775-2 (hc)
ISBN: 978-1-6642-0771-4 (e)

Library of Congress Control Number: 2020919209

Print information available on the last page.

WestBow Press rev. date: 10/20/2020

ONE

JOEL'S EYES TOOK ON SAUCER PROPORTIONS; HIS MOUTH OPENED AUTOMATICALLY then closed around the last forkful from his plate. The look on his dad's face struck him dumb. Thad's eyes blazed his countenance, horrific. He had a fork full of food but it clattered to his plate, sending bits of food everywhere. He grabbed a breath and roared, "Get out! I don't ever want to see your face again! And even more, I can't stand your mouth! You spout that *God* stuff at me all the time! I won't hear it again!"

Thad didn't notice the food on his clothes or on the table. He pounded his fist so hard his utensils danced, and his water glass bounced and tipped, spilling water on the table. He put actions to his words, never giving Joel a chance to speak. Slamming both fists onto the table, his boots thundering on the floor, he sprang from his chair. It clattered to the floor as he lunged at his son to his left.

Joel managed a few chews. His eyes grew even wider, and he nearly choked as he convulsively tried to swallow, realizing what his dad's actions meant. Everything happened so fast Joel only had the chance to drop his fork which clattered onto his plate and added to the noise and chaos in the kitchen. He sat at the table with his ankles crossed, he couldn't stand. As Thad's huge hand came at him his whole body froze.

Joel's mom sat across the table silent, glaring at him, her grown son, as if he were a child or a rebellious teenager. Leslie, his sixteen-year-old sister cringed, tears welled in her eyes. She was frightened by their dad's words and actions, but as Thad lunged from his chair, she bolted from the kitchen. Thad made all the noise, Eleanor didn't even acknowledge her daughter. She had never taken the side of her children when her husband was in a rage; tonight was no different. She didn't make a sound as Thad's huge hand wrapped around Joel's upper arm.

Joel managed to swallow as the beefy hand circled his upper arm and closed around it. Thad's hand lifted him from the chair! Joel, an adult, and no lightweight, was moving! Where did Thad get his strength? There wasn't time to push back from the table. The chair tottered; then crashed to the floor between the two men.

Joel tried to get his feet under him, but his dad dragged him backwards and sideways. His boot heel caught the edge of the large living room rug and pulled it along, doubling it over. The bunching rug sent furniture careening around the living room, and his boot kept connecting haphazardly with furniture along the way. Finally, the heavy rug and the triangle it made were so large that it came out from under his heel, but the chaos remained. No one followed behind to straighten the rug or right the furniture. Thad, in a rage, just kept dragging his son from the kitchen, across the living room towards the front door, but never looked behind him at the destruction he caused.

As the noise and chaos continued, Joel was glad he'd changed from his dress shoes to his boots. He winced as several pieces of large living room furniture hit him. In the hallway his foot connected with a curved leg of his mom's antique settee and nearly toppled it. It wobbled precariously, but remained standing. However, the seat had several things on it that fell onto his legs and feet. One large, heavy box toppled off, landing squarely on his shin, radiating pain through his entire leg. He stifled a groan.

Still relentless, Thad kept dragging him. He finally reached the front door. He yanked it open so hard it crashed against the wall. The impact of the door on the wall bounced the mirror off its hook; it crashed onto the top edge of the settee that had just righted itself. The mirror shattered, raining hundreds of sharp shards of glass down on Joel's head and onto his clothes, some even rained down on Thad, but he paid no attention. He had one goal – to get Joel outside the door of his house.

The instant he heard the mirror hit the settee, Joel closed his mouth tightly. Many tiny pieces of glass hit his face and neck and nestled in his hair. One large shard came hurdling towards his right eye. He saw it an instant before it hit him and managed to shut his eyes and turn his head. It pierced the skin only centimeters from the corner of his eye. Another groan welled up in his throat. The shard was large and heavy enough that it didn't stay embedded in his flesh, but fell away as soon as it struck. It left a deep puncture. The blood from his temple was instantaneous and the pain profound.

Thad never let go of his son. He just took another step, grunted, took another step over the threshold and with all his strength, flung his son onto the small porch. Joel's lower legs slammed into the door frame as he went through. With his hand free, Thad shook himself, sending more glass onto Joel. Joel's eyes were still closed, but he felt the temperature change that sent goose bumps up his back. The air was much colder as he landed only inches from the edge of the porch. His body bounced on the hard, unforgiving planks, another groan came from deep inside. He landed hard on his back and shoulder, forcing the breath from his lungs.

The door slammed and the deadbolt snapped. Thad stomped heavily through the glass on the bare wood floor, crunching the pieces even smaller. The heavy oak door muffled any words, but Thad started swearing to color the air blue. When in a rage the foul language was usually emphasized by fist punches and foot stomps or kicks. There were many pieces of furniture in the house with gouges in them from Thad's boots over the years.

Joel lay as he landed. His heart seemed to stop and his lungs screamed for oxygen. It seemed like long minutes before he could pull in a breath. As he tried to drag in a breath, he thought it strange that once his dad grabbed his arm he only grunted, but didn't speak. Still, until now, he'd never thrown him out, only demanded he get out of sight. Thad had used his belt on occasion, but mostly his fists or a solid back hand across his mouth, sometimes enough to cause a nosebleed or a cut lip. He'd had many black eyes and bruises from Thad's huge hand.

Because Joel's back took the brunt of his fall, he wiggled his toes, nothing snapped or felt numb. His legs moved normally although with a great deal of pain. He decided he was still in one piece. He hadn't hit his head, it had only snapped like a whiplash. The puncture still bled, but with all the pain all over his body, he wasn't thinking clearly. He raised his arm and pushed his sweatshirt sleeve against the hole, only then realizing how much his arm hurt from his dad's crushing strength and his shoulder hurt from hitting the floor.

"I can picture the black-and-blue bruise now." He sighed. "That'll be nothing to what this place on my face'll look like."

A few seconds later he was able to fill his lungs and remembered his nose was dripping because of the cold when he changed clothes earlier. He'd used a handkerchief to wipe his nose and stuck it in his back pocket then. Since he could finally breathe normally, he rolled slowly away from the edge of the porch onto his side and pulled the soiled hanky from his pocket. That was better than his hoodie sleeve to stop the bleeding from the puncture.

The change in position made him realize he had a massive pounding behind his eye. The puncture was so close to his eye that he couldn't open it. Even after wiping his eyelid it was hard to force his eye open. When he finally did, his vision was blurry. Perhaps that would clear up soon. Bleeding from his temple was much better than a puncture to his eye! That would have meant a trip to the ER.

Any trip to the ER meant money spent he didn't have. He was on his own since he was on the wrong side of the door. That brought another stark realization; the keys to his car were also on the other side of that door. He couldn't have gotten to the ER! His car was worthless without his keys.

His next breath didn't hurt, but was icy cold. Really, only his back, his arm where his dad's hand had squeezed, and his temple hurt. The pain in his shins had lessened. He put one hand on the floor to push himself up, but stayed on his knees for a bit longer. He still needed his other hand to hold the hanky to his head. However, the pounding in his temple changed to a headache behind his eyes and he felt light-headed, along with the blurry vision. The hanky was doing its job beside his eye, but the place hurt terribly; he hoped it wouldn't develop into a migraine. Still on his knees he willed strength into his body.

Since his dad had walked away from the door there was no reason he had to rush off. Without his car, where could he go? The house was in the country, several miles from the closest suburb. Without his keys, he'd have to walk. The closest place, the most logical was his Aunt Lucy's, in the closest suburb, but several miles away. Without a coat or his car he was in a bad predicament! A long sigh escaped.

Still holding the hanky to his temple, he stayed on his knees for several more minutes, hoping the light-headedness and the blurred vision would leave. At least his eye stayed open. He must look awful! His cheek was puckered and his hand was sticky. His hoodie was probably ruined. Before he covered the puncture, a small puddle had pooled on one of the porch boards. Just then a cold wind swirled around the side of the house so penetrating that he shivered. It was definitely colder outside than inside.

Holding the hanky beside his eye, he looked at the closed door, pulled in another deep breath and whispered, "Bye, Dad, Mom, I love you because you're my parents, but I guess I'll never see you again. Not unless something drastically changes in your house and your hearts. Lord God, I pray for that day! May it be soon." He bent over, tears slid down his cheeks, but he couldn't stop them, as he added, "Oh, God, keep my sister safe! My Father, she's only sixteen and Dad could hurt her so badly!"

The cloth was stuck to his temple so Joel took a minute to look around. The sun was gone, evening and dark heavy clouds had moved in, covering any stars and the moon if it was even up. The house sat alone on a country road, his dad didn't want a security light outside, even though the house sat so far from the road. That meant that the only light came from inside the house. Thad hadn't turned on any lights between the kitchen and the door, so it was dark on the porch. It was fall, only a few weeks until Thanksgiving, the days were much shorter, and daylight saving ended soon, but the evenings were short. It was that bleak time of year, no colored leaves or green grass, but there was no snow on the ground.

A strong gust swirled around him, penetrating the zip-up hoodie he'd pulled on when he changed clothes, preparing to spend the time after supper in his room studying. Of course he couldn't have grabbed his coat on his dad's frantic march to the front door. Now with the cold wind, Joel's body quaked. He quickly let go of the cloth that stuck to his temple, but his hands shook so much he had trouble zipping the hoodie. He jerked up the hood, hoping to keep the wind from going down his back because he only had a T shirt under it. It was too dark to see what his sleeve looked like, but it stuck to his wrist.

When he came home from the university, he'd changed out of his good 'professor' clothes. He hung his slacks and jacket in his closet and his tie with the others, but left his button-down shirt on the bed. He slid on his better jeans and pulled on his prized leather boots that his dad had given him during a short season of good will, perhaps for Christmas last year. Goodwill and Thad Lawson rarely went in the same sentence. The upstairs at the house was always cooler than downstairs, so he pulled on the hoodie.

His wallet with all his money, his driver's license and other important cards was in his back pocket. He was very glad; sometimes he left his wallet on his desk when he changed clothes. Before he buckled his belt he put his phone carrier on the belt, but failed to put the phone back in it. His heart sank, another groan started deep in his chest; his briefcase, lesson plans, his dissertation notes and his laptop with his completed chapters were on his desk in his room where he'd been studying until his mom announced supper.

He looked at the door again; he couldn't get back in without his keys, he had them in his hand when he came inside and laid them on the hall table when he hung his coat in the closet. He planned to stay here after supper to study and do lesson plans for his class in the morning, but if he had known what would happen after supper, he wouldn't have come to the house so early – maybe not at all. He never wanted a confrontation with his dad. All he ever wanted was to show the man his need for the Savior. He had tried again at the supper table, but this was the result. Tears of defeat stung his eyes. It seemed he had failed in his most important mission.

After all that noise and commotion during and after supper, now the house was eerily quiet. He heard nothing from behind the door. All that noise had also silenced any sounds outside. It was too cold for some creatures, too dark for others. Joel felt really alone.

Still on his knees, he sighed. His final semester at the university was only a few weeks old. He'd hoped to make it through his schooling before his dad did something, but it hadn't happened. No one could have predicted he'd be outside the locked door. After this semester and his approved dissertation, he would be free to pursue his life's work. He'd been offered a professorship at his *alma mater* and at another small university in another state, but now, he was here, in this city and homeless, with one set of clothes and no keys for his car. He pulled in a deep breath and let it out on a long sigh. Humanly speaking, the situation was hopeless.

Still kneeling, he assessed what he had – or didn't have. When he changed clothes he laid his cell phone on his desk upstairs, attached his phone carrier on his belt, but forgot to put the phone in it. He should never have laid either his keys or his phone down. Of course, he couldn't have known that. He owned both the car and the phone, he had saved his money for months to pay cash for that car and he had purchased the phone so he could put class notes and the apps that he wanted on it and his parents couldn't tell him he couldn't because his dad had paid for the plan. Any clothes, his Bible, his notes for his dissertation and his class preparations were in the room he'd called his own on the second floor of this house.

He stared at the bolted door. One set of clothes wasn't near enough. The university dress code for faculty was much higher than what he had on and what money he had wouldn't supply a wardrobe of any size. As he shivered, he realized it wouldn't buy a winter coat – the warm coat that hung in the hall closet did him no good on the other side of the locked door.

The hanky stayed stuck on his face, the bleeding had stopped, so he put both hands down on the planks and with some effort staggered to his feet. For being only twenty-five years old, he had several fresh aches and pains, evidenced by a few snaps and twinges, but nothing appeared broken. Still close to the door, he wished the headache would go away. He was glad the light-headedness and blurred vision only lasted a few minutes. He was sure he didn't have a concussion since his head hadn't hit anything, only bounced like a whip-lash.

"What should I do? It'll be so late if I walk to Auntie's she'll be in bed with the door locked. Besides, without a coat I'll be frozen long before I get there." Film covered his eyes. "I locked my car! I can't even sit in it to get warm!"

However, before he moved he heard lighter steps running to the door and crunching through the shards of the broken mirror. *Oh, no! What now?* Was his dad coming to see if he was still there? As he listened longer, he realized it couldn't be his dad; the steps were too light and moving too fast for that. Dad never moved that fast any more. It wasn't his mom, either.

The dead bolt snapped, the door opened a crack and a head appeared. His sister, Leslie whispered, "Joel, oh, wow! You've been bleeding! Are you okay? It was the mirror, wasn't it?" They both heard their dad's recliner squeak, so she held out her hands and said, "I grabbed your Bible and your phone from upstairs and here are your car keys. I'm sorry that's all I could grab, but at least you can get to Auntie's."

Joel held out both hands, not so much to take the things his sister held, but to hug her. He was so relieved to get the keys. He did put his hands on her shoulders and said, "Thanks, Sis, thanks so much. I love you." Then he quickly took the things. They both heard another heavy thump from the living room.

Leslie pulled her hands back and took hold of the door, but she whispered, "I love you, too, Bro. Take care of yourself. Maybe we can see each other at Auntie's. If I live that long!" They both heard their dad's recliner thump. He'd brought it to a sitting position and stomped his feet on the living room floor, he was never a quiet man.

Realizing as he looked at the few things in his hands, and remembering what was still upstairs, Joel blurted out, "Sis, how can I stay in school?"

"You will, God will supply, I know it. Stay the course, as Grampa says." Leslie pulled in a breath. They both heard their dad's heavy foot on the hardwood floor beside the living room rug and knew he would soon be in the hallway. "Gotta go! See you!"

"Yes, see you, Sis. God keep you safe!"

The door went shut nearly in his face, but the deadbolt didn't snap. He was sure his dad was in the hall by now, he groaned, what would he do to Leslie? He couldn't help her. "Oh, my Father, keep my little sister safe!" he agonized. "That man could hurt her so badly! God, put Your hedge around her – please!"

Now that he had his keys and couldn't intervene in what happened on the other side of the door, Joel turned and stepped off the porch onto the step. As his right foot hit the ground from the step, his knee buckled and his back spasmed, but he didn't go down. He gritted his teeth and groaned a bit. Now that he'd jolted his body there were a few other pains he noticed, especially his legs where they'd hit the door frame and his arm where his dad had grabbed him, but he determined to ignore those places. Life went on, he'd hurt worse before, even from his dad's hand or his belt and he'd survived, so this was nothing new. Life at Thad Lawson's house could be a very traumatic experience for his children.

Farther away from the protection of the house, the wind across the open field was stronger and colder, making his body shiver convulsively. He clutched his Bible to his chest and wrapped his other arm around himself. It couldn't have happened, but he wished Leslie could have grabbed his winter coat. It wasn't that old, he'd bought it last year, but it would have taken too long to open the closet door.

He couldn't run, he hurt too badly, but he hurried to his car. His mom's car blocked some of the wind, so he pushed his phone into the carrier and wished Leslie had grabbed the charger when she'd gotten his Bible. The phone wasn't much good if it was dead and he'd had it on all day, writing notes to use for his dissertation. He could go to the phone store and buy another charger, but that would be money spent he could better spend on something else.

Friday had been payday, most of it went in his checking account, and his was the only name on the account. He was sure his dad wasn't above trying to take over his bank account if he could. However, his dad was notorious in town he couldn't impersonate Joel – ever. No one had ever said the phrase 'Like father, like son'.

With his dad's statement and actions, he was truly on his own. There would be no bed or meals at this address for him ever again. His mom would not intervene, she never had in the past, and she wouldn't change, not with the expression he'd seen on her face at the table. It hurt him to think that might be the last view of her face he'd ever have.

His car was down the driveway beyond his mom's car. Limping a little, his teeth chattering, he hurried to it as fast as he could. He wasn't sure if his dad remembered he owned it or if he thought he could leave him totally destitute without his keys. The car was not new enough for a remote opener, but he quickly inserted the key and slid behind the wheel. He had the car running before he closed the door. He was glad to be out of the wind. He closed the car door, and felt instant relief from the cold. Now he faced away from the house, but saw only the darkness of night.

Into the dark and stillness, he said, "Father, God keep Leslie safe! Oh, my, she's only sixteen, but big enough Dad could do anything to her!"

Leslie closed and locked the door, turned away, but still stood beside the hall table when her dad stormed out of the living room, coming between her and any escape. His eyes looked lethal enough that if they were the shards of glass, she would be dead now! She cringed with every step he took as he waded through the mirror glass crunching under his feet. His hands balled into fists at his sides. His eyes blazing, he grabbed Leslie's arm in a vice-like grip. She knew she'd have a hand-sized bruise there really soon.

Even though he'd just finished supper, his fowl, beer breath hit her in the face as he snarled, "Did you give that man his keys?"

Thad shook her so hard, Leslie had to grab a breath, "Yes, Dad, I gave Joel his keys – and his phone – and his Bible." Glad for how strong her voice was, she added, "They are all his, he had a right to them. I know you didn't want him to have them, but they are his, he bought them all, so I got them and gave them…."

Angry, he didn't let her finish speaking before he flung her away. She spun around and her shoulder hit the door very hard. Her hand smacked the door knob; she groaned but didn't go down. Had she fallen, the sharp glass shards could have cut her quite severely. She bit her bottom lip to keep from crying out. Whenever he did something to either of his children it infuriated him if they cried. Now that her dad had thrown Joel out, she must defend herself against him. How? She had no idea! He was so much bigger, she was sure she was at his mercy.

Silently, she added, *As convenient as his keys were why didn't you grab them after you threw Joel out? They were right there on the table.*

She still leaned against the door, but made sure she watched his every move. The man was twice her size and very muscular, she'd never seen him work out, but he surely must to have all those huge muscles! Her dad took another step towards her. She tried not to cringe, but it was hard not to show fear. He hissed and some of the spittle landed on her sweatshirt. She felt it land and tried not to make a face, but kept her eyes glued to her dad's face.

Grabbing a breath, he hissed, "You… you little beast! If you were eighteen I'd throw you out, too! You go along with your brother…"

Trying not to look at the disgusting spot on her sweatshirt, but knowing she'd have to scrub that spot very soon to get the awful stuff off, she said, "Yes, Dad, I do. He's never done anything wrong to you. You hate him because he's not doing what you want him to. And he tells you about God's love. Neither of us does what you want and you hate us both. We both love God and so we try to please Him."

The man's face contorted in rage. His feet continued to crunch the glass, his weight going from one foot to the other. He couldn't seem to stand still, both hands were flexing into fists; he always became more agitated when either of the children mentioned God. He let out another breath and made some noise that Leslie was sure was something she didn't want to hear. She knew that if he could, he'd breathe fire on her.

He raised his right fist, but uncurled one finger and pointed to the stairs as he snarled, "Get out of my sight!"

"Yes, Dad, I'll be glad to," she murmured with relief.

Glad he'd sent her away with only a few bruises and still on her feet, Leslie ran passed him and never stopped until she was up the stairs and out of sight. His massive hands flexing into fists and his feet crushing and grinding the glass shards, he followed her to the foot of the stairs, but stayed at the foot of the stairs watching until she disappeared. She was never sure he wouldn't hit her, even though he never had punched her, or used his belt; he had slapped her hard enough to leave bruises, so she tried not to be that close to him – ever.

She breathed a sigh of relief and rushed in the bathroom to wash off the awful spittle. When the sweatshirt was cleaned as much as she could, she hurried across the hall and closed her bedroom door. She crossed into Joel's room, quietly closed his door and rushed around the bed to turn on his bedside lamp, hoping, since it was on the other side of the bed that it wouldn't shine under the door enough for her dad to see it. If there was any possible way, she would see that Joel had his things. Fortunately, she had her phone in her jeans pocket, she could text him.

Without Joel as a buffer, how long could she last in the same house with her dad? He seemed more... violent... more... angry and her mom never stopped him. He was never angry with her, but she always agreed with him or kept quiet, no matter what he did or who he did it to. Even her own children took a far distant place from her husband. Leslie always wondered; weren't mothers supposed to defend their children? Hers surely hadn't! Not ever!

While she mulled over her home situation, wondering how their dad could be so cruel, she was never still. If her dad found her in Joel's room, she knew beyond any doubt she'd feel the end of his belt. He had never whipped her, but he had Joel many times until only a few years ago, now he was gone! She knew she was disobeying her dad's wishes to leave her brother destitute and homeless. She didn't care; she'd do everything for Joel! She knew he'd often defended her and kept her safe from her dad's wrath and actions, taking the back-hand or a belt whipping when she knew her dad had meant it for her.

She couldn't help make a little noise, some places of the bedroom floors made noise, but she worked hard to be quiet. In this awful mood he might throw her around again, hit her or even undo his belt and whip her. Just the thought made her shudder. It didn't matter, she'd chance it! Joel deserved every break she could give him. She was determined to stay the course.

She rarely came all the way into Joel's room, she had no reason to. She stood by the bed and looked around to see what she could use. Joel had several backpacks, so she found two large ones. She emptied his dresser into one and a half. The rest of the space she filled with little things from his desk, including his phone charger. She pulled out her phone and sent Joel a text.

As soon as she did, she scooped up his laptop; the papers on his desk she knew were his notes for his dissertation and his class preparations and put them in his briefcase. There were two books open on the desk, she closed them and put them on top. It was heavy when she had it crammed full. She made sure it was tightly locked. She looked in his closet and sighed. He dressed well and had lots more clothes than she did, but then he had to, he taught college classes. She was proud of him. He had been her hero ever since she could remember, even as a toddler.

As Joel drove the long driveway he crested the hill and stopped, turned on the dome light and pulled down the visor to look at his face. He carefully peeled the cloth from his temple; he didn't want to reopen the wound. The cloth was red with a few white streaks; he stuffed it in his hoodie pocket. His right cheek and his right hand were streaked. There were streaks on his eyelids and his nose. Several inches of the sleeve of his hoodie were also saturated. He knew there were other spots on the hoodie that were dry and probably wouldn't come out. Also the headache that had started immediately following the puncture hadn't let up at all. He could use a pain killer; it might keep the pain from engulfing him like a migraine.

He looked at the clock on the dash. Auntie's was the only place to go. He needed to get cleaned up and after all that had happened his mind was in too much turmoil to study. Besides, what could he study? His notes and lap-top were still at the house. What he'd revised and decided was in its last stage was on his lap-top – at the house – behind a locked door.

He sighed, and his heart sank. He had his Bible and his phone with a few apps, but no charger, so when it went dead he couldn't do anything. Months of work were gone - inaccessible! He felt tears scratching behind his eyes, but he blinked, he refused to shed them. All that work and for what? How could he get it? He couldn't redo it! There wasn't time. In fact, there were two library books on his desk. How could he return them?

Stay the course*!* That inner voice said. He acknowledged that voice with a slight nod, but he whispered, "Lord, how do I do that?"

He never understood why his mom had gone against everything her family stood for and she'd been taught from birth. During high school she was a rebellious teen and dated a classmate from a bad crowd, making her part of that bad crowd. What surprised him, there'd never been any drug use. Not even to this day. That was amazing.

However, Eleanor acted and dressed the part, ignoring everything her parents said and usually did the opposite. He had done the same – gone against his parents' wishes – only because their demands were so evil and went against everything his Bible taught him. He'd felt the belt often because he refused to do Thad's demands. He took the belt gladly just so his dad never laid it on Leslie.

Joel knew that even though the Wilson's and Lucy came to Eleanor's high school graduation and told her where they'd meet her after the ceremony, she ignored them and walked away while her dad still talked. She hadn't met them, leaving them standing in the place after most everyone had left. Claudia had cried while they waited for the daughter who never came.

After graduation, she and Thad had wadded up their caps inside the gowns and thrown the bundles on the floor outside the room where the gowns were being collected, then ran from the building. Several other graduates had stepped on the mound, while others waded through the heap before someone realized what the heap was. There were several footprints on the two gowns and the caps were bent badly. Neither Thad nor Eleanor found their families. Everyone knew Thad was the high school's worse 'bad boy' and Eleanor left the building with him. The next day, in another town miles away, Eleanor and Thad falsified their age and married. Eleanor certainly hadn't tried to reform Thad, but taken on his ways. She rarely spoke with her family after that. Her parents and her younger sister shed many tears in the years since then.

Thad and Eleanor stayed away from their home town for nearly a year; no one had a clue where they had gone or what they had done. However, when he and Eleanor came back to town they moved into the house on some acres in the country. Thad must have made some serious connections, because it wasn't land owned by his family. If Joel understood talk around their table, his dad owned the house free and clear. Joel assumed it was true, they'd lived in the same house since he was born and no one had evicted them. Even the sheriff, who disliked Thad and came often for other reasons, never came with an eviction notice. Thad always had money. They never lived lavishly, but very comfortably. However, hardly any money went to his kids. Thad never held a steady job; he never tried to seek work. However, Joel had determined at a young age that he didn't want to know what his dad did.

Within weeks of their return to their hometown and before Thad and Eleanor were twenty Joel was born. Nine years later they had a daughter. Both children were born in the house; Eleanor never went to the doctor for either child. Fortunately, there weren't any complications. Joel had realized in elementary school that doctors and hospitals were not part of the Lawson's' lives. He was glad, even as a young child, that he and Leslie were very healthy.

Their parents tried to raise their son and daughter to be just like them, but Joel and Leslie had both turned their backs on those awful ways and found refuge with their Aunt Lucy and Uncle Josh. Two good people who prayed for them and always had the door unlocked so they could come anytime. That became a bit easier once Joel got his driver's license and a car.

This was not the first time Joel had had a run-in with his dad, it happened regularly, but he tried over and over to show the man Christian love, especially as he grew older and knew better how to share his faith. However, each time he tried Thad wouldn't listen, but yet told him he had to live in their house while he went to school, including college and graduate school. It made no sense. He was actually surprised that it had taken six and a half years after his high school graduation for his dad to finally throw him out. Still, Joel knew things had been brewing for a long time. Some of Thad's outbursts were almost terrifying.

However, his dad's ultimatum tonight meant he could never go back to the house when his dad was there. Even if he were gone when Joel came, the man might come back even minutes later and now there was no telling what he might do to his son. The man worked so sporadically away from home that Joel had no idea when or if he could return for his clothes and his other important things. Tomorrow he taught a class, an eight o'clock. He looked at his watch, there was no time to get to a store and buy some other clothes.

"What would I teach? You don't teach college classes with just thoughts in your head!"

He tried to shake his head, but he couldn't with the headache, so Joel breathed out a sigh and pinched the bridge of his nose. What he had in his wallet wouldn't buy a suit, a dress shirt and tie like he needed to teach his classes. He could wear the boots instead of shoes. Perhaps he could get a dress shirt and some decent slacks at a discount store, but that was all. At this time of night, with his headache and his appearance he wouldn't go to the discount store. His hoodie was ruined, he was sure his aunt couldn't get all the spots out. That meant he had nothing to shield him from the late October weather. Some years they even had snow!

Leslie was extremely quiet in Joel's room before her parents left the living room. However, she was still there when they came upstairs for the night. She held her breath, afraid that her dad would come and listen at the closed doors and know that she was in Joel's room, not hers. The upstairs wasn't very big and her room had a common wall with her parents' room. There was no insulation in the inside walls, any little sound was easily heard anywhere upstairs.

Joel's room wasn't over the living room, but that didn't mean her dad couldn't have heard something while he was still downstairs and that was why they came up. She looked at Joel's alarm clock; it was about the time her parents went to bed. She stood still waiting to hear where he went, but she breathed a sigh of relief when she heard their door close. He hadn't come to listen at any other door. That surprised her. Sometimes she wondered if the man could hear her and Joel breathing!

Joel finally felt composed enough to drive the country road. He pushed up the visor with the mirror and turned off the dome light. Auntie's house was in the nearest suburb, but still some miles away. He turned on the road and when he could no longer see the house in his rear-view mirror, he relaxed. Life went on, as Leslie had said, he must stay the course.

He did have the love and support of his aunt and grandparents. They had grieved and wept many tears over their older daughter's choices. They couldn't help him financially, his grandparents lived on social security and his retirement, but they prayed for him and that was more important than anything else. Auntie would let him sleep on her sofa-sleeper.

Because he taught as a TA in the science department Joel did not have an RA position, he couldn't have taken it, with his dad's ultimatum, so he couldn't afford campus housing or a meal plan. He worked less than forty hours a week, he was considered a full-time student working on his thesis, so to live at his aunt's would help him. Perhaps he'd feel comfortable eating at her table if he gave her something from his paychecks. He'd ask her about that, maybe even tonight.

Because of his parents' questionable livelihood, they lived several miles out of town, Thad wanted to live as far as possible from law enforcement. Even so, Sheriff Gibbs knew Thad Lawson on a first name basis. Joel had never asked because he didn't want to know what he did to make money and Thad certainly hadn't told him what he did. He just knew there seemed to always be plenty of money, but he had no choice as to who his parents were and up till now he'd had to live at their home. Usually, he could come and go as he pleased and most of the time his place was set at the supper table. That wouldn't happen again, his mom wouldn't beg his dad to change his mind. It had never happened before; he had no pipe dreams that it would now.

Tonight had been no different. His mom always supported her husband, never took the part of her children. Tonight she glared at Joel across the table when he started talking about something that God had done for him and Thad started yelling and yanked him from his chair. Usually, she never spoke while his dad ranted, but she obviously went along with him. Joel often wondered where her maternal instinct was. She never showed it for either him or Leslie. At nine years old he watched how his parents had treated his baby sister. He had determined even at that young age that if he ever had children he would never treat a baby like that!

If Leslie hadn't taken a chance and gotten his keys he'd have had to walk miles to reach Auntie's house and possibly collapsed along the road from the cold, but even more importantly, it would have been too late to knock on her door. He couldn't blame her for locking her door and not answering a knock late at night. After all, she lived alone in the city suburb; he wouldn't want her to leave her door unlocked. Until he got his phone she never knew when he or Leslie would come and they could never give her much warning when they could get away.

Leslie was his ally and he was glad. They always stuck together. As a young boy he'd gladly taken several whippings to keep his dad from whipping little Leslie, just because she cried. Tonight she must have run upstairs when their dad had grabbed him to throw him out or she couldn't have gotten his Bible and phone so quickly. Of course, he hadn't been aware of what else happened in the kitchen while his dad dragged him out – other than see his mom's face and see her anger at him.

He pulled onto his aunt's driveway, and let out a long sigh of relief. Those ten miles felt more like a hundred and ten. As he shifted into Park he felt his phone buzz with a text message. He grabbed the phone from his belt, flung the door open for the light and read. *Bro, come EARLY tomorrow. Clothes on back porch.*

OK, he quickly typed back. He couldn't help a sigh of relief. "Man, this is twice tonight she's come through for me! She said 'clothes' but surely she knows how important all the things on my desk are."

He sat in the car for several minutes to regroup, wishing the headache would go away. His temple hurt so badly his head throbbed with his pulse, his shoulder and his arm where his dad had grabbed him really hurt, his legs hurt when he moved them in the car. It had been hard to keep the pressure on the gas pedal all the way from his house. His back hadn't stopped hurting. He turned off the car, slid the phone back in the carrier, pocketed his keys and pushed the door further open. He shrugged, and stood up as the wind whipped around him. He headed for the front door of Auntie's modest bungalow. Staying the course meant grabbing life by the horns and living the life he was meant to live. He would do that and God would take him step by step. He had learned that at an early age at his Auntie's knee and God had not let him down.

TWO

Lucy Steel had been married to a good man, but Josh Steel was killed on the job two years ago. She stayed in the college town, but she down-sized radically in the years since he left her a widow. When she sold her home, she bought a small bungalow. Now she was closer to where the Lawson's lived in the country, in a different neighborhood but in the same suburb as her larger home had been.

"I wish I could help her, even a little," Joel sighed. She got a small settlement payment each month from the company, but she was too young to receive social security, she had a secretarial job, but she never had the chance to go to college and had only been able to take a few courses at a technical school after high school, so she had to live very frugally now with her small income. However, he knew she'd never ask him to pay her, so he must remember to insist she take what he could give her. If he must live here, he felt obligated to help her out.

He loved his aunt, she had given him his first Bible and led him through a child's version of the 'sinner's prayer', then taught him to read and study his Bible. Even as a child, the Bible verses she'd helped him memorize had guided him through many of the skirmishes he had with his dad. She and her husband were the ones who took them to Sunday school and church, whenever they were allowed to go. Her door had always been open to him and Leslie. Her small home was like an oasis and they'd come many times for a meal or to talk and regroup. She didn't live far from Leslie's school, so she came much more often than he did. Every time he thought about her he thanked God for that very important person in his life.

Joel's aunt and uncle had encouraged him to pray and seek what God really wanted him to do with his life. That encouragement meant even more after his uncle died. Joel had mourned his passing, in fact, he still felt the hole in his life because his Uncle Josh had been more of a father figure to him than his dad, because his uncle was a firm believer in his Lord and Thad surely was not. He was now in graduate school because of his prayers and their encouragement.

'*Stay the course*,' was not only Ed's motto, but it had been Josh's too.

As he took the step to Lucy's door it occurred to him that since this was his final semester and he must defend his thesis before semester break, he could then move on with his life. If he wanted, he could move out of town, now his life was his own. No, he had given his life to his Heavenly Father; it was His life to send him where He wanted! He must never lose sight of that important place God his Father held.

A sigh of relief slipped out, Les was getting his things! "Leslie must take my things past Dad's room*!*" That thought nearly sent Joel to his knees there in front of Lucy's front door. However, the cold wind that had swirled around the country house was just as strong and whistled around Lucy's house, sending Joel quickly to her step.

Lucy must have heard his car, because she opened the door and said, "Come in, Joel!" At the sight of him she gasped, "Oh, my! You're hurt! Is it bad?"

As he stepped from the cement slab into her house he said, "No, it could be a lot worse, Auntie, but I turned my head just in time for the glass shard to miss my eye. Actually, it's only a puncture and the bleeding's stopped, but I do need to clean up. Oh, Auntie, you are a sight for sore eyes!"

She smiled and asked, "Have you eaten?"

He took another step into her welcoming home, pushed the door closed and nodded. "Yes, Auntie, I managed to clean my plate before the fireworks started. Still, if Leslie hadn't taken the chance and grabbed my Bible, phone and keys I'd still be walking."

"Oh, my! It's so cold out! Look at you! You only have that thin sweatshirt!" Lucy's eyes sparkled with tears as she pushed the door to make sure it was tight. Her voice wobbling, she said, "Joel, I pray for them every day, but you're twenty-five and it seems hopeless. I know God uses every thing in our lives for our good, but twenty-five years without an answer..."

Joel hugged his aunt and kissed her cheek. He wondered sometimes if he didn't love this lady more than his own mom. He couldn't remember the last time his mom had allowed him to hug or kiss her or that he'd even wanted to! Perhaps as a small child he had, he really couldn't remember. Life at the Lawson's' hadn't been one of showing love between parents and children.

"I know, Auntie, I pray for them so much, but as Les told me when she gave me these things, we must stay the course. God can do anything but fail and we must believe that."

Lucy pulled Joel tightly against her and also kissed his cheek. She continued to hold him and he was happy to stay in her warmth. Into his shoulder she said, "Yes, but they must make the choice and that's what's hard for us to accept. Ever since – even before they graduated from high school – they've been this way!"

"Yes, Auntie, that's true."

Lucy continued to look at her nephew and shook her head. "So he kicked you out, you can't go back? You didn't even get your clothes? Is this all you have? You don't even have your winter coat? It's cold! It's almost November!"

"Sis sent a text just as I got here to come early tomorrow to get my things they'd be on the back porch, but yes, he said he didn't want to see my face again and he literally threw me out the door, that means I can't go back, who knows when he'd be gone!"

Lucy stepped from Joel's arms, but kept a hand on his arm. She looked at her nephew and Joel saw a look come in her eyes, as she said very seriously, "Joel, don't wait till morning. Go back ***now***! Park down the road, in that spot where you can see the house; wait till all the lights go out and go back for them. I have this feeling you might not get them in the morning!"

"All right, Auntie. I've experienced enough of your premonitions that I'll do that. Besides, I'd have to go back really early, maybe even before daylight, because I teach an eight o'clock tomorrow. Les is really putting herself out for me."

"Perhaps, but you've been her rock ever since she can remember." Not acknowledging that, Joel turned around in the small hallway, ready to go back to his car.

"Wait a minute, Joel, take off that sweatshirt! It needs to soak. I'm sure we can get that blood out if we soak it. Fortunately, I never got rid of Josh's winter coat, I found it in a box the other day, and hung it here in the closet until I could think of what to do with it. Surely you can wear it, it's good and warm. Wash your face and hands then get on back there for your things."

Joel nodded, unzipped the damaged hoodie as Lucy reached in her closet for the heavy coat. She put it over the door knob as Joel rushed to the kitchen to wash and Lucy went a different way to soak his hoodie. When he'd dried his face and hands, he turned from the sink and Lucy held out a tube of something and a band-aid. "Here, put this on that place to keep out any infection. It does look better now that the blood's gone." With just a tiny uplifting of her lips, she added, "Now you don't look like a scarecrow."

"Thanks, Auntie, thanks so much."

Lucy smiled and Joel took the things, did as she said, then took the coat and put it on. He felt the warmth immediately. He gave Lucy a tired smile, went back to the front door and went to his car that wasn't even cold yet. As he sat down in the car exhaustion crept into his bones and he felt the ache in those bones from being tossed onto the porch. He hoped he could make it back to Lucy's without an accident. He pulled in a deep breath, closed the door and stuck the key back in the ignition and started up. He had to remind himself that he was staying the course.

He looked back at the house; Lucy stood in the window watching, so he raised his hand and waved. He saw her hand wave and imagined she was smiling, but her face was shadowed, so he couldn't tell. Undoubtedly, she was praying that his mission was successful. He also let out a prayer, a sigh really, that he could get his things, a few clothes, perhaps. The things on his desk were irreplaceable. His dad locked the doors, even the deadbolts at night and he didn't have a key for the bolts. God would make a way somehow, he believed that.

He eased his car back out of the driveway and felt like he was a hundred years old. Between the aches he'd acquired because of his dad, the puncture wound on his face and the headache that didn't want to give up, he wondered how anyone could survive into their eighties or nineties! He pulled in another deep breath and headed back the way he came.

Staying the course, was it worth it? "Grampa seems to think so," he murmured.

Without him knowing, a window curtain moved at the house next door. A curious neighbor looked out on Lucy's driveway. It was rather late for Lucy to get visitors. Jenni wondered who it was. Only moments later before the neighbor left the room the man came back out and left. The woman hadn't seen a man at the neighbor's house ever before. She was concerned for Lucy, but the man wasn't moving like a thief, but someone who truly knew Lucy.

Recently, Joel hadn't come to Lucy's house nearly as often as he had in high school or undergraduate school, so Jenni was curious who would come to her house so late at night. The family next door was friends with Lucy and since she lived alone they often watched out for her. Lucy was glad for their friendship; she and Loretta often spent time together, since they'd moved next door. Loretta was happy to be friends with Lucy, but she quickly walked away whenever Lucy brought anything into the conversation about the Lord.

In the last few years their oldest daughter, Jenni, had moved back home after college and her bedroom window looked out on Lucy's driveway. Jenni was Joel's age. She'd been in many of Joel's classes in school and when she graduated she'd gotten a scholarship to an out-of-town university. She had gone there for her four years to get her degree, but came back to her hometown for a job opportunity and now lived with her parents next door to Lucy Steel. Joel's car on the driveway alerted her. It was late, who would come and then leave so soon again?

Joel turned enough that the streetlight let Jenni see his face. "I know him! That's Joel Lawson! I haven't seen him in forever!" Jenni whispered. "I wonder why he's come so late to Lucy's house, but now he's leaving again!"

Not knowing that the neighbor watched and certainly not caring, since he had so many thoughts himself, Joel left town and pulled on the country road to his parents' house. Just before the driveway he pulled into a pull-off beside the road where he had often stopped in the years since he'd started driving to watch the house. Several times he'd made a U-turn and gone back to town before reaching the house because of the activity he'd seen from this spot. Because of that, he'd slept in his car many times. Ever since his uncle had died and his aunt had moved into her little house he hadn't felt right imposing on her very often.

After only a few minutes, all the lights went out downstairs. He continued to sit, knowing they would still be awake. His dad could be looking out the window in his parents' room that looked out towards the road. However, Joel knew he couldn't be seen because of the trees and he'd turned off his lights when he parked.

The light was bright in the master bedroom, so he probably wasn't looking out. His sister's room was on the corner he could see, but no light came on in it. He could see one window in his room. As soon as the light went out in his parents' room he saw a dim light in his room. Perhaps it had been on the whole time, he couldn't be sure. He pulled in a breath, Leslie was taking a chance gathering up his things and she was still in his room!

Seeing the light, put action to his tired body and he opened the door. This far from the house there was no worry that his dad would hear the noise. Would Leslie have gotten his briefcase? She hadn't really mentioned that in her text. He quickly left the car and picked up a few pebbles from the side of the road. As soon as he had several quarter sized stones, he started across the field toward the back of the house.

"If Sis tries to make it past their room with a suitcase he may hear her!" He started to run as best he could in the dark. His aches and pains were a big hindrance. For several years this open area had been a corn field, so it was quite rutted and that made it very hard not to turn his ankle. The moon was behind the clouds that covered the sky and without any nearby security lights it was really very dark. At least it wasn't raining and hadn't rained in nearly a week. Mud would make the going even more treacherous. He was committed, he would stay the course.

The light was still on in his room when he reached the house; she was still in his room! Perhaps she hadn't started taking his things from his room. He pulled in a deep breath; it was a long ways across the field, even going overland. He was out of breath and his heart was pounding. His back was screaming and both legs had cramps. He hurried around back and noticed there was nothing on the back porch. Letting out another sigh, he knew Leslie hadn't tried to get by their bedroom. That was very good!

He had barely reached the back of the house when lightning lit up the sky behind him. Joel groaned, if it rained before he got his things and made it back to his car… oh, my! He could be in a world of hurt! Not only because he and his things would be wet, but he could easily turn an ankle on the uneven ground or slip in mud and get hurt even worse than when he'd been thrown onto the porch. He was watching his window so intently that he almost didn't hear the thunder several minutes later. It was barely a rumble.

Still intent on getting Leslie's attention, he threw two stones at his back window, hoping that his noise wouldn't wake his dad or cause him to do anything to Leslie in a rage. They both knew she was going against Thad's wishes to get him his things. He didn't want anything he did to cause his sister any harm! *Stay the course!* He would, he had to! Both stones hit the window but one of them slid down the screen and made a strange sound.

He took several steps back from the house so she could see him and prayed, "Father, God, please keep Sis safe! I'm not there now; it could be so hard for her. Dad can be so awful! I love her, Lord, be with her. I thank You for her thoughtfulness in getting my things."

Leslie was so intent on what she was doing that she jumped and nearly screamed when the stones Joel threw hit the window. The stone scraping the screen made a very strange sound. She stuffed her fist into her mouth to keep any noise inside. The house had been so quiet that the sound of the stones seemed magnified. Fortunately just at that moment she faced the window and saw the vague outline of the stones falling away from the window, but the sound sent her heart into overdrive. It also showed her the lightning flash to the west over the trees.

She scowled. "Not even a half hour ago I sent him a text to come for his things in the morning. Why's he here now?" She was glad he came, she'd told him his things would be on the back porch, but she couldn't find a suitcase in his closet and if she couldn't pack his clothes how would she get so much past her parents' room without her dad hearing her? She surely couldn't have made only one trip with all his things! "His briefcase weighs a ton!"

It took a moment for Leslie to finally get her brain and her feet to work together to move to the window. With the window closed she didn't even hear the thunder rumble. Joel stood back so she could see him and he motioned for her to raise the window. She did and in a hoarse whisper, he said, "Sis, just throw the things down. Knock out the screen somehow, don't try to get past their door to bring them down. I'm sure you'd never make it."

Leslie nodded and looked at the screen. She also saw another streak of lightning. That sent her heart into fits! Joel was out there, and possibly before he got all the way back to his car with his things, so would the rain! She saw how to take the screen out and as quietly as she could, she removed it. As she lay the screen aside, she heard another grumble of thunder. She hurried because of the impending storm, so Joel's worldly possessions started tumbling to the ground. The loose clothes from his closet came first and landed in a heap. Joel watched, it didn't really matter, the ground was still dry. Next came a cloth sack with several pairs of shoes. Then two backpacks as full as they could be and a briefcase tumbled out the window.

Joel sighed in relief as the briefcase came. He was sure she'd put his laptop and all his notes for his dissertation and the classes he taught in it, since they were all on top of his desk. He didn't try to catch it; there was enough of a cushion of clothes to make a safe landing. Fortunately there was a very good latch that kept the briefcase closed and latched as it tumbled onto the clothes. However, there was another grumble of thunder.

"Thanks so much, Sis," he whispered loud enough for her to hear. "I can't begin to thank you for getting these things for me. This briefcase especially! Auntie told me to come back tonight. She wasn't sure things would be on the porch in the morning."

Leslie nodded and stuck her head out the window. In a whisper that was barely above the night sounds, she said, "That might be true. Dad is in rare form since he threw you out. He hasn't really stopped cussing and stomping around since. I was surprised he didn't check my room to make sure I was in it when they came up for bed. See you Bro. Oh, by the way, he sent me up real soon after you left, so I couldn't get your coat from the closet." She looked at him a little more closely. "Is that Uncle Josh's coat?"

After another rumble of thunder he said, "Yes, it is. For some reason, Auntie still had it after all this time. Believe me, I'm glad for it! That wind is really cold tonight! I think it's picked up now that a storm's coming in. Thanks for what you've done, Sis. I'm so glad you got my briefcase, you know how important all that stuff is!"

"I'm glad I could, Bro. Remember, stay the course!"

"It's hard, but I'm trying to remember that, Sis." He smiled at her. "Get to bed and get some sleep, remember it's another day tomorrow."

"You know I will."

Joel started gathering his things as Leslie quietly put the screen in its place and lowered the sash. With the storm coming, it was urgent, so he didn't look up at her again. Even before Joel had all his clothes in his arms the light went out in his room, but another streak of lightning cracked. The lightning helped him gather his things, but the snaps were coming closer together and the thunder was getting louder, so he must hurry.

From what Les had said about their dad, Joel knew he must hurry for another reason. He must get everything the first time. He didn't dare make a second trip, not just because of the storm, but because of his dad. He took the shoe sack and stuffed all of his good shirts and ties into it until it was stuffed, slung both backpacks, one on each shoulder, took the shoe sack and put it on his back too, then tried hard to get all his clothes into a pile he could carry on one arm.

Rather than wait for another lightning flare, he felt around on the ground to make sure he had everything then picked up his briefcase. He was loaded down and staggered to stand up. The aches and pains from his trip to the porch hadn't gone away, but another snap of lightning sent him on his way. As he started across the field to his car he wondered when he'd see Leslie again. Perhaps their paths would cross at Aunt Lucy's.

It was very dark between lightning flares, the clouds were heavy and as he crossed the dirt, the lightning came more frequently and the thunder was louder and longer, perhaps it would rain soon. If the thunder and lightning were any indication, it could be a bad storm. He was intent on getting to his car, hopefully before the rain came. He didn't dare waste time, his dad could see his dark form crossing the open field, and there weren't any trees to hide him. There was a single row of trees around the pull-off, but nothing in between

Joel wondered what his dad would do in this mood if he did see him. It didn't matter, Joel had all his things and he had not entered the house. He moved on a direct path from the house to his car and never slowed once he started across the wide open area, but he did glance back several times. However, the lightning and thunder followed him. Each time seemed just a little closer and a little louder.

There was no change at the house, it stayed dark and he saw no one before he reached his car. Of course, his dad could stand at his bedroom window and see him if he'd heard anything. He hoped the noise of the storm had covered any sounds he and Leslie had made. Joel was huffing by the time he reached the road, but he quickly put his things on the back seat and the floor. He sat down behind the wheel and pulled in a deep breath, it was a long walk and not easy to navigate, especially holding so much in his arms. He was glad he hadn't turned an ankle, since he couldn't see well where to put his feet. He was especially glad it hadn't started to rain! However, he barely had his door closed when another streak of lightning snapped over him.

He started up, glad the spot was so far from the house the engine noise couldn't be heard. He quickly started a U-turn, pulled on his lights and let out a sigh of relief. "Thank You my Father, thank You for letting Les get it all and for telling Auntie to send me back." A peace swept over him, God was with him, would always be with him, every step of the way in his life, he knew that for a fact! A lightning snap seemed to add emphasis. Only seconds later the thunder roared. He hadn't even gotten turned around before the first fat drops hit his windshield.

As he drove back to town he was convinced his aunt was right, perhaps he wouldn't have gotten his things in the morning. Who knew what frame of mind his dad was in! Leslie had seemed almost scared as she threw his things out the window. His dad probably had threatened her at the door when she'd given him the things after supper. He hoped the man hadn't hit her, now that he could no longer be there, what would their dad do? He nearly sobbed; Dad could and possibly would do any number of things to her! He couldn't be there to protect her!

"God my Father, protect my little sister!" he prayed, nearly in anguish. Another snap of lightning and a loud clap of thunder bounced around outside his car and the rain came down with a vengeance. His wipers could hardly cope.

Leslie replaced Joel's screen, lowered the sash and turned off the light, then silently walked around the bed to the door. She stood and listened for several minutes before she opened the door, but her heart was hammering. During her silent wait there were several lightning snaps and roaring thunder sounds. She turned the knob, then closed Joel's door by holding the knob until she could let it go without a sound. Quickly, she hurried into her room, closed the door just as quietly, wishing there was a lock on the door. She shed her clothes in lightning speed, pulled on her granny nightie and snuggled down under her covers, hoping she could sleep after all the excitement. Her heart was still going at warp speed, but she knew no one but her could hear it.

Still she wondered if her dad had heard anything. Was he still awake? With the lightning and thunder it was possible. She sometimes thought he slept with one eye open! Maybe with the kind of work he did he had to stay alert most of the time. Neither she nor Joel really knew how he made money. They didn't want to know! Besides, Joel had hit the back window, the one farthest away from their dad's room, with the stones. To her, that noise seemed really loud! Perhaps he'd heard them. She closed her eyes, intent on looking like she was asleep if her dad came to her room. She prayed that he wouldn't. It was late; she really did want to go to sleep! With school tomorrow, she didn't want to stay awake.

However, only a few moments after she was in bed there was noise in the hallway and her heart jumped into warp speed again. It was her dad, not the storm. A few seconds later her bedroom door crashed open. Several things tinkled in the room when the door bounced against the wall and vibrated. She saw the shadow of her bedside lamp wobble and hoped it wouldn't crash down. If it did, it did, she had no way of stopping it, she couldn't move that fast. She did wish that if it crashed that it would fall another way, to start off a confrontation with her dad with an injury was not her wish. Really, she wished all this awfulness would stop!

The crash of the door against the wall mixed with the snap of lightning and roar of thunder as the rain came. Thad paid no attention, but took only three heavy steps across the room and yanked her from the bed, his big hand easily circling her arm. He paid no attention to the sheet and blankets covering her or tucked under the mattress. Shaking her mercilessly, he yelled, "You... **you**! You did it again! I heard you!"

Trying to act as if the man had wakened her, Leslie said, "What, Dad?" She blinked her eyes as she looked at him.

The man raised his free hand, but just in time dropped it before he hit his daughter, still he hissed, "Don't give me that innocent stuff! You emptied his room!" His words were punctuated by the thunder and lightning and the rain battering her windows.

Her dad held her sideways, but now it was over the hard floor. Leslie had survived his attacks before, so she braced herself for when he let her go. When he grabbed her like this she never knew if he would drop her or fling her away or even slap her before he did one or the other. She was sure he would do something and she didn't want to break a bone. A trip to the hospital was never on his agenda! So far, he had only slapped her when he was in a rage, but there was always a first time for people like him, especially now that Joel wasn't here.

In as strong a voice as she could speak, she said, "Yes, Dad, I did. Joel has gone out of his way to be kind and loving to you. He deserves everything that is his! He's done so much with his life and what he has done has happened even in spite of all you've done to keep him from it. I *will* help him all I can!" There was a snap and a roar outside the window.

Totally ignoring her words and holding her completely off the floor, he snarled, "Where is his stuff? What'd you do with it?" Still holding her arm, he gave her another good shaking. It almost felt like her arm would snap. The rain pounded on her windows and the lightning flashes were nearly constant with the thunder roaring, adding even more noise to the confrontation.

Grabbing a quick breath, she gasped out, "He got it already!" *Thank goodness Auntie told him to come for it tonight!*

"**What**!" the man raged. His voice was loud even over the storm. Violently, he shook her again, bringing tears to her eyes. She tucked her head; her face was in a shadow he couldn't see them. "He was here? In the house?" He shook her even more violently than the other times.

Leslie didn't answer him, she couldn't, he'd shaken the breath out of her, but when she didn't answer he flung her across the room. In that instant there was a huge crash of thunder just outside. His obvious intent was to have her hit the wall or her desk and that would hurt, but she determined not to let out a sound, she knew that a whimper or a cry infuriated him even more.

Just before she hit the wall she curled into a ball and slid into the corner beside her desk. It was dark and Leslie stayed with the desk between her and her dad, not making a sound and not moving, hoping that her dad wouldn't find her. Perhaps with the storm, he would leave, the lightning made eerie shadows and the constant thunder covered any sound in the house.

At that exact moment lightning cracked, thunder roared and even harder rain descended, smacking the window like bee-bees. Much to her relief, Thad didn't come after her, but turned around and breathing heavily, stomped out of her room. She watched him smack the door-jam with his hand so hard that the sound vibrated in the room. The picture she loved bounced against the wall. He didn't close the door so Leslie could hear him muttering curses at her and at Joel and at their God. He stomped down the hall and soon the door to their bedroom slammed. She guessed her mom was also still awake.

Still in the corner, Leslie whispered, "My Father, God, what will it take? My Father, Dad has been doing this to my brother for almost twenty-five years and me too since I was a baby. God in heaven, why? Will it ever stop?" Leslie took a deep breath, the lightning snapped and thunder roared, but Leslie added another sentence, "God, it's so hard to stay the course!"

She didn't expect to hear an answer, but in her room, even with the tempest outside, after her dad's bedroom door closed, a stillness came over her - a peacefulness. It was a profound feeling; perhaps even a Presence surrounded her. She sat in awe for a few minutes. It was so different from the tempest outside. Because of how she landed, her knees were bent, so she put her arms around them, but it felt like some huge, warm arms came around her. It was dark in the room, only lit by the lightning outside, but somehow – she couldn't have explained it to anyone – everything had changed. She was content to stay as she was for a few more minutes.

Auntie had these thoughts sometimes and usually they were right on. She'd had one tonight and sent Joel back for his clothes. He probably wouldn't have gotten them if he hadn't. They would have been soaked if he'd come in the morning! That's if they would even have been there! Their dad might have brought them in just to keep Joel from getting them. She knew he'd do that just for spite! After all, he had demanded to know what she'd done with his things.

During another crack of lightning, Leslie scrambled from the floor, closed her door, and climbed onto the bed for what was left of the night, hoping she could sleep. Thank goodness Dad hadn't really hurt her! The storm was still overhead and the rain was pounding the house, so Leslie pulled the covers over her head. However, she realized her feet were cold. Her dad had pulled the covers from the bed when he'd dragged her out. She quickly kicked the blankets over her. However, hiding under the covers didn't make the storm less violent! She was sixteen, no little kid. She sighed made sure she was covered, snuggled down, and closed her eyes.

The minute she stopped moving the covers she felt that profound stillness surrounding her. She still 'listened' as the storm moved on and the rain battering the window slowed. Something profound urged her to pack a backpack full of clothes, as much as she could stuff in the pack in the morning. That wouldn't be hard, usually, she had to get herself ready for school and fix her own breakfast, her parents never left their room until after she caught the bus. She wondered if they watched her from their window while she hurried down the driveway. Tomorrow she wouldn't care.

It would be easy to pack her backpack, she had several and one was very large, so she'd take it with her along with her book bag. She'd stay with Auntie. It would be a relief to get away from her dad. He had come after her twice tonight. He'd never come looking for them at their aunt's, even though she was sure he knew where they were. With Joel there already, it would be great! Even though it had been such an eventful evening, she felt that peacefulness and fell asleep almost as soon as her head hit the pillow.

Joel drove through the rain. It was really pouring! His wipers hardly took care of the windshield and his headlights seemed to bounce off the wall of rain coming down in sheets. The thunder boomed inside the car, the lightning hurt his eye. He had to strain and concentrate just to keep the car on the road, since there were no lines marking the sides and center on the country road. The noise of the lightning snaps and constant thunder made the headache more severe.

When Joel finally reached the city he breathed a sigh of relief. There were street lights to help guide him; he didn't have to concentrate quite as hard. He was so tired he couldn't wait to get to Auntie's house. Finally, he turned onto her street and was glad to point his car onto her driveway. The storm hadn't let up, even though he'd driven at least ten miles. It was raining so hard he wouldn't open the back door to grab anything and then he saw the house door open.

He scrambled from the car, flinging the car door as he took a step toward the house. Seconds later he raced through the door and slammed it shut. "Oh, Auntie! It's awful out there, but the storm didn't come until I got back in my car. The lightning started when I reached the back of the house, I wasn't even aware of the thunder until several more streaks of lightning showed in the sky." He pulled in a deep breath. As he shed his coat and hung it in the closet, he said, "Les was still in my room when I got there and threw everything out the back window. I managed to get everything at one time, putting the backpacks on my back, but the storm followed me to my car. Everything's dry on the back seat. I'll bring them in in the morning!"

Lucy went to the door and locked it, as she said, "Joel, I'm so glad! I started praying the minute you left and when I saw the lightning off in the distance I prayed even more. I knew it would be bad walking on that field, but with armloads of stuff it could be even worse."

"Thank you! I'm sure that's what held off the rain until I got back to the car. It's really a long ways across that field and with my arms so full..."

Lucy's mantel clock started making noise. She looked at the clock through the archway and said, "Joel, this has been an incredible night! Let's get some sleep."

Joel smiled at her and breathed out a big sigh, "Yes, Auntie, I'm ready for that! Thanks for all you've done for me. I'm so glad you have this couch where I can crash."

In the morning Leslie woke earlier than normal. It was still dark, but it wasn't raining. She remembered the feeling she'd had last night, so she threw back the covers, hurried into the bathroom to take her shower, do all the things a teen aged girl did in the bathroom in the morning, and brought back all her things. Rather than only one backpack, she pulled out her two largest ones and began to fill them as quietly as possible. In amongst the clothes she put several of her most favorite things, several trinkets and jewelry. Her favorite picture wouldn't fit. Now with Joel living at Auntie's, she knew she'd spend more time at her house.

By the time she had both packs as full as she could, her dresser was empty and she had most of her things from her closet. She had all of her favorite clothes, both from the closet and her dresser. She dressed in layers so she could have as much as possible. She made sure she had her phone charger and other things she knew she couldn't do without. She loaded as much as she could in her purse. She put a few things in her book bag, a pair of her favorite shoes mixed in with the books. It was quite large and could hold more than her school supplies. She emptied her piggy bank, all the money in her room she put in a side pocket of one of her backpacks. She didn't question her actions, she felt sure that feeling she'd had last night hadn't come by mistake. She continued to stuff things in those three bags until they couldn't hold another thing!

Afraid her parents would wonder why she was spending so much time in her room, although she didn't know if they woke up before she left or not, she slung both backpacks over her shoulders along with her full book bag and her purse and quietly hurried passed their door. Was her dad awake? He had heard her last night, even though she was sure she hadn't made much noise, but she heard no sound from their room, so she hurried passed the door.

There was one stair that creaked if she stepped in the middle, so she stepped to the side and ran the rest of the way down the stairs. She didn't care if they watched her go to the bus, not this morning. She left her packs by the front door. The mirror glass was still on the floor.

She fixed her favorite breakfast, even fixed a large glass of chocolate milk.

She grabbed what money she could claim downstairs and ran out the door to catch the bus. She was still several steps from the road when it pulled to a stop across the road from her driveway. She clamored on and the driver looked at her a bit strangely, probably wondering why she carried two backpacks as well as her book bag, when usually it was only her purse and a limp book bag, but, thankfully, she didn't comment.

Leslie sat with her friend, but she also didn't ask why she had so much. As soon as she sat down, she pulled the packs from her back and put them between her legs, they weren't as noticeable there. When the bus arrived at school, Leslie went to her locker to leave the backpacks. They nearly filled the locker. She looked forward to staying with Auntie. As much as she had from home, she could stay with her aunt as long as she wanted or as long as Auntie would let her. She'd treat this as a mini-vacation! To stay with Auntie really was a vacation.

The red phone rang once and the emergency dispatch grabbed it immediately. "This is nine-one-one! State your emergency!"

"Oh! Yes, please! Send something right away! I just felt the house shake! Oh, it felt like something exploded! Oh, my! It was an awful boom! Please, can you do something? Send somebody!" the frantic voice said breathlessly into the phone.

"Yes, Ma'am, what has exploded? Can you see what's exploded? Is it nearby?" The phone number started a light flashing. The dispatch immediately began flipping switches.

"Oh, it has to be on the Lawson place. You know where that is? The Lawson's are my neighbors, you know."

"Yes, Ma'am, we know, it shows on our county map where that is. We've put out the word; authorities should be there within a few minutes. Are you safe?"

"Oh, yes, I'm fine, but them… Maybe they aren't!"

"Yes, Ma'am! We have units dispatched as we speak!"

Emergency dispatch was in the downtown police station, but there were instantaneous relays to all the other law enforcement offices and fire departments throughout the city and in the suburbs. The nine-one-one exchange hadn't even finished when the horn began to blare in the local fire station and the firemen raced for their gear and the trucks. The huge doors flew open and the fire trucks and SUVs raced from the building.

The emergency call sounded in the county sheriff's office. The sheriff was familiar with the Lawson's, especially Thad Lawson. He and Eleanor had been on the Sheriff Department's 'bad' list for many years, but except for petty incidents that only amounted to a few nights in the county jail, nothing could be placed on their shoulders.

Sheriff Gibbs heard the transmission and left his office before the exchange finished. He knew that the fire department would send equipment, but that didn't mean he couldn't go. He slammed his fist on the dispatch desk, turned on his heel and rushed into the room where the deputies had their desks. He looked around and saw several of his cronies sitting at their desks.

"Guys!" he exclaimed, his face beet red, "Did you hear what came in on nine-eleven?"

"Sure did, Sheriff! You wanna get on over there."

"**Better believe it**!!" he roared. "Come on guys. We're outta here; we'll nab Lawson!"

Sheriff Gibbs stepped to his office door, yanked the keys to his sheriff's car from its hook and exclaimed, "I'm sure old Thad was doin' some concoction and it exploded in his face. We need to get in on the ground floor! Lawson won't get away with nothin'!" His cronies were all on their feet behind him, but none of them mentioned that if the explosion was bad enough that a neighbor reported it, that probably 'Lawson won't get away….'

However, one of the younger deputies who wasn't in the sheriff's pocket sat at his desk. He muttered, "Yeah, if he did something and it exploded in his face, he surely didn't get away!" Of course, he didn't say the words loud enough for the sheriff to hear him, only two of his friends next to him heard. They nodded in agreement, but Sheriff Gibbs was nearly out the door.

The sheriff's cronies scrambled after him and one exclaimed, "We're with ya, Sheriff! Right behind ya! We'll load up and get over there ASAP! We'll get that Lawson this time!"

Sheriff Gibbs slammed his car door as the others scrambled in. Three other doors slammed as he inserted his key. The poor car roared to life as the sheriff's voice filled the car. "**I wanna throw that man's you know what in the slammer forever!**"

The siren drowned out the deputy's words, "We're with ya, Sheriff! We'll get him!"

Sheriff Gibbs slammed his fist on the steering wheel as he left the cage. "It's about time that man paid for the stuff he's done over the years!"

"Agreed!" the sheriff's second in command said. The car exploded onto the street, its lights and siren going. Fortunately, there was no other traffic on the street

THREE

Joel had breakfast with Lucy and after a good cup of her coffee, left to teach his eight o'clock class at the university. Even with the usual sleepyheads, his first hour was a good session, and then he spent a very productive morning in the university library stacks. He had just left the chair to get his lunch; his stomach had already reminded him several times that it was time to eat. He was pulling his things together as his phone rang. He snagged his coat from the back of his chair and threw it over his arm, grabbed the phone from his belt and looked at it. He didn't recognize the number, but it was local, so he answered.

A very brusque voice said, "Joel Lawson?"

"Yes, this is Joel."

The man cleared his throat and said, "Mr. Lawson, this is Fire Precinct Lieutenant Winslow." He cleared his throat, before he continued, "Ah – this is terribly hard to say, sir, but your neighbor heard and felt an explosion in the vicinity of your house." Joel gasped, but the man continued, "She called nine-eleven, so we dispatched equipment and I'm standing on your driveway, sir. Amazingly, there was no fire when we arrived, but Mr. Lawson, there is nothing – absolutely nothing - left of this house! Because of the explosion only the hole for the basement is left. The stones on the driveway beside the hole are melted together into a solid mass."

Joel heard sirens in the background, but he could barely process what the lieutenant was telling him. His mouth went instantly dry and a shudder went down his back. After taking a breath, then swallowing, hoping for some moisture so he could speak, he finally croaked out, "Oh… my! Oh… oh… my! What about my parents?"

Obviously very uncomfortable, the man cleared his throat, then after a short silence he cleared it again. However, his voice obviously strained, he answered, "Mr. Lawson, I am looking at a small pile of remains here close to the hole that could possibly be what is left of a vehicle and a little further away metal remains that I recognize as the shell of a vehicle. I'm sorry, Joel, but at this time we have no idea if your parents were in the house when it exploded or not. If they left, it was on foot. From the way things look, there is no way of discovering anything that could have been in the house. With these two piles and assuming they were both vehicles…"

Joel swallowed again, his throat felt totally clogged. "Be a few minutes, I'll be there."

"That's fine, we aren't going anywhere."

After her morning classes, Leslie had just set her lunch tray down on a table when her cell phone buzzed. It was unusual to hear a phone buzzing in the lunchroom because of the noise, and at first she didn't realize it was her phone. Her friends were either still in the lunch line or coming behind her to get a seat, so they wouldn't be texting. When it kept buzzing, she realized it had to be hers; it was too close and too noisy in the lunch room to be anyone else's. She grabbed it from the pocket of her purse and swiped the face to see the text. It was short.

"Sis, don't go home, go to Auntie's. Tell you later J

OK she typed back.

For a minute she wondered why Joel would have told her to do that. He didn't know she'd planned to go there anyway this afternoon. She settled into her seat with her tray on the table in front of her. Her friends brought their trays and settled around her. As with most sixteen-year-olds, the girls were laughing and loud. Soon, Leslie forgot about Joel's text.

It was a pretty day and as Jenni sat at her desk eating her brown-bag lunch she saw the sunshine and wished it wasn't so cold. She'd love to take her lunch out to the picnic table. However, she'd barely registered the thought when her desk phone rang. Always ready to leave the station for late-breaking news and because that was part of her job, she swallowed her half-chewed mouthful, picked up her land-line and said, "Jennifer Mikles, what can I do for you?"

"Jenni!" an urgent voice exclaimed, "just now, on the FD scanner there was an explosion reported! Can you go on it? It sure is late-breaking news!"

"Sure, Alex! Where?"

The man was obviously excited and had to pull in a big breath before he said, "The report said it's the Lawson place out there in the country. You got any idea where that is? You've lived around here a long time."

"Yeah, been by there lots of times. It's a white house with a long driveway and sits all by itself on that country road. That's the place you're talking about, right?"

"Yup, that's the place!"

"I'm on it! Catch you later!"

"That's the spirit, Jenni, go for it!"

"Sure, that's me, Alex!"

While she spoke, Jenni felt her adrenalin racing through her veins; this was what she loved about her job. Alex hadn't finished when she reached in the desk drawer for her purse. They ended the conversation and Jenni threw the receiver back on the cradle, stuffed the last mouthful of her sandwich in her mouth, grabbed her water bottle, bolted from the desk and grabbed her coat on her way out of her tiny office. She ran to the newsroom, collected her camera man and a battery-powered mike, and together they ran to one of the station's SUVs.

Still buttoning their coats against the October chill, the door from the building hadn't even closed when Len yanked the keys from his pocket and hit the fob door-lock. The vehicle beeped and as the locks clicked he dove behind the wheel, while Jenni rushed to the passenger door. These two often went together on an assignment. Jenni liked Len, they complimented each other, hardly having to talk about what to say or do.

"What's happening, Jenni?" Len asked, as she slammed the door and grabbed her seatbelt. Len turned the key then yanked the stick into drive. Only seconds later they were headed for the street from the station parking lot.

Jenni pointed toward which way to head on the street. "I don't know much, Len. Alex called and said he heard on the FD scanner that there's been an explosion at the Lawson place. That's all that he told me. You know where that is, right? It's out in the country a bit."

Len winked at Jenni and nodded, but looked back at the asphalt. "Yeah, it's a good thing I've been in these parts awhile. You locals have it all over us 'feriners'. So, I guess we'll both find out together if that's all you know."

Jenni chuckled at Len's way of mutilating the word, but she said, "Yeah, I'd say! An explosion – what would have caused that?"

"Ahhh, Jenni..." Len said reluctantly. "I don't know the Lawson's, it could be, um, some kind of meth lab or such, they do explode at times. And being in the country... Or maybe it was even a faulty furnace. That can happen this time of year, since they sit idle all summer. Hard to tell. Or it could be something on the property. Does the guy have enemies? Maybe somebody lobbed a torch in the house or something. Guess we'll find out more when we get there."

"With all those possibilities, your guess is as good as mine."

As Len made the turn onto the city street to head for the country, he exclaimed, "We are on it this instant!" He floored the gas pedal, the van jerked and they left black marks at the edge of the parking lot.

Jenni heard brakes squeal as the SUV entered the city street. She grabbed the seatbelt that was already buckled and hung on. She took a deep breath and cautioned, "Len, if there's nothing there and Alex said there was a bad explosion reported, there won't be anything more or less there when we get to the place if you slow down enough you don't risk causing a problem with another driver along the way. You know, of course, it'd be sorta bad for the TV station's reputation to have to report a news van had an accident on the way to another event. Alex sort of frowns on stuff like that." Jenni cautioned.

Len sighed and lifted his foot marginally from the gas pedal. "I get it. Sometimes I wish I had sirens on this thing."

"Well, you don't, it'd be best if you didn't act like you did," Jenni said, righteously.

"Right, I gotcha." However, Len still screeched around several corners anxious to reach the road out of town. Jenni had ridden with Len enough times she stayed quiet, but held the armrest and seatbelt tightly.

Without thinking about his stomach growling a few minutes ago, Joel ran to the parking lot outside the university library, threw his things in his car, including his phone and dove in. Even in those few minutes the October wind hit him where the coat was open, penetrating his suit coat that was buttoned underneath. He quickly pulled the two parts of the winter coat together, so thankful his aunt still had it. Still for October, even with the sun shining, it was a cold day. As soon as Joel started the car he turned up the heat. The warmth felt good, but he hardly thought about it, his mind was churning.

He had to use the by-pass around the city, but in less than ten minutes he was on the country road that led to his parents' home. He hadn't expected to travel this road again so soon. When he reached the pull-off he slowed to look across the open space. He gasped, just as the lieutenant said, there was no house there at all, only the huge propane tank! It was one thing to hear someone talk about the destruction, but it was quite another to see it himself.

Last evening from this spot he could see the whole house, the lighted windows, the dark shutters against the white siding. Today, there was absolutely nothing there, just official cars, one with its lights flashing, SUVs and fire trucks. As if the whole building had been removed, something like tornado devastation pictures he'd seen where a house was sucked up into the funnel. The electrical storm was last night, there was no tornado and today was a beautiful day.

The lieutenant had said there were a few piles of rubble. The large propane tank was the only clue there had been something other than an open field. From his vantage point on the road, Joel could only see the metal skeleton of one car and the tank. At that moment, Joel was glad for an empty stomach! He continued passed the row of trees, still with his eyes glued on the spot.

The fire trucks and SUVs all belonging to the local fire department were parked in a line near the crest of the hill where the house had been and men in uniform stood around them, but no one was spraying anything. There were no flames and it wasn't smoke that was rising, it was dust being carried away rather quickly by the breeze. Close behind a firetruck was the sheriff's car, lights going and siren blaring. He could hear the siren even in his closed car! The sheriff had pulled up beside the twisted hulk of a car. Any other rubble the lieutenant spoke of was such a small pile he couldn't see it from the road.

Only the sheriff car had lights flashing and siren blaring. All the fire department vehicles were silent and dark. It was broad daylight, the car was parked! Joel shook his head. "Leave it to Sheriff Gibbs to let everyone know he's here!" Exasperated, he muttered, "What is the sheriff doing? Probably trying to throw his weight around! I'm glad I've never had dealings with him! He's been to the house enough. Even as a little kid he was around a lot."

He gulped, coughed trying to take a breath. This was much worse than he imagined as the lieutenant described on the phone! He pulled in the long driveway, but stopped behind the line of fire department vehicles. His eyes scratchy, he couldn't keep tears from falling. His dad had thrown him out last night, but he'd lived in this house, grown up here! He had a few good memories from the twenty-five years he'd spent here, but this devastation was mind-boggling!

He stepped out of his car slowly and stood there taking in the whole scene, his eyes blurry with tears. He couldn't remember the last time he'd cried, but unable to see, he swiped his sleeve across his eyes. He flinched, the sleeve hit his temple, making the wound on his head hurt and reminded him that his headache hadn't gone away. Of course, the siren from the sheriff's car did nothing to ease the pain.

Had his parents gone to their reward? "My God in heaven! What have they done?" he whispered. "Did... did they cause this or was it something else?" Of course, Joel couldn't have heard an answer, even if he'd expected one. The siren from the sheriff's car blared too loudly. His headache pounded nearly in the same rhythm.

The lieutenant turned and watched as Joel approached. When Joel arrived, he held out his hand and said, "Joel Lawson? Lieutenant Winslow."

Joel nodded. "Yes, I'm Joel. What have you found out?"

The lieutenant shook his head. "Joel, unless they got away far enough there's not enough to tell if there was anyone in the house when it blew up. These would have been their cars?"

Joel looked at the places where the man pointed and said, "Yes, that's right. That's Mom's car and I'm sure that over there is Dad's truck. He usually parked beside the house." He continued to look around and finally said, "This is unbelievable!"

The lieutenant looked at Joel a bit more carefully, scowled, pointed to his face and asked, "Were you hurt? You have a black eye! You haven't been here, have you?"

Joel raised his hand to the band-aid, not knowing he also had a black eye and said, "Dad threw me out last night. A mirror close to the front door didn't fare too well when he yanked the door open. When the door crashed against the wall, the mirror fell and broke. A shard of glass gave me a puncture wound. I still have a headache, but I'm really okay." They had to yell because of the siren still blaring from the sheriff car only a few yards away.

Lieutenant Winslow looked at Joel and said as quietly as he could, "As you can see, we have Sheriff Gibbs here and some of his cronies. They just arrived right before you came; they ignored all of us and started to look around even before they decided to talk with me. I'm sure they can't see anything more than I can see. He wasn't some friend of your dad's was he?"

Joel nodded; the sheriff was not one of his close friends. "I saw the car when I pulled up. He knows my dad quite well, not as friends, but he is *not* one of my friends."

"Wish he'd turn off that siren of his! Of course that won't happen nobody's in the car. He sure does like to make his presence known! Brace yourself, Joel that man's out for blood!" Now that Joel stood with the lieutenant, the sheriff turned on his heel and was making a bee-line towards them. His three cronies were following right behind him.

"I can see that!" It wasn't hard to see that the sheriff was headed straight for Joel and the lieutenant. His face looked like the storm clouds last night! His hands in fists were pumping.

The lights and siren continued to flash and screech because the sheriff didn't go near his car, but turned on his heel from making his own inspection that took him nearly twenty minutes. Joel and the Lieutenant watched silently. Completely ignoring the noise, he walked purposefully toward Joel and the lieutenant, his face was beet red. His three cronies lined up behind him.

"So! What's up!" Gibbs demanded, arrogantly, his eyes were mere slits. Throwing his hands onto his hips, close to his revolver, he glared at the lieutenant, as if something he'd seen or didn't see was the fire lieutenant's fault.

Winslow threw out his hand toward the site. "See for yourself, Gibbs."

"Nothin's there!" he roared.

Lieutenant Winslow nodded. "Good observation, Gibbs. You get an A+ today." It was obvious because of his sarcasm that Lieutenant Winslow didn't think too highly of Sheriff Gibbs. Looking down the row of fire fighters standing near the trucks, they also shared the lieutenant's sentiments about the sheriff.

Sheriff Gibbs seemed to ignore the jibe and said to Winslow, "So where is everybody?" Joel wasn't sure who 'everybody' was, but Gibbs could be wondering where Thad was. He wouldn't be surprised if that was true.

Not knowing the relationship between Gibbs and Thad Lawson as Joel did, the fire lieutenant shrugged, looking around at all his men. "Far as I can see we're all here. I have two of my men in the hole going through the rubble that's there. And there's powerful little of that. I have a few guys out in the field looking to see if there's anything out there. So far they haven't found anything. This young man is Joel Lawson..."

Sheriff Gibbs's head whipped around and he took a menacing step toward Joel. He glared at him as he interrupted the fireman. "So-o-o-o you're the son! What's with this?" He flung his hand out, nearly hitting Joel in the face.

Joel opened his mouth, but Lieutenant Winslow whirled into Sheriff Gibbs's face and said, "Stop! Stop right there!"

Gibbs took a step back from the fire lieutenant. They were both big men, neither one could intimidate the other. With fire in his eyes, the sheriff yelled, "What do you mean stop!" With an accusing finger pointed nearly into Joel's face and without lowering his voice, he added, "He's the son.... that's what you said! He's Thad Lawson's son! That's enough for me! We need to get to the bottom of this! Where is the old ...." the man cleared his throat "...anyway?"

A calm that belied his words, the lieutenant leaned over to get as close to the man's face as he could. However his eyes were flashing daggers as said, "I mean... Gibbs, that this is *Professor* Joel Lawson from the university. He *happens* to be the son, but he had *nothing* to do with what happened here today! *Nothing!*"

Snidely, Sheriff Gibbs said, "How do you know that?"

Checking off his fingers, the lieutenant said, "First of all, I know that Thad Lawson threw his son out of the house last night and told him never to come back. He did **not** go back! He has not seen Thad Lawson since about seven o'clock last night. Secondly, *Doctor* Lawson was at the university all morning teaching classes and only found out about the explosion when I called him! Do you have a problem with that, Sheriff Gibbs?" Winslow took a step into Gibbs' space and his voice could be heard clearly above the siren.

"Yeah!" he said, arrogantly and stepped back again. Leaning over, trying to get even closer to Joel's face, he yelled, "If he's Thad Lawson's son he's gotta know what's going on! And I intend to find out!" Doubling his hands into fists, he roared. "Since you said he's Thad Lawson's son, there has to be somethin' he knows!"

Angrily, the lieutenant said, "Good luck with that! We – me and my men are pretty sure that Thad and Eleanor both went up with the house. Got any other suggestions?"

"What caused this?" He yelled, he didn't answer the lieutenant's question, but glared at Joel, then the lieutenant, probably hoping for something with his intimidation tactics. It was his way – had been for years. Sometimes it worked, other times not. The sheriff seemed to forget when it didn't. Joel and the lieutenant knew it wouldn't now, there was powerful little to see!

Clearly fed up with the sheriff, since he obviously wasn't listening, the lieutenant said, "We don't know! No one saw what happened. A neighbor felt and heard the explosion and called nine-eleven. We came out. There was no fire, just rising dust and two small piles of rubble that were probably cars. The driveway's a solid mass, there's a hole in the ground with a bit of rubble in it. There isn't a stick of anything. So – you tell me, Sheriff Gibbs – what's your take on this white hot explosion that yielded no fire?"

Without answering Lieutenant Winslow, Sheriff Gibbs turned to Joel and took a step toward him, as he asked, "What's your take? You know the man!"

"I have no idea. I was rarely here at the house, since I graduated from high school several years ago. I stayed as far away from Dad's business as I could. Besides, why couldn't something other than humans have caused this?"

His hands on his hips, Sheriff Gibbs crowded into Joel's personal space and stared for a long time at Joel, but said nothing. When Joel didn't say anything, only looked the man straight in the eye, the sheriff realized that his tactic wasn't working. He pulled in a deep breath, and looked around to see the destruction. With a silent glare at Lieutenant Winslow, he spun around toward his patrol car, motioned his men and climbed into the car. He turned off the lights and the siren, made a quick U-turn and left. Once he turned away, he never spoke or looked back.

The lieutenant nodded and murmured in the sudden silence, "Good riddance!" As the sheriff's car disappeared, Winslow said, "Like I was about to tell you – I have my crew working on what's left in the hole, but as I say there isn't enough left to get any kind of feel for what happened. There just isn't anything, not enough to even make a guess. All that's there is metal, but nothing can be identified. I called your closest neighbor, the one who called. She confirmed that there was an explosion. She felt it and heard it, but of course, her house is too far away for her to witness anything. With the trees she couldn't even tell me if she'd seen any smoke!"

Joel nodded again, started rubbing his temples, the siren had worsened his headache and whispered, "That's the way Dad wanted it. Except that the house was already here, he'd have built it back even further from the road so no one could see it. He really had no use for people seeing what he did." He sighed, "I suppose the sheriff heard the neighbor's call just like you did. I'm surprised he didn't stick around and try to milk this thing more than he did."

The lieutenant nodded. "As long as the man's been sheriff, he knew your dad, right?"

"Oh, yes!" Joel exclaimed. He added, "I tried not to be around whenever the sheriff came around, though. Nothing good ever came from his visits!"

Still looking at everything that could possibly give a clue, the lieutenant asked, "By the way, do you have any clues? I didn't have a chance to ask before the sheriff..."

Joel still looked at the empty place where the house he'd lived in used to stand. "No, I really don't, Lieutenant. I spent all day yesterday on campus and only came back for supper, planning to spend the evening and night here. However, Dad threw me out after I ate. That's when the mirror broke and the glass hit me. My sister gathered up my things and I was able to get them because I came back later and she threw them out the bedroom window to me. I know Sis went to school today, because after you called I sent her a text and she answered, but as for my parents' activities today or last night, I have no clue."

"This is all quite a puzzle!"

Walking on the solid driveway, Joel said, "Like you said, it had to be very intense and extremely hot! This driveway was all gravel before! I can't believe this is Dad's truck! It was a year old and really one of those hot numbers that roar around town!"

"Wow! No more than is in this pile....!"

Joel and the lieutenant moved toward the hole in the ground and the man said, "Like I said, there's the hole and a little rubble, but that's all. I've called headquarters for the experts; they'll try to determine the cause." Letting out a sigh and moving his hand around the site, Winslow said, "With so little here, I don't see how they'll make a judgment, but that's on them." After a minute, he asked, "Did you say your sister got your things? Was she here overnight?"

"I... I assume so. It started storming after I reached my car with my things. Leslie doesn't have a car, so I'm sure she was here overnight." Joel's head went slowly back and forth. "I can't put my mind around this," he whispered. "This boggles my mind!"

"I know it's unbelievable! What kind of furnace was there?"

"That could have been it, I suppose." He nodded toward the tank that sat some distance away, still intact. "It was gas - propane, as old as the house and possibly Dad hadn't had it checked this year. The water heater and the cooking stove were also propane, oh, the clothes dryer also but that was electronic ignition."

The lieutenant nodded. "Who knows at this point!"

Joel and the lieutenant reached the hole, and looked in to see two firemen, their hands in gloves, looking over a small amount of rubble, several pieces of twisted metal. Joel looked around, knowing how large the house was. He shook his head and said, "This isn't big enough, Lieutenant. The house had a full basement, cement block walls and a cement floor! This is less than half that size"

The lieutenant nodded. "I wondered. The explosion made some of the walls collapse."

"Yes, must have. In fact, the furnace was where it's completely filled in, the water heater beside it. There was a small room that Dad always kept locked that I knew nothing about. It was in that part that's filled in. This part where your men are had exercise equipment. It's all gone!"

"Okay, that's good to know. I'll be sure the experts know that." They still stood by the hole as a van with the local TV station logo drove up, but Joel stayed with the lieutenant. He had no interest in talking with reporters or being seen on TV; not after the encounter with the sheriff.

"Guess we'll soon be on candid camera," Winslow said.

"Not if I can help it*!*" Joel murmured to himself.

When the news van reached the same pull off where Joel had stopped last night, Jenni pulled in a gasp. "Wow! Look over there, Len! There's nothing here! Used to, this was the only place to see the whole house from any direction, but there's nothing! This is amazing!"

The fire trucks made a line ahead of them as Len made the turn and headed up the long driveway. He exclaimed, "I'd say that's a fact!" Still looking around, he scowled, "Tell me, it's been a while since I was by here. Wasn't it a two story house, sorta large, right?"

"Uh huh. Two story frame house with white siding and green shutters. Mr. Lawson didn't want close neighbors for some reason."

"Yeah, we can only guess at that one."

Len pulled up beside another car, jammed the stick into park, and they both scrambled from the SUV. Len brought out two cameras, placing the strap of one around his neck and setting the much larger video camera on his shoulder. Jenni grabbed the mike, settled the battery-pack strap on her shoulder, left her purse in the truck and headed for the group of fire fighters that stood beside the large fire truck. They weren't frantically pulling out hoses or equipment, but standing around, their hands in their pockets against the cold. There were no flames, nothing to rescue. There was a fairly small hole in the ground, with two heads in it and several piles of rubble in the driveway. Only dust was rising from the hole and the breeze took it quickly away. There were no flames, not even the smell of smoke.

Stopping beside the fire fighters, Jenni looked around and exclaimed, "Wow! Amazing!"

One of the fire fighters nodded. "You got that right, Lady! We came flying out here expecting a full out fire and there's nothing!"

"This is how you found it? No fire, nothing?"

Nodding the fireman said, "You got it! We got here to see that hole in the ground. Just that and rubble. As you can see, there's a little dust still going up, but that's it. Never was that first bit of fire or even the smell of smoke! We aren't sure when it happened, nobody saw it. The neighbor heard and felt the explosion and called it in. Lieutenant said he's going around to talk with other neighbors."

The man shook his head. "Don't know what he can find out, there aren't any houses that a body can see. Unless they were going by on the road when it happened they couldn't tell him anything. Actually, can't see a blame thing but an open field and a big, old propane tank!"

"Oh, my! Was anyone home?"

The man shrugged, pointing to the pile of rubble close by and the metal hulk down the driveway. "Can't tell, really. Two vehicles, or probably was. But unless there was some warning and people got out and had time enough to run far enough, they're long gone. They'd had to have a good warning, that explosion sure put out the heat, see the driveway? Lieutenant is saying husband and wife were both home, so they died when the place exploded."

He also nodded around the open field around the house and said, "Lieutenant sent a couple of guys out to see if there's anything that got thrown away by the explosion, but so far, they've found nothing. I mean, there isn't as much as a stick! Usually, there's something!"

Jenni stared at the two men moving around in the hole and said, "It was a good sized house as I remember. Two stories, but it's gone! That hole's too small for such a big house."

"Yeah, that's true. We can only guess, since that's all that's here now."

"Didn't Lawson's have some children?"

The man nodded toward the lieutenant and said, "The son's here and he says he's sure his sister's at school. He sent her a text and got a reply."

Jenni looked toward the man she knew was the lieutenant and saw a civilian with him, but she couldn't see his face. "You say the son? Is that him over there?"

"Yeah, that's him."

Joel lifted his head just then to look around, turned his head slightly and Jenni gasped, "I know him! That's Joel Lawson!"

The fireman shrugged. "I guess, is that his name?"

Jenni nodded and looked again at Joel. "Oh, yes! I didn't know he was still living around here. Wow!"

She looked around. "As we came down the road we met the sheriff. I guess he was here? Why'd he leave so quick?"

Cynically, the man replied, "Yeah, he was here, big, old blustery guy! Didn't see nothin' he could haul to jail, so him and his buddies left. Had his siren and lights goin' the whole blame time he was here, though."

"Huh…" Sometimes Jenni wondered about the sheriff. It was a political position. People voted for the man. She didn't know anyone who liked him, yet he'd been in office for more years than she could remember. She hadn't voted for him the last time he won his election.

A fireman climbed from the hole and Jenni rushed over. When she asked, he shrugged and said, "Not much there. Just a small pile of rubble we couldn't identify. I imagine when the guys come from headquarters they'll take some in for testing."

Jenni shrugged. "I guess that'd be the only way to know."

Sheriff Gibbs was frustrated, it was obvious. The other three officers in the car stayed quiet, they knew the sheriff well enough that when he was in this mood nobody made a comment and certainly didn't make fun of the situation. Stating the obvious, the sheriff exclaimed, "Lawson wasn't there! I thought sure…"

"Nope, he sure wasn't, Sheriff!" *He probably died in the explosion!*

When the car reached the city limits, the sheriff showed his frustration. He flipped on the lights and siren and roared into town, through all the lights, scattering cars, straight to headquarters. Once inside the cage he jerked the stick into park, flung his door open and moving his legs was momentarily inside. The deputy in the passenger seat turned off the car, the lights and siren and pocketed the keys before he left the car. He and the other deputies left the car much more slowly. Sheriff Gibbs was already inside before the other three left the car.

Of course, the officer at the dispatch desk heard the siren outside, so he looked up when the sheriff stomped in. "So what did you discover, Sheriff? You're back really quick, seeing it was Thad Lawson's place."

"Nothin'!" Gibbs shouted.

The dispatch officer did a double take at the sheriff's harsh word. He scowled and asked, "As in nobody told you anything? You didn't see Thad Lawson because he escaped? Wasn't the fire department there? Weren't they trying to put out the fire? What'd the lieutenant have to say? What do you mean, 'nothin'?"

Sheriff Gibbs swung his arm down, as if to slash what the officer said. "No!" he bellowed. "No! There was nothin' there! A hole in the ground, two firemen lookin' around in the hole. Two piles of rubble and the fire department vehicles. No fire – nothin'!"

"Couldn't tell you what happened? NO FIRE?"

"No! Winslow had the son there and claimed he knew nothing. I swear, the son had to have the man brain-washed!"

"Why?"

Sheriff Gibbs scowled at the other man as if he was demented. "Said Thad threw him out last night, but he had a black eye! Said witnesses could verify the guy was at the university till Winslow called him. Couldn't get nothin' outta the son, neither! Said he didn't know a… blame thing!" The sheriff paced two steps, then back. "There gotta be somebody! I say it's the son!"

The dispatch officer shrugged. "Could be they're telling the truth, Gibbs, it could be, you know. If the son got thrown out last night, how would he know what went on today?"

"Don't know," Sheriff Gibbs grumbled grudgingly. Wanting to vindicate his own way of thinking, he said, "Coulda come back this mornin' and lobbed somethin' in the place!"

"Give it a rest, Gibbs. Things may come to light in a day or two."

"Yeah, guess that's so. But wouldn't the son know the man's business? I mean, really?"

"Not if he kept clear of him!"

"Yeah, I guess," the sheriff grumbled. Hardly giving the other officers the time of day, Sheriff Gibbs marched into his office and slammed the door. Slouching into his desk chair, he grumbled, "'The apple don't fall far from the tree.' I swear it!"

Joel noticed the man with the video camera talked while the film rolled. Joel quickly turned away. He didn't want his face seen on the evening news. The woman walked around interviewing the fire fighters. One man from the hole climbed out and she snagged him immediately. Joel worked hard to keep away from her. He knew over the years that his parents were on the news several times, most of those in the paper, but several times on the TV news. He couldn't remember once that it was favorable and even though he was their son, he didn't want his name brought into anything related to them. All this was devastating; he probably couldn't put three words together and have them mean anything. After all, he'd lived in this house and both his parents were missing. He looked up at the clear sky and was very glad it wasn't raining; there wasn't a storm or any storm clouds on the horizon.

Jenni walked away from the group of fire fighters and tried several times to get to Joel, but he managed to evade her. He gave the lieutenant a two finger salute and slid into his car, made a U-turn and left. Jenni watched him. She hadn't seen him since high school.... well, last night in the dark... they had both gone separate ways. He stayed and went to the hometown university; her scholarship took her to another university a few hundred miles away. She also could have gone locally, but decided the other school had a better department in her major. Getting out of town suited her just fine. Now that she was back she felt she had a better perspective of things in the mega-city that included the suburb where her TV station was located.

She sighed as Joel stepped into his car; he'd filled out into a handsome man and dressed to meet the public, but obviously had no intention of talking with a reporter. She blew out a frustrated breath and wondered if he even recognized her. Thinking about it, he probably didn't. She decided she'd let him have a day or two to grieve, maybe she'd catch him some other day.... or night. She went to the lieutenant to ask questions. The man didn't have many answers about the explosion, since there were no eye witnesses and so little left, but he did answer several about Joel. It still frustrated her that Joel had skipped out and she hadn't been able to talk with him.

After Jenni and the lieutenant had talked for several minutes, another official looking vehicle drove up the driveway and the lieutenant turned to see it. "Ah," he said, turning away from Jenni. "The experts are here! Maybe we'll get some answers. One can only hope! There's so little here and the breeze has carried off any smell that might have lingered. I know they're better at detection than I am, but still.... When all that's here is a pile of rubble..."

"Are they from your station or downtown, Lieutenant?"

Just before he started walking toward the SUV he said to Jenni, "Oh, they're from headquarters. Have to send them the news as soon as it happens, of course. Say, if you wanna know more about Joel, you might ask Sam, he's one of my guys and went to college with Joel, I think. He's just coming out of the hole."

Jenni smiled, reached to shake the lieutenant's hand, knowing that since the experts arrived her interview with him was over. "Thanks for your time, Lieutenant. Catch you later."

"Sure, not a problem," he said, absently over his shoulder as he walked down the driveway toward the SUV with the insignia on the side. Jenni followed close behind him, perhaps he'd introduce her to the 'experts' and she could interview them. Then again, there are some folks who don't like to talk to a reporter – like Joel Lawson, for instance.

Three men stepped out of the vehicle, and the lieutenant started talking immediately. Jenni stayed beside him hoping to hear something he hadn't said to her. She eagerly looked at the men as they left their car. They, in turn, took one look at Jenni holding her mike and all three turned their backs to her to listen to the lieutenant, which was very frustrating. At least at this site there wasn't much to see and not many answers, but no one wanted to talk to her at any length. She sighed – the story of her life. Sometimes she wanted to leave the profession, but other times it was challenging. She turned, wondering where and what Len was doing.

The three men who came in the SUV were intent on seeing the site, so the four men walked between the department vehicles and fanned out around the hole. Two of the men jumped into the hole that the fire fighters had left a few minutes before. Both Len and Jenni watched them and Len started his video camera, but Jenni held her mike. She'd get conversation, but no answers if she asked questions. These experts didn't want to talk to her.

After Len got all his pictures and news footage and Jenni got as many answers as she could, they left. It didn't take long to look at a hole in the ground! She was sure that if the experts came up with answers someone would let the station know. Alex's office was lined with scanners from the different city departments. They always got late-breaking news first hand.

While things at the site were still fresh in her mind, she sat at her desk, eating her lunch time apple and listened to what she had recorded, then started her report. She had a hard time only writing the facts. Since she remembered Joel and been by the house so often, it was hard to be detached. She discarded several attempts before finally settling on what she would say on the evening news. In fact, she had her boss review what she had written, hoping it was suitable.

What she usually reported – national, international news, state and city news, even events she went on herself in the city; things that happened where she had no personal interest in anyone, she had no problem being detached, but not the Lawson event. What she had seen at the Lawson place was beyond traumatic and it affected her greatly.

Her family had lived beyond that house from the time she was tiny, so she'd gone by it many times over the years, on the school bus or later in her personal car. Joel had ridden the same bus. She had never realized that something so personal would affect her so much. All afternoon she caught herself staring off into space thinking about and visualizing the Lawson site. Of course, it wasn't hard to visualize Joel only yards away from her.

FOUR

In Leslie's class after lunch one of her friends had her phone on and learned about the explosion at the Lawson house. The minute her classmate blurted out the news the class erupted and pandemonium reigned. Leslie was stunned. That was why Joel had told her to go to Aunt Lucy's house. He probably wanted to tell her and didn't think she'd find out some other way.

No one did class work that hour; the teacher quickly decided that European history could be replaced by instant breaking local news, so they only talked about the explosion for fifty minutes. Several in the class found the news on their phones and soon, pictures started coming on the screens, so they showed them around the class the entire time. Leslie felt shell shocked.

Leslie was only a body in her other classes that afternoon, in fact, nothing new circulated in those classes. A house explosion that close to home preempted anything either teacher said. For Leslie, nothing registered except what had happened to the house where she'd lived all her life and the assumption that her parents had died. Tears slid down Les's cheeks the rest of the day. It was an awful realization that the only home she'd ever known and her parents were gone!

Some girlfriends would walk her to her aunt's house, she didn't live that far from the school and several of her friends also lived in town. She loaded her back with her backpacks and book bag at her locker, and tried to dry her tears before she left the school. She didn't want to walk city streets and be crying, but she could feel them scratching behind her eyes. Her friends gave her a sad smile before they went their ways, some to the busses and others to walk home.

One of her friends squeezed her hand and another pulled her into a hug before she turned up the walk to her aunt's house. However, the minute she reached the walk to the door of Lucy's house, the lady opened the door and Leslie ran to her, threw her arms around her, buried her face in Lucy's chest and burst into tears. Lucy had tears in her eyes while she stood holding Leslie, patting her back and shedding some tears on her shoulder too.

Finally, several minutes later, on a hiccough and a shudder, Leslie said, "A-aunt-tie, why? Why? Auntie, somebody at school had their phone on and learned about the explosion and we saw some pictures somebody took. There was nothing there – nothing at all! We talked about it all afternoon! They're dead! They weren't saved! They didn't know Jesus! How... why did God let this happen? I've prayed all my life that Dad and Mom would get saved! But they're dead! It didn't happen!"

Tears slid down Lucy's cheeks, Eleanor was her older sister. Through her tears she hugged her teenaged niece and stroked her hand through Leslie's hair, as she said, "Honey, I don't know why. I have no idea what God's plan is. It's hard to understand, I know. All we can do is look to Him and let Him take us through this."

Lucy tried to stop her tears, but looking at Leslie's face, more tears flowed. "I know this is so hard for you, dear girl, they were your parents. You're sixteen, that's not very old to lose your parents; you're still dependent on them. This was such a traumatic way! But you know, I'm really glad you weren't there too!"

"Yes, me, too," Leslie whispered. "Joel texted me at noon. Was that when it happened?"

"We aren't really sure, Honey."

"Really? Why not?"

"Honey, the house is so alone on the road that nobody saw what happened only your neighbor heard the noise and felt the vibrations of the explosion. She's who called nine-one-one for the fire department."

"Oh... oh, wow!"

After several more minutes of resting in her aunt's arms, Leslie pulled back and shrugged out of the straps keeping the packs on her back, letting them slide to the floor. They were heavy. She hiccoughed, looked at her aunt and whispered, "Auntie, last night I had a feeling, like you have sometimes. I felt like I should pack my backpack and take it to school, so I packed two this morning with as much as I could, but that's all I have! I have some clothes, only what I could stuff in my bags, my phone, and my purse. I even stuffed my extra money in a side pocket of my backpack. I have all my books and school supplies; they were in my book bag! At least I got Joel's things out for him last night, but I never thought something like this could happen and I'd lose so much. Auntie, I saw the pictures the kids showed around! I couldn't believe it!" She pulled in a deep breath. "Auntie, even their cars! Like there's nothing left!"

Lucy nodded. "Yes, I was sure you'd lost everything, but I'm glad you got what you did. I'm sure it was the Lord telling you to pack your bags! Joel called me not long ago while he was there. He said there is nothing – nothing but some rubble. The cars that were there can hardly be identified, and they were both there. That has to mean your parents were both in the house."

"Oh, Auntie..." Leslie burst into tears again. "They... they never showed us any love, but I... I... they were my parents! Joel and me were both born there – I mean, they never showed us that they cared, but it was where we lived! Joel never called it home and I didn't either, but still... we'd always lived there!"

"Honey, I know, I know so well." Lucy looked at Leslie's backpacks that were stuffed so full she had hardly gotten them zipped. "Maybe we can go to Goodwill soon and see if there's something you can get. With weather like this I'm sure you need a few more warm clothes."

Leslie nodded. "Okay, I have a little money; I can get a few things."

Lucy shook her head. "No, Honey, you shouldn't pay for things. I'll help you; you won't have any money once yours is gone. I can help you. We'll work on that tomorrow."

"Okay Auntie, I love you so much! I'm so glad we could come here. You've saved my life lots of times just by being here and having your door open for me. I wanted to come today! Dad threw me around twice last night! But... but, Auntie, now they're gone!"

Lucy smiled at her niece through her tears and said, "I love you too, my sweet child. God has been good to us all these years and has never let us down and He never will. I'm glad you've come to your uncle and me whenever you needed to. We wanted to be here for you because we were sure we knew what your home life was like. I know your dad was a hard man to live with and I've never seen my sister except from a distance at school and then after her graduation when we both went to the grocery or something like that, but she never spoke to me."

"It was hard, wasn't it, Auntie?"

"Yes, child it was heartbreaking to see what she was doing with her life and how she allowed Thad to dictate who she saw and what she said. I could tell as she sank lower, but I had to leave her with God. I certainly wasn't expecting Him to do it in this way, though."

"That is for sure!" Leslie exclaimed.

"Mom and Dad often asked how they went wrong with her. I never thought it was their fault, and Josh told them she made her own choices, but I know they found it so hard to accept. They're coming for supper, so we'll pool everything we come up with over a good meal. Joel, of course, is coming when he gets done what he needs to do with the fire department at the house. If there's so little left I don't see how he can give much information, but he'll be along."

Leslie pulled in a deep breath and finally said, "Oh, I'll be glad to see Grampa and Gramma, I haven't seen them for a while. Since they moved, they live far enough away I can't get to their place and of course, only Joel would take us, but I'm glad they're coming tonight. Auntie, it's hard to even think about it!"

Still close to tears, Leslie asked, "Auntie, do Grampa and Gramma know about this?"

Lucy gave Leslie a tiny smile. "Yes, Joel asked me to tell them, so I called them. It was the first they'd heard about it so it was awful for them and so hard to tell them, but I'm sure it would have been harder for Joel to tell them. That's when we decided to have supper together. Will you help me get started? I'm not used to cooking for so many of us. Will you?"

"Yeah, sure, Auntie, I'll help you all I can. Mom didn't want my help much, Dad was kind of stuck on her cooking, but she did let me help once in a while." Leslie took a deep breath and said, "I guess we'll live here with you for a while, won't we?" Leslie shook her head. "When Dad kicked Joel out last night I had no idea something like this would happen today! Auntie, it's so hard to put my mind around this!"

Lucy put her arm around Leslie and said, "Yes, dear child, of course you'll stay here! I wouldn't think of letting you both live somewhere else! Besides, where else could you go? There isn't any place! I wouldn't make you stay in a hotel, it's not right. Joel has the sofa-sleeper and you'll have the room upstairs. Honey, take your things up there now, it'll be good. We'll get started on dinner after that." She smiled at her niece. "We'll make a good one!"

"Okay, Auntie. I'll take these things upstairs." Tears still hanging in her eyes, Leslie said, "How can Joel be there at that place? It must be horrid for him!"

Lucy nodded. "I'm sure it is."

However, before Leslie could pick up her things someone knocked on the door. Lucy went to answer and a man in a fireman's uniform stood there. "Excuse me, Ma'am; I'm Lieutenant Winslow from the local fire station. I just left the Thad Lawson property a few minutes ago. Joel Lawson said he thought his sister, Leslie would be here. Would she be here from school perhaps?" He gave Lucy something that passed for a smile and said, "I have a question for her that I think is pretty important. If you don't mind?"

"Yes, she's here. She just got in from school. Won't you step inside? It's so cold out!"

"Yes, I'll do that, but I don't want to interrupt. Still, my question is rather important. Could I speak with Leslie, please?"

Leslie came up behind her aunt and said, "I'm Leslie. I wasn't there at all, you know. I was at school all day."

The man looked kindly at the teenager and said, "Leslie, I know you were, and because of what happened at your home, I'm very glad you were! Even so, I need to ask you at least one question. May I?"

"I… I guess."

"Ma'am, either last night or this morning before you left for school did your parents do anything that seemed suspicious to you? Or maybe say something?"

Leslie shrugged. "When I got off the bus after school yesterday and came in, Dad was reading the paper in the living room and had a beer, like usual. Mom had started dinner, that's kinda the time she usually starts to cook, too. They never talk much to each other when me and Joel are there. Joel came in time to change clothes and maybe study a bit and eat, but he planned to stay. We ate, but we weren't even done when Joel said something and Dad pulled him from the table and dragged him to the front door. I ran upstairs to his room to grab some stuff. Dad slammed the door after he threw Joel out and started cussing, but he went back to the kitchen, when Mom did the dishes he went to the living room to his recliner. Far as I know, he read the paper. Nobody called and Dad didn't call anybody. It was quiet, except for supper, and him throwing Joel out, he lit into me after that, nothing really happened that didn't usually happen."

The man scowled, so Leslie said, "After I gave Joel his things Dad marched into the hall after me and flung me around, then ordered me to my room, but he never hit me. I could smell the beer on his breath. I ran upstairs and stayed in Joel's room and they came up for bed around ten. I never heard what they said or did after he ordered me out of his sight. This morning, I left for the bus before either of them left their bedroom. While I'm still upstairs I never hear them make any noise, they didn't this morning either."

The lieutenant also shrugged. "Well, I guess that answers that, I guess we'll never know what could have happened or what could have caused the explosion. Neither you nor your brother can give me any clues and there was no eye-witness."

"So there was an explosion? For sure?" Leslie asked. "You have no idea what could have caused it? The place just blew up!?"

Lieutenant Winslow nodded. "Yes, the house is gone but for a hole in the ground. From what your brother said the explosion even caused some of the basement to collapse. The hole is much too small for the size house I remember when I've been out that way. The rubble in the hole is just that, and very little of that, really. It can't be recognized as pieces of anything. Outside, some yards away from where the house sat is the metal frame of all that's left of a car. Your brother said the pile of rubble very close to the hole, but on the driveway was probably your dad's truck. There is nothing salvageable at the site except the propane tank. There are still some experts at the site trying to determine if they can find what caused the explosion."

"Oh, my!" Lucy whispered.

"Joel, my brother, was out there with you?" Leslie asked.

"Yes, he came out when I called him. He was as shocked as you. Of course, he had no idea what your parents had done."

"No, he barely finished his supper before Dad threw him out."

The lieutenant shook his head. "How can we ever know what caused the explosion? I've never had to deal with something like this. Even the neighbor who reported to us only said she heard and felt the explosion, not that she could see anything."

"I guess we can't know, Lieutenant. We must leave it in God's hands," Lucy said.

The lieutenant hesitated for a second, before he said, "Yes, Ma'am, that is all we can do. I am extremely sorry for your loss, Miss Leslie."

Leslie nodded, not sure what she should say, so she said, "Thank you."

Not long after the lieutenant left, Joel drove onto Lucy's driveway, and sat in the car for several minutes. Leslie was upstairs emptying her backpacks and saw him through the gable window and wondered why he sat in his car so long. Maybe he had a headache. Of course, she hadn't been to the site, so she wanted to hear what Joel said. She watched as he opened the door, brought his briefcase out and headed for the house. He seemed to move extra slowly.

Leslie raced downstairs to open the door. "Oh, wow! Bro, you've got a shiner!"

"Yeah, I know. I've had a few comments about it, believe me."

Lucy had already gone to the kitchen, but when she heard Leslie open the door, she came to hear what Joel would say. "Was it bad?" Leslie asked.

Joel shook his head. "Sis, there is not a thing there! Except a few piles of stuff, anybody going by that didn't know would think it was an open field. ...Well, the propane tank sits off where it was. The driveway's there, but where the house was is solid and looks like clouded glass. Those are the only clues that something was there! It's kind of like the pictures you see after a tornado where houses were sucked up into the funnel, nothing to show for a house!"

"Oh, my!" both Lucy and Leslie said.

Joel stepped in and as he put his hand on the door to close it, a siren whooped outside. He looked out to see what was going on and the sheriff's car whipped in the driveway. The sheriff motioned Joel outside. Joel pulled in a long breath, and said, "It's the sheriff again. I saw him out there at the site and listened to his accusations. I can't imagine what he wants now."

Lucy said, "Tell him as little as possible!"

"Believe me, I will! I have nothing to say, to add to what I told him out there at the site."

Joel dropped his briefcase next to the closet, stepped outside and closed the door on the cold. He stood on the cement slab in front of the door and pushed his hands into his pockets. It was easy to see that the trees along the street were blowing in the strong breeze and Joel wished he had a hat on or that the sheriff hadn't come.

The sheriff jammed the stick into park and was instantly out on the driveway. "So, what are you doing here?" he asked, angrily, walking toward Joel, his hands going to his utility belt.

"Excuse me?" Joel asked. *As if it's any of your business!*

"So what are *you* doing here?" the man repeated and pointed to the house.

Joel looked at the man for several seconds contemplating what to say. Finally, he looked the sheriff in the eye and asked, "It is important for you to know why I'm at my aunt's home? You were out at the explosion site; it's obvious I can't live there!"

"Yes!" the man hissed.

"Why?"

Exasperated, the sheriff pulled in a breath and roared, "You're a suspect!" If he hadn't yelled, the wind would have carried his words away.

"Of what?" Joel shrugged, bewildered.

As if it was obvious, the sheriff slammed his fists on his gun belt at his waist, leaned into Joel's personal space and yelled, "The explosion at the Lawson place! You lived there!"

Joel nodded. "Until seven o'clock last evening it was where I lived. You're right. As the fire lieutenant told you, Thad Lawson threw me out the front door. Last night! I left. I have never been thrown out of any place before, but I took him at his word. My sister texted me to come for my clothes. She threw them out the window. *I did not* go back in the house!"

Snidely, Sheriff Gibbs said, "He also said you were at the university this morning."

"Yes, I was."

"What for?" he yelled, losing his patience.

Joel took a deep breath, looked the man in the eye, knowing he had nothing to hide, he answered, "Sheriff, if it is any of your business, my Aunt Lucy was up and fed me breakfast. I went from here to the university where I taught two classes today, one from eight to nine-fifteen and the other from nine-thirty to ten-forty-five then I went to the library, where I was when Lieutenant Winslow called me. I left immediately when he called and went out there. Perhaps you saw me come, you were already there."

Clearly not believing Joel, Sheriff Gibbs took another step into Joel's space and said, "You have someone who could verify that?"

"Yes, Sheriff, I most certainly do. Someone I know and who knows me could tell you everywhere I was. Believe me; I do not make a practice of lying!"

"Call them!"

Joel didn't touch his phone, but looked steadily at the sheriff, but didn't retreat from him. "Look, Sheriff Gibbs, just because Thad Lawson was on your black list and he is no longer where you can touch him, doesn't mean I am cut from the same mold. As you well know, I was not usually at that house when you came to see my dad."

As Joel finished speaking another car pulled behind Joel's car. Sheriff Gibbs turned to look, didn't seem to recognize it, and turned back with his mouth open ready to say something else. However, before he could speak, the driver stepped from the car and strode quickly up to stand beside Joel. The man was nearly as tall as his grandson and out-weighed him by about fifty pounds. The scowl on his face would make any self-respecting person shake in his boots.

The sheriff glanced at the man, did a double take and looked again. Surprise registered on the sheriff's face, but before he could say anything, Ed Wilson said, "Sheriff, you were questioning my grandson for a reason?"

The sheriff cleared his throat, lifted his hat and put it back on. "Well... well... he's Thad Lawson's son, Mr. Wilson."

"Yes, and that's relevant? Thad was also my son-in-law. Tell me how this can be relevant to an investigation – that the *fire* department is conducting?"

Sheriff Gibbs gave a fake cough and said, "Well, one always suspects family first when something like this happens."

Ed Wilson shook his head. "No, Sheriff Gibbs, that's not always true, except when law enforcement has a bone they want to pick with a repeat offender whom they can't accuse any more because he isn't available. Isn't that right?"

"Umm, yeah, I guess it is," the sheriff said, grudgingly.

"Fine, you'll be on your way now?"

"Ah, yeah."

"Thank you, Sheriff. You have a good evening."

"Yeah, sure. Umm, have a good one yourself, Mr. Wilson." The sheriff didn't say anything more, but the look he gave Joel led him to believe the sheriff wasn't done with him.

Joel let out a deep sigh and whispered, "What an oaf!"

Grandfather and grandson watched the sheriff hurry to his car, slam the door and wheel the car into the street without looking back. "Thanks, Grampa, I take it you know the sheriff?"

"Yeah, you could say that. We have crossed interests on several occasions." Being on the city council for this suburb, put Ed Wilson and Sheriff Gibbs at the same meetings on several occasions. Ed Wilson never let Sheriff Gibbs get away with anything. Of course, Sheriff Gibbs didn't like Ed Wilson at all.

With the sheriff gone, Ed turned and motioned Claudia to come and at the same time, Leslie flung open the house door and raced to the car. She reached the car just as Claudia pushed the door open and exclaimed, "Gramma! I'm glad to see you! Auntie and I are making supper."

The older lady gave her granddaughter a sideways hug and said, "Leslie, dear, I'm glad to see you! Shall we go inside out of the cold?"

"Sure, Gramma, let's go!" Leslie put her arm around her gramma and started for the door. Ed and Joel followed behind and Joel closed the door.

Over her shoulder, Leslie said, "Grampa, I'm glad you came!"

Ed smiled at his granddaughter and said, "I wouldn't go anywhere without your gramma, you know that, don't you?"

Leslie laughed. "Sure I do!"

Lucy stood in the opening to the kitchen, but she asked, "Joel, what can you tell us? Maybe they'll have something on the news later."

Joel looked down at his briefcase, opened the closet door and set it inside. "Auntie, I have no idea what could have caused such an explosion! It had to be super hot and huge. The lieutenant asked me about the furnace, but that's the only thing we could think of. The propane tank is the only thing left, but it's still intact and sitting where it always sat, so it wasn't what caused the explosion. It's amazing! Since I couldn't give him any clues because I wasn't there since last night, he had nothing he could tell the experts from headquarters. I left before they came. There were firemen in the hole and a couple in the field, but nobody found any clues. There were no smells, nothing. As I drove down the road before I got there, I saw a couple of columns of what I thought was smoke, but the lieutenant said was dust rising from the remains."

"And the lieutenant said the hole wasn't big enough for the basement."

"Yes, that's right." Joel walked into the living room, slouched into the recliner and put his head back. Closing his eyes, he continued, "The part of the basement where the furnace, water heater and that storage room were is completely filled in. It doesn't even look like there was ever anything there! No cement blocks, floor, nothing!"

With his eyes closed, Joel pulled in a deep breath and said, "You know, this has been an incredibly horrific day!"

"That it has!" Lucy exclaimed. "And you still have a headache."

Joel nodded. "That is correct!" Looking toward the front door, he added, "And having to deal with the sheriff twice hasn't helped it at all. That man refuses to believe anything I tell him! He wanted me to call someone to verify every minute of my day."

"Want some headache medicine?" Leslie asked.

"Yeah, I wouldn't mind at all, thanks."

"Of course, I'll get some."

Leslie came back with some pills and a glass of water. Joel gratefully took them from her and as he took the pills, Leslie took the older lady's hand and exclaimed, "Gramma, come on! Auntie and I are starting supper; come to the kitchen and talk with us. Joel and Grampa can talk while we cook." Leslie made a face. "I really think we need to talk about something else."

"So you've been to school all day?"

"Yes, Gramma, but I didn't do much this afternoon. Joel sent me a text, but only told me to come here from school. He didn't know I'd planned to anyway. One of my friends in class learned about the explosion on her phone. That sure was a shock! Somebody posted pictures, so that's all we talked about after lunch! It's so incredible! I can hardly think that the house and Mom and Dad are gone! It wasn't a fire but an explosion it's hard to put my mind around!"

"I know, I hope Joel can explain it all."

"Gramma, he told us there isn't much there. Not enough for anyone to tell. If he can't tell us any more than that we'll never know! Actually, the lieutenant from the fire station came and asked me what Mom and Dad did last night and this morning. When I couldn't tell him anything unusual, we decided there's no way to figure out what happened. It's kind of spooky!"

Claudia Wilson hugged her granddaughter and kissed her cheek, she smiled and said, "Honey, sometimes it's not meant for us to know. Child, we must leave it all in God's hands. You and Joel are safe, that's what God wanted. I must be content. You are my darlings."

Tears clouding her eyes, Leslie hugged her gramma and said, "Yes, Gramma, I know you're right, but it's still so hard."

"Honey, I know it is. Let's help your Aunt Lucy get that dinner on the table. We can surely cook up something good!"

Leslie's tummy growled. She chuckled and said, "I think it's time!"

Lucy fixed a good meal, after all, she and Joel's mom came from the same home growing up, so they cooked pretty much alike, but Joel hadn't thought too much about that until tonight. During supper the only topic that anyone wanted to talk about was the terrible events of the afternoon. However, Joel was the only one who had been to the site and he didn't want to talk about it much, since he'd seen it first hand. He answered questions, but didn't say too much else.

Soon after Lucy and her mom finished clean-up, his grandparents left. After that, Lucy and Leslie settled in the living room, his aunt planned to read and Les had some homework to do. Joel felt at loose ends and since he didn't have his own room now, he decided to go back to the library for some study time. However, he still had a headache and the place on his temple was sore and throbbed in time with his pulse. He wasn't sure how productive he would be.

Because he didn't feel good, he couldn't concentrate, so soon after he arrived and settled down, he shrugged back into his coat and left for the park. The park was in the center of the suburb, but after dark it was deserted. After the chaos all day it suited him just fine. He walked several well lighted trails and thought about his parents. The fact that they were gone weighed on him. As far as he knew they'd never made Jesus their Savior and Lord. Since Eleanor came from such a good Christian family, he wondered if she truly had accepted Jesus as her Savior but had totally rebelled since she'd met Thad Lawson. However, he had no such thoughts about his dad. His thoughts were truly distressing.

Once he was in the park, thoughts about his dissertation never crossed his mind. But when he climbed back into his car he wondered at the wisdom of wasting the hours, he was ahead of schedule, but he wanted plenty of time to review. He wanted the thesis to be accepted the first time, without having to revise it. Still, he didn't regret the time he'd spent in the park. He felt refreshed and knew it had been therapeutic and that was what he needed tonight.

When supper was over for most people, the evening news anchor said: "Ladies and gentlemen, local news: The home of Thaddeus and Eleanor Lawson was completely destroyed by an explosion as reported by neighbors earlier today. You will notice in the following news footage that there was not enough left of the structure to know what could have caused the explosion or if anyone was in the building at the time. Only a vehicle going by on the road could see the house, so neighbors were unaware of any unusual circumstances until they heard and felt the explosion. Unfortunately, there were no eye witnesses. Experts are still at the scene trying to find out the cause of the explosion, but as we came to news time no decision had been made.

"Unfortunately, Thaddeus and Eleanor are believed to have been at home and presumed dead, but are survived by their children, Joel and Leslie Lawson. Both are students here in the city and were away from home at the time of the explosion. They will be residing with family."

Following the anchor's words, pictures came on the screen of the house, as it had been, from a county file used for tax purposes. It looked like a decent house very modern and quite large. The area around the house was landscaped, but there were no junk or dead cars around. The porch seemed in need of some repair, but nothing that couldn't be fixed with a few swings of a hammer and a coat of paint. Two late model vehicles sat in the driveway beside the house.

The next sequence was live, narrated by the man taking the pictures and showed the empty space and what was left of the basement with rubble in it. The intensity was obvious; the gravel driveway looked like solid, cloudy glass. On the driveway were two heaps of twisted metal. All the fire department vehicles sat near the hole. Firemen and several civilians stood looking at the dusty remains. None of those standing around could be identified. It was easy to see the fire fighters in their uniforms they weren't trying to hide from the camera.

"Folks, experts are at the scene and are still trying to determine the cause. As news comes in we'll pass on any new developments." Jenni looked into the camera as she reported the facts. She concluded the segment and moved on to other news. She was glad she had other things to report, seeing and talking about the experience at the Lawson property depressed her.

Jenni's last official obligation for the day was reporting the evening news. Once she signed off, her day was over. She clocked out and was glad that she could. That one experience had been so traumatic she'd had a hard time working through other things she needed to report on the news. It was by sheer determination that she had. It made her wonder how Joel could put his mind around what had happened to the house and his parents. She knew his parents didn't try to get along with their children, but this whole happening had to be mind-boggling.

Once Jenni finished reporting the seven o'clock news, she shrugged into her coat and left. Two things happened; she breathed in the cold fall air and her stomach growled loudly. She patted her stomach, climbed into her car and drove straight to her favorite drive-thru for take-out. It was after eight o'clock, so dinner time had passed by the time she got home. With the traumatic happening at lunch time, she couldn't remember what she'd eaten. Her stomach reminded her of that. She had used so much adrenalin it had depleted any calories she'd eaten.

While she was away at college her parents sold their farm and bought a house in town, so when Jenni moved back after college, rather than rent a place, she moved in with her folks, since they had plenty of room. They remodeled one end of the house for her. However, she didn't want her mom to always save a plate for her. She could easily afford to feed herself. Fortunately, her favorite restaurant had a drive-thru and was on her way home. She stopped there often to get something for a quick meal.

While she drove the rest of the way home, she hoped to put the day's events behind her. Just seeing the Lawson place was very traumatic, because she remembered Joel Lawson. That made it worse, much more personal. She was glad she lived in town now and wouldn't have to drive by the desolate site. She didn't want to watch the news segment that Len had made at the site. Fortunately, that was a different feed, but if she watched TV tonight there was a good chance she'd see it again. Her dad would watch TV, but there were other things she could do.

After eating her take-out, she wandered into the living room with a mug of hot tea. Her dad already had the TV on, but she hoped it wasn't the local channel. Perhaps there was a game or a movie to watch. She slid onto the couch and pulled her feet up onto the leather cushion. It was her favorite place in the living room and her dog, Curly, jumped up beside her. Her dad was watching a professional basketball game. Neither team was a favorite of hers, so she wasn't enthused, but it did take her mind off the day's events just a little.

She knew they'd show Len's footage of the explosion site later tonight on the local channel and seeing it live once was more than she wanted to experience. She was pretty sure that what the experts found out – if anything - would be reported sometime during the evening. Since there'd been so little there she wondered what they found. Of course, her parents would only see what was reported on the news; they'd want to see it. That was understandable.

Curly was her sounding board, so after seeing who played on TV, she whispered to Curly at her feet; "Curly, that guy whose house exploded is a really nice guy. I liked him, I knew him all through school. I wonder what his parents were doing or was it a gas leak or something? It was an explosion, it couldn't have been anything else, there wasn't anything left of the house!" Curly stepped over her legs and licked her face, but of course he didn't answer. That's probably why dogs are considered man's best friend. Jenni absently started patting Curly's head. The announcer on the TV started shouting and Jenni looked up in time to see a long shot and hear the buzzer. Of course, Marvin started yelling and slapping the chair arm. He'd just witnessed his favorite team pull out another win for the season and he was thrilled.

At the explosion site Jenni had to settle for what the lieutenant told her, which was powerful little, since there was so little left. No one had seen the actual happening, or if initially there had been fire, but there was no evidence of fire. The fire fighters couldn't tell her much more. She had looked into the small hole where the basement had been, the two firemen in the hole were more mass than what was there from the house!

She remembered going by the house many times while riding the school bus. It was a good sized house, two stories with a porch across the front. There were shrubs in front of the porch on both sides of the walkway to that porch. They were also gone along with the house! Two mangled heaps of metal gave proof of something more than a propane tank had been in the open field. Of course, the house sat far enough from the road a passer-by couldn't see the hole.

Since Joel was at the site she'd tried to get a statement from him, but he had never looked at her and tried very hard to stay away from her and her camera man, and was quite obvious about it. She guessed that was understandable, he had to be in shock, since everyone assumed both his parents had been killed. Frustrating her even more, none of the firemen could tell her much about Joel or the explosion. Lieutenant Winslow hadn't been too helpful, either.

Since she didn't care about the new game on TV, her thoughts wandered. She and Joel had been classmates, from kindergarten and ridden the school bus for many of those years. Since he boarded the bus soon after she did, he often sat with her. In elementary school they'd been in the same class and sat close because their last names were alphabetically close.

As they moved up in the grades they'd been in many of the same classes. He was always friendly, not just to her, but to everyone. He was never a bully or picked on the younger kids. As she remembered, he never was part of any 'click' or been one of the jocks on a sports team, but he was always physically fit. Maybe his mom was a good cook and fed her family well.

They had several math classes together and since she wasn't good in math, he helped her. She remembered he was as good a teacher as some of the people who stood in front and called themselves 'the teacher'. He'd not only helped her with math, but they were partners for a science fair project, probably ninth grade science, they won first place. The judges had a hard time awarding second place, but first place was never disputed, their project deserved first place.

She wasn't surprised at graduation that Joel was the valedictorian of her class. She'd envied him his intelligence, but he had never flaunted it. At graduation it was like a broken record hearing his name called for all the scholarships and awards he received. She remembered some classmates chuckling as Joel once again stood for another award. One of them had been a full four year scholarship to the local university. That had been a surprise to everyone, including Joel himself. She had been there when it was awarded and saw his reaction. He had been totally surprised, if she remembered right, he even had tears in his eyes.

When Jenni had finally gotten some information at the explosion site about Joel and his sister, either from the lieutenant or one of the fire fighters, she was shocked to learn that Joel was still a student. She knew he was twenty-five, because she was. She assumed that he had finished his undergraduate work and gotten a job in town. How could he keep on after his undergraduate work? He still went to the same university and that would definitely help him financially.

From what she knew about his parents – being arrested and doing jail time was common knowledge in town – he didn't get any financial support from that source. After all, the university he attended was a Christian institution; nobody who spent time in jail would support a relative going to a Christian university! However, she learned that he was in his last semester of graduate school and doing a dissertation for his PhD. Obviously, no slouch! However, no one knew what his field of study was or what he would do once he was finished. Probably if she'd been able to talk with him she would have found that out.

She'd gotten to know him pretty well when they worked together on the science fair project. Maybe she'd even had a little crush on him? She wouldn't have admitted that back then, but now – well it was a bit obvious how she'd acted at the time. As she remembered, Joel hadn't showed that kind of interest in her, only that he was glad for her help with the project. A lot of what they did needed two people. It embarrassed her now to think how she'd acted - like a typical teen-aged girl, him…well; he'd tolerated her, acting much more mature!

She had also gone to college right out of high school, but she'd left town to get her education. Her parents were all for that, they knew it would help her mature if she was on her own for a while. She had a scholarship, but she'd wanted to see another part of the world before she settled down. She had gone four years for her degree and come back to her home town because she'd had a job offer and now she worked for the local TV station as a reporter and evening news anchor. Until today it had been her dream job and she hoped it would be again.

Tonight, though, she couldn't leave her job behind at the station. Tonight she knew someone personally who made part of her news today. Usually, she could stay detached from what she reported, but tonight all kinds of questions circled in her mind. She hadn't gotten to talk with Joel and that frustrated her. She could only cast the blame for his avoidance on two things, either he didn't know who she was or he was too upset to talk to a reporter.

At the site she'd talked to one of the firemen who had taken some undergraduate classes with Joel at the local university. He told her that Joel was a brilliant student when he'd known him, but now he was in graduate school and doing a dissertation, but no one knew what subject he was earning his degree in or any plans he had after graduation. As she sat thinking about it, she remembered that Joel didn't ever talk much about himself. She guessed that was because he didn't want to broadcast who or what about his parents. She couldn't blame him for that he was such a nice guy – his dad… well, not so much!

FIVE

Jenni finished her tea. Then, since she wasn't interested in her dad's game and didn't want to hold her mug any longer, took her mug to the kitchen and went to her room. Curly was her dog and always wanted to be with her when she was home, so he followed her. She sat at her desk and turned the light on. Curly sat next to her begging for some love. She had been gone all day. However, after a few strokes, he slouched to the floor beside her apparently happy.

At her desk, Jenni hunted for her senior yearbook, she usually didn't want to reminisce about high school. However, she was curious about what Joel had listed as his goal in life. Just working on that science fair project, she knew he was focused on his academic work. Since he was the valedictorian, he had a special page all to himself in the year book. Had he known what he wanted to do? Had he known he'd continue his schooling after his four years of undergraduate? She wondered how he paid for his graduate work, university schooling was no cheap undertaking, but without talking to him, she guessed the yearbook was her best bet.

Jenni opened her yearbook, knowing it would bring back some memories. The first pages featured the science teacher who had judged their science fair project. He had retired that year. He was a nice guy and always seemed more than fair, not like some of the 'old battle axes' they'd had who made you fight for every good grade you got in their class.

She kept turning pages; sometimes they featured some of the outstanding students on the first few pages along with sports teams. They had a spectacular year that year in several sports, so there were several pages of different sports teams and some pictures during those events. She'd lived a bit since then, only a face or two looked familiar.

Joel hadn't been into sports, just academics so she didn't look for him on the teams. However, she found Joel, he and the salutatorian shared a page. The girl didn't plan to do anything special in life, remembering her, Jenni wasn't surprised. She was heavy on her boyfriend, as she remembered and taken secretarial courses just to get by. However, the science teacher who retired praised Joel and said he was one of his prize students all through school. As she remembered their fair project, that was no surprise. The caption under Joel's picture said he planned on going into the science field for his college major, but it didn't say what branch.

She finished reading the caption under Joel's picture. By this time, Curly had stretched out on the floor. She shook her head and said, "Curly, it figures. We took first place for that science fair project. I mean, because of Joel, it was awesome. I just came along for the ride." Curly knew she talked to him, so he thumped his tail, but he didn't open his eyes to look at her.

She'd learned just before air time for the evening news that Joel and his sister planned to live, at least temporarily with some family. Family; she remembered he'd often talked about his aunt and uncle, but now, so many years since, she didn't remember their names. She did remember that he was nearly devastated when his uncle was killed. The accident had happened while she was home on summer break one year. It was big news. Since she'd moved back, a single lady lived next door. "Is Lucy Steel their aunt? Is that why he was here last night?" she asked Curly, but this time, he didn't even thump his tail. He was off in doggy dreamland.

Jenni looked at her clock it was time for Curly's night time walk. When a car drove on the neighbor's driveway, she said, "Come on, Curly, it's time for your walk. Let's go!"

Curly leisurely got to his feet and stretched both back legs before he followed her, but Jenni was out the door of her room waiting by the back door. She had her coat on and his leash ready when he arrived at the door, so Jenni quickly hooked it on and led him outside. In the streetlight she saw Joel exit his car. She took several steps closer so she wouldn't have to yell and said, "Hi, Joel! So you're living with Lucy now? She's your aunt?"

Joel let out a long sigh. "Yes, since the explosion today Leslie and I have no other choice. Jenni? Is that you? You live here in town?"

"Yes, I have been since I came home from college."

"Wow, I didn't know that!"

"My parents moved into town while I was gone, so being the lazy person that I am, I just moved back in with them. They remodeled this end for me. I was there at the site today, but I didn't know you still lived there or were still in town."

She saw him nod in the streetlight. "Yes, it was at my dad's demands that I still lived at their house. Not my choice at all, but I did it gladly because of Leslie. She's nine years younger than me and is in high school. I have only this semester and then I'll defend my dissertation. I hope to move on after that, but for now I'm here. Aunt Lucy is kind enough to put us up. I have no idea what'll happen now. She isn't that well off that she can put both of us up indefinitely." He sighed again. "Unfortunately I don't make much as yet."

"That was an amazing thing that happened out there today! I couldn't believe what I saw – what I really didn't see when Len and I came to that spot!"

Joel nodded. "I have to agree with you." Scowling, he asked, "Why were you out at the explosion if you don't live out there now?"

Watching Curly at the curb, she nodded, "I'm with the local TV station. I was the reporter there along with our camera man."

"Oh, I didn't know what you'd done after college."

"Yes, I'm a reporter, but I'm the evening news anchor. I was the one who reported it on the evening news a bit ago."

Curly had finished his business and Joel looked haggard and wiped out, so Jenni decided not to press him for more information. "Joel, I'll let you go. It's been some day, but since you're next door, I'll see you again, I'm sure."

"Yes, that's probably true, Jenni. I hope I can get to bed a bit earlier tonight. Dad kicked me out after supper last night and then I went back for my clothes. Then with that storm, last night wasn't too long on sleep." He gave her a tired wave and headed inside.

Jenni let Curly sniff another bush and watched Joel close the door. Only moments later she saw most of Lucy's lights go off. As she went to the back door, she sighed, "He's still a nice guy." Inside, she took off Curly's leash. "Curly, I still didn't find out much more than I knew before!" Curly wagged his tail, knowing that she was talking to him but he went to his water dish for a drink. She shed her coat, closed up the house and turned out the kitchen lights.

It was time for bed. Her parents were in bed and she was ready to dream about anything other than the explosion. Since she'd just talked with Joel that might not happen. Maybe it would be Joel she dreamed about! She grinned, not a bad dream! If ever there was eye candy that was Joel Lawson! She and Curly entered her room and she closed the door. She put Curly in her sitting room, closed the door, and quickly got ready for bed and snuggled under her quilt.

Joel went in the house and locked the door. Things were so different now than last night! It had been storming, for one thing, but he had shed a few quiet tears into the pillow because of his mom and dad. Tonight they were no more. It was quiet and dark in the house. Lucy had left a light on over the kitchen sink for him, but that was all. He shut it off, but knew he could find his way in the house because it wasn't totally dark. This house wasn't in the country.

The house was quiet. Les was in the little room upstairs and probably bedded down. His aunt was in her room down the hall. He wished he could afford even an efficiency apartment, someplace he could call his own. Here he must open the sofa-sleeper each night and hang his slacks, good shirts and suit jackets in the coat closet beside the front door that was already full with - coats. The rest of his clothes stayed in a box he'd brought from the grocery store and it stayed in that same closet. He wished for a dresser just to keep his clothes organized instead of in a box! Auntie didn't have a desk, so he had to keep everything school related in his briefcase – also stored in that closet and use the library. He was grateful, but it worried him that he and Leslie had definitely doubled Lucy's food bill, which was hard for her.

Joel sighed, tomorrow was another day. A day to glorify God and do the things he must do, but life as he knew it had changed drastically. He opened the sofa and straightened the sheet and blanket that stayed on the bed when it was folded up. On top of his clothes in the closet were his nighttime sweats, so he took them to the bathroom. He touched his temple, he needed to inspect the puncture and dress it again, but he felt the need for a warm shower.

He hoped the shower noise wouldn't disturb Auntie. Maybe he should come home earlier so he wouldn't disturb her. Still, he wondered how he could do that and still get all he needed to do done. He closed the bathroom door quietly, took off the band-aid and looked at the puncture and for the first time he saw the shiner that people had commented about all day. It wasn't too bad, not like someone had punched him, but the bruise definitely circled his eye.

The warm water felt good to his skin and definitely washed away much of the sadness of the day. He hoped he could sleep through the night without a nightmare. What he'd seen this noon was like he figured a war zone looked like after the combatants had left – no, like a tornado had reached down from the sky and plucked up the house and left everything else untouched.

The puncture wound looked good, but he still put salve and a band-aid on it. He didn't want it to get infected. Only a few minutes later he fell onto the pull-out bed, managed to pull the cover over himself and died to the world.

Life went on, it always did. As Leslie had said, one must stay the course. That course was full; each day was packed with everyday existence. After making arrangements for a memorial service for his parents and a long talk with his friend the pastor of his church about what he could say about Thad and Eleanor Lawson, Joel knew he must get back to his routine. His classes needed to be taught by him, not some substitute and only he could do the research on his dissertation. Those were a must and fortunately he had most of what he needed.

He had thought about it several times and marveled at how things had worked out. It had truly been God's intervention that Leslie had gotten all his things to him. God had been in it all! He was also convinced that God had held off the storm until he reached his car with all his worldly possessions. Having Auntie send him back and also prompting Leslie to pack so much for herself had truly been God's foreknowledge. He was in awe of his Heavenly Father, only He could have orchestrated everything that had happened in those two days.

The precinct lieutenant urged him to contact his parents' homeowners' insurance company, so he had. He was not impressed with their initial response. They were quite hesitant and reluctant to tell him anything, since he couldn't tell them the cause of the explosion or any positive decisions that the experts had made, since they hadn't made any. However, the company had assured him they would send someone out to look around.

Three days after the explosion Joel taught his eight o'clock class and was in the campus library using one last research book for his thesis. Signs were posted to turn off cell phones in the library, but the insurance company representative told him they'd call back to set up a time to inspect the property, so Joel had his phone on, his ringer muted and had just closed the book when his phone vibrated. He answered as quickly as possible.

“So, Mr. Lawson,” a peppy voice said when Joel answered. “Would you be free in say an hour to meet with my adjuster at your property?”

Today he only had one class and he’d already taught his eight o’clock class. “Yes, that’ll be fine. I’ll be there. What will he want to see?”

“Well, everything, of course!” the voice replied, indignantly. “We certainly can’t make a judgment without seeing what remains of what we’ve insured!”

Joel let out a sigh. “I wondered. The first person I talked to from your company was a bit skeptical when I told her there isn’t anything there except several piles of rubble and a hole in the ground. It shouldn’t take your adjuster long.”

Joel heard clicking computer keys, but the man said, “That’s all? The policy along with the picture shows a two story, eight room house - rather large. Surely there’s something visible!”

“Yes, that is correct. However, all that’s left is some of the basement that was under that two story, eight room house. There is some rubble from the house in the hole in the ground, but nothing that can be recognized. That’s all.”

“Wow!”

“Umm, yeah, that’s a good description.” Joel tried to hide his sarcasm. “I’ll make my way to the site and meet with your adjuster. As I say, in an hour is fine, I’ll be waiting there.”

“Well, that’s great; my man’ll be there in about an hour! Show him around real good, fella! We’ll get this thing all worked out! Hey, we’re a company known for good, fast, efficient response!” Joel shook his head, as he ended the call. It was as if the man on the phone hadn’t even heard him say there was nothing there! It didn’t matter, he’d go out there and lead whomever around and let him see… nothing.

Joel put his phone back on his belt, closed up the library book and gathered his papers. He snapped his laptop closed and put all his things in his briefcase. There weren’t any windows in the library, he had no idea what it was like outside, but he could use some sunshine right now. He hadn’t had time or enough money to get a winter coat, fortunately Auntie told him not to worry, she didn’t expect him to return Uncle Josh’s coat. He could wish for some warm breezes, but being November, well above the Mason/Dixon Line, that was probably not in the forecast. He picked up his briefcase and the book; then stopped at the desk to return the book. He gave the woman a tired smile and walked out. As Leslie said, he must stay the course.

A man staggered through the woods. He wasn't quiet, so none of the woodland creatures made noise. The sun was shining, but it was cold, and he shivered, but he looked at his clothes, they were only rags and what was left of them was black, stuff he couldn't brush off. What he had on his feet couldn't be called shoes, only tiny threads holding the soles on his feet.

What had happened to him? He'd never worn rags like this! His feet, he looked at them as he shuffled through the pine needles. He'd never had stuff like this on his feet! His feet looked awful! His stomach growled. When had he eaten last? He couldn't remember when or what he'd eaten. Had he been asleep, if so why was he outside? Didn't he have a bed somewhere? What time was it? All he knew it was daylight.

There was a stiff, cold breeze blowing! The sun was out, but it didn't warm the air very much at all. He had a coat, where was it? Why hadn't he stopped to put it on? There were no leaves on the trees, only bare branches and twigs. The grass he saw was brown. The pine needles on the ground were brown. Sometimes he fell into a tree, but quickly righted himself, the bark scraped places on his body and that hurt badly. A few times he tripped over a root, but he tried really hard to catch himself before he fell. He had fallen the first time and had to push himself up. His raw hands had screamed for mercy.

All over his body were sore places, really sore places! There was black stuff all over him, was it dirt, but he couldn't brush it away. When he tried to brush those places, it hurt; somehow it was stuck to him. He hurt, his face hurt and his hands had places that were black, other places red, but some had huge, white puffy places and if he pushed on them it seemed like water moved back and forth, but they hurt like crazy. He had places on his body like that and if one of the puffy places broke, stuff ran out. He shook his head, but he stopped right away, it hurt too much. It was hard to pull in a breath; he felt that cold air all the way down his throat and deep inside. It made a whistling noise somewhere along the way to where it stopped.

His brain didn't seem able to process anything much. He couldn't figure out where he was, nothing looked familiar, just trees – bare trees. Every once in a while it felt like a gigantic boom went through his body it made his whole body shudder. It seemed his ears even vibrated! He wasn't even sure who he was, all he knew was that he was walking in the right direction, somehow he'd get out of the woods and he'd know....

Because he didn't want to see the place again, Joel walked slowly to his car. If he didn't have to be at the site for an hour he had plenty of time. Reluctantly he drove the streets away from the university toward the site of the house where he grew up. He'd never called it home; he couldn't say he ever felt at home there. Even as a child he never felt at home in the Lawson house. For many of his growing up years he thought he was an unwanted mistake. Emphatically Auntie and Uncle had told him he was not, that he was made in God's image! Auntie made him understand that God had a special plan for him. Desperate for reassurance, he'd believed her.

When he was nine years old his sister was born and he'd loved her from her first squall. He determined he'd protect her as much as any nine year old boy could protect an infant. Today they were very close. He would have been more than devastated if she had been killed in the explosion. He was glad she had responded to his text message so quickly the day it had happened. He hadn't had to worry about her. Leslie had been at school and he was glad of that. His only regret about that was that he'd only told her to go to Auntie's house and not told her himself about the explosion. He regretted she found out about it from her friends and classes.

Really, if he called any place home, it was Uncle Josh and Auntie's place. They had always given the two of them unconditional love. If Joel could reach a phone without his dad finding out and call, one of them would come and take them away from their house. After Uncle Josh was killed and Auntie moved into the much smaller house, he and Leslie always ran to her for help, protection and comfort. Many times, Joel wished he could help her more than he could, but that hadn't happened. He made little enough as it was. He and Leslie felt much more at home living with her these few days than they ever had with Thad and Eleanor Lawson.

However, he knew he must see to collecting the insurance money that they were entitled to because of the policy. After the lieutenant had told him he should contact the company Joel wondered what they should do with the money. He wouldn't build back! The whole property held too many bad memories even a new house wouldn't remove them! He had no plans to live here anyway. Perhaps he'd give a big percentage to Auntie she deserved it for giving him and Leslie a place to live. Getting Les a car might be a good thing. Of course, that was if the company would let loose of any money. After talking with two of their representatives, Joel wasn't sure that his claim would be honored at all. Since collecting the money meant meeting the adjuster at the site, he would do it and explain what he could and answer questions if he could. He felt like the site was quite self-explanatory, but he should be there for sure.

He drove from the university to the country road and came to the spot where he'd parked the night before the explosion. He looked toward the site as he had that night. It was the first and only clear view of where the house had been, but his mouth dropped open and he looked again. "There's no car there, so the insurance man hasn't arrived, but there's somebody walking around between the piles of rubble!" he exclaimed out loud, he was so astonished.

Although he'd been driving slowly, knowing he'd get there long before the adjuster, now he speeded up. Who was wandering around the place that looked like a war zone? His heart climbed into his throat, was someone trying to vandalize the place? From there to the driveway he contemplated who it could possibly be. He knew none of the neighbors would come around besides; the fire department had strung yellow tape around the hole. The woman who had called in the explosion wouldn't come to look. She had only tolerated the Lawson's as her neighbors. Thad and Eleanor hadn't been especially friendly. He shook his head, he had no idea.

Joel pulled into the driveway and as the person heard the car, he turned and started walking toward the car. Joel had never seen a person more grotesque! He continued to stare as he drove closer, but the man kept coming toward him. The taste in his mouth made him sick. His adrenalin kicked in, his heart rate doubled. He finally realized the person had been burned nearly beyond recognition and the clothes on his body had been reduced to chard rags!

"Dad!" the one word exploded out of Joel's mouth.

Joel immediately grabbed his phone from his belt and tried to punch 9-1-1 into it, but his fingers were trembling too badly. He also realized that there were tears filling his eyes and blurring them so much he couldn't make out the numbers. He had to end his first try he couldn't even hit three numbers correctly.

"Nine – one – one! State your emergency!"

He blurted out, "Please! Send an ambulance to the Lawson place! I believe Thad Lawson is wandering around the site of the explosion and is terribly burned!"

"Are you sure?"

"Yes, Ma'am! This is his son, Joel. I'm sure it's him!"

Joel heard a few clicks and the woman said, "Yes, I've got an ambulance dispatched on the way. They should be there very shortly."

"Thank you!"

The nine-one-one call was heard in all the emergency and law enforcement headquarters and if an officer was in his car with it running he also heard it. That meant that Sheriff Gibbs heard the call on his radio but, he was on the other side of the county responding to another call. Frustrated, he banged his hand on his steering wheel. "That's Thad Lawson's son! It seems he's everywhere! What's he doing there at the site? The fire lieutenant strung up that yellow tape!" He let out a sigh. "And his dad! They're probably meeting up there to cause more mischief. Wow! Man! Maybe they'll still be there when I get through with this call. Can only hope!" Sheriff Gibbs looked out the windshield and muttered, "Why'd he call for an ambulance?"

Joel and his dad were about the same height, but Thad weighed nearly twice as much and much of that was muscle, but today he looked gaunt, as if the explosion and trauma had not only burned him, but taken pounds from his body. Joel's body started trembling uncontrollably. He stopped near the shell of his mom's car, but the burned man still walked toward him. A shudder worked down Joel's back and he felt bile rise in his throat. He couldn't believe how awful the man looked. What hung on his body were only scorched rags!

He jammed the stick into park, but forgot to turn off the ignition and jumped from his car, leaving the door open and hurried towards the man. The closer he got to him, the worse he looked and Joel wasn't able to control the shudder that skinned up his back or the goose bumps that rose up on his arms. In fact, he swallowed hard so he wouldn't throw up and even slapped his hand over his mouth for a moment.

"Dad!" he exclaimed. The word exploded from his mouth.

But the man kept coming, as if he didn't hear or recognize what Joel called him. As Joel watched he saw that he wasn't walking like his dad walked, but one look at his feet showed him he had to shuffle to keep the items that had been his boots on his feet. Joel tried very hard not to show a reaction, but he knew he didn't dare touch him. There wasn't any skin colored place on his body. The man had to be in excruciating pain! Joel felt another shudder rush up his back, he could hardly look at the man in front of him, especially knowing what his dad had looked like.

The cloth on his body was ripped and charred and barely covered him. Where skin showed through it was either black, deep red, blistered or weeping. There was not a hair on his body anywhere! It was November the man had to be cold! Joel had on a suit jacket and his uncle's winter coat. He certainly wasn't overly warm.

"Dad!" Joel murmured. Again tears fogged his vision, but he would not shed them.

When Thad finally reached Joel, he was silent for several minutes, staring at him, looking him up and down. Then in a voice Joel hardly recognized the man said, "Do I know you?"

Joel looked into eyes that were like his own. They looked vacant, like no one was home. Tears glistening, but unable to speak louder, Joel whispered, "Yes, Dad, it's me, Joel, your son."

"I… I have a son?" He peered at the young man for several minutes, then looked back over his shoulder and asked, "What is this? Why am I here?"

Just about to cry from emotional overload, Joel nodded. "Yes, Dad, you're Thad Lawson. Your house was here, but there was a really bad explosion, your house blew up. This is what is left. I guess you were thrown free by the explosion. That happened three days ago."

Just then, off in the distance they heard the ambulance siren wailing. Thad looked towards town, but he scowled. "What is that?"

"I saw you when I pulled in so I called the ambulance. You need to be in the hospital."

"I… I do?"

"Yes, you're burned very badly and you probably have amnesia. Very possibly you're in shock, maybe have a concussion. Those are all things I can't take care of, only a doctor can do what you need done." The man looked so forlorn that Joel had all he could do not to reach out and touch him, but he didn't. He was afraid if he touched him he'd injure him more. He could burst some blisters or scrape off some of the charred places and maybe cause more damage. He certainly was not a medical person he wouldn't even attempt to be with Thad Lawson.

"Oh," Thad whispered and sank slowly to the ground in front of Joel.

Joel had to swallow to keep from bursting into tears as he looked at the man at his feet. Just the sight of his dad pushed his compassionate spirit well over the top. He had to force his hands to stay at his sides, stuffing them in his pockets so he wouldn't reach out. His mind told him to catch the man on his way down. He was nothing like the dad he'd seen the last time he'd been near him, the night he'd thrown him out. That night he'd been belligerent, today he was docile as a lamb. As he watched, his dad's eyes closed. He slowly went from sitting to a slump and finally the slump took him to the ground. His body curled into a fetal position.

"God in heaven! This is so hard!" Joel murmured as he watched his dad. Again the bile welled up and nearly spewed out of his mouth.

The ambulance whirled into the driveway and screeched to a halt beside Joel's car. Two men jumped out and one went to the back of the truck immediately. The doors at the back crashed open. The other man walked towards Joel and asked, "What's the problem?" Then he saw Thad and swallowed. "Oh, my!"

Joel nodded and said, "This is Thad Lawson, the house that was here was his. I guess he was thrown clear. Obviously, *way* clear! Since nobody found him. He doesn't know me and he asked what this was, so I suspect he also has amnesia as well as all these burns. It's possible he's now lapsed into a coma. There's no question he belongs in the hospital."

"Yes, sir, no argument on that!" the medic exclaimed. "We'll get him loaded immediately. This is how you found him?"

Joel shook his head. "No, he was walking around when I first saw him. We had a brief conversation before he collapsed at my feet."

Nodding toward another car pulling off the road, Joel said, "I'd go with him, but that's the insurance adjuster I came out to meet. I certainly didn't expect to find my dad wandering around this place when I drove out!"

"We'll take him in. You'll be along?"

"Yes, as soon as I can."

"Can't ask for anything better than that!"

Thad was very docile; Joel's assessment was accurate. Thad Lawson had lapsed into a coma. Nothing the men did roused him. The medics loaded him carefully onto their stretcher, laid the restraints across him and buckled them loosely because it was the law, but there wasn't a place that wasn't burned. He didn't wake up as they loaded him, but he let out a sigh Joel heard clearly. It was as if Thad's body knew someone would take care of him and he could let go.

Joel shook his head, how had his dad survived? Joel knew that was a miracle! Where had he landed? Several fire fighters had inspected the field around the house probably most of the open area and found nothing. In fact, the house sat nearly in the middle of the open area and the woods were far behind the house. In the state he was in how did he find his way from such a distance as the woods? Joel could only shake his head. God had again orchestrated all of this!

The man who pulled behind Joel's car hadn't left his car before the paramedic climbed in with Thad, the doors closed and the driver climbed behind the wheel. He started up, made a U-turn, turned on the siren and raced away. Joel watched, amazed. How long had Thad been awake? How had he walked from the woods? His body looked tortured! Joel shook his head. "No other option, God walked him from the woods so someone – me – would find him – today!"

The driver's door on the Towne Car finally opened, but the man in the black suit and power tie watched the ambulance race away. Joel didn't move towards the car, he was in his own world of shock. Finally, the man lifted his briefcase from the passenger seat and left the luxury car, walked up to Joel and asked, "Who was that? Why was there an ambulance here?"

Joel looked at the well dressed man and wondered momentarily how much of the settlement the adjuster kept. He quickly dismissed the thought it wasn't what a Christian should consider. "It was my dad. He's the owner of this property, I found him wandering around the site. He was terribly burned I didn't see a place that wasn't. He didn't know me or what happened then he collapsed at my feet. We thought he'd died in the explosion the other day along with mom. The medics and I agreed that he'd lapsed into a coma before they arrived."

The man held out his hand and said, "I'm Emil Rhoades, from the insurance company."

Joel nodded. "I assumed you were. I'm Joel Lawson. I'm the son of the people who owned this property." He waved his hand towards the destruction. "There was a house here until the other day. The neighbors heard the explosion and felt it, but of course they didn't see anything, since only someone passing on the road can see the house." He pointed to the pull off up the road and added, "That's the only place you get a clear view of the house."

Standing on the driveway, far from the yellow tape, Emil exclaimed, "Nothing's here!"

"That's right."

"Well, let's take a look!"

"That's fine. That's why I'm here to help you look around and answer any questions." *The sooner you leave the sooner I can.*

The man placed his briefcase gingerly on the hood of his shiny, black car and opened it. The top-most paper was an eight and a half by eleven print-out of the Lawson house. Without speaking he picked it up and looked at it for some time, then turned his head and looked at the empty space and saw the propane tank some yards away. He cleared his throat, looked at Joel, looked back at the picture and said, "This is what was here?"

"Yes, that's the house that was on this piece of property until three days ago. I do not make a habit of telling falsehoods!"

The man shook his head, laid the picture back in the briefcase, then picked up a pad of legal paper and a camera and slowly pushed the top down on his briefcase. He didn't look at Joel, but started for the hole in the ground. Since he didn't speak, Joel didn't speak, just followed him. Joel wondered what kind of inspection the man would make; he didn't look like the kind of man who deliberately got his shiny black shoes dirty.

Back in town, a man skidded around the corner into Jenni's office at the TV station. She was listening to something through her earbuds and busily typing into her computer, but she saw the movement in her doorway, so she quickly clicked her mouse to save what she'd typed and yanked out the earbuds, that stopped speaking when she clicked off her mouse. She looked up and stared at the man in her doorway. She'd never seen her boss look so wild-eyed before.

"Jenni!" he exclaimed from the doorway. "Jenni, listen up!"

"So, are you the wild man from Borneo?" she asked. "What has got you so agitated, Alex! I've never seen you like this!"

Inside her little room he dragged in a breath, threw out his hands dramatically exclaiming, "Jen! Unbelievable! Amazing! Only a reporter will believe something so bazaar!" He pulled in another breath and added, "You won't believe what I heard on the scanner!"

Jenni laid her earbuds beside her computer and said, "Okay, what's the secret, Alex!"

"Believe this! I mean, *believe* this! Hospital dispatch just sent an ambulance to the Lawson property! Joel is there for some reason. The emergency dispatch said he claimed he'd found his dad wandering around!"

Aghast, Jenni stared at her boss. "What! Alex, you have got to be kidding! I mean, you saw the footage Len had, there was nothing left! *Nothing*! It happened three days ago! How in the world! His *dad*? Besides, I saw some of the fire fighters out in the field around the place – they didn't find anything!" Jenni gasped. "You're *sure*? Joel called for an ambulance?"

"I know!"

"Alex, I'm on my way!"

"Good job, Jenni!"

Alex left and Jenni sat and thought for a minute. Joel might be the only one on the property by the time she arrived and she had no assurance that he would be. It would take her several minutes to reach the site and he could leave with the ambulance. She wouldn't need a mike or photo coverage; in fact, he might not speak to her if he saw any of those things today. Besides, why did she need any of that? Rather than hunt anything down that would give Joel enough time to leave, she grabbed her purse and knowing she had a pad and pen, jumped from her chair. Maybe this way she could get some answers from Joel himself. She could only hope. She had no idea why he had gone to the site or how long he would be there. However, if he was there, she intended to ask some questions and hopefully get some answers. At the last minute, she remembered to grab her coat from the hook and dashed towards the door to the parking lot.

Joel shook hands with the arrogant insurance adjuster. They had covered the site even the empty field, taking pictures, but the well dressed man wouldn't get near anything that might soil his clothes. Emil couldn't deny the destruction of the house that their company had insured. So after as thorough an inspection as the adjuster was willing to make, asking many questions, some Joel had no answers for and filling out his paperwork, the man closed his briefcase.

He made no promises, since the explosion hadn't been ruled as accidental or purposeful. Of course, the company was out to save themselves money. Joel shook his head; there wasn't enough of anything for the fire department experts to make a calling. The adjuster could only put down what he saw, which wasn't much. The company would probably stall for months.

The adjuster had barely closed his door when another car traveled down the road and turned into the driveway. Joel muttered, "It's like Grand Central Station! This is a quiet country road! Nobody comes out here. When will I ever get to the hospital? At least it's not the sheriff! Thank goodness!" It was a private vehicle; Joel had no idea who was stopping.

Jenni stopped in the spot where the ambulance had been, so Emil started up, and made a U-turn. Jenni put her car in park and made a silent inspection of Joel. He still had a black eye that seemed even darker today. He was probably six inches taller than she was. He had sandy brown hair that he kept rather short and had no hair on his face. That made it much easier to see his features, including his high cheekbones, his kissable lips.... and his blue eyes. In the few days since she'd seen him here before she didn't change her opinion – the man was eye candy!

Joel was not smiling as he faced the road. Finally, she stepped from her car. Not recognizing her at first, Joel walked toward her car with his hand out to shake. Just being at the site depressed him and dealing with the adjuster was depressing, but of course, he must speak to whoever this was. Perhaps they were in the wrong place and he could get them to move on soon.

It was obvious to Jenni that Joel didn't recognize her. On the other hand, Jenni sported a smile big enough for both of them, as she said, "Joel! We're back at the site again!"

Joel stood still for several minutes looking at the beautiful woman. Her hair was shoulder length and with the sun, it sparkled a rich mahogany. However, even with a rich, creamy skin color, her eyes were blue. She dressed well and her clothes showed off her nice curves. Even Joel, in the state of mind that he was, could appreciate what he saw.

With a small smile, perhaps only the lifting of a corner of his mouth, he said, "Jenni, forgive me! I had no idea! Oh, my, I remember you were a lovely young lady in high school, but my goodness, you are a very lovely lady, even more now! I surely didn't see you well the other night at the house. You're with the TV station? I didn't know that! Yes, maybe you did tell me. I've had a hard time the last day or two processing everything. What can I do for you?"

Jenni blushed at Joel's compliment, but she said, "Thank you, Joel. How are you doing?"

Joel thought for a minute. He shook his head, she had no mike, no recording device, no reason not to answer honestly, so he said, "You know, I'm not sure, really. It's been such trauma to Leslie and me it's hard to put my mind around it. Nobody has figured out what caused the explosion, it's still such a mystery! And there was nothing here! Nothing at all! Just a few minutes ago, I found my dad wandering around the place. Now that was beyond incredible!"

"Your *dad*?" she gasped. It was so hard to comprehend. "How in the world...?"

"Yes, it was him. I can't believe it myself and he was burned almost beyond recognition. But I inherited my eyes from him, he looked at me, so I know it's him."

"How could he have survived?"

Joel shook his head. "I have no idea! Every place I saw was burned and there was no hair on his body. He has amnesia, he remembers nothing. Before the ambulance came he collapsed and lapsed into a coma, so it had to be adrenalin that kept him going. I must say the explosion must have thrown him so far away that no one found him. The firemen looked in the field, but not in the woods, so he must have been there." He nodded towards the trees a good ways away. "I'm assuming he was knocked out for a while and when he came to he wandered back here. Today was the first time I came back, so I don't know how long he's been here."

"This is incredible!"

Joel took a few steps and leaned against his car. It was warm, so he turned his back and put his hands down on the hood, since he didn't have gloves. He looked at Jenni and said, "Yes. It has to be a miracle! I don't know what else to call it."

Feeling a bit uncomfortable with that line of thinking, Jenni asked, "You didn't always, umm, get along with your dad, did you?"

A tiny smile crossed Joel's mouth. "Actually, I think Dad didn't *want* to get along with me. We clashed every time we were within speaking distance and have for most of my life." He placed his fingers over the band-aid beside his eye and added, "He had thrown me out of the house the night before the explosion and told me he never wanted to see my face again."

"So you only had the clothes on your back? Wow! And that bruise? What's that from?"

"Yeah, the mirror in the hall didn't make it when Dad sent the front door crashing into the wall. A shard of glass punctured this place and obviously gave me this bruise."

SIX

"OH, MY! IT COULD HAVE HIT YOUR EYE!" JENNI EXCLAIMED.

"Yes, but I saw it coming and turned my head enough so it didn't. At least the piece of glass fell away and didn't get imbedded in my temple."

Jenni could tell Joel didn't want to talk about that, so she changed the subject and asked, "The lieutenant said you're working on your PhD, did you lose all of your work? How awful!"

Joel leaned heavily on the warm hood of his car and shook his head. "No, Leslie has less than I have. She was at the house, texted me to come for my stuff and took the chance to empty my room before she went to bed. She threw it all out my window, so I got everything except my winter coat. She only has two backpacks full of things she took to school with her."

"Wow! Oh, my!"

Joel looked away and said, "Yes, it's incredible! When Dad threw me out, Leslie snuck my keys, phone and Bible to me before I left. I went to Aunt Lucy's and Les sent me a text to come for my things in the morning, they'd be on the back porch. However, when I told Auntie, she told me to come right back. It's a good thing! Remember the storm we had? Les told me that after I left with what she threw out the window, Dad roughed her up and demanded to know what she'd done with my things. God told Auntie to have me go back! I got there in time for her to send the things out the window. She didn't have to truck them passed his bedroom, he'd have heard her! Another thing, I think God also told Leslie to pack her backpack with clothes before she left for school. She doesn't usually take more than her book bag to school."

"Joel," Jenni whispered, "that truly is incredible! This whole thing boggles my mind! Doesn't it you?"

Joel looked back at Jenni and said, "Yes, it truly does. I believe that for a fact. Only God would know what would happen the next day. It was an awful thing that the place exploded. We all assumed that my parents were killed, but obviously not, but God knew and 'In all things, God works for good…' I have to accept that."

"Wow!" Otherwise, Jenni had nothing to say. She could only stare at Joel. How could the man have such faith in God? Since she was a little girl she'd never considered God much in her life. He hadn't seemed too close, too interested in what she wanted to do. She didn't go to church or have anything to do with Christian things. Her parents hadn't really been church goers; they'd go for a Christmas service or maybe at Easter. She had always figured that if her parents didn't think too much about God or doing things with church, why should she.

When they were in school, Joel didn't speak about his home life, but people knew what he and Leslie lived with. Thad Lawson was notorious in town. The kids at school, especially, but others too knew how often Joel and Leslie went to their aunt and uncle's to get away from the awful home. She wondered, his relatives must have taken them to church. His parents surely wouldn't! Still she couldn't believe that he'd kept his faith. It was so hard to believe and to say that 'In all things, God works for good…' she couldn't put her mind around it, but Joel had!

After several minutes, Jenni said, "That's another thing. The day of the explosion I talked with the lieutenant. He knew you are still in school, but he didn't know your plans. You say you're about finished writing your thesis?"

Joel shrugged. "I'll get my PhD at the end of the semester in Geology, if my committee approves my dissertation. I have a position lined up in a sister school… Perhaps it's the one you went to. I'm anxious to start."

How could he remember what school I went to? Jenni scowled. "But if you go that far away, what will happen to your sister and now your dad? You say he has amnesia, but suppose with all that's wrong he never gets right again." She raised her hand and pointed to the empty site. "What'll happen to this place? Will insurance expect you to build it back?"

Joel sighed and shrugged. "Jenni, I don't know those answers. I found Dad less than an hour ago and sent him to the hospital because he was so badly burned and had amnesia. I've never seen anyone burned that badly! I need to talk with the doctors for an assessment before I can do anything and

Les can always live with Aunt Lucy until she graduates." After another sigh, Joel continued, "For so long I've wanted to leave here, but for several reasons I couldn't and finish my education. But in January there was supposed to be light at the end of the tunnel."

Knowing that Joel wouldn't talk to her much longer, she asked, "So what happens if you can't take that position because of your dad?"

He lifted his hands from the hood and stuck them in his pockets. He shrugged and said, "I don't know, Jenni. I'll cross that bridge when I come to it. If he must be institutionalized, I guess I'll deal with it when that time comes. Right now, that is one too many irons in the fire."

Joel looked at his watch and Jenni knew her interview was over. She said, "Joel, it's been good to talk with you again. This whole thing has been amazing! Maybe we can talk again soon, since we're neighbors now." *I can only hope.*

Joel nodded. "Possibly. I do get home from the library pretty late and you do walk your dog at night." He put his hand down on the fender and added, "The paramedic asked if I'd be along soon, so I must get to the hospital. It was good to see you, Jenni."

Jenni smiled and said, "Yes, that's true. Thanks for your time, Joel."

"Sure," he answered, less than enthusiastically.

Jenni wished they could renew their acquaintance, but not today. The man had so much on his plate he couldn't think straight. His mind had to be on his dad at the hospital and surely where he was headed. Jenni went to her car and at the same time, Joel turned from his fender to the door. His car was still running. They both got in and as Jenni watched Joel pulled the door shut, but put his forehead on his steering wheel, but didn't move the stick. He had to be exhausted with the weight of his responsibilities. He was the only one to deal with them.

It was a terrible weight of his parents' house totally demolished, dealing with an insurance adjuster. Now his dad reappearing with so many problems, his sister and all he was doing to finish his education – a dissertation – a PhD! The man was amazing! He'd said he'd already made arrangements. That meant he'd worked through a memorial service for his parents and now his dad was alive! She started up; glad for the few minutes they'd talked. Jenni left before Joel lifted his head from the steering wheel.

Joel sighed, listening to Jenni's car start up, then retreat on the gravel driveway and sat in the stillness for several more minutes, not even moving, but let the warmth from the heater warm his bones. Even leaning against the warm fender hadn't banished the chill. He couldn't remember ever having so many irons in the fire, not even when he had to deal with his dad about his education. Actually, that had been on-going since high school.

Thad only finished high school and saw no reason for his son to go on. He was opposed as soon as he'd found out that Joel wanted to go to college. As his graduation came close he and his dad had many discussions, mostly, Thad cussing. Thad was determined that Joel was finished when he graduated from high school and let him know in no uncertain terms! On the other hand, Joel had been just as adamant that he would be going on to college. Joel had been mildly surprised that his parents even came to the commencement, but they had.

However, Thad had nothing to say after the ceremony when he'd found out how many awards Joel had gotten. Unbelievably, Thad had insisted he live at their house while he went to school, even graduate school. Joel still hadn't figured that out, even all these years later. "Of course, it doesn't matter now, there's no house to live in and no dad to enforce the rule."

Still with his head on the steering wheel, Joel whispered, "It was three days ago that the place exploded. Not one of the firemen found anything but the little bit of rubble and that was in the hole. How long has Dad been awake and walking around here? It's cold; he could have pneumonia on top of everything!" Unless his dad woke up at the hospital and could remember something with a clear mind, everything was an unanswerable question!

What Jenni had asked was a viable question. What would he do if his dad couldn't live on his own ever again? Leslie would be fine at Auntie's and once Joel got settled into his new position he could send her money for Leslie's room and board as well as Les's spending money, but his dad.... He couldn't ask Auntie to care for him, he was her brother-in-law. Even if he paid her, he couldn't – he wouldn't ask that of her! "Besides, she doesn't have the room; she only has one bedroom downstairs and a tiny one inside the eaves. That would not work at all!"

Besides who knew what Thad's personality would be! He could be belligerent, with moods turning violent instantly or docile as he was today. And just because the man was alive didn't mean all his external injuries, was all the injury there was. The explosion could have affected him internally, profoundly. Obviously it affected his voice. It could be permanent or temporary, who knew? Thad could still die! He had lapsed into a coma here at the site.

He jerked to a sitting position, grabbed the steering wheel tightly and gasped out the words, "Could Mom be out there too? Oh, wow!" He pulled in a deep breath and on the exhale, he said, "That would be totally amazing!"

Jenni was long gone. He sat alone at the site. He started shivering as his body felt the heat so he turned up the heater fan another notch; he'd been outside for some time and still was chilled. How long had his dad been awake in this cold with only rags on his body? Even though he didn't want to, he sat staring at the desolate site. The propane tank looked so out of place.

He struck the steering wheel with his palm and exclaimed, "I spent an hour with Pastor working on a memorial service for Dad and Mom! That'll have to be scrapped!"

Before he took the stick out of park he pulled out his cell phone. That thought about his mom wouldn't go away. What had his parents been doing that his dad was thrown out? Could they have been together and both been thrown out? He guessed it was a viable question and his mind wouldn't let him ignore it. "God in heaven! I need Your help!"

He sat a few minutes debating who he should call. Not the sheriff! Just the little he'd dealt with him recently didn't make him his new BFF! He'd learned recently that one of the deputies was in his high school class. Not great friends, but they still knew each other. He punched in the number for information, inquired for the non-emergency number for the sheriff department then dialed it, hoping someone other than the sheriff himself would answer

"Sheriff's Department, can I help you?" a gruff voice answered.

"I hope so. Would Roger Williams be there?"

"Ahh, yeah, he's here. Could I tell whose calling?"

"Yes, it's Joel Lawson."

"Yes, sir, I'll connect you."

"Thanks."

Shortly another voice said, "This is Roger. I can't believe you're calling, Joel! You're one of the original good guys! Never in trouble! What's on your mind?"

"Roger, are you sitting down? I hope so, you'll never believe this!"

"Umm, yeah, I'm sitting. Still, in my position you'll have to go some to surprise me."

Joel smiled, but he said, "An hour ago, maybe a bit longer, I came out to meet the insurance adjuster here at the site, but when I looked across the field from that place on the road, I saw somebody walking around. Believe it or not, it was my dad!"

"Your *dad*! No, you're not serious! Just because I know you, I drove by the other night. All that's there is rubble, a hole in the ground and the propane tank. You have to be kidding!!"

"Oh, yes! He was burned awfully and couldn't remember anything, but it was him. My question that I called about, I wonder if Mom could have been thrown out. I guess Dad was thrown so far into the woods nobody looked that far. What do you think?"

"Wow! Wow!" Roger cleared his throat. "Wow! I guess that's a possibility!"

"Maybe it's worth looking into, but nobody went with Dad to the hospital and I should go, but what if Mom's out there alive?"

"I'll talk to Sheriff, see if we can't get a team out there and scour those woods! If she's there, umm, alive or not, we'll find her!"

"Thanks, Roger. I'm on my way to the hospital now."

"I'll let you know."

"Thanks, I'll appreciate that."

"Hey, not a problem!"

Taking another look at the desolate site, Joel pulled in a deep breath and wished his headache would let up. He'd forgotten to bring some pain reliever, again. He put his car in reverse, made the swing and headed out of the driveway, intent on getting to the hospital that was several miles away. It had been over an hour since he'd watched the ambulance leave with his dad. He wondered what they could have done before he arrived to give consent.

He let out a sigh. "Right now, I could wish that there was two of me! This one really wants to run away!"

The business that kept Sheriff Gibbs busy on the east side took a very long time. Several times he cursed under his breath; wishing things would shape up faster. He was frustrated; Thad and his son were both at the explosion site! If he could apprehend one or both, it would make his day! Those two had to be into something, he was sure, especially now that they were both there. He wondered where Thad had been hiding while he, his men and the fire department had all been at his place. It sure would have made it a lot easier if he'd been around that day!

Almost two hours later he wrapped up his business on the east side, and finally headed across the city towards the Lawson site. When he came to busy intersections he wasn't above using his emergency equipment. It helped to take his frustration out on the unsuspecting citizens with his lights, siren and fast car. He really made record time. If the son was there with Thad he would confront them both and find out what they had done the day of the explosion! And both of them there? That was something he couldn't let get away! He surely was not convinced the son was any better than the father. "He talked a good line, but I got ways!" he muttered.

The sheriff took advantage of his official car and made it around the by-pass in record time. If another car had acted as he was, he'd have arrested him for reckless driving! He turned off on the country road, anxious to reach the pull-off where he could see the site. He slowed to nearly a crawl and took a long look through the trees at the clear view of where the house had been. "What!" he grumbled. "There isn't a car in sight! And nobody's here!"

He pulled up on the driveway as close as he could to the yellow tape, shut off the car and stormed to the tape sealing off the hole. A few pieces of the rubble had been moved, but as far as he could see nothing had really changed. There was no evidence that Thad or Joel had been at the site. Frustrated, Sheriff Gibbs slapped his hand on his gun and clamped his mouth shut on the words weighing on his tongue. He spun on his heel, stomped back to his car, sat down, and slammed the door against the cold, wondering what he could do now that he was here.

He turned the key so he could get some heat and his radio squawked, calling for him. When he answered, Deputy Williams said, "Sheriff, a minute ago I answered a call from Joel Lawson. He just left the explosion site because he found his dad and sent him to the hospital, but he wondered if his mom could be out in those woods."

Barely keeping his frustration under wraps, Sheriff Gibbs lifted his eyes to look at the tree line a ways away and said, "Yeah, I'm here now. Thought maybe those two would be here still. Come on out, all of you guys who can. We'll scour these woods and see what we find!"

"Be there real soon, Sheriff!" Of course, the deputy had no idea by the words he said what the sheriff's true intentions were.

Sheriff Gibbs let go of the mike on the two-way radio and hit the steering wheel, frustrated even more. He turned off his car again, pocketed the keys and hit the steering wheel again. He scowled; Joel had sent his dad to the hospital? Why? What was wrong with Thad? "An ambulance? Come on, what's with the theatrics?" His mom in the woods? What was all that about? Why would his mom be in the woods? With his mind-set, Sheriff Gibbs couldn't put his mind around Thad being injured or his wife being in the woods.

Agitated, he couldn't sit still, so he left his car and stomped to the hole; then looked into the woods a hundred feet away until he heard cars on the road. He walked down the driveway and greeted his men as three cars emptied out. He asked the deputy what Joel had said then set up a search party using a grid so that every foot of the woods behind the house was covered. If the woman was hiding in the woods... "**I tell you what! we'll find her**!" he muttered.

Some time later, Joel pulled into the emergency parking lot and rushed into the ER.

The receptionist recognized him and said, "Joel! They need you right away! Here, you need to sign this form for consent."

Joel nodded, scratched his name beside the X, but then rushed to the cubicle where she directed him. He stepped into the room and saw two women in scrubs and a man in a long white coat looking at the still form of his dad. Someone had removed the rags from Thad's body and draped a hospital gown over him and covered him with blankets. An IV dripped; somehow someone found a place that wasn't burned too badly and big enough to thread the needle into a vein. A blood pressure cuff circled his other arm. However, nothing else was happening. The doctor and nurses stood around the gurney, but now that he'd arrived, they were looking at him.

"Oh, my!" he murmured, as he rushed in the room. Thad surely didn't look any better.

The doctor waited for Joel to look at him before he asked, "This is your dad? What happened?" Obviously the doctor didn't watch TV. "Why didn't you come with him?"

Not liking the accusing voice the man used, Joel said, "Sir, three days ago there was an explosion at the place where I've lived. My parents' home was totally demolished. *Totally.*" He added emphatically. "Everyone assumed that my parents were both in the house and had been killed in the explosion. Today I went to meet the insurance adjuster at the site and went there for the first time since the explosion. I found my dad wandering around and called the ambulance. He collapsed and lapsed into a coma before the ambulance arrived. However, while they were there the insurance adjuster came, then a reporter from the TV station on his heels. I have just now gotten away. I'm sorry I couldn't get here any sooner, but I guess that's how life works."

Still looking at Joel, his eyes showing how angry he was, the doctor said, "No one else could have come?"

"No, no one. My sister is a sophomore in high school there are only two of us."

"This happened three days ago? No one looked around?"

Trying not to let the arrogant man's attitude affect him, Joel said, "Yes, of course! Firemen looked around for quite some distance from where the house was, but didn't find anything, no debris, no bodies, and certainly not this man." *This doctor reminds me of the insurance man I just got finished dealing with!*

The doctor shook his head and waited a minute, as if pondering Joel's words. "This is amazing! We've been waiting for you to come, but I've already written some orders, so we'll proceed now that you've given consent. We have a resident burn specialist who will need to evaluate and see what we can do, if anything. He's in a coma, how did you find him?"

"He wasn't when I first arrived, so I called the ambulance. He said a few words to me then collapsed at my feet. After that I realized he'd lapsed into a coma."

"This is truly amazing!"

"Yes, I totally agree with you."

The doctor hit a few keys on the computer next to the gurney and very shortly, two men came, whisked the gurney that Thad was on away, and Joel watched him go. He turned to the doctor. "So what happens now?"

"I assume the specialist will do his evaluation and then speak with you. You might need to stick around for a while," he added, rather sarcastically.

"Yeah, I'll do that." Joel turned from the doctor, watched the gurney and shook his head. *Does the man think I'm so incompetent or have so little regard for my dad that I'll leave?*

With Thad not in the room, the others started to leave. The doctor didn't speak to Joel, but walked out, totally ignoring him. With his attitude, he reminded Joel of the sheriff. The two nurses, seemed friendlier, they both smiled and one said, "If you're hungry, the cafeteria's on the ground floor. You can leave your cell number with the clerk up front, if you're needed, whoever can call you. If you've had all that in your morning, you're probably ready for a good meal."

Joel sighed. "Thanks, I feel like I've been run over by a freight train and come out worse for wear." Touching the band-aid on his temple, knowing the shiner was still dark, he added, "I've been nursing a dull headache for several days. Probably a cup of coffee and some food would help. I'm sorry I couldn't come with my dad, but I had no idea when I went out there to meet the insurance adjuster that he'd be there! I was as shocked as anyone could be."

"We realize that." She smiled at Joel again. "Not all of us occupy such lofty places in the universe as others."

Joel smiled back at the friendly nurse and said, "Thanks, I needed that."

"Yeah, I had that feeling. Sometimes we wonder where the bedside manners went."

"Mmm, that would cause one to wonder." Joel followed the women from the small room and went back to the clerk at the front desk.

It was lunch time again and Leslie put her tray down quickly on the table because she heard her phone buzz with a text message. It had to be Joel; all her friends were also in the lunch room. She grabbed the phone from her purse, wondering what was so important, especially while she was at school. She swiped the face to read, *Sis, you'll never believe this, but I found Dad at the site! He looked awful! He's at the hospital being evaluated and I'm here now, too. J*

Leslie stared at her phone; then read the message again. She sat down hard on the bench, not facing her food. She stared at her phone and tears came to her eyes. She was so in shock she didn't think to wipe them away, so when one of her friends put her tray down, she looked at Leslie and asked, "What's the matter, Les? You're crying you look like you've seen a ghost! Come on turn around, your food's getting cold!"

Leslie couldn't speak; the tears kept sliding down her cheeks, and dripping off her chin. She looked at her friend and slowly shook her head. Still without speaking and tears still sliding down her cheeks, she held out her phone to show her the message. The girl took the phone and read the words, looked at Leslie, looked back at the words and exclaimed, "What! Wow! You've got to be kidding! After all you've told me Joel told you! Come on! Unbelievable!"

The tears still falling, she whispered, "I… I… really didn't want him to live, but he did!" In an even quieter whisper, she murmured, "God, I'm sorry, I'm so sorry. Forgive me for those awful thoughts."

There in the noisy cafeteria a peace and a stillness came over Leslie. She felt those arms, ones she'd felt the other night. Those same big, strong arms came around her for comfort. She looked around the large room; everything was as it usually was. People were calling across the room, others busily eating, but Leslie wondered how no one else but her felt what she felt. She swiped her eyes, but for several more seconds tears slid down her face. As her other friends came to the table with their trays her friend showed them Joel's text. Everyone was shocked.

Joel left his cell number with the clerk then hurried to the cafeteria. He was very hungry and it was later than he usually ate, some food might help his headache. Everything he took was in disposable packages, even the large coffee. He had no idea how long the doctor needed to evaluate his dad and then want to speak with him or where that could happen. However, he knew that if everything was in disposable wrappers he could meet the burn doctor anywhere.

Before he started eating he sent Leslie a text. She needed to know about their dad before anything went on the air. She'd learned about the explosion from someone's phone, and pictures on social media. That was a terrible blow for her. This would be a shock, but she'd hear it from him. He was twenty-five and all that happened was mind-boggling. What was it doing to Leslie? He had no idea. She was sixteen and a girl, her personality was very different from his.

He finished eating and was gathering up all the packages from his lunch when his phone rang. He answered and a woman said, "Is this Joel Lawson?"

"Yes, Ma'am."

Very matter-of-factly, she said, "This is Dr. Fredrickson, the burn specialist here at the hospital. When and where could I meet you?"

"Ma'am, I'm just finishing my lunch in the cafeteria. I could meet you anywhere."

"That's good. I could use a coffee and some lunch myself; it's been a rather hectic morning. I'll be right down."

Joel threw his trash away, went to the elevator and waited only a few minutes until a lady in a white coat over scrubs, with a mask around her neck, stepped off the elevator and smiled at him. Even with a surgical cap on, she was a beautiful woman. Joel was surprised how young she was. She held out her hand and said, "I assume you're Joel Lawson, I'm Evangelyn Fredrickson. Let's get that coffee. I think meeting and talking in the cafeteria is a good place."

Joel took her hand and shook it warmly. "Yes, I'm Joel. I just finished my lunch so I'll try and find us a quiet table so we can talk. Will that work for you?"

Smiling at Joel, she said, "Oh, sure! I'll hunt you down as soon as I get some caffeine. Maybe even a sandwich."

"That's fine, Dr. Fredrickson." They walked into the cafeteria together, but Evangelyn hurried to the coffee dispenser and Joel looked for an empty table. It was still lunch time, so the cafeteria was quite full. However, he found a small table in a quiet corner. As he pulled out the chair he wondered what her evaluation would be.

As a non-medical person, Joel felt sure they couldn't do much for his dad. At the site he hadn't seen a spot on Thad's body that wasn't burned. Most of what he saw wasn't blistered, but charred! He was amazed that someone found a place to insert an IV needle, he hadn't seen any place flesh colored. Someone was incredibly good to start an IV! Nothing was done to Thad in the ER. He couldn't believe the attitude of the doctor he'd already encountered.

Dr. Fredrickson soon joined him, she doctored her coffee and said, "May I call you Joel?" He nodded, and Evangelyn continued, "Joel, your dad is very bad. I can't emphasize that enough. Not only are burns nearly covering his body that are third degree and would have to be surgically cleaned and dressed, but it's evident that there was quite a bit of internal damage that we must assume was caused by the explosion. I understand you spoke with your dad?"

Joel nodded. "Yes, very briefly, he said a few words which led me to believe that he was amnesic as well, before he collapsed and lapsed into a coma. He didn't know me; in fact he didn't even know he had a son. But those few words sounded nothing like I've ever heard him speak before. Even when he wasn't angry, his voice sounded nothing like it did this morning. It was kind of like his voice was coming from inside a barrel. It was really strange."

"That is because his vocal cords were damaged. I'm told this explosion occurred three days ago and no one found Mr. Lawson until today?"

"Yes, that's correct. Actually, as far as I know, no one has visited the site since the explosion the other day, so I don't know when he actually woke up. I was amazed!"

"I am too. I'm surprised that he even woke up and that he came back to the site."

Joel nodded and said, "Yes, that amazed me, too. Perhaps God had it all orchestrated so that I would find him. So what are you saying?"

Evangelyn took a mouthful of her sandwich, then a swallow of her coffee before she said, "Joel, I'm sure you spoke to your dad for the last time this morning. Amazingly, the paramedic got a blood pressure reading and got the IV going, but things have deteriorated dramatically since. In fact, his blood pressure dropped even as they transported him. It was a significant drop. Since coming in it has dropped considerably more and like I say, not only is he burned extensively, but we're sure there is extensive internal damage. If I were to put him under anesthesia and try to remove all the damaged skin and anything else damaged by the explosion, just on the outside, I'm not sure he would survive. Mr. Lawson is very ill!" Evangelyn said emphatically, finished her sandwich and wiped her mouth with her paper napkin.

"So what is your recommendation, Doctor?"

Lifting her cup, but not drinking, she said, "Joel, I'm afraid your dad will soon pass away. He must have a strong constitution to have survived at all! Especially as cold as it's been these few days. Really, I think our only option is to keep him comfortable until he does. I cannot in good conscience subject his body to any treatment that I know would be required."

"I understand. Is there any way I could see him and stay with him?"

Evangelyn held her cup to her lips, but nodded before she said, "Yes, certainly, if you wish. I have no problem with that. I've sent him to the Burn Unit on second floor. That's the place he will be monitored most closely. If you want to make your way there, I'll call up an order that you be allowed to stay with him as long as you wish."

"Thank you; I'd appreciate that, Dr. Fredrickson."

Evangelyn finished her coffee, held out her hand and Joel shook it. "It's sad meeting under these circumstances, Joel, but it's good to meet you." She looked him in the eye, saw the band-aid and the large bruise and scowled. "Goodness, Joel, what happened to you? You weren't in the explosion were you?"

"Oh, no, this happened the night before. Dad threw me out. As the front door crashed into the wall the mirror on the wall didn't make it, but a shard of glass hit me right there."

"Wow! It could have hit your eye!"

"Yes, it could have, but it didn't. Anyway, thanks. I appreciate the time you've taken to see both Dad and myself. This whole thing is unbelievable."

"Yes, it is."

Evangelyn and Joel stood up. The doctor gathered her things and pulled her phone from her pocket. She pressed one number and turned her back to Joel, so he left to take the elevator to the second floor hoping it was close to the Burn Unit. He didn't know the hospital well. From what the doctor said he felt an urgency to reach the unit. The elevator came immediately. He stepped into the Burn Unit waiting room. A few steps away was the door into the unit itself.

As he pushed the door open a nurse met him and said, "I assume you're Joel Lawson?"

"Yes. Is my dad still living?"

"Come with me. Mr. Lawson, you need to suit up. He's deteriorating fast, but at least put on a sterile mask and gloves."

Joel had the two things on in record time then looked at the nurse. He felt the urgency to be with his dad even more now that he was so close. The nurse took a breath, turned quickly and grabbed a chair from the nurse's station. She dragged it along as she led Joel to a small cubicle next to the nurse's desk. Much to Joel's surprise, there were no machines hooked up to the person in the bed, he had expected several. Only the same IV that he had seen in the ER was hooked up to him. Thad's breathing was shallow, but Joel could see his chest moving. Joel had never touched his dad, but with all the blankets he wondered if they were to try to warm him up. From the cold he might be hypothermic. He had been in November weather for three days!

In a whisper, she said, "He's deteriorating fast, Mr. Lawson, since arriving. The transfer from the stretcher to the bed was traumatic. Be quiet if you speak, so you won't startle him."

The nurse stopped at the end of the divider, but Joel nodded and took the chair she'd brought up as close to Thad's face as he could. The nurse didn't go into the unit at all and Joel didn't sit down, only bent over the man, but didn't whisper. In a very quiet, clear voice, even through the mask, Joel said, "Dad, God loves you. He wants to forgive your sins today and take you home to heaven to be with Him. I wish you could hear me and tell me that you accept God's free gift. We've talked many times about it you know what God wants, Dad."

Much to Joel's surprise, Thad opened his eyes and looked at his son. His eyes didn't have a vague look, they were clear and bright. They never wavered from looking at Joel. "Yes," he murmured. "I… believe…. Jesus… died… for… me." He looked at Joel for another instant, then his eyes closed, his chest raised once and the word "Son," came on that exhalation. His chest never rose again. His head slowly turned toward Joel, but Joel felt sure a peace settled on Thad's face – a look he'd never seen before whenever he'd looked at his dad, not in all his life.

Joel hadn't sat in the chair! He looked at his dad and wondered how he had survived. Then a realization hit him. A whisper exploded from his mouth, muffled by the mask, "God's been chasing him for years! He wanted Dad to confess his sin!" Joel's eyes lit up and he stood basking in that realization. A second later he whirled around the end of the cubicle and said to the nurse standing behind the desk, "Ma'am, I believe Thad Lawson just drew his last breath!"

"Oh, my!" she said. "You barely made it here!"

"Yes, but I did!" *I am so happy I did! Father, God! I* am *in awe! You are amazing!*

After giving the nurse the information she asked for, and she assured him the hospital would take care of notifying the proper people to take care of Thad's body, Joel left the unit and immediately pulled the mask from his face. The room he entered was the Burn Unit Lounge and it was quiet and empty. He sank into a chair and pulled off the gloves and realized that the headache he'd gotten almost instantly from the mirror shard hadn't gone away in three days but had ramped up and was pounding behind his eye. It hurt enough that he wished he carried some pain relievers with him. In fact, it hurt so much worse that he laid his head back on the cushioned top and closed his eyes. His headache was so powerful he knew he'd never fall asleep, but he had to savor what had just happened in the unit.

He had much to do still on his dissertation – finish reading, writing, then revision, but it would have to wait. Right now, he needed to see his pastor and then his Auntie and probably Leslie, in that order. How in the world could he explain what he had just experienced! Events starting after class this morning were so incredible he certainly couldn't go back to the library to work through some dry, science tomes!

He left the hospital fifteen minutes later. Today was Friday, the end of an incredible week, one he couldn't even imagine living through, but he had. He knew Pastor Tom had shortened hours on Fridays, but he hoped the man was still in the office this close to lunch time. He didn't know if Tom took off the whole afternoon or just a few hours. What he had just experienced he must share with someone and who better than his pastor?

He couldn't help it, one minute he was shedding tears, but the next minute the grin encompassed his face. He found himself wiping a tear while he was grinning! God sure did some amazing, incredible things! When he arrived at the church he saw several cars still parked in their usual spots that meant that the staff was still there. He breathed out a sigh of relief and parked close to the walkway into the church.

Joel shut off the car and with a tear glistening on his cheek, but a smile on his lips he hurried up the walk and rang the buzzer to be let into the building. It buzzed, so he went in and the pastor met him. "What can I do for you, Joel?" Tom asked.

Joel didn't answer, just walked passed him into the pastor's office and sank into a chair. Tom followed him in and closed the door. Joel watched him silently until he sat down. Joel cleared his throat and a tear slid down his cheek, but he dashed it away. Finally he said, "Tom, I just came from the hospital! I had the most incredible experience I've ever *ever* had! Absolutely nothing like it in all my twenty-five years!"

Instantly perplexed, Tom looked Joel up and down, but sat forward in his chair and put his elbows on the desk. He scowled and asked, "Why? What's the matter? Are you ill? Actually, for all you've been through you seem quite well." He nodded and added, "Except for that place on your head; that is.

You have quite a shiner, my friend! When did that happen? I don't remember seeing it the other day when you came. Only the band-aid."

Joel waved his hand he had something much more incredible to say. "Tom, I think the shiner's from the trauma from that glass shard and maybe some blood leaked around my eye. That shard hit with a wallop. I can't say for sure and haven't had time for a professional check. People started noticing the next day, but it's gotten darker since I saw you." Joel took a deep breath, leaned forward on his arms, and exclaimed, "Pastor, you will never, ever believe this!"

Tom grinned at his friend and held out his hand as an invitation. "So convince me! You've done a pretty good job of that over the years. Believe me, Joel I have great respect for you, always have. The events that've happened this week are enough to boggle the mind!"

Joel grinned at his friend. "I'll try not to bore you, Tom."

As Joel told the pastor the events of the morning, the man slightly older than Joel looked at him, his mouth slowly falling open. Joel finished by telling him the last encounter he'd had with his dad only moments before and Tom swallowed. "Joel," Tom finally said in awe, "What an amazing thing! After all these years, oh, my!"

"I know. I'm convinced that God did all that so that Dad would admit to me that he needed Jesus' blood to take away his sins. Another opportunity came up, so I used it. That was why he'd thrown me out the night before the explosion."

"Isn't God amazing!"

Before Joel could speak again his phone rang, he was about to ignore it, then thought perhaps it was Leslie. He would need to tell her the rest of the story very soon. He grabbed the phone from his carrier, but he saw the sheriff's department number, so he said, "Oh, that's the sheriff's department perhaps they have word about my mom."

"Well, sure, go on and answer! It can't be any more wild than what you've just told me!"

Joel chuckled. "Wild, huh!" He swiped the phone, "Roger."

"Joel, Sheriff ordered a search as soon as I told him what you'd told me. Believe me; he had as much trouble believing what you said as I did. I had to assure him that you were totally trustworthy, since he didn't know you." Joel held any comment on that sentence. "All the deputies, every one of us, went to the woods behind the site and covered every inch of those woods. We found nothing, no debris, nothing. Oh, we found a place where leaves and pine needles were matted down, it could have been where your dad was, but that was all we found."

"Thanks, Roger that relieves my mind. At least I can be sure Mom died in the explosion. Of course, I finally followed Dad to the hospital, but I was only there maybe an hour and a half before he died, too. I guess we'll never know what really happened the other day, but that's in God's hands. Thanks so much for your help."

"Not a problem, Joel. Glad you called me."

SEVEN

"THANK YOU FOR GOING TO ALL THAT TROUBLE," JOEL SAID.

"Hey, we do all we can for this county!"

"Umm, yeah." *Maybe you do, but not all from your department do!* It made Joel wonder what reaction the sheriff had when he got the news. He was a bit surprised that the sheriff hadn't shown up while he was there. He wasn't convinced that the sheriff believed Thad hadn't thrown a bomb at the house. He was pretty sure the sheriff believed that Thad was alive and well….

While Joel put his phone away, Tom said, "So I guess we'll have a funeral for your dad and a memorial for your mom?"

Joel shook his head. "Actually, Tom, it's ironic, but Dad's wishes were that he and Mom be cremated. That's another reason I think God had him come out of the woods. So let's go with the memorial service we originally planned." Joel let out a long sigh – the headache was ramping up. "It's been some week! I can't remember when I've had so many irons in the fire!"

"That's fine, Joel. We'll keep things just as we'd planned with the service tomorrow. Maybe after that you can get back to some kind of normal."

Joel smiled at his friend. "I can only hope. Of course, staying with Aunt Lucy and sleeping on her sofa-sleeper, is not what I'm used to, but it's better than the alternative. Her house is so tiny there's no room for a desk, I must study and make lesson plans at the library. I only get snatches of time, so I'm there pretty late. So far, not before Auntie and Les go to bed."

"Yes, but it is temporary."

Joel nodded. "That's if I get this dissertation finished when I'm supposed to. The way this week has been…" Joel sighed. "It's anybody's guess."

Tom chuckled. "I have no fear that you will get it approved at submission with flying colors." Joel hadn't told his pastor much, but Tom knew about Joel's many accomplishments in his academic career. He had been contacted only yesterday to ask Joel a question. No time like the present to do that. Tom leaned back, resting on the chair's back legs, crossed his arms across his chest and said, "By the way, you're still determined to take that job out of town… out of state? Didn't I hear that our illustrious local higher education factory wants you to stay here?"

Joel sighed. "Yes, Tom, you've heard right. They do want me to stay. It's been almost weekly since semester started. One or another from the department stops to ask me. Until this week it was not an option, I wanted to get away because of my parents, but that's been removed. Right now all I can say is, we'll see."

"Just so you know, your department chairman asked me to urge you to give them some consideration. Actually, he was very urgent about asking!"

"He was that dogmatic about it?"

Tom nodded. "That's a good word for it, yes. Of course, he never mentioned salary…"

"Tom, it was never about salary, but my parents, Dad especially. As long as I can keep body and soul together until the Lord calls me home, I'm satisfied." Joel started to get up, so Tom did too. Joel sighed and said, "Just after Dad threw me out Les came to the door with my keys, phone and my Bible. She told me something Grampa has told us and that is to stay the course. It's an incredible course! This week has been so incredible I'm not sure I'm living it!"

"Isn't that the truth, Joel! Sometimes it's beyond our comprehension. Yes, that's good advice. I'll remember that, thanks."

Joel looked at the clock and said, "I know you're off soon, I'm glad you were here when I came. We'll see you tomorrow, Tom. I need to go see Aunt Lucy and tell her about all this."

"Yes, I can imagine! Two o'clock is when the paper says the memorial will be. Do you have any pictures or anything you'd want to share?"

Joel shook his head, heading for the door. "Tom, there were never any pictures taken. We did not have a happy home or do anything happy together, not as long as I can remember. Dad didn't want keepsakes of his family. As far as I know, there never were wedding pictures!"

Tom took Joel's hand and shook it warmly. "Joel, I know you didn't live in a happy home. However, God has watched over you and Leslie, it is remarkable!"

"Thanks, Tom, you've been a life saver over the years and I appreciate it a lot."

Saturday afternoon at two o'clock, Lucy and her parents, along with Joel and Leslie sat on the front row in their church auditorium for the memorial service. The organist played some quiet music as the church filled up. Quite a few of the church people came to honor Joel and his family. Only moments before the service started a man and woman Joel didn't know came and sat across the aisle in the front seat. The church was full.

After the couple sat down, Lucy leaned over to Joel and whispered, "Wow! That's Thad's parents. You know that, don't you?"

Joel shook his head. "I never saw them before in my life! Knowing what my dad always looked like and how he acted, they look like respectable people."

"Yes, they do. Perhaps that's why Thad never had anything to do with them."

"I often wondered why we never knew his parents. I knew he was a local man. However, I'd learned early on not to ask questions. I thought perhaps they'd moved away."

"I never got to talk to Eleanor, not once she went into high school; she wouldn't come home until really late so she didn't have to talk to any of us. After she graduated, of course, it was even worse, so I never knew what you knew or didn't know. I never thought to ask you."

"Thanks for telling me, Auntie."

"Of course, Joel! I wouldn't have kept it from you had I known."

Joel nodded. "I'm sure that's true."

Pastor Tom didn't have much to say about Thad and Eleanor Lawson other than what Joel had told him. The couple had never come to the church. Until Joel bought his car, they made sure their children didn't come regularly for services or youth activities. Eleanor left anything religious as soon as she started going with Thad in high school – long before Tom came as the pastor. When Tom took the pastorate, Joel warned him not to visit; Thad would have gladly tossed him out, never allowing him to say more than his name and occupation.

However as he ended his remarks he looked around at the full church and said, "Yesterday, to meet with the insurance adjuster, Joel went to the explosion site. Very much to his surprise, he found his dad wandering around. He was disoriented and very badly burned, but very docile. Before the ambulance arrived to take him to the hospital Thad collapsed and lapsed into a coma at Joel's feet. Sometime later, Joel arrived at the hospital, but only a few minutes after Joel arrived Thad went to the Burn Unit and Joel was allowed to stay at his bedside."

A smile broke across Tom's face. "Folks, Joel, as he often has in his life at his parents' home, spoke to his dad about his soul there in the Burn Unit. Friends, I'm happy to tell you that Thad Lawson; only seconds before he went out into eternity woke up and told his son that he believed that Jesus died for him. Therefore, we commit his and Eleanor's souls to Christ Jesus."

The lady across the aisle burst into tears and her husband quickly put his arm around her. No one saw them, but the man also had tears in his eyes.

The pastor dismissed with prayer, but as soon as the service was over, Joel stepped across the aisle and said, "I'm Joel. Aunt Lucy tells me you are Dad's parents. I never knew!" Leslie stepped up beside him and Joel put his arm around his sister before he said, "This is my sister, Leslie. We are happy to meet you and so glad you could come to this service today!"

There were tears in both their eyes and the lady had a large hanky in her hand, but the man already had an arm around his wife. Absently, Joel realized that he looked somewhat like the man before him. Just as he knew his dad at the explosion site because their eyes were so alike, so the man who sat before him had eyes just like he and his dad.

Eagerly the man took Joel's hand and held it. His voice quivered, as he said, "Joel, we're Steven and Mary Lawson. We've wanted to know you ever since you were born, but weren't allowed, your dad adamantly refused, even though we begged. When we found out that your mother was pregnant with your sister, we begged our son again, but were shut out immediately."

"Oh, my!" Joel said in awe and shook his head. "Oh, my! Unbelievable!" he whispered, again. "I'm finding out some very incredible things, just this week."

"Wow!" Leslie murmured.

Giving the couple a smile, Joel said, "Believe me, we will not turn our backs on you now that we know! It's great to have another set of grandparents!"

"Thank you, Joel. It has been hard, but we've kept up with what you've done with your life and we are so proud of you! We will support you, both of you, any way we can."

"I truly thank you, sir!" Joel said sincerely.

Steve stood and brought his wife with him. They gave their grandchildren watery smiles and Steve said, "Joel, it is truly an incredible thing to finally meet both you and your sister."

Mary had more tears sliding down her cheeks. She stepped forward, took Leslie into her arms and hugged the girl close. Still with her arms around her granddaughter, she looked at her grandson and said, "Oh, my! I can hardly believe! It is so special to know we have such wonderful grandchildren! Steve, we are so blessed."

"Yes, my dear, it is truly awesome!"

In the very back of the auditorium was a young woman who came to pay respects. Her boss learned about the memorial service at the church. Since he knew that Jenni knew Joel personally, he told her she needed to come. That she might be able to find something out that was news-worthy, especially since the deaths were broadcast on TV. She was reluctant to go, she didn't like funerals, this was in a church, which she didn't visit often, and it felt strange to be here. Besides, she didn't want to put anything on the air to dishonor Joel. However, being the reporter that she was, she came and was attentive to every word and action in the service.

However, she hadn't taken a pad of paper or a pen from her purse, only sat clutching it tightly, but she was well aware of all that went on in the large auditorium, especially Joel and his family. She watched Joel, then his sister scramble across the aisle to speak with the other couple.

She sat in the seat as others around her stood up to leave. She hardly noticed them step over her. This service was far out of her area of expertise and certainly out of her comfort zone! What the minister said about Thad's last words weighed heavily on her mind. In drawing his last breath he told Joel he knew Jesus died for him! As the preacher said those words he smiled and acted joyful! She glanced at Joel and he nodded and smiled; Lucy even smiled. What made that so important? She shook her head, the words meant nothing to her and yet they seemed to mean everything to Joel's family and especially to the lady across the aisle! If Joel and the preacher were happy about it, why did the woman burst into tears?

Jenni knew Lucy, because they were neighbors, and Joel, no one else. She wondered why Joel was so anxious to meet the people across the aisle. He nearly leaped from his seat, and crossed the aisle to speak with them. Jenni noticed that the woman still held a hanky and dabbed at her eyes. Jenni shook her head. People acted strange in church! Jenni slipped out of the building while Joel spoke with the couple. She had no intention to make herself known to Joel.

As Jenni started her car she hoped tonight when she walked the dog he'd come home and she could ask questions. She must get to the station and prepare for the evening news. Hopefully she wouldn't have to do much. She must convince Alex there was nothing from the memorial service. She knew, if she didn't understand all that was said and done many who watched the news wouldn't either. She reported news on the local station – a cross section of the city's population watched. If she tried to report something she didn't understand those watching and listening would also get the wrong view and that she didn't want to happen – not to Joel.

Joel's car was already on his aunt's driveway when Jenni came home from the station. She had convinced Alex that there was nothing said or done in the service that she needed to air on the news, even though that's why he sent her. There were some things Jenni still mulled over and didn't understand, but they didn't need airing. She always felt that funeral services should be private times for families and close friends. Even though the Lawson deaths were very public, the memorial service was private; a time for people to remember the ones who were lost and what had happened. They didn't need news coverage. Jenni was convinced of that.

When Jenni left her car with her purse and take-out, she wondered how she could talk to Joel. Walking Curly for his late night business it didn't seem like Joel would come outside, especially now that he was here already. What reason would he have? She was sure he didn't see her as a 'special' friend. She sighed and went inside. She was hungry, her stomach had growled several times since she'd put her take-out on the passenger seat only a few blocks away. Sometimes she wished that as a single girl she didn't have to work but could pursue the man of her dreams.... Well, did she consider Joel Lawson the man of her dreams?

However, as she sat in the kitchen eating she heard a car start up. She couldn't see Lucy's house from the kitchen window, but the car was close enough she was sure it was Joel, perhaps he was leaving for the library and she could walk her dog when he came back later. Tonight especially she had things she wanted to ask him about. She knew he was the only one who could answer to her satisfaction. She determined to listen carefully for when he came home. The things she'd heard and what Joel had said yesterday bothered her almost as much as the explosion. She ate another mouthful; her stomach let her know it wasn't satisfied yet.

Her mom came in the kitchen and poured herself some lemonade, then sat with Jenni. Loretta said, "Lucy has company now. Who are those two people? Are they living with her?"

Still trying to satisfy her hungry, noisy stomach, Jenni said, between bites, "Yes, Mom, remember that house that exploded the other day? The one close to where we used to live?" When her mom nodded, Jenni said, "That's Lucy's nephew and niece. They're the children of the people who died from that explosion. Their mom was Lucy's sister."

Loretta scowled. "Oh, my! Didn't you report on the news yesterday that some man was found wandering around that place?"

"Yes, Joel had to go out there for something else and found his dad. Alex heard about an ambulance dispatched to the place so he sent me out to get the particulars. I went out there and talked to Joel, but he'd already sent his dad to the hospital. The man had been thrown out of the house by the explosion. It was far enough from the site that the firemen didn't find him. Joel said he was burned almost beyond recognition and he only lived for a short time after he arrived at the hospital. Today was the memorial at Joel's church. Alex asked me to go, so I did."

Loretta's eyes were bright as she leaned toward Jenni and asked, "So did you report anything? Surely there was something at the memorial service that you could talk about. I mean, that explosion was something! Your dad and I watched your news report that evening."

"No, Mom, you know I only report the news on Saturday, my back-up does most of the work, so no, nothing happened or was said that I felt I should put on the news. I really felt strange knowing that Alex wanted me to report something from a memorial service. It didn't seem right, like I was intruding on their private life." Jenni put another mouthful in her mouth.

Loretta waved her hand at her words. She scowled, perplexed. "Tell me if I'm wrong, but isn't that what a reporter does? Report things from people's lives? Surely something happened that you could have reported! I mean… as I remember, Thad was… an interesting character. Surely there was something…. I, umm, know of a few things he did, even in high school! In a memorial service don't they tell about things in the dead person's life?"

Jenni shook her head. Her mom's opinion of her work hurt. "Mom, lots of things happened at the service, but I didn't feel right blasting them over the air and besides, it was a private service, I couldn't do it." Jenni could still hear the car driving away.

Loretta grinned and changed gears when she said, "That guy seems about your age, Jen."

Jenni sighed; she knew exactly what her mom was thinking. "Yes, Mom, we do report things from people's lives, but sometimes it's best to leave private things alone. That's the way I felt about the memorial service. To answer your other question, we were in the same class in public school, starting in kindergarten and rode the same school bus until I got my car as a sophomore. When I went away to college he stayed here and went to the university here."

Giving her daughter a big smile, Loretta patted Jenni's hand and said, "Get over there and get reacquainted! Why, he's a really good male specimen! You aren't getting any younger. What kind of work does he do? Is he well placed? Why's he living with Lucy?"

Sighing again, her mom was really acting like an eager beaver! She smiled at her mom. "Yeah, Mom, you ask so many questions, but I'll go over there as soon as he comes home from the library tonight. You know I always walk Curly before I go to bed."

Loretta looked at her daughter, wondering at the tone of her voice. "The library? Why's he going to the library so late in the evening? On a Saturday? Is it open on Saturday night?"

Jenni put the last mouthful in her mouth she chewed and swallowed and said, "Mom, it's the university library where he goes. He's almost got his PhD. He's working on his dissertation for it. I'm sure he goes to the university library to work on it. Obviously he has lots of research and only the university library has what he needs. He has writing to do after that. If the library's open, he'll probably be there, since that's where the research books are."

"Ah, I see. Well, that's great! He could make lots of money and support you really well, you know. Jenni you need to look into that!"

"Mmm, yeah, Mom. I'll be right on that."

"You really need to go meet him!"

Jenni had finished eating, so she picked up her glass and took a long swallow of her tea. Her mom's attitude about Joel and about her work didn't sit right with her and she needed a minute to get her thoughts together. She set the glass down and took a deep breath, let it out. She looked at her mom and took another deep breath. The last words and actions that the preacher said about Thad still weighed on her mind maybe her mom could answer her question.

Jenni shrugged. *In for a penny, in for a pound.* She asked, "Mom, you and Dad never go to church, just on the holidays. Why? Besides, why do you bother to go even then? I never could see the sense in that."

Instantly, Loretta acted very uncomfortable and cleared her throat. "Well…" she said, but ran out of words immediately.

Jenni waited, when Loretta didn't continue, she said, "When I saw Joel at the site, when he found his dad, he talked about things that were foreign to me, but were close to his heart."

Loretta cleared her throat and shrugged, trying to act nonchalant. She looked over Jenni's shoulder and answered, "Well… your dad and me didn't think it was that important. Sundays are one day when we can sleep in and do what we want. And… umm… well… Your dad's worked his whole life in the company and well…. we didn't feel the need. Things have gone our way all our married lives, you know." Loretta cleared her throat again. "Christmas and Easter… well, it's kind of the thing to do, you know? Christmas and baby Jesus and… well… Easter had all those palm branches and hallelujahs."

Determined to find something out, she said, "Mom, Joel's pastor told us something right before he ended the service that I can't get out of my head. He said that just before he died that Thad opened his eyes and looked at Joel. He took a breath and said, 'I believe that Jesus died for me.' Then he died. Is that important? The preacher and Joel both seemed so happy about that."

Loretta cleared her throat and Jenni saw her swallow. "Yeah, umm, maybe it is important…." Loretta stood up, actually, she jumped up, very agitated and wanting to get away from Jenni's questions. Quickly she left the table. As Jenni gathered her boxes, Loretta turned away and said, "I'll go watch my show now, it's about time." Jenni watched her, shaking her head, but didn't say anything. It was Saturday; her regular show wasn't on on Saturdays. It was as if her words caused her mom's conscience to bother her. Everything she said made her mom uncomfortable. Loretta hurried into the living room and instantly there was noise from the TV.

Those few words Joel had said to her out at the site kept churning in her head. 'In all things, God works for good…' That along with what the preacher had said about Thad's last words troubled her. She wondered if Joel had just said those words or if he'd quoted from the Bible. Jenni didn't have a Bible, but she thought maybe there was one somewhere in the house, but she had no idea where. She was curious enough that if she had a clue where a Bible was she might look for it. Could God be that interested in a person that He'd use ***all*** things in a person's life? Even bad stuff? That was enough of a reason to try to talk to Joel.

Between those words and what she'd heard at the service and her mom's reaction just now, she was perplexed. Why should it matter if Thad believed that Jesus had died for him? Why did the preacher make a point of saying those words? He made a point of saying the exact words. Another perplexing question: why did Joel and the preacher smile and act happy and the woman across the aisle burst into tears? Who was the lady on the front row? Joel moved across the aisle in a hurry. It was very obvious she wouldn't find out the answers here in this house. She must hope that Joel would come back at the time when it was appropriate to walk Curly. Again she decided that he was the only one who could answer her questions to her satisfaction.

Joel had taken Lucy and Leslie to the service and his grandparents had met them at the church. The church people were kind to supply a meal after the service; and not only the side of his family that he knew attended, but Steve and Mary Lawson stayed. It gave Joel and Leslie time to get to know them a little. Joel found out that the Lawson's were Christian people and that's why Thad had nothing to do with them, even forbidding them access to his children.

Joel realized during the meal that it was another way for Thad to persecute his parents and his children, although Joel and Leslie didn't know he was persecuting them. His eyes became scratchy when he thought about Steve and Mary begging his dad to let them know their grandchildren. He wondered how Lucy, Ed and Claudia had gotten to know him and Les, with his dad so adamant! Of course, they were his wife's side that could be the reason.

During the meal at the church, Steve Lawson told Joel about an apartment building that he and his wife owned closer to the university where Joel studied and worked. Steve invited him to come see an apartment that was open. Joel didn't want to slight his Aunt Lucy, but he thought that now the order to live with his parents didn't confine him that as a twenty-five year old, living in his own place might work well for him.

Joel brought Lucy and Leslie back to Lucy's home from the service and his grandparents followed. However, Joel was quiet thinking, about what Steve had offered him. It surely wouldn't hurt to go look at the apartment. He was not making a commitment. However, he had to admit that if the apartment fit into his plans, his meager budget, and lack of furniture; he'd take it. A tough order to be sure, at least he could have his own space. Perhaps even a desk!

Back at Lucy's they talked about the service over iced tea. Thad's death-bed commitment was quite a conversation piece at the meal at the church among the people who served. Nearly everyone in their suburb knew Thad Lawson. It was an awesome thing, it took Joel completely by surprise and he was there at that death-bed! He wondered if things had been different if he would even have recognized God's hand in it all. How could he not!

However, once his grandparents left he felt the need to get away for a while. The house was too tiny for any quiet thinking. Jenni's car was still ticking because she had just come home when Joel went out and left. He had decided that even if the apartment was only an efficiency and he had to sleep on a sofa-sleeper, at least no one else would be using the room. He also hoped he could have a desk where he could spread out his things to study and work. Never having a place to call his own made it hard to feel completely at home at Lucy's.

He loved his aunt and would never hurt her, but with Leslie also living there, he didn't feel right. Besides, he'd tried to convince Lucy to take some money for his and Leslie's room and board and she would have nothing to do with it. Still, her house was so small that the living room felt crowded with the sofa, a few small tables, a recliner and a stand with a small TV on it. He'd never called the Lawson house 'home', but it was much bigger than Lucy's bungalow. He wouldn't say it out loud, but he felt claustrophobic when he was there with both his aunt and his sister. If the TV was on there was no where in the house to get away from the sound.

Joel called his granddad then drove across town to the address that Steve gave him. Since he didn't know his granddad he wondered what he was getting into. However, since it was so close to the university, it was in a good section of the city. It was an unusual set up. The building they owned was among other apartment buildings and looked like several around it, but each building was owned by someone different, a cooperative. Steve stood outside the building, smiling, waiting to greet his grandson. Joel parked, hurrying to meet his new-found grandfather.

He grasped Joel's hand, grinned, and said, "Joel, you have no idea how happy I am to finally meet you! We saw all the news on TV, but we still didn't know how we could meet you. We saw in the paper about the memorial service, so we decided to come."

Joel nodded. "I'm so glad you did! I really feel honored to finally meet you." Feeling uncomfortable, Joel asked, "What should I call you? You are my granddad, but would you rather I call you something else? Little kids must call their grandparents by those names, but, well…." Joel finished his thought, "I'm an adult, maybe that makes a difference for you."

The smile left Steve's face and his eyes glistened, as he said, "Joel, I would feel honored if you want to call me 'Granddad'. Since Thad was our only child and we only met today, I have never been called that in my life."

Joel smiled at the older man and exclaimed enthusiastically, "Well, consider yourself 'Granddad' from now on!" Feeling the need for a hug himself, Joel put his arm around the older man and squeezed. "I also feel very honored to have such a fine man to call Granddad! Both of my granddads are fine men! I'm just sad that it's been this far into my life for me to discover you! Your son did you no favors!"

Steve immediately reached around Joel as well. He made no secret about the tears that glistened in his eyes. He sniffed and pulled a handkerchief from his pocket to wipe his eyes. "I will happily consider myself your granddad, thank you! Oh, by the way, I think your grandmother would be pleased if you'd call her 'Nana' if you don't mind."

Joel's happiness seemed to overflow. Still with a grin, he said, "Sure, our other grandmother wants to be called gramma, so Nana it is! So, what have you got, Granddad?"

Steve was so pleased that he gave Joel a huge grin as they went in through the main door. "The place I have is quite large, on the ground floor. The lay of the land slopes so the back of the building is exposed, but the front only partially, so this apartment has an entrance and patio on the back, but in front there is dirt part way up the outside wall and the windows look out on the lawn. That arrangement helps keep the temperature moderated."

Steve took Joel down a few steps from the main door, and unlocked a door on a dark hallway. Joel entered the apartment through a short hallway, with a door that he assumed was a coat closet. A few steps later he walked into a large room. "Oh, my, this is huge, Granddad!"

Using his hand to point out the different areas in the room, Steve said, "Yes, this is the living space, with designated areas for the kitchen, dining area and the living room. You see the patio door from the living room out onto the patio. That one door also locks with a key, so you can go in and out there. There are several parking spaces just for these ground floor apartments. The two bedrooms and bath are back there."

Joel walked around the apartment, looking behind closed doors to find lots of closet space. The bathroom was large and had a washer and drier as well as a large linen closet and both bedrooms were large, probably bigger than his at his parents' home, but the view out each one was… dead grass and the root-swell on the trees. However, that didn't bother Joel. Bedrooms were only for sleeping anyway.

He stopped for several minutes to look out the huge patio door and liked what he saw. Finally, he said, "Granddad, this is way more space than I'd need! Even so, I would have two problems that I can see immediately."

Steve scowled and said, "Really?"

Joel nodded. "Surely this would cost way more than I can afford and I don't have that first stick of furniture. I never owned any myself and after the explosion there isn't anything."

"Well, my fine grandson, I would be overwhelmed with gratitude if you would consider it a gift from your nana and me for as long as you need it. Since we haven't been able to give you one present for any of your birthdays or Christmases that would suit us just fine. Your other problem; very often people move out and leave furniture, so this complex has a storage building where we store decent furniture when we clean out an apartment. So your problem is solved, all you need to do is say when and what you want and we'll have people on hand to move you in."

Joel spun around and looked at the older man stunned. He spread his arms, a bit like a child and came to his granddad. After a hug, he exclaimed, "Granddad, I am overwhelmed! This is amazing! I will accept your offer. Let me get this by Aunt Lucy, Leslie and my calendar and I'll call you next week. As you can imagine, my calendar is bursting and this week has really been a huge setback in my research and writing."

"That will be just fine." Steve swallowed before he said, "Joel, you have no idea how much it means to me… to us, to have you enter our lives! After trying so hard to be allowed to know you and to know that it was not to be. To have Thad turn against us so totally was devastating and then to deny us our grandchildren was heartbreaking for both of us, but especially for Mary. She has cried many tears over her wayward son."

"Oh, Granddad, actually, I was shocked when Auntie told me who you were."

Very seriously, Steve said, "Joel, I'm sure that your dad was determined never to let you know anything about us. Even in junior high school he was rebellious. He would have no part of his Christian upbringing and that hurt us immensely. Mary often asked what she had done wrong in raising him and having him turn out the way he did."

"I understand, Granddad. Actually, my other grandparents asked the same questions about my mom, but my Uncle Josh always told them in no uncertain words that it was not them but my mom's own will that had taken her astray. I would say the same to you. It was Dad's own sinful nature that listened to the words of the Devil that led him astray."

In awe, Steve whispered, "Thank you for saying that, Joel. That means so much! Believe me, I will tell Mary what you've said, it will mean so much to her."

Joel nodded. "I'm glad I could tell you that."

Soon after the tour, Joel and Steve went to their cars and Joel sat for several minutes as Steve drove away. "Less than a week ago Dad threw me out of the only home I ever knew and said to never come back. I found refuge in Auntie's home, but I didn't want to be a burden. The next day my parents' house was blown to oblivion and my parents were both killed because of that. Les also had to move into Auntie's bungalow that could only accommodate one or maybe two people comfortably." Because of the lack of space and privacy he was very uncomfortable there, but knew with his finances he couldn't move out. To have had to rent a place would have stretched his finances almost to the breaking point – he still wore a borrowed coat.

Now, today, he had met two fine people he should have known all his life, but because of things beyond his control had never known them. Now he'd been offered a spacious place to live, rent free and furnished. It was incredible! Life as he knew it was gone, right along with the house he'd lived in for twenty-five years! How amazing!

Before he started up, he murmured, "Thank You, Lord! Thank You, thank You! I am totally overwhelmed by Your blessings!"

Joel still mulled over what he'd been offered when he arrived at Lucy's house. It wasn't as late as he often came from the library, but it was dark. After all, it was only days until Thanksgiving. His dash clock said it was barely nine o'clock. He pulled up in the driveway and looked at the house next door. Just as there were several lights on in Lucy's house, Jenni's house had many lights still on. People were not heading off to bed yet. He wondered if Jenni would be walking her dog any time soon, but it was earlier than she'd walked him on other evenings.

Still thinking about what was offered; Joel opened his car door but sat in the seat and looked around the quiet street. Sitting in the dark he decided the wind was calm, it wasn't a bad temperature to stay outside for a few minutes and not go in the bungalow right away. Leslie and Auntie were probably watching TV, but he wanted to savor his blessings for a few minutes in the quietness of the neighborhood. Things that had happened this week were totally incredible he had to savor them alone. Until they went to bed the house wouldn't be quiet.

In the corner made by the driveway and the sidewalk the street department had cut a dead tree over the summer and left the stump quite high. It looked high enough to sit on, so Joel decided he'd sit for a few minutes. He left his car and walked down the driveway. To have another set of grandparents boggled his mind! And to think they had wanted to know him and Leslie all their lives, but were not allowed! And now he had the option of a spacious place to live! God was pouring on the blessings!

Joel sat down on the stump and bowed his head. "My Father, I am in awe of You! Everything that has happened this week has been from Your hand. The fact that Dad was at the site; that he woke up at the hospital – all of this was against all odds! You had to do it all! That is so obvious. I thank You from the bottom of my heart!"

Jenni and Curly had just entered her room when she heard Joel's car pull onto Lucy's driveway. She hadn't planned to go straight to bed, sometimes she went to her room to be alone and think. Her parents had remodeled so she had her own bath and a tiny sitting room, with a desk, her TV and a comfortable chair as well as her bedroom. She still had questions that didn't have answers. A glance at the clock told her it was too early to walk the dog for the night, but Curly didn't care. It wouldn't hurt to spend a few minutes outside. If Joel stayed out, why not?

She closed the door so that the room was dark and didn't turn on the light. She could see outside better with the darkness behind her. She walked straight to the window and pushed her hand behind her curtain to look out on the driveway. Much to her surprise, Joel didn't go immediately into Lucy's house, but went down the driveway and sat on the stump of the old dead tree. Why would he do that? It was cold! It was November! Surely Lucy had a chair in her house more comfortable than an old stump! However, Jenni wouldn't look a gift horse in the mouth! Curly surely could use a walk. Joel was staying outside, … well, she was on her way!

Jenni turned and said, "Curly, it's early, but Joel's still outside and I want to talk to him, come on, I know you can make your juices flow." Curly followed but didn't voice his opinion.

Quickly, Jenni went to the kitchen. She didn't want to talk with her parents. She pulled on her coat and snapped on the leash and was out the door. She'd make sure that Joel's time outside included some time with her! She didn't allow Curly to stop until she had walked the strip of grass to the stump, where Joel still sat looking up at the cloudless, star-studded sky.

"Hi!" Jenni said, breathlessly, as she nearly dragged Curly down her driveway. Obviously the dog had taken her seriously.

"Hey, Jenni! Your dog needs to walk this early?"

Jenni cleared her throat and said, "Well, he'll walk any time I want to walk him, but I wanted to ask you some questions."

"Sure, ask away! I'm working on my PhD dissertation, so I probably don't have all the answers yet, but… wait till January!" He raised his fist in the air and grinned.

Jenni laughed. "I'm sure you have lots more than I have. You said something out at the site yesterday that really has me puzzled and I wanted to ask you about it."

"Sure, what did I say?"

A gust of wind whirled a few strands of hair across her face, but she pushed them behind her ear. "You said, 'In all things, God works for good...' Really? Joel, you didn't get along with your dad, he kicked you out and then the house exploded and they were killed. How can you say God works for good? None of that is good! I mean, really? Surely you can't see that as God's will!" Curly walked over to Joel and sniffed his pantleg, then lay down beside him.

Joel reached down and dragged his fingers through Curly's dark coat several times. Curly, of course soaked up the attention. Joel smiled and said, "Nice dog."

Only a minute later, Joel pulled one leg up and placed his heel on the stump, then crossed his arms on his knee, but he looked up at Jenni very seriously, as he said, "Yes, it's hard sometimes to believe that everything that happens is part of God's plan. Some of those things I really don't want as part of my life, but the Bible says, as God's child, everything that happens makes me into the person I am or will become. God uses all those difficulties, hardships, set-backs to make me a stronger person and that is good. If everything I experience was just a smooth sail on a glass lake I'd be a wimp."

Jenni's words nearly exploded from her mouth, "But I haven't had near the stuff happen to me that you have! I don't think I'm a wimp!"

"No, you're not that, but you've had other things come into your life to make you a mature person, Jenni. Different things affect our lives in very different ways." *Besides, if* you're *not God's child,* **God** *wouldn't use your experiences to mold your life.*

Jenni nodded, but didn't speak for several minutes then she took a deep breath. The other thing she wanted to ask really had her puzzled. "I had another question for you and it's bothered me a lot just this afternoon."

"Okay, shoot! It sounds sort of serious."

Jenni looked away and spotted Curly. She still hesitated and took a deep breath before she said, "I guess maybe it is, Joel. Umm, I came to the memorial service. My boss said to come to see if there was anything news-worthy." Before Joel could react, Jenni held up her hand and added, "I didn't report anything this evening, Joel. I worked hard to convince him there wasn't anything I needed to report. I think a memorial service is a personal time for family. Anyway, why was it so important for your preacher to say that your dad woke up and told you he believed that Jesus died for him?"

Joel was silent for several minutes. It seemed quite obvious to him that Jenni didn't know her Bible, but more importantly, she very probably didn't have a personal relationship with God, the Father or Jesus Christ His Son. Because of that, he was convinced that this was probably the most important thing he would ever say to Jenni and he wanted to say it just right. Joel didn't want to bring offence, but Jenni needed to know the truth. He didn't look at Jenni; instead he looked up at the sky, wishing he could see his heavenly Father.

EIGHT

HE PULLED IN A DEEP BREATH BEFORE HE SAID, "JENNI, WHAT MY DAD DID ON THAT last breath was *the* most important thing he ever did!" Joel pulled in another deep breath and let it out before he asked, "Jenni, if you were to die tonight do you know for sure that you'd go to heaven?"

Jenni coiled Curly's leash around her hand, gave Joel a glance, but looked away quickly and looked across the street into the darkness. Very uncomfortable, she finally said, "How can anybody know that! How does anybody know there is such a place called Heaven?"

As kindly as he could, Joel said, "Jenni, I've held the Bible dear to my heart for most of my life and the words in it I believe with all my heart are God's words to mankind. Throughout the Bible He says there is a heaven and a hell. When a person dies, his body goes in the ground, but a part of him – in each one of us - that makes him a living, breathing person, that makes him unique, that no one can see - that part lives forever. That part, his soul, will go to either a beautiful place where God is, that is heaven, for ever and ever or his soul will go to a terrible place called hell where God is not. A soul that goes there will be in torment for ever and ever."

Curly wandered off, stretching Jenni's arm out from her side, but she didn't notice. Instead, she asked, "Really? You truly believe that?"

Joel smiled at her and said, "Yes, Jenni, I do. God says it over and over in the Bible that here on earth, as a living person we have to make a choice. We must choose to either spend forever in heaven with God or in hell forever where God is not. It is a choice that each person, individually must make."

"Well, sure, I choose heaven!" she said, excitedly. She almost added, *Of course! If there's a heaven and a hell who wants to go to hell!*

Joel nodded and slid his foot off the stump before he said, "You see that's why what my dad did yesterday just before he died was so important. He had to admit he couldn't get himself to heaven. Jesus, who is Himself God and is totally without sin, died for Dad's sin. He took all that evil stuff he did all his life, all that anger and the evil words he's said over the years, everything evil in his heart that he didn't even say out loud, to that cross and paid Dad's sin debt so that Dad could go to heaven, but Dad had to admit that Jesus had died for him. As far as I know, he had never done that in all his life.

"Jenni, each one of us must admit our sins, our inability to pay our own sin debt and let Jesus take it to His cross. That is the only way anyone, any human being, can go to heaven."

Uncomfortably, Jenni said, "Joel! This is heavy stuff!"

"Yes, it is. Like I said, those words Dad said were the most important words he's ever said in his life. They turned him from going to hell, a place so awful that God said was meant for the Devil and his demons, completely around and sent him to heaven. I expect to meet him there. Actually, I believe that God was chasing Dad and that's why I found him yesterday. God intended for Dad to confess his need for a Savior before he died." Joel pulled in a breath. "It's possible God wanted *me* to hear him say those words. I am utterly grateful to God that I did!"

Jenni cleared her throat, pushed that clump of hair back behind her ear again and straightened her spine so it was as straight and unyielding as a board. She pulled on Curly's leash and in a totally different voice, said, "Umm, thanks for talking to me, Joel. I guess you've answered my questions, but I'll have to think about what you've said for a while. I'll see you again, Joel. Ah, Curly, it's time to go inside. Come on, I know you've done your business."

Joel saw Jenni's body language as well as heard her speech and knew that she had no intention of making a decision tonight. He swallowed a sigh and said, "Yes, Jenni. I'd like to invite you to our church for the service tomorrow." He couldn't help the slight wobble in his voice. He knew she wasn't rejecting him but his Lord.

Rather abruptly, she yanked on Curly's leash hard enough that he took several running steps, as she said, "I'll pass, Joel! Good night!" Tossing her head, she hurried down the driveway to the house. Joel still sat on the stump, but watched Jenni nearly drag Curly back to her house. Only seconds later Joel heard the door on Mikles' house shut very decisively.

It was a quiet neighborhood. There were cars in many driveways. Nothing stirred on the street. There were still lights on in the houses and Joel could see places were a TV was sending out blue light. Probably some would stay up to watch the late news. There was a streetlight two houses down and one across the street, but Joel sat on the stump for several more minutes.

He sighed and knew what he'd said to Jenni had made her think about things she may never have thought about before, but they were so very important. It could make the difference between what his Aunt Lucy was and what his mom had been. He also knew his words had upset her, but obviously she wouldn't act on her thoughts, not tonight.

As the door closed, Joel bowed his head and said, "God in heaven, use my words in Jenni's life. I believe she needs to be saved, but only You can do that. Please, Lord, defeat the Devil in her life. If I'm not the one to lead her to You, please send someone to her who will."

Lights were going out in the houses close by, and Joel pulled in a deep breath and stood up. He had sat on the stump long enough he was chilled. The breeze was starting to penetrate. He needed to be on the other side of Auntie's door before she locked it. She had promised him a key, but it hadn't appeared. Thinking about it now, he probably wouldn't need one, not since he'd be moving into his own place in only a few days! He would come see her, probably eat some meals here, but he wouldn't be here every day. He wondered if Leslie would stay here or go with him. If Leslie stayed, he knew he'd be back to check on her. He loved his little sister so very much! As children from an abusive family, they had a special bond.

Joel pushed out a long breath, stood up and brushed off his coat. He'd sat outside for quite a while, but it was time to go inside. Now that he was standing, the breeze tussled his hair. He turned to take the few steps to the cement slab in front of Lucy's door but he looked at Jenni's house. What he told her was so important, but she wasn't ready. He knew which room was hers; he'd seen the light go on after their late night talks. The light was on in that room now. He shook his head; it was obvious she didn't share his faith in God his Father and His Son, Jesus.

As things stood, in a few days there would be no late talks with Jenni because he wouldn't be here. Perhaps before he moved he could share with her again; or perhaps not. Jenni needed to know she was going to heaven; she needed to confess her need of a Savior. Perhaps it was Joel's place to plant the seed and someone else to water and God would get the harvest.

Jenni was a nice young woman, but if she didn't share his faith, she was not for him. Over the years he'd lived at Thad Lawson's house he'd suffered too much to put his faith aside for someone who wasn't a believer. And after what he'd found out today, after meeting his grandparents that his dad had denied them, that was even more important. He would stay the course, that all-important course included his Savior. Besides, he hadn't even initiated these meetings with Jenni, she had been the one to approach him, every time, not that he was opposed, but he would not make a special effort to come see her when he moved. He went in Lucy's house and locked the door behind him. He would pray for Jenni, perhaps at another time she would be open to letting Jesus take her sins to His cross. He would pray to that end.

Joel felt the furnace running as he shed his coat and hung it in the closet. The house was quiet, Leslie was behind the closed door upstairs and Lucy was behind the closed door to her bedroom across from the bathroom. One light greeted him when he walked in. He turned it off and went back to the front closet for his nighttime sweatpants and went in the bathroom for his shower. He needed to dress his puncture wound. As far as he could tell there was no infection, it didn't hurt, but he needed to dress it. The headache had finally subsided, that was a relief!

His aunt had never said that the noise he made taking his nighttime shower bothered her. Even so, he didn't want to disturb her, so he closed the bathroom door quietly. She was a wonderful lady! Over the years she had been such an influence in his life. After just meeting his other grandparents, he wondered how Auntie and his grandparents were in their lives for as long as he could remember. Perhaps he'd ask her in the morning. He shook his head. Joel realized that his dad was not only antagonistic and belligerent, but... cruel, maybe was the word. Keeping his children from his parents was a cruel thing to do to them. It would have been one thing if they'd lived miles apart, but they lived in the same city, the same suburb!

It was time to call down the day. He would do that with a warm shower; at the end of an action packed week, one he could never have fathomed in his wildest dreams. The new week would start with church tomorrow and the rest of the week play out as a normal week. He might only be twenty-five, but he could live quite well without all the mind-boggling events he'd lived through this week. Maybe he could take some of those irons out of the fire! He was looking forward to getting his dissertation finished. He knew there was one more topic that would be his last chapter that needed to be addressed. Hopefully that could happen this coming week.

After closing the bathroom door, he turned on the water to warm up and said, "Life this week has been unbelievable, but God's hand was in everything! He is an awesome God!"

He stepped into the warm water, letting the chill from his time outside leave his body and let the events of the day wash away. It felt good to relax. After a nice, warm shower, the band-aid on the puncture wound hung on by only a tiny spot, so Joel took it off and threw it away, put a little salve on the place, but left off the band-aid. Now was probably a good time to let the air get to the wound. It was mostly healed.

After he brushed his teeth, combed the rats from his wet hair he hurried back to the sofa-bed. He couldn't wait to get horizontal! He soon was and in Lucy's comfortable living room, he managed to pull the light blanket over him. He let out a long sigh. Tomorrow was another day, it would come, they would live it; he would stay the course. Fortunately, he could spend some of it in God's house. He closed his eyes and let sleep claim him.

In the morning, Joel was reluctant to stir, but the aroma of Lucy's delicious coffee brought him around. That dear lady was doing so much for them. When Leslie came downstairs, the three of them met at the breakfast table and after Joel said the blessing, he said, "Auntie, I need to run something by you. After the service yesterday I began to wonder about this and couldn't come up with an answer."

She took a swallow of her coffee and reached to cover his hand. She smiled and said, "Okay, fire away! You know I'm always interested in what my nephew has to say."

Joel breathed in the aroma from his breakfast plate, put a forkful of his aunt's scrambled eggs in his mouth and savored them. He grinned, before he said, "Mmm, Auntie, these eggs are great! The coffee you fix is super! In fact I have only praise for all the meals you've fixed for us. By the way, did you know that the Lawson's own an apartment building here in the city?"

"An apartment building! No! I hardly know them, just to know who they are. Even when Josh was alive and we went more places I can't remember ever seeing them. So no, I didn't have any idea! My goodness that is something! Where is it?"

"While we ate at church yesterday, Granddad told me about it and said he had an open apartment. He invited me to see it, so I went over after Grampa and Gramma left. The building is in a complex a few blocks from the university. If I wasn't too lazy, I could walk to campus. It's in a nice neighborhood. Really, I couldn't believe the size of the apartment he offered me."

"So that's where you went! I wondered what you two talked about so seriously at the dinner. But when I heard you come home from wherever, you didn't come straight in. Joel, I know it's cramped. You don't have your own space and there isn't room for a desk. You know you're welcome here any time. Whenever you want to come is fine, but I know you would be more comfortable in a place of your own. Can you afford this? How about furniture?"

His grin widening, Joel said, "Auntie, he says they have a storage building full of left behind furniture in the complex. He says they only keep the best things that are left and that I'm welcome to use anything I need to fill the apartment. He also said that since they were never allowed to give me birthday or Christmas presents that they didn't want any rent for it. I really couldn't believe it when he told me all that!"

Lucy set her coffee cup down on the table with a thunk and exclaimed, "Oh, my! That is amazing! Of course, take him up on it! Really, even to furnish it? That is amazing! Joel, I had no idea, that's for sure! This is just one more thing to add onto an incredible week!"

"Yes, Auntie, that's so true."

Leslie looked totally forlorn as she asked, "What about me?"

Joel smiled at his sister, took another mouthful of eggs and said, "Sis, the place has two bedrooms, so you could come, too. It's a really nice place and seems pretty quiet. But you'd have to change schools it's definitely not in this district. Like I say, it's only a few blocks from the university and you know that's on the other side of town."

Lucy quickly said, "Dear child, you are more than welcome to live with me! You have that place upstairs and we get along really well together, but if you want to go with Joel, I won't stand in your way at all, so it's up to you."

Leslie let out a long sigh, "Auntie, maybe later I'd want to change schools, but right now, with all that's happened, I'd like to stay where my friends are. So it's okay for me to stay here?"

Lucy laid her hand across Leslie's hand and smiled at her. "Of course, child, I'm more than happy to have you!"

There were tears in Leslie's eyes, as she said, "Thanks, Auntie, thanks so much! Bro, when will you move?"

"Not tomorrow, Mondays are so busy, since I teach all morning, but maybe Tuesday. I'd like to be on hand when the furniture is moved. I have no idea how that works. I'm to call Granddad and let him know, I'll do that tomorrow." His grin hadn't dimmed as he looked at Leslie and added, "Oh, Les, our other granddad said he would be very pleased if we'd call him Granddad and our grandmother Nana. I was sure you'd have no problem with that, so I agreed."

"Well, okay, it'll seem strange to have more than one."

"Yes, but he said it'll be a first for them to have grandchildren and they're thrilled!"

Tears came to Leslie's eyes as Joel said those words. "Our dad wouldn't let us know our grandparents! They are his mom and dad!"

"I know. It hurts me too, Sis."

"It's unconscionable what that man did to you both!" Lucy exclaimed.

Joel cleaned his plate. "Auntie, if Dad was so against us knowing his parents how did you and Grampa and Gramma know us? I can't remember a time not knowing you."

"It was your grampa. He told Mom and me over and over that he wasn't going to let Thad push us out of Eleanor's life. Thad had her so poisoned that she did everything he told her, nearly to the letter. Dad said that even as we waited there at the school after her graduation when she didn't show up. Mom was heart-broken!

"One day he and Mom were grocery shopping when Eleanor was there. They noticed she was pregnant with you. She tried to ignore them, but Dad walked up, blocked her in, using her shopping cart so she couldn't get away and insisted she tell him when you were to be born. He did it kindly, but he was forceful and Eleanor would always listen to her dad. He was tireless in pestering Eleanor that they had to tell him when their son was born. It made Thad furious!"

She grinned at Joel and continued, "They didn't want to, I know, but Dad wouldn't let them off the hook. Of course, once you were born, El had you with her, so Mom and Dad got to see you, even as a baby. You know that you were both born at home. That was one reason; they didn't want anyone to know, but we wouldn't let it go. I was still in school, so I didn't get to see you for several years. Once I was out and going with Josh, I made sure I got to know you!"

"I am so glad, Auntie! What would we have done, Leslie and me? We wouldn't have known about Jesus at such a young age. And all the times we had to get away! It was like an oasis in the desert, that's for sure."

"I know, that's why Dad was so insistent! I remember he and Josh went to their house after Leslie was born and informed them that the four of us planned to be part of their children's lives, there would be no quarrel! Your dad was angry and tried to throw them out, but it didn't happen, it was two against one. I really don't think Dad and Josh told Mom and me everything."

Joel shook his head. "Auntie, we are eternally grateful!"

Leslie nodded. "Auntie, what would we ever have done if we hadn't been able to come to your house when it got so bad at home?"

"Child, I don't know, but I know that God takes care of his own. He used us to be part of His plan for your lives and I'm very grateful for that."

"So are we," Leslie sighed.

Joel also reached for Lucy's hand and added, "Absolutely, Auntie! Especially this past week I *know* that God is an awesome God!"

Only a few minutes later the three were ready for church, so Joel opened two doors on his car and took Lucy and Leslie to their church for both Sunday school and church. Joel was happy to go to his college and career class, his pastor was the teacher and they were great friends. Of course, Lucy went to the ladies class and Leslie loved her teens class, she had several really good friends there. Finally, things were normal! Joel was even convinced he'd be able to spend his time working on his dissertation as he wished.

Jenni had a hard time getting to sleep Saturday night. She had much on her mind, what Joel told her while they were outside was a heavy weight around her neck. When she came inside she hadn't wanted to think about it but she did all night. It was early morning when she went to sleep and Curly was frantically scratching at her door after the sun was up by a few hours that finally woke her. She sighed, sat up slowly and reluctantly, pushed her feet into her slippers and pulled on a fleece robe, then opened the door to let the dog into the back yard.

After a longing look at the bed, she went into her bath for a warm shower. When she was ready to greet the day and her parents, Joel was opening doors on his car for Lucy and Leslie. All three were well dressed and Jenni decided they were on their way to church. "All that happened last week! They were in church yesterday and they're going again!" she muttered. "What's so stimulating about going to church so often? I can't imagine!" She looked at Curly sitting at her feet, his tail flashing back and forth. "You! I suppose you want your breakfast!"

She opened her door into the living room and her dad had the TV on, but he still had on PJs and his robe. "Ah, there's my favorite girl! What's on for your day, Jen?"

"Not a whole lot, Dad, but could I ask you a couple questions?"

"Sure! I've always been a good listener, you know." He winked at Jenni; they both knew why he was a good listener; the other female in the house made him do it.

Jenni curled up in her favorite corner of the couch and her dad muted the TV. It was rare that Jenni could talk with her dad alone. She didn't rush to the kitchen for a cup of coffee. She took a deep breath and said, "Dad, I asked Mom a question yesterday, she got uncomfortable when I asked. She really didn't give me a straight answer, so I'm hoping maybe you will."

"Sure, I'm all ears!"

Jenni cleared her throat. "Well, you know that Lucy, next door, has her nephew and niece living with her now because their parents were killed in that house explosion last week."

"Yeah, you reported it when it happened. From the looks of that footage, it was a really horrendous explosion, too!"

"Right. Well, I've had a couple of talks with Joel, here when I've walked Curly and also out there at the explosion site the other day. Anyway, my boss wanted me to go to the memorial service they had for his parents and the preacher said something I couldn't forget. I kinda wanted your take on it."

The man made a face, but it was gone in only an instant and because Jenni wasn't looking at him, she missed it. "Okay, what'd he say?"

"Well, actually, Joel found his dad alive out there on Friday." Marvin sucked in a breath, obviously he hadn't heard about that. "He sent him to the hospital right away. We heard about that at the station, so I went out and talked to Joel for a bit. After that Joel went to the hospital and was at his bed and heard his last words. Dad, the preacher said the man opened his eyes, looked at Joel and said, 'I believe Jesus died for me.' Joel said…"

Marvin slammed his hands down on the arms of his recliner and nearly came out of his chair in one movement. "WHAT! What did you say?" he asked intensely.

Jenni looked at her dad; she'd never seen him like this! His face was beet red, he was half standing, but his knuckles were white from holding onto the chair so tightly. "What did you say?" he repeated through his clenched teeth.

Really concerned, maybe her dad was having some kind of attack! She'd never seen him like this before. "Dad! What's the matter?"

His eyes blazing, the man demanded, "How old's this preacher?"

"He's young, Dad, just a little older than Joel. Why?"

The man sagged back into his chair, let out a long sigh and said, "Jenni, don't *ever* ask me stuff like that again! It's not fit conversation in this house!"

Jenni looked strangely at her dad. "Um, sure, why not?"

"Because, God stuff… just isn't good…"

Still perplexed and a bit worried about her dad's reaction, Jenni wiggled around in her place on the couch and said, "Of course, Dad, I won't mention it again, Dad. Sorry."

"Yeah, okay." Marvin quickly slumped back into his chair, and hit the button on the remote so that the TV started blaring again. He never looked at Jenni, but glued his eyes onto the weatherman. Jenni shrugged and went to the kitchen for that cup of coffee.

As she poured a mugful she mused, "Well, my question made Mom uncomfortable, but Dad… he didn't even let me finish what I was saying and he got downright hateful about it! Wonder what that's all about?" She shrugged. "Guess I'll never know." She cleared her throat, "…not unless I ask Joel." She cleared her throat again. *Maybe not tonight – maybe tomorrow?*

Monday morning Joel was excited about moving into his own place, but he had to teach his eight o'clock class. It was Geology 101. As he drove to the university, he did some deep thinking; he had to make a decision about his future. He had a choice; he could go or stay. He was graduating, after all. Geology 101 was near to his heart. Perhaps he needed to re-think his tentative commitment to that other university. They wanted him to teach geology – since that was his major – but leave out any reference to God, the Creator and His part in making those rocks. To leave out creation and also Noah's flood was totally opposed to what he believed.

The thought of evolution and the earth being millions of years old went totally against what he read clearly in the book of Genesis. Even if he didn't have to use the word in his classes, it would be implied if he couldn't talk about God as the Creator. As he thought about his preparations for his classes, he made reference to God the Creator almost daily! Joel knew he couldn't compromise his beliefs! After all he'd been through last week and the miracles he'd witnessed during that time, there was no way he could leave God – his heavenly Father - out of anything he taught. He realized it was almost exactly like his decision about Jenni last evening. If God wasn't in it – it wasn't for him!

For months he thought he would agonize over his decision – whether to teach in the other state, on that secular campus or to stay here, at this Christian school. When he was first approached to take the TA position he had a long meeting with the chairman of his department and then later when he formed his doctoral committee for his dissertation, he had another discussion with the chairman of that committee about his views on geology. Thankfully, everyone was in favor of his way and the content of his teaching and dissertation. Here he could teach the course as God wanted him to teach it, there he could not.

"Father, God," he breathed as the students straggled into the room, "thanks, that was easy. Before, I know I let my relationship with Dad color my thinking, now I see that. Really, there was never a choice, I see that, too." Now he must find the time to let that other school know his decision. Maybe he'd Email them soon. He had told them he was seriously thinking about the position, but there was no reason to put off letting the other university know his decision. They needed to know so they could hire another person as a professor. He would also give them his reason. He might as well give a word of testimony along with his rejection.

He packed up his briefcase after class, put on Uncle Josh's winter coat and headed to the library for the two hours before his next class. Outside, the sun was shining and the wind fairly calm, so he decided to call his granddad to see about a time for the move he was anxious to make. There was a bench on the way to the library that was in the sun, he would call right now! He had already put Steve Lawson's number in his phone, so he sat down and hit the number.

On the third ring a man's voice said, "Hello?"

"Granddad, it's Joel."

There was joy in the man's voice as he said, "Oh, I'm glad to hear from you, Joel! So will you take us up on our offer?"

Joel's face was nearly cracking with the smile, as he said, "Absolutely, Granddad! It can't be today, I'm covered up. Mondays are always like that, but I can free up tomorrow. Would that work for you?"

Letting Joel's happiness enter his own soul, Steve said, "Tomorrow will be fine, Joel. When could you meet me?"

Knowing he couldn't act like a little kid, although his legs itched to be dancing on the sidewalk, especially since he was sitting in plain view on the college campus, nearly a professor and not a kid any more, he still exclaimed, "Oh, any time, Granddad! Right after breakfast… well no… I teach an eight o'clock. How about nine thirty?"

Steve chuckled at Joel's enthusiasm. He'd wished since Saturday that he and Mary could have known Joel and Leslie as they grew up. He and Mary had talked about what wonderful young people they were even though they'd been raised in such a home, there had to have been a godly influence from the other side of the family. However, God had brought them together finally and he and Mary would be eternally grateful. It was an awful way to bring it about, but God had made it happen and He'd brought the wayward son home. Knowing that made their joy overflow! He would be thankful that he could know Joel and Leslie from now on.

Those thoughts had put a lump in Steve's throat, so he cleared it before he said, "That would be perfect, Joel. Meet me at the storage building and we'll do a walk through to see what furniture you want. We'll get you moved tomorrow!"

"I'm excited, Granddad! I talked to Aunt Lucy and Leslie. Auntie has no problem with my moving out, she knows how cramped it is and Leslie wants to stay in her school district, but I'm definitely in!"

"All righty then, we'll see you tomorrow, Joel."

"Yes, sir, I shall be there!"

Chuckling, Steve said, "I knew you would be!" Joel put his phone away and nearly skipped down the walk to the library.

That evening, Joel came home late from the library, time had gotten away, but he finished the section he wanted to get done. However, Jenni didn't come out to walk her dog. Joel was disappointed; he hoped to talk to her again before he moved, but she obviously wasn't ready - not to talk about the serious topic of where her soul would spend eternity. Her window was dark. Perhaps she'd already walked her dog, he wasn't exactly sure of the time. Auntie's place was out of his way, he wouldn't come here often any more, but he would miss their evening chats. Undoubtedly God had other plans for him that didn't include Jenni Mikles, at least not now.

He went inside, intent on a shower to wash the day's grit away and opening the sofa-bed as he'd done for several nights. However, there was a pile of folded clean clothes on the central cushion. He grinned, his dear aunt had washed every piece of dirty clothing all he had to do was put them in the box he'd take to his new apartment. He must thank her in the morning.

Before he fell asleep on his feet he went for his shower. The house was quiet Leslie was in her room and Auntie in hers. Joel didn't like being a night owl, especially since it wasn't his home, but with all he had to do, time was getting eaten up. Thanksgiving was just around the corner. That was his deadline to finish writing his dissertation. With a week's vacation most of the library was closed. He knew there were several reference books he still needed to use.

Only the general areas of the university library would be open to students during Thanksgiving vacation with restricted hours. He'd seen signs saying the stacks, where he studied, would be closed for the week. Checking out reference books wouldn't happen. He definitely wanted to have his dissertation finished by Thanksgiving. If he remembered right the canteen would also be closed, another trial – another reason to be finished with his need for the library by Thanksgiving. If – that was a big little word – all went well, it could happen.

Tomorrow there wouldn't be any studying. Moving and arranging furniture and buying what he didn't have would be an all day job he was sure. Especially since he had no sense about what he wanted, what went together, all that stuff. He surely hoped there was enough furniture in the storage building to furnish his place somewhat; of course he had nothing to bring in. His meager checking account might find itself empty at the end of the day. He really had no idea what he would need to buy. He took a quick shower, glad the puncture wound was healed and the shiner gone. He tossed the pile of clothes in his box in the closet and fell into bed.

Before he closed his eyes, he murmured into the darkness, "Father God, thank You again for all Your blessings to me. Be with me and help me to stay the course."

Joel was excited about having his own place. He rushed from his early class Tuesday. He was leaning against the storage building when his granddad walked up. He was grinning, but Steve laughed and said, "You're not anxious to get moved in, are you, Joel?"

Joel chuckled and said, "You could say that, Granddad! It's a good thing I was so tired last night, I slept like a log!"

Steve unlocked the door and led Joel into a huge room. "Well, come in and look around. I'm glad for this nice weather the furniture won't get wet or ruined today. We can take our time looking for things that you'll want in your apartment and get it on the truck at our leisure."

Joel followed Steve and stepped inside the massive room, but stopped after one step. The room was nearly overflowing with all kinds of furniture. "Wow!" Joel exclaimed, "This is better than a furniture store! I can't believe all that's here."

"Yes, it is amazing what people leave behind and of course, none of us owners ask for any reasons. We only ask for the keys back. If they don't clean out the unit, we also keep their deposit. We don't advertise our apartments are furnished, but on occasion people will just walk away from an apartment. The people who were in that apartment before you did just that. Let me show you what I had to pull out of that place and see if it won't be a good fit."

Incredulous, Joel exclaimed, "Really? People just walk away from an apartment and leave the furniture? Incredible! Lead on Granddad! I'm right behind you."

Steve had a pick-up truck and soon he and Joel had agreed that everything that Steve had emptied out of that same apartment was perfect. There was even a large desk that Joel knew would work well. A maintenance man that worked at the complex joined them. Joel knew his granddad had asked him, but he helped them load every piece of furniture back on his truck. Joel couldn't wipe the grin from his face as the truck made its way from one building to the other.

He wasn't much for placing furniture, but as Steve guided the pieces into the apartment, it started looking like an attractive place to live. Joel even had a queen sized bed in which to sleep! Of course, that meant he must buy sheets, pillows and blankets along with two sets of curtains so people wouldn't look into the ground floor windows when he was in the bedroom.

By lunchtime the apartment was furnished and Steve said, "Joel, you're a big man, how about we go home to eat lunch with your nana and me, then you can go back to finish up?"

"I would love to do that!"

"All righty then, let's be about it!"

Joel was curious to see where his other grandparents lived. Steve led Joel to a fairly new, but very nice neighborhood of single homes. Mary Lawson came to the door when she heard the vehicles' doors and when she saw Joel; her grin spread as she ran down the porch steps and threw her arms around her grandson. Joel hadn't lost his grin from when he saw his granddad at the storage building, so he spread his arms and welcomed the hug that Mary gave him.

"Joel! Welcome, welcome! You must bring your sister some time!"

"I will, Nana. We really want to get to know you."

Matter-of-factly Mary said, "That goes more than double for us!"

Lucy had insisted that Joel had to come for supper. By the time he drove up at six o'clock to eat and get his few things, his bank account was nearly empty. He must wait for another paycheck to get a drape to cover his patio door. However, he felt he had done well with what he had. He'd saved some cash to buy groceries to fill his belly and keep him fueled for studying and class preparation until his next paycheck. It wasn't enough to get more than the essentials, but he knew he wouldn't starve. He'd learned how to squeeze pennies long ago and he was more than willing to keep on. Just to live in the beautiful apartment was well worth it.

While he did his high finance of buying things for his apartment, setting aside grocery money, he'd decided to leave some money for his aunt. She had put both Joel and Leslie up and fed them for the week and he was no skimpy eater! He knew that her income wasn't all that great. However, he knew he must be creative, he couldn't just hand over some money – she would refuse it. Some people were that way. Before he left her house with his box of clothes, suits, shirts and shoes and his briefcase, he had figured out where to leave the money so she wouldn't find it until he was gone. As he walked out, he still hadn't lost his grin all day!

Late that evening when Jenni decided to walk Curly Joel hadn't come back to Lucy's house. She still wondered at her dad's reaction to her question, but she couldn't help being perplexed by it all. She finally did walk the dog, making him wait until he was antsy to get out before she attached his leash and headed out, but Joel didn't come back to Lucy's. She had to admit, she was disappointed that he didn't.

In fact, after taking her morning shower the next morning, Jenni looked out her window and Joel's car wasn't in Lucy's driveway. She knew she hadn't gotten up that late that she'd missed him. She sighed and wondered how long it would be until she ran into him again. Where could he have spent the night?

When Jenni arrived home after the evening news and getting take-out she saw Lucy walking her garbage container on the driveway out to the street. She hopped out of her car quickly and as Lucy came back, she said, "Hi, Lucy! When will Joel be in this evening?"

Lucy smiled and said, "Jenni, he moved into an apartment closer to campus yesterday. He came here for supper last evening, but I really doubt he'll make it a habit to come around now that he has his own place. It is across town of course and I'm pretty sure he intends to cook his own meals. You two were having chats when he came back from the library, weren't you?"

Jenni sighed and felt a knot tie up in the pit of her stomach. She might never get the answers she wanted now! "Yes, I've known Joel a long time. We used to ride the same school bus all through public school. It was great to chat when I walked Curly at night."

Lucy smiled. "It's a bit far to walk him to where he lives now. Sorry he didn't tell you."

"Yes, but I guess that's how life is sometimes."

Lucy nodded. "I've known that to be the case, Jenni. Life gives us many ups and downs as it goes along. God gives us what He knows is best for us."

Jenni swallowed a sigh of disappointment. As Lucy left and went inside, Jenni reached back to her passenger seat for her take-out, walked slowly to the back door and went in. She knew she and Joel hadn't parted on very good terms the last time they talked. She had to admit it was her fault. He'd been kind in everything he said, she'd been so abrupt with how she left him, but she had been really uncomfortable with what he said. Now she was more than uncomfortable, after how her dad had acted, she really didn't know how she felt.

She realized that was true even more now that she'd talked with both of her parents. Their reactions shed light on why she didn't know much about things done and said in a church. With her dad's reaction, now she wondered why they went to church on those rare occasions. However, she would honor what her dad demanded she would never raise the questions again.

She'd still been speculating on Monday, so even though she'd heard Joel come home, she hadn't gone out. It seemed now the chance had been taken away. Joel might come for a meal at Lucy's, but never would come around that late at night. Being the seven o'clock news anchor didn't get her home while Joel would be here for a meal, either. Unless he stayed to chat with his aunt and sister, she'd surely miss him.

She quickly hung up her coat, found her silverware, opened her take-out containers for her dinner and sighed as Curly flopped down at her feet. She took some quick bites to curb her growling stomach and said, "Well, Curly, I'd say that was a really short chapter and it just got its last period." Curly heard his name, so he wagged his tail, content to have his mistress at home.

Friday morning, Evangelyn's beeper went off as she took her shower, but she didn't hear it. Her phone was beeping with a text message as she came from her bathroom. She quickly activated it to see the text: *Doc, burn victim transported, received in ER from local house fire. Waiting your eval.*

She sighed, knowing they needed to know she'd received the message, she typed back, *OK, be there shortly.*

She moved into high gear to finish necessities. Being the only burn specialist in the hospital meant she was always on call. She'd been the burn specialist since she took the job. It had been six months, but she felt like she'd been at the hospital and tied to her job for years, not months. "Why are Fridays usually the worst day of the week?" Of course, she didn't get an answer from her quiet apartment walls.

NINE

VERY SOON SHE HEADED OUT WITHOUT HER USUAL BREAKFAST BAGEL AND COFFEE, but grabbed a banana from her fruit bowl. As she made sure the door was locked, she looked through the glass longingly at the empty coffee maker. Perhaps she'd invest in a coffee brewer that started when a timer went off and a huge to-go cup. She could at least have coffee to go that way. Especially today, it was barely light and it was very cold. A hot cup of Joe would taste really good.

However, no one at the hospital evaluated a burn patient. She must determine if the person was critical or not, so she had to get there as quickly as possible. Perhaps she'd get away after her eval for some nourishment in the cafeteria. Sometimes burn patients couldn't wait that long; it could be touch and go. The severity of the fire could cause the victim terrible consequences – even internal. Smoke inhalation was always a potential threat to add to burns.

Friday, Joel had another eight o'clock class to teach, so he had to be up and out early. Not as early as when he'd lived at his parents' house, now he could savor his coffee and have a second cup. He didn't mind the early hour; he'd never been a sack-rat, even as a child. He'd been anxious to be up and out – anything to keep away from his dad, but he often took his little sister, so their dad didn't abuse her. Now that was behind them; what a relief! However, the best part that he'd shared with Pastor Tom, Auntie and Leslie was that Dad had told him that he believed that Jesus died for him! Like the thief on the cross, Thad Lawson would be in heaven!

Today was payday, he was anxious to stop by the discount department store and find a drape large enough for his patio door. That was his first priority. It would stay open when he was gone, but once he was home he could close the drape if he wanted. He was on the ground floor and many people walked on the parking lot. Also, there was the matter of a cookbook.

Since he moved in he saw people walking dogs or walking away from the complex on the parking lot and people getting into their cars. He felt self-conscious walking around his apartment in his nearly worn out sleeping sweats. He'd had them a long time and the sweats were totally comfortable to sleep in, but they weren't something he wanted people outside his apartment to see him in. Still, he had every right to be comfortable in his home.

As he ate breakfast Friday morning he glanced outside and thought he recognized a lady unlocking her car. He strained to see her, it wasn't totally light, but he saw some of her features with the lights on the parking lot. She was dressed in jeans under a stylish winter coat. She looked vaguely familiar, but he couldn't place where he'd seen her, but it hadn't been long ago. She was a striking blond, her hair curling around her face and lying by an inch or two onto her coat collar. He wondered why she didn't wear a hat, it was cold, but she wore neither a hat nor gloves. However, she left in a nice, quite new car before he figured out how he knew her. While he got ready he contemplated where he might have met her, but he never figured it out.

He hadn't been very close, so he hadn't seen her features well, but even from his table he could tell she was a beautiful woman. One thing he was pretty sure of, she wasn't in a class he taught. He'd never seen her at the library even though he spent so many hours there. Those two places were where he spent most of his time, so it puzzled him where he would know her from.

He reached for his coffee carafe and warmed up his half cup and decided that if he was closer he might have seen her better and maybe remember where he'd seen her. Perhaps he'd meet her sometime they were obviously neighbors. If she parked on this parking lot, she undoubtedly had an apartment not far from his and on the same level.

He had been in the apartment since Tuesday but only to put his head on a pillow Tuesday night, because his new grandparents had fed him lunch, at least his granddad had called it lunch! It tasted like a meal fit for a king! In the house where he grew up the same meal would be considered 'dinner'! Auntie had done the honors for supper. Even so, he'd slept like a log every night since he'd moved in. His new bed fit him well and was a much bigger place to sleep than the sofa-sleeper Lucy had. He'd never been a cover hog, but it felt good to stretch out.

One thing was a privilege; he could do some of his studying at his desk, which meant he was home for a much longer time. It was quiet with no distractions! What a delight! Last night he came home early enough to fix his own supper! That had been an eye-opener! Maybe he should buy a cookbook along with the drape. He'd had little chance to cook for himself. Thad had expected his meals fixed the way his mom fixed them. Leslie didn't have much experience.

Until Wednesday he didn't realize how much better he slept since he left the library so much earlier. Being able to spread out his things on the desk inspired him. When he finished studying he didn't have to stuff everything in his briefcase, but could leave the things he didn't need in the morning on his desk! What a treat! In fact, everything about this place was a treat.

When this semester started Joel set his goal to finish the first draft of his dissertation by Thanksgiving. The university was closed that week; he could get a lot done. With that much finished he'd have the final thesis by Christmas. His committee chairman told him his defense was scheduled for the Friday before Christmas break. He would be on the faculty roster as Doctor of Geology for the spring semester. That thought was incredible. After all the events of last week he wasn't sure if that would happen. However, after the time he'd spent the last two nights at the desk in his apartment, it would. He was determined to stay the course!

He admitted that life was good, God was good. 'In all things... God...' Some bad things happened last week, but also many good things. Still, he missed his sister. He was her self-appointed guardian since he was nine years old and he missed her, but she'd made up her own mind. She hadn't blindly followed him, but made her own choice to stay at Auntie's. She'd had a traumatic week too. Their dad had abused her twice the night he'd thrown Joel out. She was nine years younger than he was, so losing her parents at sixteen was a lot different than at twenty-five. He knew that whatever affected him as a twenty-five year old man affected a sixteen year old girl much differently.

He also missed his talks with Jenni. It was good to reconnect with someone he'd known for so long. However, God would take care of any social life he had. He wasn't looking for a serious relationship until he finished his schooling. For a long time, along with praying for his parents' salvation he'd prayed that God would direct his steps to the lady He wanted Joel to have for his wife. At this point in her life, Jenni was not that one. He would continue praying and stay the course. Ever since Leslie had told him that he'd kept it close. He felt he was on the course God had set for him he would do his best to continue.

He finished breakfast, checked to see if he had everything for his class and his hours at the library. He decided to stay long enough to work with the reference books then come home! It was a new feeling to see a few books and papers sitting on his desk. As he locked the door, he murmured, "Thank You, Lord for all Your blessings in my life."

He sat behind the wheel and turned the key. The car chugged to life, so he let it warm up. It seemed really cold today the sun hadn't been up maybe twenty minutes. He took those few minutes to pray, "Everything last week was so incredible! Still, Lord, I won't mind if it's not that dramatic the rest of the year." Now that he lived so close to campus, the car hardly warmed up. From one parking lot to the other only took minutes and he'd park his car for the day.

Evangelyn pulled out of the parking lot, but it was a ways to the hospital. On the way what awaited her made her think about the man she evaluated last Friday. Thad Lawson was by far the worst burn victim she'd ever seen. She remembered his name because his burns were so extensive. She wasn't sure what covered his body were truly burns from a fire! Chemical burns from the explosion could have caused the horrific places. She hadn't heard if the cause had been determined. As she remembered, there wasn't any fire at the site; not when the fire department arrived. She didn't know explosives, what could cause such devastation without causing a fire?

When she arrived home the evening of the explosion she saw the clips on the TV. Except for the propane tank it seemed ludicrous to think there had been a house in that open field! She wasn't surprised that the experts couldn't decide what had caused the explosion, since there was nothing but a few piles of rubble and a hole in the ground. She wondered how the man had survived. She was not surprised that he had died so soon after she sent him to the Burn Unit. She was still astonished that he hadn't died instantly as his wife obviously had.

Another thing that puzzled her; he was found three days later! If he hadn't died from the explosion, why hadn't he died from exposure? She hadn't seen them, but someone told her he only had rags on his body. It was the first of November! She put in her notes he was burned over one hundred percent of his body. The rags had not protected him. She didn't include anything internal. Without putting him through many traumatic tests how could that damage have been evaluated? It couldn't have happened! The man was too close to death! Just to hear his son tell her how different his voice was had confirmed her suspicion that he had extensive internal damage. She would leave it at that. After all, the man had died soon after her eval.

"How could he have lived?" she murmured. "Any kind of explosion kills so many people and then he was out in this cold… for three days!"

By now, she followed another car obviously going to the hospital. It was almost time for shift change, with the day shift nurses fresh for the day. On Friday, she'd talked with Thad's son and he'd impressed her. He seemed like a good person and concerned for his dad. For a work day, he was well dressed in a suit and tie, made her wonder what he did for a living. He seemed young to be an executive, but then, now-a-days anyone could be independently wealthy.

He waited for her, eating lunch. He hadn't come flying in, in a uniform from his job, or smelling of cigarettes, for that matter, breathless to meet her and hear what she had to say. Then not really knowing how to take the news that she had for him or know what questions to ask, but in a hurry to get back to work, since his boss didn't know he'd taken off. That had happened more often than she cared to remember. Often when that happened the child would just shrug, at a loss to know what response to make, tell her to do what needed to be done and run out again – without seeing the parent at all!

Still thinking about Thad and his son, Evi pulled into the doctor's parking lot. Young Mr. Lawson was concerned enough that he asked to stay with his dad, even though he knew the man was dying; he looked grotesque! When she first saw him it sent a shudder down her back. She wondered if his son had really looked at him before he sent him to the hospital, but he'd said he had. She knew that many children wouldn't want to spend time with a parent, especially one looking so bad, not even if their death was immanent, but Mr. Lawson's son hadn't hesitated. She admired him for that. He had seemed like a very intelligent and caring man.

Evi parked and looked at the sky where a hint of sun rays was coloring the horizon. It would be a beautiful day and she'd miss it. OR suites and the Burn Unit didn't have windows to the outside. She entered the hospital and went to the locker room for clean scrubs then took the elevator to the OR suites where she'd been directed. Of course, she stopped in the scrub room to scrub and put on the sterile uniform before she stepped into the room where the patient was. There was always the threat of infection and no burn victim needed even a hint of an infection! She hadn't been practicing medicine that long, but no patient of hers had acquired an infection that she knew about. She hoped to keep it that way for a very long time!

She often told herself she was glad they didn't take pictures of you in full sterile uniform. It wouldn't win her a beauty contest! Of course, she wasn't in it for fame or fortune. Her little sister's friend had died in a school fire and she and others had been burned very severely in the neighborhood elementary school that had burned to the ground when she was in high school. Evangelyn had determined to right that wrong if she could. Now she was considered one of the burn specialists in the city, but she'd put her heart and soul into her profession. It was a long haul, but she'd fulfilled her requirements sooner than many in her field.

She determined to put other things from her mind and stepped up to the gurney that held the patient. The woman was awake, but had received a dose of pain medication before Evi had arrived. Evi saw that this woman's condition was not life-threatening. She was glad – thinking about Thad Lawson had given her an adrenalin rush. Now, she breathed a sigh of relief. This surgery would take three hours, but she was sure the woman would survive. There would be some scars, but she would heal well. This woman's burns were definitely not from an explosion as Thad Lawson's had been. She was also breathing easily, no smoke inhalation.

Evi made her assessment and pulled down her mask to smile at the patient, who gave her a crooked smile. She stripped off her gloves, and told the OR supervisor she would talk to the family before any treatment. The supervisor assured her they could do the surgery in that operating room in an hour. Evangelyn nodded, wadded up her gloves then left the OR.

In the anteroom, she took off all that sterile stuff and put on her long lab coat over the scrubs she'd wear the rest of the day. They would take the patient somewhere so the OR could be sterilized for the surgery later on. If the surgery started at nine o'clock, it should be finished by noon. She could handle that quite well.

As two OR attendants wheeled the patient from the room and grateful for the hour's time, she hurried to the cafeteria for some coffee and a bagel, or something more substantial so she felt strong enough to do the surgery that would take the rest of the morning. Her stomach growled at the thought of food. Evi realized that the banana hadn't even touched the edge of her hunger. So often she couldn't take the time to eat, so she did every chance she could. She knew she was a long way from being overweight! Being as in-demand as she was made that a laughable thought.

Joel parked in the Science Building parking lot, expecting to walk to his classroom and prepare for his class of bodies that would wander in. Being the eight o'clock class, on Friday morning, meant there were only one or maybe two students who came in with a flourish, greeting him and asking about anything. The other twenty-nine or thirty wandered in, as if they weren't sure if they were in a fog or the night before day. Some even still had a bed-head! Many walked in with a large to-go cup, the coffee smell was strong in each of his early morning classes Friday was no exception. In fact, there had been a few times when that coffee had ended up on a test paper handed in and made for a messy stack to work through to correct them.

However, he rounded the corner from the door into the building and standing beside the door to his classroom stood the Science Department Chairman. It looked like he'd been there for a few minutes, leaning against the wall with his arms crossed over his chest. Joel's steps stalled for a minute until he saw the friendly smile on the chairman's face.

"Hello, Dr. Winsted! I didn't expect to see you this early! Actually, it's usually a motley crew who straggle into my Friday eight o'clock class. Can I help you?"

The doctor took one step towards Joel and said, "Joel, your letter of acceptance reached my desk yesterday afternoon. I was truly excited, but I was sure you were already at the library, so I didn't try to track you down. I am exceptionally pleased that you've decided to throw your cap in with us!" The good doctor put out his hand and grasped Joel's. "Joel, I am so pleased to welcome you. We will set up a schedule of classes for your next semester in a few days."

"Th-that's great!" Joel stammered.

Before Joel could say anything more, the doctor continued with a smile, "Believe me, the compensation you will receive well surpasses what you have been making as a TA."

Joel smiled and shook the man's hand. Compensation wasn't really a concern, only getting done with the thesis on time. "Remember, Dr. Winsted, I haven't defended my thesis or had it approved." He smiled at the older man. "I should think that would be the all important happening first. And that won't happen until a month from now."

The older man chuckled and put his other hand on Joel's shoulder. "Joel, believe me, I have no worries about that! Not one! Welcome aboard."

"Thank you, sir thank you so very much!"

"Oh, you are most welcome! We are all so happy that you've decided to join our faculty! The geology department will thrive, I'm sure."

"Well, we can only pray that'll be true."

"Oh, did Henry tell you he's waiting for your final draft? The publisher is excited to get your thesis. So as soon as you finish and print your copies make an extra so he can pass it along. The publisher told Henry that the release date will be before next school year! Believe me Joel; we're excited to add it to our science library as soon as we get that first, autographed copy."

Joel looked at his mentor. Astonished, he swallowed and closed his mouth before he finally was able to say, "Dr. Winsted, really? I don't believe it!"

"Oh, yes, believe it, Joel!"

A few minutes later the two men split. Dr. Winsted went back to his office; to his desk, messy with paper work that only a department chairman can do. Joel felt like he'd seen enough papers to last him a good long time! Being chairman of a department wasn't on his bucket list. He went in his classroom glad that he was early enough no student had arrived. He was grinning as he set his briefcase on the desk, but before anyone came in he danced a two-step and shot his fist into the air. God was good, He was good ALL THE TIME!!! That was something he could never, ever doubt again! Sleepy heads, bed heads and coffee spills couldn't set him back today!

Evangelyn sat down at the small table and doctored her coffee, when a colleague, carrying his own tray, came to her table and said, "Hey! Mind if

I sit with you, Evi? This place is hopping! I mean, it's only breakfast, look at the crowd! Talk about noisy! Wow!"

"Sure, Derek, have a seat, but it is Friday and people gear up for the weekend on Fridays. Sometimes those end up as accidents. I'm stuffing this in my mouth before I scrub for surgery. One of those accidents ended up on my plate. We got a burn victim in early this morning that I'll do soon. I can't imagine what she was doing so early to get so many third degree burns! I'm glad she wasn't in that life or death stage."

Derek set his tray down and pulled out his chair. "So you can get this one fixed up?"

"Yes, it'll take a few hours, though. I hope to preserve as much skin texture as possible, but her arms are fairly involved."

Taking a sip of his hot coffee, Derek said, "I heard about Thad Lawson last week! That was something that he survived the explosion! Has anyone determined what caused it?"

Evangelyn shook her head. "No, I never heard, except the blurb that said he'd been found alive. Of course, when I saw that on TV I knew he'd died. I was amazed, astonished while I did my eval that the medic on the ambulance found a place to start an IV! The man had burns over one hundred percent of his body! Our man had to be creative to find a place to take a blood pressure as well as start the IV. I guess starting an IV in a moving ambulance is an art."

Slathering butter on his hotcakes, Derek said, "I believe that with all my heart! I'd never attempt starting an IV in a moving vehicle! You talked with his son, isn't that right?"

"Yes, I couldn't give him any hope, but he asked to stay with him until he died. I heard the man lived a few minutes after his son arrived. I did feel sorry about that, but I warned him!"

"That's true. Do you know who his son is?"

Evangelyn cut a piece of her French toast, but didn't put it in her mouth. She shook her head and scowled. "I have no idea. We didn't talk about that – just to know he was the man's son. In fact, I've forgotten his name."

Dumping lots of syrup on the hot cakes and watching the steam rise Derek pulled in a long breath. "These smell great!" Spreading the syrup, he added, "The man is Joel Lawson. Actually *Doctor* Joel Lawson. He'll finish his PhD next month with honors and stay as a professor in the science department. The hometown university is thrilled to have him join the faculty as a professor of geology. Joel's graduated with honors at every level, starting in high school, despite the harassment he's received from his dad. That man was opposed to his son going on after high school! But he had nothing to say once all the awards were given out."

"Really?" Evangelyn exclaimed, taking another long sip of coffee. "But he's getting a PhD, wow! If he's that intelligent, surely it showed before he graduated from high school! Why wouldn't his dad want him to go on? Most parents have high aspirations for their children."

Derek nodded in answer to Evi's question and chuckled. "I guess since you're not hometown you don't know Thad Lawson, but he's been infamous in the city for a long time. From what I heard, it was like a broken record at that commencement Joel got so many awards, including a full four year scholarship to our hometown university! I guess when his dad found that out he never said another word and Joel went on."

"Really! Wow!"

Taking one last mouthful of her toast, then finished her coffee, Evangelyn wiped her mouth, scowled and said, "You've said a mouthful, Derek, I had no idea! The man seemed very concerned about his dad. If there was that much antagonism between them why would the son want to spend the last moments of the man's life with him? He asked intelligent questions, too."

"Yes, he would. His life is reflected in what you said. Joel is a humble man despite his many achievements and his more than stellar academic work. I've heard he's an excellent teacher as well. Even as a TA his classes are full so the university feels its getting a great deal."

"So he must defend his thesis soon?"

Derek cut through the stack of pancakes and put a generous amount in his mouth, then let out a contented sigh. After he chewed and swallowed, he took a swig of coffee. "Yes, it's scheduled the Friday starting the university's Christmas break. He'll take the professor position already given him for the spring semester. He should learn about it today or Monday."

Scowling, Evangelyn asked, "They've already assigned him, even though he hasn't defended his thesis? Universities don't usually do that, do they? Some of them that I know of don't even want one of their students to teach at their school."

Derek cut another large forkful of his hotcakes and stuffed it in his mouth, chewed and swallowed. "Nope, they were anxious for Joel to accept.

Actually, his thesis is scheduled for publication and the university plans to put it on their library shelves as soon as it's released. He was approached by another university out of state, but he finally decided to stay here. I think it was his dad's death that clinched his decision. Knowing Thad Lawson, I'm not surprised Joel wanted to get out of town." Derek leaned back in his chair and took a swallow of his coffee.

Scowling, Evi said, "But this is a suburb of a huge city, there are other universities close by! He could have moved to another suburb and gotten away from his dad. So he really didn't get along with his dad? I'm surprised about his concern. He asked specifically to stay with him until he died. I wondered, because the man looked grotesque! I mean… with all that burned flesh… I made it a point to find out if he had really looked at his dad. I've seen children who wouldn't come in the room with a dying parent, yet Mr. Lawson's son asked to be with him!"

Derek wiped his mouth, and took a sip of coffee to clear the syrup taste, before he said, "That has amazed me for years! Joel lived at home until the explosion and for most of his life has tried to persuade his dad to be a Christian and the man would have nothing to do with that."

Contemplatively, Evangelyn said, "I wonder if that's why he wanted to be with his dad so much there at the end." She shook her head. "But the man was already comatose when he arrived at the hospital! No one could rouse him."

Derek stuffed a large mouthful of hotcakes in his mouth then washed it down with coffee, contemplatively he said, "You could be right. Some people do make a deathbed decision."

"Yes, they do, but the man was already comatose when he was transported. Would he have awakened before he died? Nothing I did roused him. His blood pressure was falling; even in the ambulance!" Evi shook her head. "When would he have done it? Out in the country? The son told me he'd talked with him, but he said he was confused and amnesic."

Very seriously, her fellow physician said, "Evi, have you never heard that God can do anything that He wants to do, when He wants to do it?"

Evangelyn nodded, "Yes, I've heard that and I've seen it happen."

Derek nodded. "Yes, so have I."

"Did you hear about something like that happening? Knowing how bad Thad Lawson was I can hardly put my mind around that!"

"No, I can't, but Joel being the man that he is, wouldn't have broadcast such a thing."

Evi wiped her mouth and asked, "How do you know him so well, Derek? If he's finishing his thesis, he's younger than you. You probably weren't even in school with him."

Derek wiped his mouth and grinned. "Well, Evi, I'm a local hooligan, not that I was bad, you understand." Evi smiled. "I was a few years ahead of Joel, but he was in my school district. He made waves in junior high. Even in our school district, students of his caliber were noticed. His home life, too. Thad's name was in the papers and he spent jail time, too." Derek shook his head. "Several times we heard about the way Joel defended his little sister – it was outstanding!"

"Really?"

"Yes, he'd stand between his dad and his sister and take a whipping with the man's belt that he planned to give the little girl."

"Oh, my! Yes, he must truly have been dedicated to her!"

Evi stood, picked up her trash and said, "I'm on to surgery! I'll be in that sterile outfit."

Derek laughed. "Have a great time! I know how revealing those are." Evi grinned and threw her trash away, but as she left the cafeteria for the OR suites, she sighed, life went on.

She reached the waiting room outside the OR and saw a man and a teen aged girl there. Evi walked up and asked, "Would you be Mrs. Edwards' family?

"Yes, we are."

Evangelyn held out her hand and said, "I'm Dr. Fredrickson. I'm doing her surgery soon. I'm sure she'll do fine, after surgery she'll be in the Burn Unit for a week or so until she heals."

"Oh, I thought Dr. Fredrickson was a man who'd do my wife's surgery."

Evi was used to words like that. Dark ages ago only men were considered intelligent enough to be a surgeon, so she smiled and said, "Well, since I'm Dr. Fredrickson, you'll have to put up with me, I'm afraid, Mr. Edwards. I'm on my way to scrub for her surgery now. I'll talk with you later. It'll be about noon when we're finished."

The man nodded. "Thanks, Doctor. I hope you can fix her up real good. I guess Nina and I'll be here waiting."

Evi smiled back at the man. "I guess you will."

Evi walked on, but she hadn't gone far when she heard the girl whisper, rather loudly, "She's real pretty, Dad, don't you think?"

"Nina, pretty don't get people cured."

"No, that's for sure," Evi said, under her breath. "Best forget all that, Evi," she grumbled. It was a typical reaction. Maybe some year down the road she'd get used to it.

Evangelyn did the surgery, taking several hours; it was not a question that the woman would survive. She wanted to keep as much skin texture as possible. After surgery she sent her to the Burn Unit where all her patients went. She had stripped off her gloves when her stomach told her it was time to refuel. She quickly stripped off her sterile outfit and hurried to the OR waiting room to speak with Mr. Edwards and his daughter to assure them that surgery went well. From there she ran to the cafeteria for lunch to bolster her flagging energy. There were several in the Burn Unit that she needed to watch closely, but lunch came first.

She was glad for the unit; it was much easier to keep infection from overwhelming her patients or spreading if it got started. All visitors had to dress in sterile gowns and masks before they saw a patient. If anyone presented with any signs of an infection they were not allowed through the doors. All her patients were in the unit, making it much easier to see them and write orders. She knew the staff and they knew her, which was good. When she first came to the hospital she'd insisted on the unit, they'd had to redo an area on the second floor to meet her specifications, but she was very glad the administration had.

She thought about her conversation with Derek, about Joel Lawson. She remembered Thad Lawson's son was anxious to be with his dad until he died. Why? If in life they hadn't gotten along and the father willingly whipped his son, why would the son want to spend the last moments with him? He looked grotesque it couldn't be he wanted to gaze on the dying man! Could what Derek said have been his reason? She hadn't heard about anything as dramatic as the man waking up, but if Joel Lawson was so humble maybe he hadn't told any staff after he arrived. If something like that happened how could Joel have kept from talking about it!

Well, her life was wrapped up in hospital life, ever since her student days. She'd gone year 'round in her undergraduate school to get through. From what Derek said Joel was smarter than she was; she'd just started earlier. Once a patient was discharged, whether by recovering or by death, Evangelyn never saw them or their family again, only on very rare occasions, perhaps as an outpatient. Perhaps as her practice stretched out over some years she might have some repeaters, who knew? Usually, people didn't try to repeat a burn situation.

In her experience, a patient was ready to enter life as he'd known it, perhaps with some modification. Having Mr. Lawson die made it almost impossible for her to ever see Joel Lawson again. She was sure that was so with Dr. Joel Lawson especially. What would they have in common? They had 'doctor' in front of their names, but that's where the similarity ended.

After leaving the cafeteria, she went to the Burn Unit. She had plenty to do to care for her other patients. The same nurse that was on last Friday when Thad Lawson was there was also on today. Out of curiosity, Evangelyn saw her and decided to ask her if she remembered anything about that short time. If she remembered the man by name perhaps Amy did also.

Amy saw the doctor come through the doors and smiled at her, then readied the computer charts that she knew Evangelyn would need. However, Dr. Fredrickson came to the desk and leaned on it. Amy looked at her questioning, "Doctor, did you need something?"

"Amy, I wanted to ask a question. This is just out of curiosity."

"Sure, what is it?"

"Remember that Lawson man who was so bad and only lived for such a short time?"

Amy nodded. "Yes, we had such a time transferring him! I thought we'd lost him. No longer than he lasted, we should have left him on the gurney. He might have lasted a bit longer."

"But his son came up after he arrived, right?"

"Yes, I had him suit up, but he didn't even get to sit at the man's bedside before he told me that he'd drawn his last breath."

"Do you know if he said anything to his dad or if the man woke up?"

Giving the doctor a strange look, Amy said, "Why no! In fact, the son took only a second to suit up. He walked up beside the bed, but I came to the desk to give him some privacy. I saw him stand over the man – I saw his head over the partition, but see him speaking… no he had a mask on. And the patient? Surely he was so bad he wouldn't have woken up! Your notes said he was comatose when he came in and was still in a coma when he came here. It was only minutes after that the son told me he had died. I was amazed he'd even made it here in time!"

Evi nodded. "Thanks, Amy, I wondered. I know he was comatose, but his son was so insistent to be with him."

"Sure, not a problem. I'll probably remember that man for a while. As bad as he was it's hard not to have nightmares!"

"I know what you mean!" Letting a shudder work down her back, Evi said, "It's the same with me, there wasn't a place on his body that didn't have awful burns on it. It doesn't take much to make me think about him. Another doctor and I even talked about him today!"

Amy pushed the rolling computer towards Evi and said, "That's true! That's why I remember him, that and how bad he was."

Still thinking about Thad, Evi turned from the desk and entered her code in the computer, then her first patient's name. She hadn't learned anything new, only that Joel had come to be with his dad. He had a mask on, which was standard procedure. He could have spoken to his dad; he didn't sit down, could a comatose patient understand something said through a mask?

After she checked her notes – looking at her picture - she went to the treatment room to scrub. She put on the sterile mask and gloves as one of the staff wheeled in her first patient. All afternoon was the same. As Evi finished with one patient, the staff member wheeled him out while Evi stripped off the gloves and entered her notes. Moments later she went to scrub and put on another set of sterile gloves, while another staff member brought another patient.

One time in the OR never took care of a burn patient's burns. As the burns started to heal, Evi had to clean away excess crusting, it was almost a daily routine and she must redress the wounds with an antibacterial compound and sterile dressings. Until all the crusts were gone, the procedure had to be done every few days, but it ensured that the burns healed properly, without infection. Because she was so diligent she hoped that each patient healed infection free.

When her last patient left the treatment room her day ended. It had started early making a long day. Evangelyn sighed with relief and stripped off the latex gloves she'd worn for her last patient. No new patient came in the ER through the day and she was glad. After looking in on another patient, she headed for the locker room to change back into her own clothes.

Doing the kind of surgery that the woman that came in so early required drained her. She felt like she hadn't had enough food. Once in a while, when she was this tired, she wondered at her choice of careers. Usually, that thought went away with the next breath. She had wanted to be a doctor who made a difference ever since high school. Her passion was still caring for people and making a difference. If she ever lost that she knew her career would be washed up. Still she wouldn't be upset if the hospital hired someone else for the burn department to help her.

Evangelyn hurried to change from the scrubs back into her clothes, grabbed her purse from her locker and with a growling stomach was anxious to get to her apartment to fix supper. She did take long enough to throw the dirty scrubs into the bin. French toast, two coffees and even a good solid sandwich didn't give her an over-supply of calories for all she'd done. From the locker room she took the waiting elevator up to the entrance that led to the doctor's parking lot, so she hurried out of the big room. In the little box her growling stomach was magnified.

She spent so little time in her home, she was glad to go there this early. She glanced at her watch and sighed as the elevator stopped, this time in November she'd missed out on the sun completely. She loved to see the sunshine; it brightened the day, and lifted her spirits when she saw it. However, all she'd see today were the last faint rays and maybe a few colorful clouds.

Maybe after supper she could read a book for pleasure or watch TV without her conscience bothering her. That would be a welcome change. She was glad when she came to the city, accepting the hospital position that this apartment was advertised in the paper and she could move right in. By the time she closed up at the training hospital there wasn't time to look, only in the newspaper and call – which she had and taken the apartment sight unseen.

She liked her landlord, Mr. Lawson, very much, he was cheerful and helpful. He found some furniture to fill her apartment, to supplement the few pieces she had. What she brought in the small pull-behind trailer looked rather skimpy in the large apartment. She was grateful and excited with the furniture; most of what he supplied was much better quality than she could have bought. At this time in her life student loans were the bane of her existence!

She sat down in her car, but before she started up, she mused, "Mr. Lawson – could he be related to the man who died last week?"

The man who was burned was so disfigured it was impossible to decide how old he was, especially without hair and so much charred skin and she hadn't checked, but his son was close to her age. She guessed her landlord could be old enough to be a grandfather. She shrugged, perhaps the subject would come up sometime and she might remember to ask him. She turned the key and the car purred to life. Really, what were the chances she'd see the man and also remember to ask that question? Not very high.

The only disadvantage about this apartment was the distance from the hospital, but she'd gladly live with that. She knew several of the single doctors lived in the apartment building close to the hospital, but she was glad she wasn't one of them. She pulled onto the parking lot for her building and just ahead was a car that she didn't know. It was pulling into the next spot. That apartment had been empty for several months, but she had noticed a car there the last few days. It had been there this morning she remembered. She must have a new neighbor. As she whipped into her spot, the young man climbed out of his car. He reached back and pulled out a briefcase and a large bag, then locked his door. He still stood facing her as she shut off her car.

"That's Dr. Lawson!" she exclaimed.

"Now I know who she is!" Joel said to himself, as he locked the car door and fingered his ring of keys for his apartment door key. "Does the good doctor live in a ground floor apartment in the same building as me? That's amazing! I wouldn't have believed it."

His image of a medical doctor put her in a house more fancy than his new grandparents lived in in a gated community, not one to live in a ground floor apartment. Obviously he watched too many medical shows with rich doctors on TV, but she drove a car much nicer and years newer than his. Maybe she didn't have the advantage he'd had of doing his education on scholarships and grants. Perhaps she lived in an apartment because she had school bills to pay. That was reason to be thankful, something he hadn't thought about recently. Without the scholarships his education would have ended with high school graduation, as his dad had wanted.

As Evangelyn left her car, Joel raised his hand and called, "Hi, Dr. Fredrickson! Are you coming home or just visiting?"

Pointing to the next apartment to Joel's, Evangelyn said, "No, I live here. Did you take that apartment recently?"

Joel smiled and nodded. "Yes, granddad offered it to me at my parents' memorial service. It was the first time I met my dad's parents. This is such a nice place, I'm thrilled with it!"

She nodded. "Yes, it is a nice place."

By this time Joel and Evangelyn had walked to the front of their cars. Joel shifted his briefcase so he could shake hands with Evangelyn. Evi shook his hand, but picked up on something Joel said immediately. Incredulous, she asked, "You're telling me you just met your grandparents the other day? Surely you knew you had grandparents! How could you not?"

"Yes, at my parents' memorial service. My dad never mentioned that he had parents. Of course, I assumed that he did, but I had no idea that they were alive and lived here in the city. I learned early not to ask questions like that. My aunt, my mom's sister, told me who they were at the service. Of course, I made fast work of making their acquaintance!"

"Oh, my! Your dad was really something, wasn't he?"

TEN

JOEL NODDED. "YES, HE WAS, BUT I MUST HOLD IT IN MY HEART THAT AS HE BREATHED his last that his heart was changed. I want to thank you, Doctor, for letting me go to be with him as he died."

Incredulous, Evi scowled and turned to Joel. Seriously, she said, "It was a reasonable request! Why thank me? I'm glad he was still alive, since you wanted to be with him. As I understand, he almost died between the time I sent him to the Unit and when you got there."

"Yes, Ma'am, I got that impression from the nurse who met me. I could tell from the urgency in her voice when she instructed me to put on the mask" Very seriously, Joel added, "But just before he took his last breath he opened his eyes and looked at me with recognition and said, 'I believe that Jesus died for me'. Those seven words brought me great joy! I had prayed most of my life to hear him say those words. He took another breath and as he let it out he said, 'Son'. He never called me 'son' before, it was his last breath. His eyes closed and was gone."

"Wow!" Evangelyn exclaimed in awe. "Wow!"

He laid his briefcase and the bag on the hood of his car. Leaned back on the warm car, then looked at the building, not at Evi, he nodded and said, "Yes, as I turned to tell the nurse that he had died the realization came to me that God has pursued my dad for a long time. All my life he hated it every time I would mention anything about my faith. In fact, he would get intensely angry and demand I get out of his sight! I understand now that God kept him alive through that explosion so I could hear him tell me that he finally believed. I believe that with all my heart. It gives me an assurance that Dad will be in heaven when I reach there sometime in the future."

Awed, she squeaked, “That is an amazing thing!”

“I believe you’re right, Doctor.”

Acting a little distressed, Evi said, “Oh, please, I’m not much older than you! Please call me Evi. We’re neighbors now, surely when we see each other around you can call me Evi.”

“Of course, and I’d be happy for you to call me Joel. Of course, you did call me that at the hospital, but please, as you say, we’re neighbors.”

Evi gave Joel a beautiful smile. “I’ll be pleased to do that, Joel. So you had lived with your aunt until you came here?”

“Well, until the day before the explosion I lived at my parents’ house. Dad demanded that I live there while I was in school and since I still am, I did, but the night before the explosion he threw me out, literally.”

Raising her hand to her temple, Evi remembered Joel’s injury when she said, “Yes, I remember you had that place and a black eye when I saw you there at the hospital.”

“Yes, that’s right. After that, Sis got everything out of the house, so I lost nothing for which I’m very grateful. My briefcase with my dissertation notes and my lap-top with what I had completed on it and my class preparations were there. If she hadn’t sent me a text that she was gathering everything, I’d have lost it all. That day the house exploded I couldn’t have gone, I teach classes all morning. Even if I had tried I might have been there when the house exploded.

“We both lived with our Aunt Lucy last week after the explosion. Her home is so small I was sleeping on the sofa-sleeper in the living room and had no place other than the library to study and prepare lessons.” He grinned. “However, last week was an amazing week!”

He raised his hand toward his apartment. “This is so cool! Granddad even helped me with the furnishings.”

“I was glad for some furniture too. He was very generous. I had a few pieces that had sentimental value.” Evi breathed out a sigh and said, “I got a call on a burn victim early this morning, so I didn’t have much to eat today and my stomach is protesting. I’d better get inside to fill it. I’m glad we met, Joel, under better circumstances, maybe we’ll see each other again.”

“That would be great, Evi! Have a good evening.”

“You the same, Joel!”

Evi gave Joel another beautiful smile and took a step towards her apartment. "First things first! I have no idea what's on the menu, but I'll find it quickly!" she exclaimed, to cover the loud grumble of her empty stomach.

Joel chuckled. "Yes, I have that at the top of the list, too. I must rustle something up. Sometime before I go to bed I must hang this drape to cover my patio door. It's such a big area and at night it's really dark." Pensively, he added, giving Evi a grin, "Although, I wouldn't have seen a pretty lady going to her car early this morning if I'd had one and it was closed."

Evi turned quickly to hide the smile at Joel's compliment, but she was pleased. She took another step toward her apartment and Joel picked up his things from the hood of his car. Minutes later they were in their apartments. Joel smiled as he put the bag with the drape on the closest chair then took his briefcase to his desk. He was home early and in his quiet apartment. It was a good feeling. He was early enough there was light in the sky; he'd eat and stay home!

Now he knew someone in the apartment complex! His next door neighbor! How cool was that? She was the lady who had gotten in her car early this morning. Of course she wasn't in any classes he taught, nor used the university library. She was beyond that – she had graduated. He sighed soon he would too, at least the library part. Truth be told, he wouldn't miss the hours he spent in the library, reading books… and more books and writing pages… and more pages!

Before he started his supper he went to his hall entrance to check the mailbox with his apartment number on it. If he did that now he could stay inside until after breakfast tomorrow. It was at the main entrance along with mailboxes for the apartments that used this entrance. He'd checked it each day since he'd moved in, but wasn't surprised that he hadn't gotten any mail. He'd only turned in his change of address Tuesday afternoon when he saw the mailman going into the building across the parking lot. He opened the box, and saw that he had a letter.

"This is impressive!" he muttered. The return address was from the state laboratory. He was sure it was findings from the explosion, but what would it tell him? The lighting in the small hallway wasn't good, so he turned back and took the few steps down to his apartment and went in, closed the door and went to his kitchen table to read what the letter said. They surely hadn't had much to test! However, he was anxious to find out what they had come up with.

Joel opened the envelope and pulled out a single sheet with an impressive letterhead.

> "Mr. Joel Lawson:
>
> This letter is in response to an inquiry made by Lieutenant Winslow of your local fire department. Findings from tests on debris taken from an explosion site that we understand was owned by Thaddeus and Eleanor Lawson, who were deceased at the time of the explosion, that you now own, have been released. We were instructed to send results of the findings to you.
>
> We wish to inform you that there are traces of what tested to be propane gas on the largest piece of the debris that was sent to our lab. We were informed that the house had both a furnace and water heater that operated on propane gas. Our technicians have determined that the explosion was caused by a malfunction of either the furnace or the water heater, but that neither of these appliances survived the explosion….."

Joel sat back in the chair, picked up the paper again and read the letter through a second time. "Amazing!" he murmured. "Mom or Dad didn't cause the explosion. They weren't doing anything illegal, at least nothing that caused the explosion. Now the insurance company has no reason not to pay the claim. Thank You, my Father! Thank You for this letter! It really relieves my mind to know positively that they didn't cause it. I'm sorry that they lost their lives, but I'm very glad that Les wasn't there. Thank You! I'm also thankful I've finally gotten to meet Granddad and Nana because this happened."

Joel made his way to his desk, he would save this letter. He felt the need to talk to someone, and wondered who to call. Without too much thought he hit Steve Lawson's number on his cell phone, but because his stomach let him know it was supper time, he stuck the phone next to his ear and went to the kitchen to find something to eat even as the phone started ringing.

When his granddad answered, Joel said, "Granddad, I got my first letter here at my apartment, but I needed to share it with someone and thought that I'd call you."

"That's fine Joel, what is it?"

"Granddad, it's from an impressive lab that did tests on some debris from the explosion site. They determined it was a malfunction of either the furnace or the water heater. There were traces of propane on the largest piece of debris that they tested."

Joel could hear Steve let out a loud sigh. Obviously digesting what Joel had read, it took Steve several seconds before he said, "Joel, thank you! Thank you so much! We can rest better knowing that it wasn't anything that either Thad or Eleanor did that caused that explosion. We certainly can't find out what the malfunction was, but it wasn't something your parents caused."

"Yes, I have already thanked God for that. Until something like this proves the matter our minds always think the worst."

"Yes, that's true. As soon as your Nana and I realized the news on TV was talking about their house Mary wondered what or who had caused the explosion. Since no one witnessed what happened, we knew only testing something from the site could really tell. Since there was so little left, we wondered if anything could be tested. Believe me she will be very glad to know."

"Yes, Granddad, I wondered about that. The lieutenant asked me there at the site what kind of furnace was in the house. I must say that was the first time I thought that propane was the cause. It was reasonable that whole part of the basement was completely filled in."

Steve said, "Joel, it was awful what happened and I'm truly sorry that Thad and Eleanor had to lose their lives, but now we are finally able to know each other and that is both amazing and makes Mary and me overjoyed for the privilege." Steve took a deep breath, before he said, "We both know that something very drastic in his life would have to happen to change your dad's ways. Thank you for calling to tell us. We'll talk with you again, Joel."

"Bye, Granddad, I'll see you soon."

"Say, how's life at your apartment?" Steve asked before Joel could hang up. With a smile in his voice he asked, "Are you adjusting to apartment life?"

Steve heard the happiness in Joel's voice, as he said, "Oh, Granddad! It's terrific! I love the place. It is so comfortable! It's close to school and that's a plus and I haven't slept better in a very long time. All this furniture you brought in is super. I sure am glad those people left it."

Steve chuckled. "I'm glad, Joel, enjoy!"

"I am, Granddad. I can work on my class preps and my dissertation here. I only have to do research at the library. I was never sure of what would happen at the house in the country and at Aunt Lucy's there wasn't a desk. Here, this desk is great! I can spread out and it's quiet."

"Joel, you bless my heart! Again, thanks for calling."

"Yes, Granddad, see you sometime."

Saturday morning Evi went in to the hospital to check her new patient. She was glad she was doing well. Before she left for home she checked her in-house mailbox that she hadn't checked the day before. She never got much mail, but she always checked every few days. In her box was a beautifully embossed envelope. Her name was in fancy calligraphy, there was no question it was meant for her. She'd never received something so fancy. She opened it and read:

> "The honor of your presence is requested at a reception for the newly appointed Chief of Staff of the hospital at the Convention Center, starting at seven o'clock on the Saturday following Thanksgiving. Light refreshments will be served and those attending are encouraged to bring a guest. This will be a black tie affair, dancing will be part of the entertainment. We look forward to seeing you there. No RSVP is needed."

The invitation was signed by one of the hospital board members.

Backing up, she slouched into a lounge chair, and read through the invitation again. She exclaimed, "Black tie! Why don't I wear my sterile outfit? That should look formal enough! I mean, after all! That, scrubs and jeans are about all I wear. Do I even own a dress?" she added. On a sigh, she asked the empty room, "Who could I ask to go as my guest? I haven't been living and working here that long, I hardly know a soul! I sure don't have a boyfriend!" She scowled. "I don't even know if there's a single doctor on staff! Who in the world could I ask?" A little voice whispered, *How about* Doctor *Joel Lawson? He's your neighbor, isn't he?*

"My neighbor," she whispered. She cleared her throat. "My **very** handsome neighbor."

Shivers went down her back at the thought. She and Joel had only met informally the night before! Still holding the invitation, she sat back in the comfortable chair and even put her feet on the low table in front of her. She had a minute she'd give this some thought. She'd had coffee with breakfast, but she could go for another cup right now. What she knew of Dr. Joel Lawson was very impressive! Well… and the man was also very impressive! She guessed he was about six two or three and very well built. She liked his light brown, wavy hair… umm, maybe to thread her hands through? *Where had that thought come from!*

She smiled, as she continued to think about the man she'd met only twice, but who had made a deep impression on her. He would be the kind of teacher she'd be willing to sit on the front row of class… with her chin on her fist, staring dreamily… and be very attentive, to say the least and make no bones about watching his every move!

"Evi!" she scolded herself. "Stop that!" *Thank goodness I'm alone in here!*

She'd been concerned about her patient, Thaddeus Lawson. When she'd met with his son at the hospital and at their apartments it was turning from dusk to darkness, so to see the color of his eyes was impossible,… but well… she wouldn't mind having him escort her to the black tie reception for the new Chief of Staff! Dancing? Oh, my…. She cleared her throat. "I'd have to approach him to go with me! Maybe I dated some in high school and college, but recently? Do women do that – ask a *man* for a date?" She cleared her throat again. "Do I approach Dr. Joel Lawson to go as my date?" Without answering herself, she stuffed the invitation in her pocket and stood up with a huff to leave. There were several days before the reception; she could work on that for a while. Maybe she'd better work on her intestinal fortitude?

On Monday morning, Joel finished teaching his eight o'clock class of sleepy students. The coffee aroma was gone, and a few had run their fingers through their hair enough to take care of the bed-head, but as usual, Joel really did make the session quite interesting. He watched the last student reach the door, but was still putting his class notes in his briefcase after class when Dr. Winsted walked in the open door of his classroom right after his last student sauntered out. Joel pulled the top of his briefcase down, but looked up noticing the movement.

Quite surprised, Joel exclaimed, "Dr. Winsted! This is a surprise, I only saw you last Friday. What can I do for you this morning?"

Grinning, the man came to the desk and sat casually on the corner. Crossing his arms over his ample chest, the doctor said, "Joel, in less than a month we'll be colleagues. I'd like you to call me 'Fred'. If that doesn't sit right as least 'Dr. Fred'. That's second best, at least until you get used to it. The whole department's on first names and you qualify. Anyway, here's what I came to tell you. The university faculty is invited to a reception at the Convention Center the Saturday after Thanksgiving for the new Chief of Staff of our illustrious local hospital."

Joel scowled and looked at his mentor, as he snapped the locks on his briefcase. "Dr.... umm, Fred, how could I be part of, umm, the faculty? I'm only a TA, I'm not really part of the faculty until next semester. And that only happens if my committee accepts my dissertation as it's written. There is the possibility that they won't, you realize."

The man with a fringe of gray hair above his ears looked at Joel and said very seriously, "Joel, believe me, I have it on good faith that your thesis will be accepted the day you present it. There is not one question in my mind about that! There are many of our faculty and several scientists at other universities who have followed your scholastic advancement who are anxious for your dissertation to be published. Make no mistake about that what-so-ever, Joel!"

"Wow!" Joel murmured.

"I know one guy who's not a professor, but the CEO of a prestigious organization who's contacted me about your progress." Fred cleared his throat. "In fact, he asked if you're available for a lecture series. These fellas are aware that what you present is of the highest caliber. I have confidence that your thesis will be accepted as is." He chuckled. "Joel, you are a feather in our cap and we're anxious for you to be part of us. So, consider this as your own debut, if you will."

Joel shook his head and put his hand around the handle of his briefcase. He started to stand but what the doctor said seemed to zap his strength. Instead, he slumped back onto the desk chair and looked at the man incredulously.

"You have got to be kidding! A lecture series? My own debut? That is a total stretch, believe me!"

"Not at all, Joel! Oh, it's black tie. You don't have a wife, but we're to bring a guest…."

Joel sighed. "Dr. Fred, recently I moved into my first apartment from my aunt's little bungalow. I had no furniture; the landlord graciously filled the apartment with left-behinds. I emptied my checking account buying curtains and such things I didn't know I needed. Actually I had to wait for my last paycheck to purchase a drape for the patio door. That and food for my belly have exhausted my resources. Now you say I must get a black tie? I understand what that is. And a date? Do I pick one of those off a tree? Between all that's gone on in my life and the work I've been doing on my dissertation, finding a date boggles my mind!"

The doctor grinned and said, "Yup! You'll get paid the day after Thanksgiving; you'll have enough to rent a tux. It's not that expensive to rent one for an evening – you'll do fine!"

"Oh, sure!" Shaking his head, he added, "And a guest?"

"Easy!" Dr. Winsted rubbed his own substantial midsection and said, "You're so handsome and so in shape, Joel, finding a date won't be any problem for you."

Joel picked up his briefcase, silently grinned at his mentor, his eyes twinkling. He rounded the desk and held out his hand for the doctor to precede him from the room. "On that note I think I'll split, Fred! Somebody else uses this room after me."

Fred grinned as he turned toward the door. "Not a problem, Joel!"

Joel still grinned as he followed the doctor from the room. The man was piling on the compliments! It had started on Friday when he came to tell him he'd join the faculty next semester. How could it be true? Scientists on other campuses were following his progress? A lecture series? That was hard to believe, although it was the science department from that other school that had contacted him to come as a professor. He'd chalked that up to… well who knew? He wasn't going there, so it didn't matter. But a lecture series? Who could that be? A prestigious organization? He wracked his brain but couldn't come up with a single name. The good doctor must be pulling his leg! And a date? Where would such as that materialize?

Jenni sat at her desk in her tiny office on Monday. She'd thrown away a can she'd emptied from the cooler in the break-room of her favorite liquid refreshment from her morning break when her computer signaled some international news coming in. That supplied some of her bread and butter, before the voice started; she turned to her computer and opened a new page, then put in her earbuds. She started typing immediately as the news came in for her news segment this evening. It was either feast or famine, some days she sat with nothing, then other times it was frantic. The words had barely finished when she saw movement at her door.

She looked up, it was Alex. "So Alex, what can I do for you?" she asked, hit her mouse to save her work and pulled out her earbuds. "You look like you're about to jump over the moon!" Since he was already moving toward her chair, she added, "Sure, why don't you come on in and make yourself comfortable?"

"So Jenni," the man mimicked, and sat down, a huge grin directed at her. It was obvious he wasn't comfortable; his long legs were cramped against Jenni's desk when he sat down. Her office was only big enough for one file cabinet, her desk, a computer extension and a swivel desk chair and the one vinyl chair she'd managed to squeeze into her tiny office. She'd had maintenance put up a board with knobs so she could hang her coat. He immediately stood, moved the chair, and sat. Jenni sat quietly watching.

When he was finally comfortable, he put his left ankle over his right knee and asked, "How'd you like a long break from your evening news over Thanksgiving?"

Did I notice the man didn't say I could have vacation? Hmmm. Skeptically, she leaned back in her swivel chair and asked, "How does one accomplish that? I realize news is preempted by football on Thanksgiving, but a long break? How does that work?" She grinned at her boss and added, "I did notice you didn't say 'vacation' but 'long break'. Alex. What's in it for me?"

He looked at Jenni and grinned before he said, "I'm thinking we could give your back-up that Friday and Saturday. How does that sound? Hey, that'd be a four day weekend!"

"Yup, that's so," Jenni agreed, still sounding skeptical. "I have a feeling that's not all. Tell me, Alex, my shoulders aren't as broad as yours, but I can handle it. You know me!"

"Uh huh," he said, grinning.

Alex put his elbows on the chair arms, put his fingertips together in front of his mouth and said, "It seems there's a black tie reception for the hospital's new Chief of Staff at the Convention Center on Saturday after Thanksgiving starting at seven. I think you and Len could cover that event as long as you had someone to cover your evening news. You'd do that, right?"

Jenni leaned back, crossed her arms across her chest and thought a minute, before she raised her right index finger, tapped her cheek and said, "So actually, I'd only get Thursday and Friday off because I'd have to be back in town for this shindig on Saturday evening is it?"

"You were always such a sharp cookie, Jenni!" Alex grinned. "I knew you'd figure it out in one and so you did."

Jenni nodded, disgusted. "Oh, yes, that would be me! And who am I supposed to be interviewing and watching for especially?"

"The Chief of Staff, Jenni, but anyone else who's there. If it's at the Convention Center it'll be a massive affair! Jewels'll sparkle, and the latest fashions will be everywhere! Of course, anybody who is anybody'll be there. I'm sure the mayor… You'll have a heyday!"

Jenni sighed, looked at her boss and shook her head. "Black tie? You've got to be kidding! I'm supposed to be dressed to the hilt, stilettos and all, but carry a mike and battery-pack. Keep an eye out for all these celebrities… Hmm, that'll be great!"

"Hey, you'll have a captive audience!"

Shaking her head again, Jenni said, "Oh, yes! I can't wait!"

"Oh, the invitation says the entertainment includes dancing! Jenni, you will have a ball!"

"Uh huh! I'm thrilled to pieces! Dancing with a mike and battery-pack, oh boy!"

Alex chuckled. "You'll figure it out, Jenni, I'm convinced."

"Oh, yes, so am I, Alex! And Len with his huge camera!"

Still smiling from talking to Fred, Joel walked around the corner and down the short hallway that led to the side door to the faculty parking lot and reached for the handle to pull open the outside door, intent on getting to the library to finish the chapter he intended as the last one for his dissertation. He would get the research and his rough draft finished before Thanksgiving break! Joel pulled on the door handle and had his leg up to take the next step, but just outside the door, a man, dressed all in black stepped in front of him, blocking his way completely.

Joel was still thinking about what Dr. Fred had said, but the man's shoes were massive and weren't moving, so Joel looked up surprised. Instantly his throat was dry and his eyes turned to saucers as he looked up… and up.

Joel was a good sized man, even in high school he was tall and well built, but the man in front of him dwarfed him. Not only was his shoe size big, but Joel thought maybe the man couldn't get through the doorway without turning sideways or ducking so he wouldn't hit the top doorframe. Even Joel, at six foot two had to look up. Joel was glad he hadn't let go of the door.

The man had on a black hoodie under a black vest. A hoodie and a vest? It was nearly winter! The temperature hovered in the low thirties! There was a thin skiff of frost on his windshield this morning. The hood was overly large and hung low so Joel couldn't see the man's face. What he could see was covered with the blackest beard he'd ever seen that hung several inches below his chin. Strings of oily black hair came around the edges of the hoodie and mingled with the beard. Something else Joel noticed, the man had a large nose ring and also had a piece of jewelry piercing his lower lip. Joel shook his head and looked again. Nothing the man had on looked too clean. However, what arrested Joel's attention were the man's black, cold eyes that stared at him, unblinking. That look made a chill slide down Joel's back.

Pulling in a breath, Joel squared his shoulders, gripped his briefcase, but still holding onto the door he asked in his strongest voice, "Can I help you? Do you need to come inside?" Joel couldn't imagine the man had business in a university science building, so he didn't move from the doorway, so if the man moved he'd have to plow into Joel if he intended to get inside.

The man had both hands in his pockets, but didn't move his head, so the hood still hung over his forehead onto his eyebrows. All he moved was one foot to widen his stance in the doorway. "Yeah," he growled, "hear your old man's dead."

Joel pulled in another deep breath and said, as loudly as he could, but it still came out strangled, "How would you know that?"

With a sneer, the man hissed, "You're T Lawson's brat!"

Joel straightened his spine and stood as tall as he could. "T Lawson's brat?" He'd never been called that in his life! 'T Lawson's brat' sounded like something someone would spread around an elementary school playground, not in a university science department building.

The man leaned into Joel's space a little and breathed foul breath into his face. "Yeah, that's what he called you a time or two!"

Joel didn't move from the doorway, but leaned back to breathe some decent air. The breath from the man's mouth was foul. He wasn't sure what the smell was, but it was nothing Joel had ever smelled. Joel wasn't sure if the man was chewing tobacco or not. Nodding, he said, "You're right. My dad died from an explosion over a week ago. It was public knowledge, people saw the result on the TV and heard about it on the radio, perhaps it was even in the papers. The fire department and the sheriff were there. Yes, most everybody knows he died."

"He owed me and my buddies money!"

"I'm sorry."

His dark eyes looking like lasers, glared into Joel's eyes. He snarled, "Don't give me that innocent stuff! You're the son! You're his brat! You gotta know somethin' about his business! He left it to you! I intend to collect what's mine!"

Joel gripped the door handle harder, but also held his briefcase fiercely. It was a hard case, full and quite heavy. He could use it as a weapon. Unfortunately he had no other weapon. However, he glared back at the man. He would not let this bully get the better of him! He had lived with his dad for twenty-five years! The man hadn't touched him or tried to take anything.

Joel took a deep breath, he was determined not to show any fear. In a clear, resounding voice, he said, "Mister, I had no dealings with any business my dad was engaged in! I wasn't interested in what he did and he wasn't interested to let me know what he did. If there was money involved I knew nothing about it! He hasn't given me any money since I was a tiny boy or told me where he kept any. Just because I'm his son doesn't mean I know anything! I have no idea what you're talking about and I will not be blackmailed with any scheme you may try to pull! If you'll excuse me, I'm on an important mission!" However, Joel didn't take that step over the threshold. He knew a building provided much more protection than a parking lot.

The man didn't move his feet, but moved his right hand inside his pocket noticeably and just above a whisper, he snarled, "Cut the big mouth, Lawson!

I'm here to collect and that's now! Hand it over! Hand over that money! All of it! NOW!" The man looked down.

As if it's hiding in my briefcase!

Joel didn't take his eyes from the man, but he noticed the hand movement. That, with his words and the way he spoke sent shivers up and down Joel's spine. Still not wanting to show he was intimidated, Joel said quite loudly, "It won't be from me, Mister! Like I said, I had no dealings with Dad's business. I didn't know anyone he dealt with. In fact, I'm sure I never saw anyone he had dealings with! When I was young, he made sure I wasn't there when he made deals. I never saw anyone to know them. When I got older, I made sure I wasn't there most of the time. If he had money or a will that included me I knew nothing about it. Any money he might have had or a will perished in the explosion, along with any merchandise he might have had at the house! I am not about to take that place, for you or anyone else. Leave me alone!"

When the thug saw that Joel wouldn't comply, he lifted his foot to take a step. He wasn't sure what the thug would do, but he still held the door. He quickly took one step to the side and slammed the door with all his strength into the man's face. He heard a grunt outside and some muffled words he didn't think he wanted to hear or understand. Joel knew the man's momentum had brought him into contact with the door he'd slammed quickly and quite hard. Knowing that the door locked to the outside as it engaged, Joel took another step to the side, well out of the way of the door and against the wall and waited, but let go of the door handle immediately.

The thug could see the door opened by a key pad; the man didn't try to open the door. Joel didn't know why he waited, but he didn't want to be in line with the door. However, seconds later, he was glad he'd removed his hand from the handle and stood against the wall. There was a gunshot blast and Joel shook his head. He was so close to the sound of the shot and the slug hitting the door that it momentarily deafened him and echoed in the short hallway.

Instantly, a hole appeared in the door as the bullet shot pointblank came through the heavy door. The solid door stopped the bullet and it dropped at Joel's feet. He did not bend over to pick it up, he wasn't sure another wouldn't follow it. Another might do more damage than the one at his feet. Incredulous, he leaned against the wall and looked at the mangled bullet, then at the hole in the door. However, there was light outside that hole, the man obviously took off.

"Wow!" Joel muttered. "Incredible!"

Joel's loud talking had alerted someone back at the corner that something that shouldn't be happening was and they called the building security. They were still on the phone when the gunshot blasted the door and they yelled, "HURRY! Somebody just shot a gun!"

Joel rubbed the side of his head trying to get his head and hearing back to normal. He wasn't aware of the frantic feet scrambling to get away from the intersecting hallways. The headache he'd had because of the glass shard and had finally gone away, sprang viciously to life, along with ringing in his ears that seemed overpowering. He didn't dare shake his head or move from the spot. He closed his eyes, hoping that would help. He still held his briefcase tightly.

Several minutes later, Joel's hearing straightened out. He heard nothing outside the door, but heard running feet behind him. He turned and leaned against the wall, but looked up and saw several men in navy blue uniforms coming towards him. The man in front took a deep breath, skidded to a stop and asked, "What's going on? We got a call said someone was shot!"

Knowing, that the man was asking him, Joel said, "When I opened the door to leave a man blocked my way and threatened me. A very large man. When I slammed the door in his face he pulled a gun from his pocket and shot the door. I never saw a gun while he talked to me. He was dressed in black and his hood covered part of his face. A beard covered the rest of it."

"You know him?"

Joel shook his head. "Never saw him before in my life. I have no idea how he knew who I was, but he knew my dad or said he did. I certainly don't have any way of verifying that! I had no dealings with anything my dad did."

"A black hood?"

"Yes." Other security men ran up breathlessly.

One last man skidded around the corner to join the other security men. Six men crowded into the tiny alcove. The officer reached for the door handle, and said, "We're after him! We'll get this crook! Man! Look at the hole in the door! He didn't pull the gun on you?"

"I would be glad if you did catch that thug! No, he didn't pull the gun while I had the door open, I never saw it." Joel exclaimed, still leaning against the wall.

He was trembling; his hands were icy cold, but there was a fine sheen of sweat on his forehead and on his upper lip. Thad had struck him with his fists and his open hands and also used his belt trying to bend Joel to his wishes, but he'd never threatened him with a gun. Joel didn't know if his dad had a gun, but to have the gun fire so close and the bullet land mere inches from him made him tremble like a leaf in the wind.

The officer turned from Joel, but yanked the door open, stopped on the threshold and looked both ways. "Guess he's gone! Ah, there, running down the block! Let's go, men! Maybe we can catch him and get this figured out!" The man took one step over the threshold.

"You stay, we'll get him!" the next man said and put his hand on the first man's shoulder to pull him back, then started out the door. The other officers followed without a word. All of them started running, but the man had a good head start.

The first man nodded and stepped back, but held the door for the others. Four men filed through the doorway and took off. As the door closed, the security man turned back to Joel and held out his hand. "I'm Bruce Ludwig, head of security. Can you tell me what happened?"

Joel nodded. He took a deep breath to calm himself. He cleared his throat and pointed to the hole in the door before he said, "First, Mr. Ludwig, the slug he shot through the door was on the floor beside me, but I believe the door brushed it away when you opened it. It left this hole, but the bullet itself was rather mangled. You might want to collect it for evidence."

The officer pulled a small baggie from his pocket and turned it inside out around his hand. "Yeah, we'll need everything we can get! That was a smart move closing the door in his face! Since he had a gun, if you hadn't it's anybody's guess what he'd have done to you! Wow! Look at the hole it made!"

Joel stared at the hole, before he said, "I didn't know he had a gun. His hands were in his pockets when he talked to me. I saw him move his hands, but I never saw him before!"

As the man looked for the bullet the door had pushed away, Joel added, "I'm Joel Lawson. I teach here in the building and was on my way to my car when the man accosted me. I was shocked to find him so close!" Joel chuckled without humor. "Most of my eight o'clock students come in half asleep, but that guy sure wasn't!"

Mr. Ludwig found the bullet and picked it up with the bag around his hand, then turned the bag the right way and put it in his pocket. "But you don't know him."

Joel shook his head. "Like I said, I never saw him before. He accused me of being involved with my dad's business, which I never was. There was always antagonism between my dad and me, we never got along, and so I never knew anything about his business. He said that now that my dad's dead that I owed him."

Mr. Ludwig scowled. "How'd he know to come here after you?"

"Sir, that is a good question, I have no answer."

The man sighed. "Perhaps my men can catch him. There were four of them, but the thug had a good half block head start. He must have turned and run the instant he pulled the trigger." Mr. Ludwig nodded. "I did see how big a man he was, but he was sure moving fast!"

Joel nodded. "It'd be good if they caught him. Yes, I think he was the biggest man I've ever seen! He filled the doorway. After the shot, I saw light behind the hole, I figured he'd run."

"You just closed the door in his face?"

Joel nodded and shifted away from the wall. His trembling had finally stopped and his ears weren't ringing. "Yes, because he took a step towards me. I had no idea about a gun, I didn't know he had one, but I didn't want to be where he could do something to me. Obviously it was good I did, perhaps he planned to unload that gun into me, since I wasn't cooperating."

The man in blue nodded. "Yes, that's a good possibility. Come with me, I need to get your statement." He grinned. "That means I got forms to fill out."

Joel let out a long breath, there went a couple hours of research. "Yes, of course, Mr. Ludwig." As they started walking, Joel added, "Yeah, with all that and then that gunshot so close it set my ears ringing, I could use a chair."

"I can believe that! That bullet coming through that solid door and echoing in this small space could make a good amount of noise!"

Mr. Ludwig took him to the security office and asked his questions, filling out a lengthy report. Dr. Winsted came as support, but Joel knew that all the time he'd anticipated being at the library had evaporated. Joel was enough on edge that he knew it would take time to collect himself to teach his second class.

After the interview, Joel looked at his watch and swallowed a sigh. It was time to teach, he didn't have time to hunt for a water fountain. He'd have to run the length of the building to get in the room on time. He moved quickly through several hallways to his classroom. At one corner was a drinking fountain, so he stopped for a drink that would help.

He was having a hard time bringing his mind back to the material he was to teach and certainly the invitation to the reception had long ago left his thoughts. He prayed as he walked into the room. He needed a clear mind and to be free of thoughts about the thug. For a change no one was early and Joel breathed a sigh of relief. He hefted his briefcase onto the desk and sank into the chair to grab another breath.

"Whew! Never thought something like that could happen! I sure hope those guys can catch him. Still, I have no idea what he's talking about." He had just opened his briefcase to take out his notes when the first student sauntered in.

However, the other officers couldn't catch the man before he jumped into a car that idled at the curb several blocks from the science building. It squealed its tires and darted immediately in front of another car on the street. That car squealed its brakes trying not to hit the get-away car. The officer closest to the car tried to focus on the place for a license plate as the car sped away, but he couldn't see anything. The other men came along side and frustrated, they watched the tail lights vanish. Winded, they all took much longer to get back to the security office. They were all disgusted their mission was not accomplished.

ELEVEN

After class, Joel followed his last student from the classroom to find Mr. Ludwig's second in command and Fred talking in the hall outside the room. Fred voiced his concern, as Joel stopped beside him. "What! You're telling me Joel has to worry that the man'll come back again? You guys didn't catch him?"

Mr. Ludwig's side-kick hung his head. "No, Sir, we saw him jump in a car several blocks down the street. The license plate was either missing or so dirty that we couldn't see anything. We reported the make and model, but often that doesn't help much in a metropolitan area like this. We never got a clear view of the man's face, since we were chasing after him."

"Well, that's the pits!" Fred exclaimed.

"Yes, Sir. We're genuinely hoping it won't happen again."

"Oh, for sure!" Fred said, and Joel nodded.

However, considering the type of threat it was, he was pretty sure the man would be back or one of his 'friends'. While he and Mr. Ludwig were filling out the report they discussed the possibility. Something that puzzled them both was how the man knew that Joel would be in the university science building. Surely Thad wouldn't brag about his son's achievements – considering the way the man had treated his son over the years! Joel had no illusions of that!

"T Lawson's brat!" Joel muttered to himself.

The security officer reached for Joel's hand and said apologetically, "Sorry about that."

Joel shook the man's hand. "Yes, I'm sorry, too. I wish you could have caught him. However, I'm sure he's not working alone. He told me, 'me and my friends,' and you say there was a get-away car. I have no idea what he wants. Dad never told me about his business."

The man left and Fred put his hand on Joel's shoulder. After a sigh, Fred said, "I guess this isn't over, is it?"

"I guess not. I have no idea what the man's talking about, but I guess Dad did some shady things while he owned the house. There was a room in the basement that he kept locked. I never saw inside. It was beside the furnace and water heater, so whatever was in there went up in the explosion. It was in the part of the basement that was completely filled in. That guy said Dad owed him money. In this case the saying is *not* true, 'Like father like son' believe me!"

"Yes, Joel, I know that for a fact, I never had any doubts. Keep a lookout, Joel. We do not want our newest professor hurt in any way. You know you have our backing all the way!"

"Thanks, Doc!"

Fred shook his head. "I wish they'd caught him, surely he'd have let something slip or let you know what he was after. To know that you were here at this time is unbelievable!"

"I can only hope that'll happen soon."

Now that he'd taught his classes for the day, Joel finally left the science building. When he reached his car he walked all the way around, but it seemed undisturbed. Even the gravel on the pavement wasn't disturbed. He wondered, since the man was already at the door if he'd done something to his car. He was relieved as he opened the door and started up and nothing happened. Even though he never was a TV addict, the police shows he watched showed more violence than what he experienced today. However he could do without something like what had happened. Violence was not something he liked; living with his dad was bad enough.

As he drove to the library his stomach growled and even though he hadn't felt that hungry, he knew he needed to eat. He did not want to get sick! It was past lunch time, but he knew the library canteen was open. It had generous hours and many students took advantage of that. He was one of them today. When he arrived, he took a long time to choose things to eat; he was still distracted by the events of the morning and couldn't make up his mind. After eating his lunch and drinking a large coffee, Joel did manage to clear the incident from his mind enough that he spent a productive afternoon at his favorite desk in the stacks. He made himself focus on the work and determined that today he would finish his research for his dissertation.

His stomach growled as he closed the book. He'd lost track of time and was surprised he was hungry again. He sighed, looked at his notes, counted the pages and decided that was all the research he would do. With this many notes he could write his last chapter, then do his revision. He had the rest of the week to get it all into sentences and paragraphs and enter it in his lap-top.

As he slapped the research book closed, he exclaimed, "Whew! A job done!"

His stomach growled again, so he stood and grabbed his coat. He would go home to fix his supper. Eating something he fixed appealed much more than a second meal from the canteen. The rest of the week he could write the last chapter, whether here or at home, it didn't matter. Next week, when the library was closed he'd work on his lap-top, at home. He hadn't been able to do any of the rest of the work at home, but there were no distractions in his apartment. *Unless you open the drape and a lovely neighbor just happens to get in her car....*

Completely ignoring the little voice in his head, he muttered, "Whew! I'll be glad to put this place behind me! I think that chair has conformed to my backside long enough!" In fact, to let the whole world know he was finished, he pushed the chair under the desk with a flourish.

He loaded his briefcase, dropped the book on the librarian's desk and headed for his car. He patted his noisy stomach and whispered, "Hold on, I'll be home in no time and I'll get something to fill you up!" He had to smile, his stomach growled again, maybe a bit impatient?

He hurried to the parking lot, anxious to get home. He was surprised the sun was still up. So much had happened it seemed like two days since he'd left home that morning. It seemed the saga of the Lawson family had not ended with the memorial service for Thad and Eleanor.

He wondered how his dad made a living. Since he was at home so much, Joel often wondered how he had money for expenses and keep a large house and so many acres so close to a large city. Neither he nor his mom ever seemed to be on drugs. He surely would have recognized the symptoms. He was amazed that over the years his parents, neither one, smoked, but his dad always had at least one beer at suppertime. He had never seen his dad drunk.

He could be very wrong, ever since he was in school he tried hard to stay out of the house as much as possible and out of Thad's way whenever he could. It was possible that he didn't know much about what Thad did, he certainly didn't know about any people he had dealings with. The sheriff came occasionally, but from his observations it never was a friendly encounter.

Evi spent most of her day in the Burn Unit. No new patients came in for evaluation. Therefore she had no new surgeries. One patient wasn't doing as well as she thought he should several days post-op. She spent extra time with him and found he had other physical problems. They were serious enough she called in another physician. He requested the patient be moved from the Unit, Evi won and the man had stayed. The other doctor must suit up to see his patient.

Her stomach growled she had skipped lunch. Now that she was off, she anticipated another quiet evening, as she turned onto the parking lot for her apartment. She still hadn't figured out how to ask Joel to be her date for the reception, but she was a big girl, she would find her nerve and ask him. It gave her the willies thinking about walking up to his door to knock and ask! She never had many dates in her life and she was sure she never had been the one to ask.

Anxious to be home, she breathed a sigh when she reached the parking lot. Another car turned behind her and its lights shone in her back window. She wondered if it was Joel, they'd come home at the same time last Friday, maybe this was when he usually finished his day. If he would defend his thesis in December he must have it mostly finished. As she turned into her spot the other car started turning, Joel was home. She didn't look that way, but he looked at her.

She turned off the key and sat for a moment. Maybe there was silence in the car, but her heart was roaring in her ears! She took her time collecting her purse. Her hands were clammy, now was her chance to ask him for a date – without knocking on his door! It was now or never, she must gear up her nerve! She cleared her throat, wiped her sweaty hands down her coat and opened the door. Procrastinating, she clicked the lock on the door instead of using the fob.

"Come on, girl! You can do this!" she chastised herself, in a whisper.

Joel shut off his car, grabbed his briefcase and stepped onto the asphalt. As Evi stepped from her car, he waved and smiled. "Hi, we meet again, Evi!"

he called across the cars. That little guy on his shoulder whispered, *Hey, now is a good time to ask her to go to the reception downtown!* He shrugged that shoulder; there was plenty of time to ask. He'd do it real soon.

"Hi, Joel!" Still feeling uncomfortable, the roaring hadn't left her ears, but knowing this was her chance, she held her purse in a death grip and blurted out, "Can I ask you something?"

"Sure, go ahead," he said, with an easy smile.

She waited until they both reached the front of their cars before she said, "Well…" she cleared her throat and tried again, "I got this invitation the other day and I'm supposed to bring a guest to this reception and… and I wondered…"

Joel grinned at her and said, "Are you talking about the reception for the new Chief of Staff for your hospital?"

"Umm, yes, you know about it?" Unconsciously, she ran her hand back and forth across the opening of her purse.

Joel nodded. "Yes, the science department chairman got an invitation for the faculty, so he invited me to come. Would you like to go together?"

Losing all her self-consciousness, Evi grinned and exclaimed, "Yes, sure!"

Joel chuckled. "I guess it's a date then."

"Great!"

Standing so close, they each heard the other's stomach growl. Self-conscious, Evi put her hand over her stomach, but Joel only smiled. "I guess our bellies want us on a mission. That's more than a week away, we'll meet again and can make plans for getting downtown."

"Great! I'll see you soon."

Joel nodded. "Yes, I'm sure of it, Evi."

Again they escaped to their own apartments. Evi especially nearly ran from the front of her car onto her patio. She didn't want to embarrass herself again with a growling stomach. However, Joel hadn't made it to his desk to deposit his briefcase on it when his phone rang. He pulled it from its carrier and looked to see who called.

A grin immediately creased his face. "Hello, Granddad, what can I do for you?"

"Joel, since this will be the first ever Thanksgiving with our grandchildren, we wondered if you and Leslie could come for the day? As early as you can so we can get better acquainted."

"Granddad, that sounds super! I must call Les and see what's up with her. Can I call you back to let you know for sure?"

Steve, always excited to talk to his grandson, said, "Of course, Joel, that's fine! If the subject comes up, any and all of the other side of your family are welcome. We'd love to get acquainted with your aunt and your other grandparents, but especially Leslie. What better time than over a Thanksgiving meal?"

"Great! I'll let you know for sure real soon."

"Mary and I are looking forward to it! Oh, by the way, no one has any allergies, do they?" Steve chuckled. "If I remember right, you ate some of everything there at the church."

Joel also laughed. "Granddad, Les and I were always glad to eat what was set before us. There was no lack, but we were always grateful. As far as I know, even my grandparents are quite healthy and have no allergies. Not that I'm aware of. Auntie has served a wide variety."

"All righty then, we'll wait for your call. Mary's so anxious she's already started a list with 'turkey' at the top. I'll say, long ago when she fixed roast turkey there was none better!"

"Granddad, I will let you know as soon as I know!"

Joel ended the call, set his phone on the table and quickly set about fixing an omelet. His stomach was too insistent to be filled to think about doing anything else. He found out quickly that an omelet was easy to fix and filled his empty stomach. However, his mind was active on another subject; he had a date for the gala downtown next Saturday! He chuckled, he hadn't really… well neither of them had asked the other. Evi had said enough that Joel knew what she was talking about and suggested they go together. That wasn't asking for a date, was it?

As he added the chopped peppers, chopped mushrooms and ham chunks to the melted butter, he sighed, "So I'd say I need to find some store that'll rent me a tux and whatever goes with it so I can take a beautiful woman to a black tie event." When the veggies were cooked he added the whipped eggs and cheese. As the good aroma entered his nose, he loosened one side of the cooked eggs and flipped it over the veggies.

"Lord, I live next door to a beautiful woman. We've agreed to go to this gala together. I feel badly about Jenni and I haven't seen her since I moved. I guess it's in Your hands, Lord."

Evi stepped on her patio, still smiling. She really hadn't asked Joel to be her date. He'd been invited to the gala, so they'd go together. Right? She unlocked her door and set her purse on the table inside the door and looked around her quiet home. She blew out a long sigh, life was a mystery. How did one figure it out? She pulled in another breath, she was twenty-nine. Shouldn't she have figured something out by now? Maybe the mystery wasn't hers to figure out.

Something Joel said came to mind as she made her supper. He said that after his dad died he realized that God had been chasing his dad for a long time. "Did God do that? Does He really take that much interest in one man?" If that were true… it made Evi shudder, then God had gone to a lot of trouble to make sure that Thad Lawson said those words to his son. Goose bumps rose up on her arms as another thought came into her mind. If that was so, Thad Lawson couldn't have died until Joel was there! Even three days after the explosion; in a really cold time in November! She had to admit, she'd never, ever heard of such a thing! It was a scary thought!

If God knew that much about one man, what does He know about me?

Not wanting to think that thought, Evi pulled a loaf of bread from her bread box, some spreadable butter from her fridge and a couple slices of cheese. She took a skillet from the wall and set it on the stove to warm. A grilled cheese and a bowl of tomato soup sounded like a good way to finish her day. She felt the need for some comfort food and that combination was her favorite. Her mom had always made the best grilled cheese sandwiches as she grew up.

Tomorrow was another day, with its challenges, but this evening she could kick back – unless they called from the hospital. Right now she wished she could turn off her phone and vegetate. She had worked with burn patients all day. Wasn't there a chance she could let it all go without a guilty conscience? The work in the burn treatment room was time consuming and tedious and she did it all day. It never seemed to get done, there was always another burn patient who needed worked on. Like it or not, she was it, the buck stopped with her!

She warmed her soup in the microwave as she grilled the sandwich in the skillet. The aroma teased her nose and her stomach grumbled. While the grilled cheese cooked she poured a large glass of iced tea – without the ice, since it was winter. After she sat down to eat her comfort food, her head went back as if someone slapped her. "I am going to a formal gala with a handsome man! What on earth will I wear? I don't even own a 'little black number'! And shoes? Oh, my! I won't be able to make a double payment on my loan this pay check!"

That funny little urchin that sometimes sat on her shoulder whispered, *What about your scrubs?* "No sir! Not even close!" she blurted into the silence.

Jenni had the day off. It was probably last Thanksgiving when she had a Thursday off. Not many of the local TV station staff worked on Thanksgiving Day. Network football pretty much took over the channel. Alex said her backup would cover whatever news didn't get dumped for football, so Jenni was trying to sleep in, but Curly wanted nothing to do with that. Jenni made the mistake of not making sure her sitting room door was closed tightly and Curly used it to his advantage. Now he had his front paws on the bed, licking her face wanting her to get up and get on with her day. And probably let him outside*!*

She opened one eye, brought her hand out from under the covers and pushed him until his feet fell off the bed and he whined, as she said, "Yuk! Curly, get lost! I wanna sleep!" From the end of her fingers, Curly again whined so pitifully that Jenni finally sighed. "All right – you are so spoiled! See, I am getting up, but I sure don't want to. You better be nice to me the rest of the day! I'm not even sure I'll give you any treats today, since you woke me up! Boy, it's Thanksgiving Day, I have the day off and you got me up early!" Jenni reluctantly sat up.

Curly flopped down beside the bed and Jenni was sure he gave her a doggy smile. With a sigh, she said, "Yeah, right! Now that you've got your way… you lay down!"

After getting dressed – sort of - Jenni wandered into the kitchen to put the dog out in the back yard and found Loretta there fixing herself a cup of coffee. While the coffee machine did its thing, Loretta said, "Thought you planned to sleep in."

"I did, but nuisance here, wouldn't let me," Jenni grumbled, walking to the door. "I told him he has to be nice to me the rest of the day. And if he doesn't he won't get any treats!"

Loretta chuckled. "Oh, sure! I have visions of that, don't you, Curly?" Curly wagged his tail, since he'd heard his name. He made a bee line to the back door.

Jenni went after him and opened the door for him to go in the back yard. As she pulled some dry cereal and the jug of milk from the refrigerator, she noticed that her dad wasn't around. It was quiet, the TV wasn't on. Her dad was gone already. In the presence of her mom, she swallowed a sigh. Where else would he go on Thanksgiving Day? Fishing was out; he had to be at work. She was convinced her dad worked too much. He couldn't even get Thanksgiving off?

Loretta slid into a chair and asked, "So what happened to the handsome man next door?"

"Lucy said he moved to an apartment closer to campus. I haven't seen him or talked to him since. He hasn't been back, not when I'm here."

Loretta gave her daughter one horrendous scowl and said, "Girl, you should have latched on to him! If he's still in town, you could have moved with him!"

Jenni wouldn't look at her mom, but shook her head. She pulled her favorite mug from the cupboard and filled it from the coffee carafe, then filled her bowl with cereal and dumped enough milk that every flake could learn to swim! "I'm sure he wouldn't go for that at all!"

"What do you mean? Everybody your age's doing it, why not him? I kinda knew Thad Lawson…I mean, him and Eleanor were something else in high school! They belonged to that gang that all wore black hoods. Anybody knew if there was trouble they could count on it being Thad Lawson and his gang. So what's so different about the son? They're from the same mold, right? Isn't there some kind of saying – 'the apple doesn't fall far from the tree'?"

Jenni sloshed milk into her coffee and shook her head. "Everything, Mom, everything! No! They are *not* from the same mold! From what I know about Joel and his dad, Joel isn't even the same kind of fruit as his dad! He would never do that." Jenni replied emphatically.

Skeptically, Loretta said, "You mean 'cause he goes to church? …So?"

"Yes Mom, because he goes to church. It means a lot to him. Not only because his dad was so cruel to him and his sister, but he's built his life on what he believes and he's been going to that Christian university all this time. Remember I asked you about what his dad said as he died, that 'Jesus died for him'?"

"Ah, I remember you asked about that." Loretta took a long sip from her mug then held the cup in front of her face, trying to hide how uncomfortable Jenni's question made her feel.

Getting up, Jenni didn't notice her mom's discomfort instead she went to the back door to let Curly in, then to the carafe and filled her cup with more coffee. She closed up the milk container and put it back in the refrigerator and then said, "Well, I asked Joel about it when he came home that night. We talked for quite a while about things like that. He told me it was *the* most important thing his dad had ever told him. He told me about heaven and hell, Mom. He talked about the Bible and said some things that really made me uncomfortable! No, he'd never take me into his apartment – not as a live-in. I know that for a fact."

Still uncomfortable, Loretta squirmed in her chair and wiped her mouth, then took hold of the mug handle and swirled the mug on the table before she exclaimed, "Well, I'd say you missed out, girl! You told me he's gonna be a doctor! He'll make really good money! Come on, girl, get with it! You wouldn't even have to work."

Jenni looked at her mom and noticed her body language. "Maybe I did miss out, Mom, but it's not the first time and probably won't be the last. Joel said some really amazing things when we talked those few times, it's stuff I'd never heard you guys talk about. I needed to think about them, but then he was gone."

"So have Lucy tell you where he lives!" Loretta exclaimed, still trying to be overly flippant. "I'm sure she knows where he went and you have a car…"

"Mom! I wouldn't do that!"

They both heard gravel crunching on a driveway close by and Loretta slapped her cup down on the table, spilling several drops, jumped up and ran to look out the living room window. "Oh, that's his car! There's Joel! Grab your coat, girl, get on out there!"

"Mom, stop!"

"Why?"

The word had barely left her mouth when they both heard a siren whoop close by on the street. It was loud enough inside the closed house that Loretta jumped, even though she saw the sheriff's car. Jenni rushed to the window to look out with Loretta. Joel's car was in Lucy's driveway, but the sheriff's car pulled in right to his bumper. Lucy, with a large shoulder bag and Leslie were already outside as Sheriff Gibbs jumped from his car and taking long strides walked up beside Joel's car on the driver's side. Both Jenni and Loretta stood staring out the window.

Barely above a whisper, Loretta said, "Uh oh, there's trouble!"

"You got that right, Mom!" Jenni agreed. "It looks like the man's out for blood – Joel's blood to be exact!" Musing out loud, Jenni said, "What could the sheriff have to say to Joel on Thanksgiving Day? In school Joel was always such a good guy – he was never in trouble. I'd almost want to say he was teacher's pet in elementary."

Loretta smirked. "Has to be juicy, knowing Thad Lawson!"

"Mom, I told you, Joel had nothing in common with his dad!"

Loretta winked. "You never know!" Jenni didn't answer, only watched intently as Joel motioned Lucy and his sister back inside. The sheriff reached Joel's car in about three steps.

Joel heard the siren and saw the white car turn behind him. Sighing, knowing this wouldn't be a quick dialogue, he motioned the ladies back inside. Joel looked in his outside mirror and swallowed, willing his temper under control. After the last few encounters he'd had with the sheriff, it was anyone's guess what the man planned to say! He hit the door lock with his elbow and murmured, "Lord, keep my mouth, give me the words You want me to say to this man! You know how he tries very hard to push my buttons! And just by association, I know he hates me and wants to pin *something* on me! It would be bad if I lost my temper!"

The sheriff's long strides brought him quickly to Joel's car, so Joel put down his window barely two inches, not even half way and said, "What can I do for you, Sheriff?"

The man pounded on Joel's roof, looked into the car and glared at him. "Like I said the other day, you're a suspect! What'd you do? How'd you get the fire lieutenant in your pocket? He was all over me and defending you the other day!"

"Really? How can you say that?" Joel answered quietly, not answering the sheriff's accusation, but working hard not to show any reaction to what he said. In fact, he took his eyes from the sheriff and shut off the car. This confrontation would probably be rather long, the sheriff had no qualms about wasting his time, but that didn't mean Joel needed to waste gas.

With another whack on the roof the sheriff's face turned red as he shouted, "You're the son, why wouldn't you want to get rid of the man who held onto millions? I mean, off-shore holdings, stuff like that!"

That was the first Joel had ever heard about such a thing, but trying not to react, he said, "Really? You know that for a fact?"

His voice almost a roar, Sheriff Gibbs reached for the door handle, but saw that the door was locked. Instead he bellowed, "Get out of the car!"

"Why, so you can arrest me?"

The sheriff gulped. That was his plan, but ordinary people weren't supposed to read his mind! "Y-yes-s-s-s!" he hissed. The man balled up his hands, then released them, but balled them into fists again and smashed his fist on the roof again.

The sheriff's whacks on the roof were so heavy and so loud it was all Joel could do not to jump each time. He stayed seated, acting as calm as he could, with the door locked and spoke through the partially open window. "I don't think so, Sheriff."

The sheriff's hand that he'd reached out with was still balled into a fist. He acted as if he wanted to smash Joel's window. Instead he bellowed, "Do as I say!!"

Joel didn't move. "Why?" He kept his left arm casually on the window ledge and his right wrist draped over the steering wheel, hoping the sheriff saw a casual look. His heart was pounding. After a lifetime of his dad's accusations and abuse, Joel hated confrontations.

Trying another tactic, Sheriff Gibbs said, "Okay, tell me your version! You don't think Thad had millions? Off shore accounts, stuff like that?"

Shrugging, as if it was common knowledge and he had nothing to hide, Joel said, "Well, first, I never knew anything about Dad's business. He never volunteered that information ever in my life and I wasn't interested enough to ask." He gave the sheriff a half smile and added, "Oh, since the explosion totally obliterated the house and I'm still around because I wasn't there, tell me, would I be driving this fifteen year old, standard issue car if I had access to millions?"

Sheriff Gibbs pulled in a deep breath; dealing with Joel Lawson was totally different from any dealings with Thad. Instead of truly answering Joel's question, he said, "Oh, ah-h-h-h, sure." There was a hint the man was having second thoughts. However, he quickly regrouped and said, "Okay, so tell me what you were doing the day of the explosion and the day before. It's gotta be there somewhere! Has to be!"

Again Joel shrugged. "Like I told the lieutenant from the fire precinct at the site; the day before the explosion I spent the day teaching classes at the university across town and when I wasn't teaching, I was at the university library on the same campus doing research for my thesis. Any one of my students or the library staff can verify that. They all know me and I didn't try to hide. What was there to hide, anyway?

"I found a good stopping place, so I left the library about five o'clock and went to my parents' home. As I'm sure you know, that takes about fifteen minutes going the bypass. I went to my room on the second floor, changed clothes, spread out my things from my briefcase on the desk planning to study during the evening after supper. My sister, Leslie was there and since she's still alive, she'd know. Mom called us to supper about six and I had finished a plateful of food when my dad started yelling at me, clamped his hand around my arm, dragged me to the front door and threw me out, telling me never to return. On the way, a big mirror crashed and one of the glass shards punctured my temple. I'm sure you saw the evidence in that black eye that I had when you came to the site the next day. Everyone else saw it.

"Later, at my aunt's house, my sister sent me a text to come for my things, which she threw out my bedroom window, let me say it again, which is on the **second** floor, but I was never **inside** the house, it was locked up. My dad locked it after he threw me out. There is someone who knew me who can verify where I was all day that day, even when I ate lunch. The only time I was alone was when I was driving, which was only minutes of time. In fact, you pretty much know how long it takes to get to their house. I've been aware of many of the times when you came to visit when my dad was alive."

Joel looked at the man, his look intense and said, "The day of the explosion I was on campus all morning. That can be verified, by students, staff or faculty. I was there until the lieutenant called me after they had arrived at the explosion site. Up until that moment I had no idea that something had happened at Dad and Mom's house. I never saw my mom again, nor my dad until three days after the explosion when I came back to accompany the insurance adjuster on his inspection and my dad was there walking around. He was terribly burned, amnesic, didn't know me and didn't know where he was."

Snidely, the sheriff interrupted, "Keep talking, Lawson! I don't believe a word you're saying! You're blowing smoke. I mean, ya coudda lobbed dynamite in some cranny with a long fuse – who knows?"

You should know how that works! Joel said to himself.

Joel hesitated a minute. Something felt like a prompting that said, *Tell him about your dad – Gibbs needs to hear what happened.*

Joel took a deep breath, he hadn't told many people about that time at his dad's bedside. This man had insulted him, why should he tell him something so awesome, so personal? *Tell him...* Joel looked the sheriff in the eye, took another breath and said, "Sheriff, did Roger Williams tell you about my call to your department three days after the explosion?"

"Yeah, what's that got to do with anything?" the sheriff said angrily. "So we searched – a wild goose chase – I might add, all over them woods. So what's that got to do with this?" The man gestured between him and Joel.

Still reluctant to tell the nasty officer something so personal, Joel pulled in another breath. "Well, you see, I went out there to meet the insurance adjuster and my dad was there terribly burned and amnesic. I sent him to the hospital right away."

"Yeah, so?"

As if he hadn't interrupted, Joel continued, "Well, I followed him a bit later and spent his last few minutes of life with him there in the hospital Burn Unit. Sheriff, you know what happened just before he died?"

Sheriff Gibbs cleared his throat and said, brusquely, "'Course not! Why'd I know that? I wasn't there! Get on with this tale you're telling me, Lawson!!"

"Sheriff, he was barely breathing, but he opened his eyes, looked at me, totally alert, knowing who I was and said, 'Yes, I believe Jesus died for me.' He closed his eyes, took another breath and whispered, 'Son.' Sheriff, he did not take another breath after that. Also, sheriff, that was the first time in my life he ever called me 'son'."

Totally uncomfortable, the sheriff looked at his feet, shuffled them twice. He cleared his throat, coughed several times, lifted his hat, pulled his hand through his hair, down across his face, slapped his hat back on his head, then put his finger between his tight collar and his neck and yanked his collar so hard the top button popped off. He cleared his throat again and in a voice unlike Joel had ever heard before he said, "I..." he swallowed, "...I d...don't believe it."

Not surprised at all, but seeing how uncomfortable he became, Joel said, "Really, Sheriff? I'm sorry to hear that. It is the way it happened."

Going back to what Gibbs had said before, Joel asked, "Sheriff, why do you say that I'm blowing smoke? After what I just told you...."

Totally back in control, or wanting Joel to think so, his eyes blazing, the man slapped his hand on Joel's roof again and blurted out, "I got it on good authority! You lobbed a torch into the house...!" The sheriff was obviously rattled. He clamped his lips together, his eyes wide, realizing he had revealed much too much information to someone he considered a suspect.

Not showing any reaction, Joel asked, "When would I have done that, Sheriff?"

The sheriff bent over, like he wanted to get in Joel's face. "Right before the explosion! Of course!" he bellowed. "Lawson, if you're so smart you're some kind of a professor, you don't need me to tell you that!"

Still being very calm, Joel said, "I see. Truly, Sheriff Gibbs, this is all very interesting! Who is it who saw me do that, Sheriff?" Waiting momentarily and watching the sheriff squirm, Joel added, "The lieutenant told me there at the site there were no witnesses – no one saw the explosion, the neighbor felt it and called 911, but that's not true?"

"I'm not at liberty to say."

Getting a little irate himself, Joel exclaimed, "Right! Of course not! Why am I not surprised you'd say that! You've made this horrendous accusation against me, but can't tell me who passed that information on to you!"

Sheriff Gibbs cleared his throat and said, "Yes," very quietly.

Showing his superior intelligence and much restraint, Joel tapped his index finger on his chin and said, "So..., let's see... probably someone using a voice enhancer called your cell phone and since you want to find something against me, because you hated my dad so much,... who, by the way... on his deathbed told me *he believed Jesus died for him...* you jumped on that anonymous tip. Never mind that the voice you heard didn't sound like a real voice. Am I right, Sheriff? Is that the way it was?" Not expecting an answer, Joel looking shrewdly at the sheriff, said, "So what you're saying makes the letter I got the other day from the state laboratory false. I guess you didn't get such a letter, perhaps it only went to the **fire lieutenant**."

That got the sheriff's attention. He'd opened his mouth to say something. Instead, he nearly danced in place, he'd never heard about a letter. "**What letter?**" he yelled and slammed his fist on Joel's roof. Momentarily, Joel was distracted, wondering if the sheriff's hand would be red or swollen when he left. His car... a dent in the roof?

Joel, keeping himself under strict control, something the sheriff was not, shrugged and said, "I told you, Sheriff. I received a letter from the state lab telling me the results of their testing of some of the debris from the basement. I know you've been there since the explosion, so I know you saw that some of the debris was gone from the hole in the ground. Did it never occur to you that in removing debris from the hole the fire department planned to have it tested?"

Trying to force his hand in through the small opening next to Joel's face, but finding his hand was too big the sheriff pulled his hand back and slammed it on the roof - again. That action made Joel reflexively jump a little, but also wondered what he had intended to do if he had gotten his hand inside. In fact, Joel wished for a second he'd had his finger on the window control and put it up even more, but that wasn't the right thing to think about – not as a Christian man who wanted to give a good testimony – even to the obnoxious sheriff!

The sheriff was so agitated he danced in place, then at the top of his lungs he roared, "This letter… this letter that you *alleged* that you got, **what does it say**? I'm the law! You *must* tell me! I have a right to know!"

"Does it matter? Will you lay off abusing an innocent citizen if I tell you?"

"Of course!" The man stood there with his fists clenched. Probably forgetting that he'd admitted he was harassing an innocent citizen.

Nodding knowingly, Joel smiled, knowing he had finally gotten the upper hand, said, "Well, Sheriff, I'll turn the tables. I'm sure if you ask the right people you'll find out. Actually, let me suggest you go talk to the fire station lieutenant. He got a copy of the letter. I was about to take my aunt and sister to see other family for Thanksgiving Dinner. You'll excuse us, won't you Sheriff? You'll need to go immediately to the fire station, of course. I'm sure he'll be there and welcome you." *Actually, **it's** a good chance he's **not** there, since it's Thanksgiving Day!*

Slamming his fist down on Joel's roof again, he bellowed, "Don't get smart with me, Lawson! I'll be back! I'm *sure* the lieutenant has that copy!"

"Yes, I'm sure he does, Sheriff. Oh, you have a good Thanksgiving! Enjoy some turkey with your wife, won't you?"

Sheriff Gibbs gave Joel the dirtiest look he could muster, put his hand on his belt close to his revolver, but didn't touch it and started muttering under his breath. He whirled on his heel, slammed his fist on Joel's roof once more for good measure, so hard Joel wasn't sure the roof wouldn't be dented!

Taking one step, he kicked Joel's back tire with all his might, rocking the car. He pulled his foot back and stood on the other foot for a minute, then with a noticeable limp, stormed back to his car. He yanked the door open, climbed in and slammed the door behind him so hard that the car shook. The sheriff turned the key, but flattened his foot on the gas pedal and the poor car roared. Joel was really glad both his siren and his lights were off and he didn't turn them on. It would not have been a quiet neighborhood. Joel shook his head the man was nearly beside himself with rage!

"Lord, was that really what you wanted me to do?"

Yes! It was! All of it! That calm voice assured him. Joel shook his head as he watched the sheriff leave.

Lucy was watching, so as soon as the sheriff got in his car she opened the house door. She and Leslie walked out. As the sheriff turned his head, Joel motioned to the ladies to come. As they reached the car, he flipped the knob to unlock the doors. They got in and he locked the doors again. He wouldn't give the sheriff any excuse to get to him personally.

He sat and watched his rear-view mirror as the sheriff gunned his car back into the street, without looking to see if there was traffic. "Whew!" Joel exclaimed, "I'm glad he had it in reverse!" Fortunately, there wasn't any traffic and the car roared onto the street. The brakes squawked and the car jerked again as the sheriff yanked the stick into drive. Only after he was out of sight did Joel start the car and pull the stick into reverse, look both ways and back more slowly onto the street. He was glad he could turn the opposite direction from the way the sheriff went. Who knew if the man was going to the fire station or not!

Leslie also looked out the back window and watched the man leave. Shaking her head, she asked, "Bro, how can you be so calm? That man's awful!"

As he accelerated, he said, "Sis, I know he's wrong. He's trying to fluster me so I'll admit to something I didn't do so he can arrest me. You know he hated Dad and was frustrated every time he only managed to pin some misdemeanor on him. I'm not saying Dad didn't do stuff that should have sent him to prison, but Sheriff Gibbs could never get any evidence. He wanted so badly to send him to prison, but he never could. That's why he's coming after me."

Lucy said, "Let's forget that nasty man and enjoy some time with your grandparents!"

"Yes, lets. I'm ready! I am so ready to spend time with people who are nice, friendly and family for Thanksgiving."

"Believe me, I am, too! I will gladly forget about that bad encounter and focus on the real reason for this day."

"Yes, it is Thanksgiving, after all and we have lots to be thankful for. These two people we're going to see are one of the best reasons!"

"I'll be glad to get to know them," Leslie added.

TWELVE

Even with their house closed up, Loretta and Jenni could hear what the sheriff said since he was yelling so loudly. It was easy to see his body's actions, even though they missed some because he was on the other side of Joel's car. But it was enough to know he was responding to whatever Joel said and they could see his hands pounding at intervals on the roof. However, they couldn't hear anything of what Joel said. He sat calmly inside the car the entire time.

Loretta looked at Jenni, her eyes full of dread. "Can what he says be true?" Loretta squeaked. "That was awful! Could it be true that he would throw something into the house to make it explode so he could get his money?"

Looking fiercely at her mom, Jenni asked, "You think Joel would be so calm if he was? I doubt it, Mom. Think about it! He'd have to run away from the house like lightning to not be hurt in an explosion! I really have a feeling that Sheriff's trying to get Joel riled. I don't know, maybe he had dealings with Joel's dad and thinks he can pin stuff on him because of his dad. Knowing what little I know about Sheriff Gibbs, I wouldn't be surprised."

"Well, yeah, I suppose. Like I told you, Thad Lawson was a really bad character when we were in high school. Maybe his son…."

"You know," Jenni said, "when somebody's in the wrong they always try to make the other guy look bad. I'm sure that's what the sheriff's trying to do."

Loretta nodded slowly and said, "Yes, that's probably true." Only then realizing what her daughter really said, she gasped, "But the sheriff's the law, wouldn't he be right? Are you sure that's true? Surely Sheriff Gibbs…"

Jenni couldn't believe her mom could be so naïve and looked at her astounded. "Mom, really? He's human! Have you never heard of 'dirty cops'?

In nearly every department across the country there are men and women who'll sell their souls for money. It's on the news a lot!"

"Yeah, I guess I have heard of that happening. But *our* sheriff? In our suburb?" Loretta looked at her daughter shaking her head.

Jenni couldn't believe the denial she saw on her mom's face. "Mom, puleese... give me a break!" Jenni said. "Of course, 'our sheriff' is just as libel to be a 'dirty cop' as the next guy. He's been in that office so long it's not hard to imagine!"

"Oh, no! Surely you're wrong!"

Moments after the sheriff's car roared away Joel backed out of the driveway. Loretta let out a long sigh. Acting as if she hadn't heard Jenni's words at all, Loretta gave another long sigh and said, "There he goes, Jenni! Surely he would have waited if he'd seen you coming out!" Obviously, her obsession with Joel and her need for a husband for her daughter far outweighed any scene the sheriff made.

Wanting a change of subject, Jenni said, "They're probably going to his grandparents' for Thanksgiving. You know, I wish your folks didn't live so far away. I'd love to see them more."

"Maybe we'll get the chance for Christmas. Since your dad has to work today, I think he's scheduled off for Christmas. You've been at the station long enough, surely you can get some time off. You'd need a good long weekend, of course. There's a little time, why don't we work on that? That does sound like a good way to spend Christmas."

"Maybe so, Mom. I'm taking Curly for a walk," she said, pulling her coat from the closet. Curly saw the coat and raced to Jenni's side while she grabbed his leash. As she snapped it on, she said, "Curly lets go for a long walk. It's not a bad day out even without the sun. Maybe we'll smell turkey roasting some place. Maybe you'll see some of your doggy friends. Won't that be cool?" Curly wagged his tail and waited patiently until Jenni had the door open.

"Be sure to be back by two, your dad'll be home and we'll have Thanksgiving Dinner at your favorite restaurant. I'm glad you didn't eat much for breakfast, I know the restaurant has a great spread for Thanksgiving Dinner."

Jenni took a deep breath and stepped outside after Curly without answering her mom. Loretta was treating her like she did as a kid in elementary school! What did she think that Jenni was so fat she couldn't eat a big meal for Thanksgiving? Or that she was so irresponsible she wouldn't come home on this special day? From outside the door she said, "Yes, Mom, I'm remembering. I'm sure I'll be cold before then and we'll be back in plenty of time."

She walked Curly to the street and waited as he did his business. Sometimes she wished they could have family in and could fix a turkey and all the fixin's here. She'd love to smell that turkey roasting. It always made the house smell so good. She wouldn't even mind being part of the preparations, she was a decent cook, just didn't like to.

From the street she and Curly walked on and Jenni pulled in a long breath of the crisp air, and smelled turkey on the breeze. "Curly, it's gonna snow one day soon." Curly wagged his tail and pulled Jenni as fast as she could move toward a fire hydrant. "Yes, get your business done so we can head on around the block. It's Thanksgiving, Curly, but I'm not sure I have much to be thankful for." She sighed. "I missed out on a really handsome man, Curly. I wonder if he has a girlfriend." Curly was pulling and Jenni had to jog to keep up. Her breath came out as steam as she ran. Maybe he was smelling those turkey smells wafting around the neighborhood.

Joel let out a long sigh as he drove away from Lucy's house. Yet another confrontation with Sheriff Gibbs! Would the man ever leave him alone? Yet again, he decided the saga of Thad and Eleanor Lawson wasn't over. He wondered how many more confrontations he would have before it was over. He hoped the adrenalin rush and the negative thoughts were gone when they reached the Lawson's house. It was Thanksgiving Day, not a day for negative thoughts. Thankfully Steve Lawson's house was on the other side of town.

He was glad to get the sheriff out of his hair and also glad he hadn't lost his temper at the outrageous things the man said. *His dad with millions*? *Off-shore accounts*? *Him lob a torch into the house*? *Laughable! All of it!* He'd known for a long time that the sheriff hated his dad. Some times when he reached the pull-off and could see their house, he turned around to head back to town because those were times when the sheriff was there, his lights flashing. Over the years Joel made it a priority not to be in the same place as his dad and Sheriff Gibbs. They were like gasoline and a match! It was anyone's guess which visit whose turn it was to be the gas!

A thought crossed his mind, but then he quickly dismissed it. Still it came back – *Who let that thug know I was at the science building at that time? And to call me 'T Lawson's brat'!* The sheriff really had been at the house in the country many times – maybe it hadn't always been to try to get some dirt on Thad Lawson! Could that possibly be true? Why would the sheriff even think Thad had millions and off-shore accounts? Joel turned into the Lawson's neighborhood and shook himself; he didn't want to think those thoughts anymore.

Lucy and Leslie had agreed to spend Thanksgiving Day at the Lawson's. Lucy wanted to get to know them, they seemed like nice people at the dinner after the memorial service and Leslie was excited to know her other grandparents, they didn't seem anything like her dad who was their son. The Wilsons said they'd come later, probably for the meal and a few hours. However, the three in Joel's car were excited to spend the day getting to know Steve and Mary.

Both of the Lawson's met Joel, Leslie and Lucy at the door. Mary was so excited to see her granddaughter that she threw her arms around her even on the porch. "Oh, Leslie, I'm so happy to meet you and get to know you!" Mary exclaimed.

A bit uncomfortable, since she didn't know the lady and definitely not used to someone hugging her, since her parents never did, Leslie put her arms loosely around her grandmother and gave her a tentative smile. "I… I'm to call you Nana?" she asked.

"Absolutely! I think it's super having a granddaughter… and a grandson! Come on inside, all of you." She kept one arm around Leslie and ushered the others into the house. "It's really cold today! But it's warm in here."

The house was filled with the delicious aroma of roasting turkey. Other delicious smells were added to fill the house, but the turkey, mixed with the warm oven air, put a wonderful essence in the air inside. Joel took an appreciative deep breath and hoped his stomach wouldn't embarrass him before they sat down to the dinner he knew wouldn't be for several hours.

Immediately, Mary commandeered both Lucy and Leslie to the kitchen. With a huge grin, she exclaimed, "Come on, girls, we have a Thanksgiving dinner to get on the table! Oh, you have no idea how terrific it is to have you all here!" Her eyes glistened as she added, "Other years we'd go out to eat. Fixing turkey dinner for two is rather lonesome."

"I'm sure it is, Mary," Lucy said. "I agree, Thanksgiving Day and dinner, especially are meant to spend with family. Now we are and we are all part of God's family."

"Absolutely! It is so wonderful!" Mary agreed. She let out a long sigh. "I hoped for a long time that this day could happen."

Steve walked Joel into the living room. They sat down near each other and Steve asked, "So what's going on in your life, Joel? Are you as busy as a cat on a hot tin roof?"

Making himself comfortable in the upholstered chair, Joel pulled in a deep breath and said, "Of course, I'm doing the usual things, teaching my classes and spending hours in the stacks. My department chairman came by and visited twice at class time and gave me lots of encouragement. One of those times was to tell me he'd received my acceptance of the position offered to me here at the university. He's treating me as if I'm already part of the faculty, but we all know that's not true until I defend my thesis next month. However, I do have my research finished, so now I can concentrate on polishing the finished product."

Steve nodded and said, "Which probably doesn't need that much polishing anyway."

Joel didn't acknowledge that statement, but took another deep breath and said, "However, a week ago Monday a thug greeted me as I tried to leave the science building after teaching my eight o'clock." Steve's mouth dropped open and he sucked in a breath. Joel nodded and continued, "We never exchanged names, well - he called me 'T Lawson's brat', but never said who he was or how he knew who I was. He accused me of being involved in Dad's business and demanded money. He told me that Dad owed 'me and my buddies' money and said I had to pay right then. When I smashed the door in his face, he shot a hole in the door. Security from the building never caught him, but he's never been back. I still wonder how he knew that I'd be at the science building at that time and especially to know my name!"

Steve pulled in a breath. "Wow! He called you T Lawson's brat? What in the world?"

Joel nodded and shook his head, leaned back in the chair, crossed his ankle over his other knee and looked at his granddad. "What happened today might be worse! Just as I got to Aunt Lucy's, Sheriff Gibbs pulled up behind me and whooped his siren for good measure. I can't believe he'd know I'd be there today at that time. I've only been back there a few times since I moved. But he accused me of lobbing a torch into my parents' house that caused the explosion! He said I would to get my hands on the millions that Dad had in off-shore accounts!"

Steve scowled, leaned forward and looked intently at his grandson. "Wow! Sheriff Gibbs – that old coot! I wish he could be fired! Our town needs to get rid of him! So I guess things haven't been quiet. Here I thought once the memorial service was over that would be it."

Joel shook his head. "No, not at all, Granddad! I had that wrong idea too. I don't know about Les, but I was hoping that was true. Really, for her sake, I hope all this harassment has been aimed at me and none of it at her! She's had a hard time just coping with the explosion and our parents being gone! And the night before, Dad had abused her twice before she went to bed! I'm glad I was so close to being finished with my dissertation before all this happened. It's been sorta hard to concentrate, if you know what I mean."

Steve nodded. "Yes, I'm sure!"

"I have finished all my research, and last night I put the final period at the end of what I intend to write. Now I'm starting on revising what I've written so I can get it printed and give copies to my committee. They have me scheduled for the presentation the Friday before Christmas break. I'm so thankful I can do that revising at my apartment where it's quiet."

Steve cleared his throat. "Would you make me a copy, Joel? I'd really love to read what you've worked so hard on for this degree. Since I've never had the chance to hear or read anything else you've written or presented, it would be an honor."

"Sure, Granddad! That's no problem." He grinned at the older man. "What's one more ream of paper among friends?"

Steve grinned. "Yes, indeed!" Steve's expression changed and he asked, "Tell me, Joel, if you'd lobbed a torch into the basement and the house exploded, wouldn't you have gone up with the house? How could you have gotten far enough away from the house in time?"

Joel put his elbows on the arms of the chair and rested his fingers against his chin before he said, "Yes, you're right, Granddad! I can run pretty fast, but not that fast. And here I stand, without a singed hair anywhere on my body!"

Steve nodded. "That's kinda what I thought. Like I say, that man needs to retire or get fired! No more friends than he has I can't imagine how he got reelected this last time!"

"Yes, Granddad, I'm with you on that!"

Evi sat at her kitchen table Thanksgiving morning, drinking her coffee and wondering what to do for the day. Where she sat gave her a view out her patio door so she could see any activity on the parking lot. She still had on her night shirt and had no idea what to do with twenty-four hours of down time. She fudged a little on two patients and sent them home a bit early since it was Thanksgiving. The two worst patients in the Unit that she couldn't release didn't need a visit today, but would need attention tomorrow. Often she wished for another burn professional who could take on some of the tasks a specialist didn't have to do. Maybe, if she could train whoever, they could do some of the initial evals. She knew a PA could also do some of the on-going work each burn patient needed as well – like what she would do tomorrow.

If she'd had more time off, or had someone else who could take on some of the work, she could have flown to Bangor for the long weekend with her family. She was sure she'd be the only one absent from the big dinner her mom always fixed. Now that she'd finished her training, her family counted on her coming home, but it wouldn't happen - not this Thanksgiving. If someone at the hospital didn't take on some of the tasks, she wouldn't get home for Christmas. She hadn't gotten home at all in the years of her residency and clinicals. That had been a very long time. She had seen her brother, he'd come to see her on a week's vacation.

While she sat at the table and looked out the patio door, Joel left his apartment. Before he reached his car a gust of wind blew his sandy blond hair. He looked mussed up enough to be kissable… She sighed and took another sip of her cooling coffee. She knew he had family, he'd told her that, and the news on the TV said he and his sister would live with family now that his parents' house had exploded. He was probably going to spend the day with his family.

As he got into his car she guessed that since he lived here alone that his sister still lived with her family. How old was she? She'd never seen the girl or woman. Was she as pretty as he was handsome? She took a deep breath and let it out, then finished off her cold coffee and made a face at the mug. Cold coffee left a lot to be desired.

A few days ago they met at their cars again, and decided when to leave for downtown on Saturday. She'd supply the car for the drive. Joel had assured her that it was easier from this suburb to drive downtown to the Convention Center than to take the interurban train and make a transfer to reach the place. She didn't know that, but she took his word for it, since this was his home town. Of course, neither mentioned they'd be in evening attire and a long train ride would be inappropriate. She still had to get said 'evening attire'. She sighed, looked into the empty cup and shook her head. Going alone to shop for evening wear sucked, big time!

She finally stood, put her mug on top of her dirty dishes, and took her little pile to the sink. Tomorrow was black Friday, perhaps after seeing to her patients, she'd join the crowds and go to some department stores to find something to wear to the reception. Black Friday was never a favorite day of hers. She hated waiting in line and then watching something she wanted disappear as someone snatched whatever it was off the rack ahead of her.

"Maybe I'll find something on sale that I can wear again. That and a pair of shoes…."

Still wondering what to do with her day, her cell phone rang. Since she was in her nightshirt, that didn't have a pocket, she had to hunt for it. Finding it in her bedroom and hoping it wasn't the hospital, she answered glad to see it was a friend from her teaching hospital. "Allison! Wow! It's great to hear from you! We haven't talked in forever!"

"Hey, Girl, are you alone today just like me?"

Evi sighed and said, "Yes, I have two patients I couldn't leave for four days, while I flew to Maine for the holiday. I'm here and you're all alone today, too? Wanna get together for the afternoon and have that turkey dinner?" She went back to the kitchen splashed water in her mug, and said, "Yeah, spending Thanksgiving alone sucks!"

Evi's friend chuckled. "That was kinda why I called you, girl. It seems really bad to be alone on Thanksgiving, doesn't it?"

"Oh, for sure! Hey, you'll need to give me a minute; I'm still in my nightshirt! Believe me, I will not appear anywhere in public in this thing!"

Allison giggled. "Hey, no problem, so am I! It's the same one you wore in school?"

"Uh huh."

"Umm, yes, that one…"

"Yeah, that one that needed retiring *before* I came to med school!"

Allison chuckled. "Yeah, I remember."

Evi and Allison decided to meet at the mall that was half way between their two homes, at one time it was a regular haunt for them. They were intent on sharing - time together, gossip about mutual friends and a big meal. They would meet close to the restaurant where they'd eat. However, when they parked and left their cars, the aroma coming from the restaurant nearly took them in right then. Standing on the parking lot, they ran to each other and hugged then took a big sniff, the wonderful aroma engulfing them. They nearly ran to another entrance so they weren't tempted so early in the day. After all, who could make a dent in shopping on a full stomach? Not two single girls, intent on window shopping throughout the mall!

They knew many of the stores were closed, some because it was the holiday, but others had people working because tomorrow was 'black Friday'. However, there was a boutique across the promenade from the entrance they came in that was open and had a lovely evening gown displayed. Evi gravitated to it and her friend said, "Evi? What's with the interest in that gown? Thought you wore scrubs most of the time or that great sterile outfit you love so much."

Evi looked at her friend disgusted and said, "You have got to be kidding! Girl, you are out of your mind!"

Evi sank onto a bench, but turned so she could see the gown in the window. Allison saw where she looked and sat beside her. After a minute when Evi stared at the gown but said nothing, Allison said, "Okay, spill, girl. What's going on? What's with that longing look?" When Evi didn't answer, Allison said, with a twinkle in her eyes, "Ah, do I detect a man issue?"

Evi sighed and said, "Yes, you guessed right. It started a couple of weeks ago."

When Evi didn't add anything right away, Allison said, "Okay, it's like pulling teeth, here! Come on, spill!"

Acting uncomfortable, Evi finally took a deep breath and said, "Well, this guy's dad was burned so badly that he died maybe forty-five minutes after I did his eval, but I talked with his son. He seemed really nice and quite interested and asked intelligent questions about his dad. Then a couple of days later one of the doctors I've met told me about him. Impressive!"

"O-o-kay..." Allison made hand motions, trying to speed things along.

"Well, anyway, now this guy's my neighbor..."

"Is he cute?"

"Allison, you wouldn't be-lieeeeve!"

Allison chuckled and drew one leg up onto the bench. "Ah, so, we're talking about the drool department! So what's with a formal gown? Your first date's to some formal shindig?"

Evi looked down at her hands, then back at the lovely gown and muttered, "Well, umm, it's not really a date..."

Allison scowled, truly bewildered. "Evi, you're thinking about buying a formal for 'not really a date'? Clue me in here, girl! Why on earth would you buy a formal gown for 'not really a date'? You have got me totally bumfuzzled."

Evi's eyes strayed to the beautiful gown and she sighed. "Okay, it's like this. Umm, Joel's almost a professor at the university close to where I live. He'll defend his doctoral thesis before Christmas. His chairman asked him to go to the reception for the new Chief of Staff of my hospital." Evi raised her hands then let them fall as if she had no choice. "I'm supposed to go to this thing. It's formal and we're going together, since we're neighbors."

"Ah, I see, so you're not really going on a date, but you're really going on a date to this reception. Is that what I'm hearing?"

Evi nodded. "Yeah, but it's formal, so I need to get a formal."

Allison stood up and held out her hand. "So, come on, the store's open, let's go get that formal from there in the window! There's a clerk, what's keeping you?"

"And shoes..." Evi added.

"Well, of course! You can't wear tennies with a formal gown!" Finally, Allison had Evi grinning as she stood up.

After spending some time in the boutique trying on the formal and buying shoes - totally inappropriate shoes for November, Allison and Evi, lugged the big clothes bag all over the mall for several hours. They were afraid that if they went out to put them in Evi's car that they'd eat too soon. They hardly resisted the aroma before, now the temptation would be worse.

Finally, several hours later, they stood in line at the restaurant with the awesome aroma waiting to be seated for their Thanksgiving dinner. The line included several families, but finally, it was their turn and the host led them to a booth. All the seats were full of people enjoying their dinners as Evi stuffed the clothes bag in ahead of her on the bench and Allison laid a much smaller bag with a shoe box in it on her seat.

They sat down and the host handed them menus. He smiled at the two pretty women and said, "Your server will be here shortly, ladies. Would you ladies like some wine with your meal? I can get you a wine list if you'd like."

"Umm, no thanks," Evi answered, knowing that would be something extra beside the price of the meal. She couldn't afford that. Seeing the price tag on the gown and add the price of special shoes made her gulp, she knew she couldn't make two loan payments let alone splurge on a bottle of wine to go with the Thanksgiving dinner she had to pay for. Life as a newly graduated medical professional left most physicians nearly destitute.

They took a few minutes to check the menus, but Allison laid hers down and said, "So, tell me about this Joel guy you're not going on a date with."

Evi grinned and laid her own menu down, what was there to order if you planned to get Thanksgiving dinner with all the fixin's? "You really are stuck on that, aren't you?"

Allison grinned and shrugged at her friend. "Well, it does seem sort of silly how stuck you are on saying you're not going on a date when you really are. Anyway, tell me about this guy, he's obviously made an impression on you."

"Yes, he really has."

"So-o-o-o-o? You say he's really handsome, obviously he's really intelligent, so come on, spill already!"

Evi grabbed the salt shaker and shifted it back and forth between her hands. She watched her hands as she said, "Like I said, I met him there at the hospital because his dad was so bad. I mean, he almost died on the way to the hospital! His blood pressure nearly bottomed out. Did you hear about a house exploding a while ago?"

"Uh huh…."

Evi tossed the salt shaker back and forth and didn't look at her friend. "Well, it was his dad. The man was comatose when he arrived. He never woke up while I did the eval. Oh, he… he had burns everywhere on his body! When I wrote up my eval I had to say his burns covered a hundred percent of his body. I wasn't sure they were fire burns, maybe they were chemical burns, but I couldn't imagine how the paramedic got an IV going!"

Allison made a motion like she was pulling her own teeth and said, "O-kay... Girl, in case you can't tell, it's not the man but the son I wanna know about. Why in the world are you taking so long to tell me about this Joel guy?"

Evi pulled in a deep breath and said, "Well, Joel really impressed me at our apartments the other day. He thanked me for letting him spend time with his dad before he died."

Allison scowled and asked, "Why should he thank you for something like that? Clue me in here. Isn't family encouraged to spend the last minutes with their dying relative? Most families feel like it's an obligation they must do!"

"Yes, that's true." Evi glanced at her friend, then at the shaker and tossed it back and forth again. "But..., he asked specifically if he could. Any more, I don't mention it, quite a few don't want to watch a family member die, but they feel obligated. I know it's hard and people aren't geared for things like that. And someone grotesque with burns... As soon as we finished talking, he sort of ran from the cafeteria to the elevator! I asked him there at the apartments why. My friend told me that Joel's dad was really a bad guy and beat his son with a belt. He threw him out of the house the night before the explosion! I wondered why Joel was so concerned and wanted to stay until his dad died. Lots of children wouldn't want to stay for less than that!"

"Yes, I know that's true."

"But Joel told me the other day that just before he breathed his last, his dad woke up and clearly told him he believed that Jesus died for him. Joel was thrilled!"

Allison's face lit up and she clapped her hands once, before she exclaimed, "Wow! Awesome! If that was the kind of man he was, it is awesome and Joel had good reason to be thrilled! Oh, wow! That thrills me, too! A death-bed decision for Christ, how awesome! That would be a once in a lifetime experience!"

The server finally arrived and quickly the girls gave their order for the real deal on the turkey dinner. The server took the menus, but Evi hardly noticed. The instant he stepped away, she folded her arms on the table, stared at her friend really perplexed, while she asked, "Why?"

"Why do I think it's awesome? Why was Joel thrilled?"

"Yes."

Allison's eyes were shining and her smile spread across her face. "Actually, the answer to both questions is the same, Evi. I believe God woke the man up so he could tell his son that he believed God's Son died on a cross to take his sins away so that he could go to heaven. Joel is obviously a Christian, so that knowledge thrilled him. I'm thrilled, even though I don't know them, because that means one more soul is in heaven and not in the awful place called Hell."

Evi waited a few seconds and tossed the salt shaker back and forth again. Perhaps she didn't know whether Allison would say anything else. "That's important?"

Allison placed her hand on Evi's arm. Evi looked at Allison's hand, then to her face. Seriously Allison nodded and said, "Evi, it's so important! We're never guaranteed one more breath. You know that! In the field we're in, you've had to deal with the death of a patient and the family experiencing it. Do you know for sure that when you die that you'd go to heaven?"

"Well, no, can anybody know that?"

Excitedly, Allison answered, "Sure! Oh, Evi, of course! If you realize that you've done bad stuff in your life and it bothers your conscience; that means you know you're a sinner. Jesus, who is also God, died on a cross just so He could take all those sins we've done and cover them with His blood. Because of that, God says you're forgiven of your sins and you can spend forever and ever in Heaven and don't have to go to an awful place called Hell."

Allison pulled in a breath. "You see, Joel knew by his dad's actions and words all during his life that he wasn't going to heaven, but after he said he knew Jesus died for him, the man had accepted God's gift of forgiveness and could go to heaven. Evi, that's *awesome*!"

Evi sat and thought about it for several minutes before she said, "I see, but I need to do that, too? I haven't been a *bad* person."

"No, but you have done sinful things just like I have. If you've cheated on one exam or lied to someone, God says you're a sinner. Evi, everyone has done stuff like that. It's how we naturally live our lives, but a while ago, somebody showed me how wrong that was and I accepted God's gift of forgiveness, so I know I'm going to heaven. That's all you have to do, Evi, is accept God's gift of forgiveness for your sins and you can go to heaven!"

Evi nodded, "Help me?"

"Of course! I'd love to, girl!"

The two girls still had their heads bowed when the server brought their meals. He cleared his throat and Evi was the first to raise her head, but Allison's was only seconds later. They both had huge smiles for the server, but

Evi's completely covered her face, she pulled her hands off the table and said, "Super! You've got our dinners. It smells good, just like the smell outside."

The server smiled and said, "Yes, Ma'am! Enjoy!"

"We will!" Allison answered.

Both girls dug into the meal that covered their platter-sized plates. The turkey and dressing sent out that delicious aroma and both girls were quiet for several minutes as they cut into their meat. Neither one said much until they picked up their napkins, wiped their mouths and breathed out a great sigh of satisfaction. Thanksgiving dinner was always good and it surely wasn't meant to be eaten alone. However, today for Evi was a day she'd never forget.

When the waiter came back, he took their plates and they ordered pumpkin pie and coffee. Evi even splurged and ordered a dollop of whipped cream on her pie. After savoring the first mouthful of the delicious pie, Evi said, "Mmmm, that is soooo good! Allison, aren't you almost through with your studies? Your clinicals or do you have more?" Evi didn't know she'd touched a bad place in Allison's life. Immediately she saw tears glisten in her eyes and was unhappy that she'd caused them. "Oh, Alli! I'm so sorry!"

However, Allison swallowed and said, "Pretty much, but I have more than a year to finish. I'll have to get another loan to finish. Dad said they can't help me anymore; I must either take out a loan big enough to cover everything or drop out for a while. I hate the thought, but there isn't a thing I can do. Mom and Dad aren't made of money and med school isn't cheap!"

Evi's cup rattled and nearly toppled as she put it haphazardly on the table. She grabbed for her friend's hand and squeezed it, as she exclaimed, "Allison! How perfect! Well, no, for you that is heartbreaking, but really, only this morning I was wishing for a PA who could split some of the work with me! I'm on call twenty-four/seven and nobody in the ER evaluates a burn patient. I can't imagine what they did before I came! Surely somebody made some kind of assessment even if all they did was send the patient on to another hospital!"

Evi shook her head. "It doesn't matter what time, day or night when they come in! I'd barely gotten out of the shower the other morning when I got a text that they had a burn patient. She wasn't critical; they could have at least cleaned her up! The only reason I had to stay in town this weekend, well besides the gala, was the two patients in the unit I need to see tomorrow. You know a specialist doesn't have to do that, a PA easily could. What do you say?"

"You could hire me?" Allison asked dubiously.

"I'd have to run it by the powers-that-be, but as I said, I'm pretty much on my own."

"Well, go ahead. As it is now, I sure can't finish without something changing."

"I'll put in that word tomorrow!"

Allison smiled at her friend. "That's great, Evi, thanks."

"Hey, it'll benefit me as much as it will you, you know!"

Joel and Leslie ate a marvelous Thanksgiving dinner with their aunt and two sets of grandparents. The meal lived up to the aromas. Because they all ate so much, they decided to wait for dessert. Besides, Steve knew there was football on TV. Of course, Lucy, Claudia and Mary weren't that interested, but after they cleared the table, put left-overs away, loaded the dishwasher and washed up what pans were dirty, they joined the men in the large living room for an afternoon of getting acquainted. The men even muted the football game!

It was sad that Thad refused to let his children know his parents, but now the restrictions were gone. Steve and Mary had a super day. Several times Mary caught herself daydreaming as she looked at her grandchildren. It was a privilege to have them in her home. Many times over the years she'd wondered how they grew up. With her son in trouble so much, she wondered how his children were raised. She was thrilled at the memorial service when she met the two finest young people she could hope for and to know they were her grandchildren. It was icing on the cake when the pastor told about Thad's death-bed confession and that Joel was responsible.

It was much later, when Mary, Claudia and Lucy decided that enough time had passed for dinner to settle and went to the kitchen. Mary started coffee through her coffee maker, hoping to cover the noises the ladies made getting dessert ready. They whispered as Lucy went to the freezer for the ice cream cake Claudia had brought. Fortunately, Ed was a bit hard of hearing and the men had to speak up for him. However, the two granddads knew what was going on.

Claudia found a basket and heaped several colorful presents in it. By the time the coffee was done, Mary had some colorful mugs and cream and sugar on a tray. Lucy found another tray, some plates that matched the dinner plates and had pushed twenty-six candles into the cake. She carefully put the beautiful cake on the tray and lit the candles. They conspiratorially grinned, and lined up, each holding their burden and decided it was time to crash the discussion in the living room between three men and Leslie. Leslie didn't know about what was to come.

"... Happy birthday, Jo-el, happy birthday to you!" everyone in the room sang the song the ladies started when they entered.

His mouth hanging open, Joel looked at the little procession. When he was able to get enough air to let words come out of his mouth, he exclaimed, "Wow! You guys are amazing! You guys remembered that today is my birthday!"

"But of course!" Joel's grampa exclaimed.

Joel looked at the three ladies and realized he'd been the one to pass the invitation around, so he said, "You were all in on this! How did you..."

Claudia looked at her grandson and tisked her tongue. As she set the basket of presents beside his chair, she said, "Young man, I have a phone and I know how to use it. Since we knew about the invitation, we've talked back and forth. I must admit it's harder with cell phones than looking in a phone book for the land line, but it can be done. I've always said, 'Where there's a will, there's a way.' And there was a will! So let's be about this cake before it melts. Make your wish right quick and blow out the candles!"

Joel looked at the beautiful cake, there were twenty-six candles stuck in amongst some colorful flowers and in the center Joel's name was written in bold, red, stylized letters.

As Claudia mentioned, the candles were burning, so Joel said, "Yes, Gramma, I'll do that." He sighed, "But you know, it gets harder each year."

"Humph!" Ed exclaimed.

Joel took a deep breath and blew. All the candles went out, but then he grinned and asked, "Why the sigh, Grampa? You don't think it's harder to blow out the candles each year?"

"I'm glad we gave up that foolishness at our house years ago," he groused.

Having fun at his serious granddad's expense, he turned to his gramma and said, "Gramma! Don't you put candles on Grampa's birthday cakes each year?"

"Joel," she answered, very seriously, "do you truly want to get me kicked out of my bedroom on July fifteenth next year?"

Still with a twinkle in his eyes, Joel said, "Well, no, now that you mention it, Gramma. So it's that serious! Wow!"

"Oh, yes!"

"Well, I feel for you, Gramma! That would be a sad way to spend Grampa's birthday."

"Absolutely!"

Mary filled all the mugs and handed them out. Claudia cut the cake and as they ate it, Joel opened the presents that his family had gotten for him. He looked around to each one with tears glistening in his eyes and whispered, "You folks know that this is the first birthday celebration I've ever had! Each one of you... you are all wonderful people! I thank you so much for your love for me. I'm overwhelmed!"

Mary had tears trailing down her face. She was too choked up to speak, but Steve, his eyes also glistening, said, "Son, you're an incredible young man! It isn't every young person who tries so hard to overcome such hardships as you've had! It is our pleasure."

Joel swallowed and whispered, "Thank you, Granddad, thank you."

After they finished eating the ice cream cake, Mary brought a carafe full of coffee that had finished brewing and poured the three men a second cup, then the four ladies took the other dishes to the kitchen to clean up. Leslie went with them this time. By now there was another football game on the TV, but nobody was interested, so Steve turned it off.

THIRTEEN

THE MEN STAYED IN THE LIVING ROOM SIPPING THEIR COFFEE AND ED ASKED, "So, don't I recall that the university's pretty much closed down this week? What have you been doing with all that spare time, Son?" Ed grinned, knowing his grandson wouldn't be lazy.

"Grampa, I won't have any until Christmas break! I've finished writing my thesis, but I must revise it to its final form and now that I have my own apartment I'm doing that all week. It's tedious, I've read it through so many times, but I must have it perfect so it'll be accepted the first time. My appointment to defend my thesis is the Friday that Christmas break starts. I should get it done and printed before that. My department head and my committee chairman have told me it'll be published and on the university book shelves before next school year."

"Wow! That's spectacular, Joel!"

"Grampa, it's daunting!"

Joel added, "The other thing going on this week, my department chairman invited me to a reception for the new Chief of Staff for our local hospital on Saturday, so I must use tomorrow to rent a tux. Since I don't have one, my chairman told me I can rent one for not too much."

"Rent you a tux?" Steve asked.

"Yes, this reception is formal, and happening at the big Convention Center downtown. From what my Chair said, I'm to wear a tux and take a guest. I don't have a tux or ever had a reason to get one. My neighbor is a doctor at the hospital, so we're going together."

"Your neighbor…" Steve grinned at his grandson. "Are you talking about that lovely lady next door to you?"

Joel felt his cheeks warm as he said, "Yes, Granddad, Evi and I are going together. Of course, being employed at that hospital, she is expected to go."

"You need a tux." Steve motioned Joel to stand and said, "Stand up, let's see what's up. Maybe we can find a remedy for the tux problem." Joel stood up, but Steve also stood and looked Joel up and down, taking in his broad shoulders and narrow waist, his height, everything. "Just as I thought. We're almost the same size. Let's go down the hall a minute. I have a perfectly good tux I haven't worn in a while and those things never go out of fashion. There's no reason why you can't have it. I'll bet you'll need such a thing several more times before I will. Once you're on the faculty you'll be out at public events much more often."

"Granddad, I couldn't possibly…!"

"Well, you can to!" he interrupted. "Come on, I know right where this thing is and we'll get you outfitted right away!"

Ed brought his feet under him and stood up, picked up his coffee cup and exclaimed, "Sounds good to me! Get on down the hall, Son."

"Grampa," Joel whispered, "you're not even on my side!"

Ed chuckled. "Hey, take what he offers! You won't have to spend money to rent one."

"Okay," Joel said, reluctantly.

All three men carried their cups of coffee as Steve led Joel and Ed down the hall to a massive bedroom. Joel had never seen a bedroom so huge. Inside the room, Steve went to a door and opened it into a walk-in closet. He turned to the men, waved his hand at a grouping of chairs and said, "Have a seat wherever until I find that thing so Joel can try it on."

Joel and Ed found seats in a grouping by the window while Steve flipped on a light in the closet and started shoving clothes back and forth. Joel tried to hide behind his coffee mug. He took a sip, but then held the mug in front of his face. His right leg wanted to bounce, but he planted his heel firmly on the floor. He might be nervous, but he was twenty-six years old today!

A few minutes later, Steve came from the closet carrying a large clothes bag. He grinned at the uncomfortable young man and said, "Come on, Joel, shed you stuff and try this on. Let's see what a handsome man looks like in a tux!"

Totally embarrassed, his cheeks flaming, Joel had never shed his clothes in front of anyone, especially his granddads. Joel set down his mug on the little table, stood and quickly shed his jeans and sweatshirt. At the same time, Steve unzipped the clothes bag and pulled out the hangers holding the black suit, snowy white shirt with ruffles and long sleeves and a black tie. Down in the bottom of the bag he fished out a black cummerbund that would complete the outfit and let the clothes bag fall to the floor. Again he grinned at the uncomfortable young man.

Seeing the black strip of cloth in Steve's hand, Joel asked, "What is that thing, Granddad? I'm to wear that, too?" He grabbed the pants and pulled them on.

Ed chuckled and said, "Son some of us need that to hold parts that expand so they aren't as obvious when we get past your age. At your age, it'll only finish out a picture of perfection."

Joel's cheeks bloomed darker, as he said, "Will you guys stop! I'm really embarrassed!"

"No need, go on, suit up!" Steve exclaimed.

Steve handed Joel the shirt and helped him button it, since the lacy strips down the front hid the buttonholes. After Joel pushed the shirttails down, he pulled the pants into place and fastened them. Steve still held the cummerbund, so he stepped behind Joel, put the pleated material around his middle and fastened it in the back, adjusting it over the trousers. So far, everything fit perfectly. Still grinning, Steve handed Joel the bowtie and watched him use the mirror over the dresser to put it under the small collar and then adjust it. Last of all, he grinned and handed Joel the jacket and buttoned the one button, then smoothed down the shiny lapels.

Joel's cheeks were still flaming as he looked at the finished product in the mirror. He pulled in a deep breath, pulled his hand down across his face and continued to stare at his image, but lifted his eyes and looked at the men in the room. Finally, he turned around and said, "Granddad, I feel totally out of my element here! I'm to wear this thing for a whole evening?"

Ed laughed. "I guarantee they won't let you take it off half way through, Son! I must admit, you do look dashing!"

"Thanks, Grampa, I needed that," Joel muttered.

"Come on!" Steve said and picked up his coffee mug, heading for the door, "Let's go show those ladies what a handsome man looks like!"

All Joel could do was groan. "Oh, Granddad!"

Pushing Joel ahead of them, the three men walked back into the living room just as the ladies came back in from the kitchen, holding their own cups of coffee. "Oh, my word!" Mary said. "Look at this handsome man! Girls, what do you say?"

"I'd say it's a sin for a man to look so good!" Claudia answered. She held her mug and sank into one of the chairs.

"Well, maybe not a sin," Mary said. "But, my word, you do look dashing! I declare you will be the prince of the ball!"

Under his breath, Joel said, "I think it's a sin that a guy has to wear such a thing! Gramma, I have lots of suits, I even have a black one I could wear!"

"Now that is not true!" Steve exclaimed, since he stood so close to Joel and heard what he said. "Every man has the right to be dressed up fit to kill a room full of lovely ladies! Don't you agree, Ed? They want to do it to us men all the time!"

"I sure do! I agree totally! Joel, as they say, you will knock their socks off! That outfit is grand and don't you say it isn't, young man!"

Joel sank into the chair where he sat before they went hunting for the tux and said, "Grampa, I'm only going as Evi's escort. I'm just a TA, I don't have my PhD yet, really… This whole thing is way out of my league! I mean, do you know how many dates I've ever had?"

Steve's heart clenched, hearing what his grandson said, but he exclaimed, "No matter, you will do that university up proud! I guarantee it!"

Joel groaned again, "Oh, my!"

Leslie came to her brother, looked at him in adoration and whispered, "Bro, you're the most handsome man I know!"

Joel breathed out a sigh. "Thanks, Sis."

Joel didn't like being the center of attention, even though he was with his family. Really wanting to hide, Joel raised the cup to his face. Then showing how uncomfortable he was; set the full cup down on the table beside his chair without taking a sip. He looked around at the others, then sprang from the chair and rushed back to the bedroom and shed the tux. He quickly put his comfortable clothes back on, gathered up the clothes bag to put the tux back in the bag.

"Thank goodness we're driving a car to the reception!" he muttered and shook his head. "Riding the train in something like this would… well, it'd be unconscionable!"

He'd barely whispered the words when Steve stood in the doorway and said, "Now then, young man, you are to put that in your car and take it home! I do not want it back."

"Granddad!"

Steve nodded emphatically. "Yes, sir, you will be the talk of the city! I guarantee it and I for one, cannot tell you how proud I am of my grandson!"

"Thanks, Granddad," he said, humbly. He carefully put the shirt on a hanger and the black suit on another, then put them both back in the clothes bag. He hung the bag on the doorknob, since Steve had closed the closet door.

Under protest, a half hour later, he laid the clothes bag inside the trunk and carefully put his presents beside it, while Lucy and Leslie got in the car for Joel to take them home. He climbed behind the wheel as Ed helped his wife into their car and Steve and Mary stood on their porch and waved. Joel was quick to admit that he hadn't enjoyed a holiday this much as long as he could remember. Steve and Mary knew they would be cherishing this day for a long time.

Joel pulled into the driveway beside Lucy's house and saw the light in Jenni's room. He missed the late night talks they'd had when he lived with Lucy and he wondered how she was doing. Now that he lived across town he doubted he'd see her again. However, whatever happened was out of his hands. Lucy and Leslie opened their doors, said goodnight and hurried into the house. Joel waved to them and backed out; he still had to get across town to his place.

Joel woke up Friday morning to a reality. Because of who and what his parents were, he hadn't dated in his twenty-six years. Friends in high school and college told him about their experiences and exploits, on dates, youth activities and double dates. He chalked that up to good information. Even so, he wondered what his plan for his date with Evi should be. Would she expect flowers? Should he ask her what she'd wear? How could he do that? Did a guy rush up to a lady's place, knock on the door and ask what she'd wear? Probably not!

As he started his coffee he knew he had many more questions than answers. He had no idea where to get the answers. He wished the lady he would escort to the gala was more than a passing acquaintance. They'd had one meaningful conversation! That was at the hospital when she told him his dad would die very shortly, the first time they'd met. That was not something you based a date on! They had communicated in Evi's professional position and this reception was certainly not in that role, other than it was her hospital that was sponsoring the reception and she needed to go because she was staff and he because his chairman had invited him. He chuckled; their conversations were peppered with words and noises about their growling stomachs! The last two times they barely spoke about going to this gala.

It was barely light Friday morning, but he'd showered and dressed before he opened his drape. He was astonished to see movement outside. He moved so he could see better and saw Evi going to her car in her usual jeans and smart-looking coat. Incredulous, Joel muttered, "Is she going to work? All I ever knew people to do Friday after Thanksgiving was stand in line at stores to find a bargain! It's too early for that. Well, no, from what I've heard, foolish people line up and wait for hours for bargains on black Friday! Really, what is the point of that?"

Before he could get his brain to function sensibly, she was in her car and gone. She hadn't seen him; at least she hadn't looked in his direction. Joel shook his head, filled his mug with the last of the coffee and headed for his desk. He needed to do more revision work. If Evi was gone, all the more reason to concentrate on his writing. After all, at this point in his life it was the all important subject. He had to get it into perfect shape the first time.

There were people counting on him to do that. He still couldn't put his mind around what Fred Winsted told him about the scientists interested in his work. He only knew of one other science department who had any interest in him. Even more incredible was that someone wanted him for a lecture series! Right now he wondered how you put together a lecture series. Before that became a reality he needed to ask Fred how to do that and what he needed to do for it.

Some time later, he leaned back in the desk chair to think and rest his eyes. He raised his cup, but saw that it was empty and dry. He'd been working for hours, but the sky outside hadn't gotten very much lighter since he'd sat at his desk. Just for the exercise he got up and made another pot of coffee, then filled his mug and went to his patio door to look out at the gloomy day for some diversion and sipped from his mug, then went back to the desk.

He looked at the words on the little screen. Fred Winsted told him that his thesis committee chairman had already engaged a publisher to get his thesis into book form before the start of the new school year! He had until the middle of December of this year to get his thesis finished and the publisher would have it into book form before the end of August next year?

"Amazing!" Joel exclaimed. "Totally amazing!" Joel could hardly put his mind around that thought. He, the son of a man who barely scraped through to graduate from high school, because he didn't want to be there, a published author! Another thought nearly boggled his mind. In only days he'd defend his thesis for his PhD and become a professor at a University known throughout the country!

Evi left her apartment at day break Friday morning and noticed that Joel's drape was open and the light was on over his table. Of course, she didn't turn her head to look into his apartment – not to see if he was there – of course not! It was the day after Thanksgiving! Why on earth would he be up already? She knew institutions of higher learning in the mega-city were all closed for the holiday. They might not have been closed for the week, but surely they were closed from Thanksgiving through the weekend! Why was Joel up so early?

"Maybe I'll ask him tomorrow on our long drive downtown." She cleared her throat and inserted the key in the car door lock. "And maybe not…"

Evi was so enthused when she talked with Allison about being a PA that without even thinking about the date or time, she called her own boss at home last evening when she got home from her time with Allison to see about hiring her. Surprising Evi totally, the doctor asked that she and Allison come to his office to talk today. He told Evi since it was the day after the holiday and the hospital population was low because only those who were too sick to go home were there; it was a good day for a long talk. He would only tell Evi that they'd talk, not that he'd hire Allison. Evi knew that each hospital had a board of directors who had to give the okay to create a new position at the hospital, but having a long talk with her boss was a good start.

Evi quickly called Allison, they decided to meet for early morning coffee and strategy talk then meet with the doctor. Both Evi and Allison hoped the long interview would result in a job for Allison. Evi was determined to do all she could to create a position for Allison – she must convince the man how very much their hospital needed another professional in the burn department. After that she must see her two burn patients and make sure they were doing well.

As she left her car in the doctor's parking lot she muttered, "Yes, a PA could do that, too. If I'd had one already I could have gone home."

During the late afternoon Joel looked up from his lap-top to look out his large patio door at the gray clouds hovering and had an inspiration. He was tired of working through his thesis for so many hours and decided to take a break. Over the months, every time he added something to his work he'd read through what he'd written, so now it nearly put him to sleep. He would do it, but it might take a while. He closed his computer and stood to stretch. It felt good!

In the kitchen he pulled out his trusty cookbook that he splurged on the Friday after he moved in and paged through the index. Nana had given him a plateful of left-over turkey that he was sure he could make into dinner for two. He found a recipe he thought he could handle and started in, but at the same time looked out the patio door. Who knew when Evi would get home on the Friday after Thanksgiving Day? She left so early on a usually lazy day.

It was barely light out, she'd been gone all day and he almost missed her. He rushed to his patio door, opened it and called, "Evi, have you eaten yet?"

"No, I'm on my way in to see what's on the menu."

"Hey, instead come have dinner with me. My nana gave me so much turkey to bring home I know I can't eat it all. Will you join me?"

"Really?"

"Oh, yes!"

"Well, give me a minute and I'll be back."

"Great, just come on in."

The minute Joel stepped back into his apartment Evi wanted to take back her acceptance. With her hand shaking, she pushed her key in the door and walked into her silent apartment. Excuses bombarded her. She was tired... her hair needed washing... they didn't know each other very well... what could she wear...? she didn't have anything she could take... she was a nervous wreck! She was sure there were many more things that if she took enough time, she could beg out of accepting Joel's invitation. After all, they were going together tomorrow... night! ...to a gala! "Girl, you are twenty-nine years old! Buck up!"

She shed her coat and looked at herself in the mirror on the back of the closet door. "Oh, my! Don't I look a wreck!" However, she went in her bedroom, found a clean pair of jeans, her newest and favorite sweatshirt and hurried to the shower. After a relaxing shower, she put on her clean clothes, slipped on a pair of shoes – not tennies - and combed out her hair, added a little make-up and went back for her coat.

As she pulled it on, she said sternly, "Evi, Joel is just a man! He will not poison you. You are going for dinner in his apartment, because he has invited you. It's a good way to get to know your neighbor! Nothing will happen, the drape will be open. Woman, you are twenty-nine years old, come on! Chin up! Shoulders back! You are not a wimp! Hutt! One... two...three... four...!" She buttoned her coat and marched out the door to her patio.

Joel set his table for two, nothing fancy, but the glasses of ice water did sparkle. The Wilson's had given him a lovely set of dishes as a house-warming present and these he'd placed correctly on the table. He told himself he wasn't anxious for her to come, but he stood to the side of his patio door so he could see when she came out onto her deck.

His heart gave a lurch when her door opened and the light back-lit her gorgeous blond hair. His smile spread as she walked across her deck, down the step, across the narrow grass strip then climbed his step. He pulled the door open and exclaimed, "Come in, Evi! Welcome!"

She swallowed a sigh... so much for escaping... her stomach growled... she cleared her throat, loudly... "Thank you, Joel."

She stepped inside and being a woman, looked around. It was well furnished, but she remembered their landlord supplied the furniture, it looked nice and Joel kept it spotless. Joel looked at her, appreciating what he saw, but she looked back at him and smiled. When he saw her eyes, his smile burst across his face. He decided taking Evi to the gala would not be a chore!

"Thanks for coming, Evi. I had a feeling we needed to know each other a bit better than as doctor and family member or neighbors in apartments next door to each other - like ships passing in the night, when we'll be spending a long evening together," Joel said, as he took her coat and placed it on the back of his couch close to the door.

Evi chuckled. "Yes, you're right. So far, that's all we've done. It seems like a coincidence that we've come home at the same time so often."

"So what took you away from home so early on black Friday? Are you into that standing in line for hours waiting for that illusive bargain thing?"

Joel led her to his table and pulled out a chair for her. As he seated her, she said, "Oh, Joel, I've had a very exciting two days!" She shook her head and picked up the paper napkin. "Listen to me! An exciting day spent at a local mall yesterday and at the hospital today?" She chuckled again. "Pathetic!"

Joel chuckled, but he said, "More than I did today! I haven't even been to the mailbox! Care for some tea?"

"Sure, that's fine." Joel poured two glasses, brought them to the table, then pulled out his chair, settled onto it and pulled himself to the table. He smiled and removed the lid from his one dish meal and ladled out a serving on her plate. "Joel, this smells great and looks yummy!"

"Thanks, it's my first attempt at a casserole. I hope it tastes as good as it smells and looks. Of course, you can't go too far wrong when it's turkey! Do you mind if I say grace?"

"Oh, no, that's fine."

Sincerely, Joel said, "Thank You, Father God for this food and for the delightful company." He raised his head and asked, "So, tell me, what was so exciting?"

Evi couldn't resist the aroma, so she took a mouthful, chewed and swallowed, before she said, "Mmm, this is really good, Joel! I guess I was really hungry!"

"I'm glad you enjoy it, Evi."

Taking another mouthful, Evi said, "To answer your question, yesterday morning I was having a pity party over my cold coffee when I saw you leave. I was sure you were spending the day with family and mine's in Bangor, Maine! Too far for a one day trip. I have two burn patients in the unit I couldn't leave for more than a day, so I couldn't go home to family. Just when my pity party reached its lowest point, my phone rang and it was a good friend from my student days. She was behind me in school, but she's far from home, too. We decided to spend the afternoon at the mall close to the hospital where I trained."

She grinned, "We parked close to the restaurant where we planned to eat and it smelled so good we ran to another entrance so we wouldn't be tempted, even before we window shopped in the mall. Except that entrance was right across from a little boutique that was open and had a beautiful gown in the window. It really was lovely and on the mannequin… well, I just stared!"

Joel smiled and said, "Yes?"

Evi let out a sigh. "Stupid me, I stood there and drooled! What could my friend think? And for goodness sake, I'm sure she thought I was an idiot standing there drooling at that gown! She asked me why I was looking so longingly at that gown, so I had to tell her I was going to a formal evening with my neighbor."

"Yes?" Joel encouraged.

Evi gave her handsome neighbor a disgusted look, took a long sip of her tea and another mouthful of casserole, let out a sigh and said, "Of course, nothing would do but I had to tell her about my neighbor. She wouldn't let that go for anything." She grinned and Joel noticed a little pink on her cheeks. "Of course, she had to know how 'hunky' my neighbor was."

Joel burst out laughing, in fact two tears slipped out onto his eyes lashes that he quickly wiped away. "Evi…! Go on!" Curbing his laugh, but barely, he said, "This neighbor… this 'hunky' neighbor surely isn't me!"

Evi nodded, her blush was full blown by this time. "Uh huh. Nothing would do but I had to tell her all about you!"

"Oh, my!"

"Joel," she said, seriously, "after we spent time in the boutique we talked, we spent several hours walking through the mall and we talked that whole time. But after we went in the restaurant we talked about work. What you told me about your dad's last breath has stayed with me ever since then. It really made an impression on me! I told Allison, actually, I don't remember making my order for dinner. She surprised me; she was thrilled about your dad! Joel, even before our dinners came, she helped me ask Jesus to take my sins away!"

All laughter aside, Joel said, "Evi… oh, that is super! Praise God! I'm glad I could help you that way! That means we are both God's children! I'm thrilled that you did that."

Evi nodded. "Yes, praying brought such peace to my heart; I've never had that before."

"I'm so glad, Evi!"

During their conversation, they emptied Joel's casserole dish and Evi leaned back after wiping her mouth. She looked at her empty plate, then at the bowl and exclaimed, "Wow! I've never eaten so much! That was delicious, Joel and look, we cleaned out that bowl!"

Joel's eyes twinkled, as he said, "I see that. I'm glad you liked my experiment. It was my first attempt at more than an omelet. You said today was exciting - at the hospital?"

Evi took a long swallow of her tea and said, "Well, part of my pity party was that I'm all alone in the burn department. If someone is burned no one sees them until I see them, no matter what hour, day or night. Of course, it means I'm on call twenty-four/seven. Lots of times someone who's not a specialist could take care of non-critical patients or do treatments on recovering patients in the Burn Unit. Those patients aren't critical. Someone who's not quite finished with clinicals can do that. It would mean I wouldn't be on call twenty-four/seven. Someone like that is called a 'PA'."

"Yes, I know that perfectly. I'm a TA at the university.... until semester break."

Evi nodded, letting Joel know she understood. "Allison and I talked about it over our pumpkin pie and she has to drop out of med school because she's out of money or she'd have to take out another loan. It's hard to pay back so much and her family can't help her, so I called my boss and he asked us to come in today so we could talk. You know, I guess we made a good case! He was impressed and said he'd take the matter to the hospital board, but he's pretty sure she'll get hired! I'm thrilled! I'll probably be able to sleep through the night most nights."

"That's truly awesome, Evi! You know, even as a new Christian, God was answering your prayer. That's one thing about my job, I have to bring my briefcase home at night, but there's no 'on call' in my profession."

Realizing Joel had given her a way to ask, she said, "My doctor friend at the hospital told me a little about you and said you're working on your thesis, but in what?"

"Geology. Since I'm a Christian, my views are different from the majority of geologists, who think that the earth is millions or billions of years old. I believe what the Bible says about the earth being only about six thousand years old and that God created the world and everything in it in only six days. Six twenty-four hour days. Because of that, I'm glad I'll be teaching here at this school. Their beliefs are the same as mine. I'm very much opposed to teaching the theory of evolution and that the earth is billions of years old."

Evi swallowed, this view was something she'd never heard before. "Oh, wow! I'd like to hear what you have to say about that some time."

Joel smiled. "I'll make sure you do, Evi. It's a subject that's very dear to my heart. By the way, now that you're a new Christian, do you have a Bible you could read?"

Evi scowled. "No, no I'm pretty sure I don't have one. Is that important?"

"Oh, yes! Not only is it so important to know that your sins are forgiven, but it's very important to know how it all started. That's found in the Bible. Evi, I can probably get you one without any problem. I'll see what I can do about that."

"Really? That would be great, Joel!"

Joel pulled in a deep breath he was twenty-six years old! Why should he feel so out of touch with women of his own age? He still wasn't sure this was the proper thing to do, but he'd either sink or swim. "Evi, I'd like to change the subject if you don't mind."

"Okay..."

Joel's cheeks warmed a bit, but he said, "Forgive me, Evi, but since my family was what it was and it was no secret around town what my dad was. I haven't dated much, really, not at all, so I'm not up on some of the proper things, but could I give you a corsage to wear with your gown? You told me about the gown you drooled over surely it needs a corsage to go with it!"

Now Evi's cheeks turned a little pink, as she said, "Oh, you don't have to do that, Joel! We were both supposed to go to this thing we're going together because we're neighbors."

Joel cleared his throat. "But I'd like to, Evi, if you would?"

Evi's smile sparkled in her eyes. "If you do, I'd feel very honored!"

Joel's face burst into a smile, it was so broad it nearly hurt his face! "Consider it done, then! What would you like? What color is your gown?"

"I'd love to be surprised! But my gown is blue."

Joel's hand crept onto the table, but he didn't move it far enough to cover hers. She watched its slow motion then swallowed a sigh when it didn't come as far as her hand. "Thank you, Evi. I'll be honored to be your escort." Joel realized he'd moved his hand, but just before he placed it over Evi's he realized he didn't have the right. They were still only neighbors. Perhaps after their date tomorrow evening, he could feel right taking her hand in his.

Evi raised her hand, making sure to hide any discomfort she had and covered a yawn, but embarrassed, she said, "Oh, my! It's been a long day and I was busy all day. I think I'd better find my bed before I fall asleep here at your table. Joel, thank you so much for asking me in. I feel much better going with you tomorrow. I feel like we know each other so much better."

"I the same, Evi. Thank you for coming to help sample my experiment. I must admit it was good. Perhaps I'll get the chance again." They stood up together and Joel hurried around the table to snag her coat. "I'll see you tomorrow at the time we agreed, or maybe a few minutes before," he said and smiled. "Believe me, Evi; I'm looking forward to tomorrow evening!"

"I am too, Joel," she said shyly.

Even though they lived side by side and their decks were only a few feet apart, Joel snagged his own coat and walked Evi the few steps to her door. She opened her door, but then turned a smile on Joel he thought lit up the sky, as she said, "Thanks, so much for inviting me in, Joel. That casserole was truly delicious. As you say, you can't go wrong with turkey! I look forward to tomorrow. I'll see you then."

"Yes, Evi, I'm sure we'll have a good time."

Evi went in her apartment and closed the door, but she smiled at him through the glass. Joel smiled back, then turned back to his own apartment, so she started the drape across the glass, but slowly enough she could watch Joel as he disappeared into the shadow between their decks. As the drape closed, Evi smiled and whispered, "I know I'll be the belle of the ball! I'm probably the youngest and newest member of the staff, but to have Joel Lawson as my date will put me in a class by myself! I can't wait!" *Date?* "Yes! A date!"

She shed her coat, draped it over her own couch and headed for her bedroom. As she got ready for bed, she murmured, "Sweet dreams, Evi. If you dream about Joel Lawson, they will be sweet!" Still smiling, she pulled the covers back on her bed and lay down on the flannel. She pulled the covers up and sighed. Could she dream of Joel Lawson?

Joel also went in his apartment, closed the door and pulled the drape. He realized he was grinning, but it didn't want to leave. It was an incredible evening! He was so glad he went with his hunch and invited her in. He and Evi had an excellent time of getting acquainted and talked so freely together. He couldn't remember being so at ease with a woman, unless he considered his sister, aunt and grandmothers. Even his late night visits with Jenni hadn't been so much fun!

Something else that seemed totally incredible – only yesterday Evi had accepted Jesus as her Savior! Again, because of who his family was and also because he and Leslie only had the bare essentials after the explosion, Joel only had his own personal copy of the Bible. However, he would try within the next few days to get a good one for Evi that she could read and study from. Perhaps they could have some Bible studies together.

He started to clean up his kitchen, but when he picked up the empty casserole dish he chuckled. They were so wrapped up in their talk together that they kept eating the food until it was all gone. That didn't stop them! They kept on talking. He looked at the clock, no wonder Evi was about to fall asleep! It was close to eleven o'clock.

Joel woke up at his usual time Saturday morning. However, he determined before not to work on his dissertation today. In fact, he had worked all day Friday of this holiday weekend. He needed a break. He dressed and made a pot of coffee, then sat down to eat breakfast. He knew he had one errand. He asked Evi if he could buy her a corsage, but she asked to be surprised. He sat back in his chair, took another swallow of coffee and shook his head.

He remembered asking her and how his heart sank when she asked to be surprised. On this kind of thing he was not good with surprises! He had no idea what was appropriate to give her. In fact, she said her gown was blue; he was so naive, he didn't know what would go with a blue gown! He wondered who normally told a guy these things or was he just supposed to know? "If I'm 'just supposed to know' somebody forgot to clue me in or maybe I forgot to take that class." Maybe he was smart in academics, but social skills? Not so much!

It hadn't been his dad who'd passed on that information to his son! For the past decade or more he and his dad rarely had a civil word for each other. During that time he often wondered if that was his fault, but now he knew it was because God was after Thad!

He washed up his breakfast dishes and decided to visit Lucy; perhaps she knew what he should do. After all, she had been married maybe Uncle Josh had done nice things for her. From his memories of his uncle, he knew the man was totally different from his dad. Not to mention that Uncle Josh had been a committed Christian man who loved his wife. He hoped she could at least help him in some way, he didn't even know what colors really went together! How bad was that! Joel shook his head, it was bad!

Maybe his mom worshipped the ground Thad Lawson walked on, but he surely had never done anything nice for her – not that he knew about! There was never any evidence of something he'd bought her in the house. She had a plain wedding ring and that was all he could remember. As he said on Thanksgiving, they never celebrated birthdays at the Thad Lawson house. None of them ever gave gifts to each other except at Christmas. Those presents were mostly utilitarian, not given out of love. They never went anywhere as a family, there hadn't even been a camera that he knew about!

As he left the complex he wondered if it was appropriate to take the corsage when he went to pick her up or before so she could pin it on her gown. "Man, you are twenty-six years old! You're a graduate student! Shouldn't you know these things before this?" he grumbled. He shrugged. "Nope, not in my memory bank!"

He thought back to his friends in high school and undergraduate school, all guys, most of them not dating anyone. Come to think of it, none of them had ever talked about getting a girl flowers, certainly not a corsage! However, he remembered pictures of the girls in prom gowns in high school and some even at graduation had corsages. Who had given them the flowers? Had it been their parents or their dates? He shrugged, not something he knew. He could only hope his dear, sweet aunt would know. Surely she would impart some of her knowledge on him!

Joel pulled up in Lucy's driveway and saw that Jenni's car was in her driveway. He wondered what time she usually went to work. When he'd lived with Lucy he always left her house before Jenni left for her day. It was the first time he'd thought about her in a couple of days. He wondered what she'd be doing this evening. Then he remembered she was the evening news anchor, she'd probably be sitting in the newsroom giving out the news, but it didn't matter, he was excited to take Evi to the reception and that was why he was here. He really wanted to do something special for her. He dismissed his thoughts about Jenni, left the car and took the few steps to his aunt's door and knocked.

Lucy answered, looked up into her big nephew's face and said, "Joel! We only saw you on Thursday, what's the deal?"

Lucy stepped back and Joel walked in, she quickly closed the door against the cold, while he shed his coat and followed her into the living room where Leslie played a game on the TV. Joel and Lucy sat down in the tiny room in the other two chairs and Joel said, "Auntie, in answer to your question, I'm here to ask advice. I really think I'm in over my head! I sat at my breakfast table and all during my breakfast I thought about this and came up with nothing!"

When she heard what Joel said, Leslie paused her game and turned to listen. Lucy pushed her thumb into her chest and said, skeptically, "You want to ask advice from me? Joel, you're the one who's been to college and has all that education! Why do you think I have answers to something you can't figure out yourself?"

Joel shook his head. "Auntie I'm so out of my element! This surely isn't about anything academic; still, I don't know everything, really! You know I haven't dated! What Dad was and how he treated people never was a secret and I never felt free from that. I'm supposed to take Dr. Fredrickson to the reception for her Chief of Staff. It's downtown at the Convention Center, it's a really big to-do! Granddad gave me that tux and she'll be beautiful in an evening gown! I need to give her a corsage, but what? I have no clue! All she told me was her gown is blue."

Leslie grinned, her big brother, this guy with all the smarts, didn't know about corsages for a date! She immediately jumped into the discussion, almost giddy, she asked, "How much do you want to spend, Bro?"

Joel shrugged and looked back and forth between the two ladies. "I don't know, have no idea! That's why I came to get some advice from you guys. Are they expensive? If they don't cost much are they shabby? Besides, do you walk into a florist and tell them you need a corsage? Do they know? I sat in my apartment and thought and thought, but nothing came to me! All I know is that she has a gown and it's blue! I thought maybe because Uncle Josh was so different from Dad that you had some experience with things like this, Auntie."

FOURTEEN

"DO YOU WANT TO GET A WRIST CORSAGE OR ONE TO PIN ON HER GOWN?" LUCY asked.

Looking totally innocent and throwing his hands out in a helpless gesture, Joel asked, "A wrist corsage? What's that?"

"It's hooked on a bracelet that goes easily on her wrist," Lucy answered. "Since it's cold out and she'll wear a coat to get wherever it is you're going, maybe one of those would be better. She could keep it in the box, so it won't freeze and put it on once you get to where you're going where she'll take her coat off."

"Okay," Joel said. "Maybe that's a good idea. So tell me what colors – oh, what else do I need to know? You see how much I don't know? Auntie, you see why I came to see you? I offered to get her a corsage, but she wanted to be surprised!"

"What does she look like? How old is she?" Leslie grinned and added, "If she's an old hag... You said she's a doctor, right?" Leslie nearly laughed. Her big, handsome brother going to a black tie affair with some old hag? Nope, wouldn't happen, not in his lifetime!

Joel sat back and looked at the TV screen that had the frozen game characters in strange positions. He thought for several minutes. Then his face turned a shade of pink, he shook his head and said, "Les, she's a lovely lady, maybe a few years older than me. She has blond hair with a bit of wave down onto her shoulders and blue eyes. Umm, she's quite trim and shapely," he answered uncomfortably. He felt his hands want to demonstrate, but kept them perfectly still.

"She's the doctor who met with me there at the hospital to explain Dad's condition right before he died and since I moved, she's my neighbor." He cleared his throat. "Last night I invited her to share Nana's turkey, so while we ate she told me her friend led her to salvation because of what I told her about Dad's last words. I was thrilled!" Red color blooming on his cheeks, he added, "I think she's a lovely lady. We've gotten home at about the same time several times. I've enjoyed our talks. Last night was really cool! We talked and talked!"

Before Lucy could answer, Leslie exclaimed, "Bro, I'm glad Granddad gave you that tux, you will be spectacular as her partner!"

Joel let out a long sigh. "Sis, I'm nervous enough about this, you don't have to add to it, you know! Good grief!"

"Joel!" Lucy exclaimed. "Stop! You will do fine, be yourself. Just because you don't feel secure in what you're doing, doesn't mean you can't handle it. Life is full of scary things, we always live through them."

Joel let out a long sigh, his eyes glistening because of the overload to his emotions, he said, "Auntie, I'll try. You know because of Dad I never dated, I always felt like his specter was hanging over me. I tried to be friendly with everybody, but I never dated. So now I feel like a fish out of water!"

Lucy put her hand on Joel's wrist. "I know that, Joel. I know what he was like, I know you're a bit nervous, but you will do fine! Really, remember all the things you had to take care of the week of the explosion. You did it all! And you did it just fine. Actually, I was amazed at all you did and you never seemed to lose your cool. And with the sheriff…"

Joel pulled in a deep breath then blew it out and tried to relax as he looked at his aunt and said, "Thanks, Auntie, I'll try to do you proud."

"Oh, I have no worries about that, Joel!"

"Thanks, both of you. I'll remember what you've said."

Joel stayed and chatted with Lucy and Leslie long enough that Lucy invited him for lunch then he left for the florist. When he came back out of Lucy's house Jenni's car was still parked in her driveway. Joel wondered when she'd be going to work, but she didn't come out and he didn't go to her door. He had never initiated those talks they'd had. Life went on, for all he knew, nothing in her life had changed. Until he learned differently, he would leave it to God.

He got in his car and started up. According to Lucy and Leslie, he should have no trouble getting the right corsage for his date. With all the advice they'd given him, surely he could. However, Joel wasn't near as confident as the two ladies in his life as to what he would be doing once he got back to his apartment. In fact, his hands were a bit clammy once he was alone in the car headed for the florist. He only hoped they had what he needed. In fact, he felt more confident about his trip to the Bible bookstore than the florist!

Saturday morning, Evi woke up excited. She remembered the tail-end of her dream – she had dreamed about her 'hunky' neighbor! As she lay in her bed she seriously debated turning off her phone. Wouldn't it be awful if they called her from the hospital that she had a critical burn patient and couldn't go to the gala because she had to do emergency surgery and then had to stay with the patient because their life hung in the balance? Having that thought made her shudder. She sighed, turning off her phone wouldn't keep that from happening and if it did, someone from the hospital would be scouring the city for her, but she sure could hope and pray that people would keep out of the line of fire, at least for today. She glanced at her clock and turned over for another snooze, she could at least pretend she wasn't on call today.

She really had nothing else on for the day and she'd been getting up quite early all week long. Her days, except for Thanksgiving Day had been packed with hospital related happenings. After she got up she wondered when Dr. Morris would let her know if Allison would be hired. If they hired her that would relieve her worry about being on call twenty-four/seven.

By the time she made it out of her bedroom to fix her coffee it was light out. She could tell by looking out through her curtains that the sun wasn't shining, but it wasn't raining or snowing, for that matter. Bangor might have snow! But she was here. The forecast she'd heard didn't give any prediction of rain for today. She wanted to pray that God would keep the rain away, who wanted wet stringy hair to go with a brand new evening gown? And besides, she'd probably be the newest and youngest hospital staff there, she wanted to make a good impression.

She couldn't remember when she'd been so lazy and gotten up so late! Even though it was such a bleak time of year, she'd rather have her patio drape open and let in what light there was, than have it closed and have to use the artificial light. She hurried to start her coffee maker, then went to the drape to open it and saw Joel get in his car. She didn't wave, by the time she had the drape pulled enough he had backed around and was heading for the street.

She watched the car reach the complex entrance and his brake lights come on and her heart gave a lurch. She cleared her throat, encouraging her heart to beat normally and said, "Girl, do not panic, it's early, he's probably got an errand, he will be back in time to drive us downtown!" However, reassuring herself did nothing to relieve her mind that her escort hadn't skipped town. Surely Joel wouldn't do that, not after having her in for supper last night!

She thought about that time at his table and sighed, "I wish he'd put his hand over mine. What do his hands feel like? Oh, my." She sighed again. "What would his lips…."

Anxiously she waited for the coffeemaker's last wheeze then poured her mug full. She slid onto a chair at her table and sighed, "What will Joel think of my gown?"

Some time later, Evi decided that maybe she ought to eat some lunch. It was only refreshments they'd serve at the reception, not dinner. However, when she went to her refrigerator and looked in she decided that even her usual comfort food wouldn't settle her stomach, she was that excited. She pulled out her pitcher of iced tea and poured herself a glass; that was all her stomach would accept. Besides, she was really thirsty. As she gulped the drink she tried to remember when the last time was she'd had a date. College? Med school? She shook her head, she could not remember. Med school had been a maze of classes, days of following doctors and l-o-n-g nights of ward duty. How could she have dated?

Maybe an hour later she decided to start her preparations. After all, washing her hair, drying it with a curling iron and applying makeup, that she never did on a daily basis would take a bit of time. And her nails! She hadn't done them in months. She cleared her throat, her shoes were three inches tall, but mostly straps. She'd have to paint her toenails! When was the last time she'd done that? It was impossible to remember that piece of trivia!

She had finally admitted that she was going on a *date* with Joel Lawson and she was excited. Last night eating dinner together had made that a reality. She was between her bedroom and the bathroom door when she heard a light knock on her patio door. She looked that way and her treacherous heart skipped a beat when she saw who was at the door. Her 'drool department' date stood there!

By the time she walked across her living room to the patio door she felt like she would soon hyperventilate! Joel was at her door! It was several hours yet before they were to head downtown! Why was he already at her door? She could see him clearly through the large, glass door; he wasn't dressed in that 'black tie', but still…. He was smiling at her. That's all it took, her stomach did a tiny flip. He had a small white box in his hands! She looked more closely; he had a paper bag covered package under his arm.

Joel was still nervous as he parked in his usual spot. They had helped him at the florist and he was excited about his purchase. Now it was time to see if Evi liked what he'd gotten for her. He took the little box and his other purchase and went to Evi's patio door. He saw her inside and smiled as she came toward him. Just before she opened the door, a gust of wind picked up a clump of Joel's hair, but he paid no attention. The breeze was cold, but it didn't really faze Joel, not as the lovely lady walked towards him. She opened the door and smiled. That smile made his heart kick into overdrive!

Before she could ask, Joel said, "Evi, I brought your corsage early. I hope you don't mind and I really hope you like what I have for you."

Blushing, she motioned him in, but took the box and stepped aside. It was cold, so he stepped in and closed the door. He waited silently as she opened the box, but she gasped as she looked at the delicate orchid. She looked up at him, her eyes, shining and the smile on her face was payment enough for all his worries. In a whisper she said, "Joel! This is lovely! Oh, my! Thank you. I know for sure I've never had an orchid before."

Joel grinned and said, "You're welcome, Evi. I was also going by the Bible Book Store and happened to remember I promised you a Bible. So here it is."

"Great, Joel! Thanks." She still held the box with the orchid, so he set the other package down on the top edge of her couch.

Not knowing what else to say or do, he said, "I'll see you later, Evi. I need to get ready." There was no reason to stay, so he opened the door, stepped out and closed her door behind him. He had a bit of work to do before he was ready to escort such a lovely lady to a grand gala! He knew she would look beautiful! Again this afternoon, he couldn't erase the grin on his face!

In fact he chuckled, he was convinced that Evi was as excited to go with him to the gala as he was to go with her. He nearly leaped in the air to click his heels as he hurried across the patios into his own apartment, intent on doing the best job with his washcloth, shampoo and razor. As he took those few steps he wasn't really sure if his feet were taking him from her deck to his or if he was floating! Well, surely his feet were walking on solid ground! After all, it wasn't like he was a hormone –driven teenager!

"Joel," he admonished himself, "What is your problem? This is only a first date!" *Mmm hmm, but it is with a beautiful lady* ***and*** *you are excited beyond words!* He went in his apartment and... jumped in the air and clicked his heels! He freely admitted that since their time together last evening that they weren't just 'going together' but they were going on a DATE!

However, Evi didn't move from the door. Of course, Joel didn't see that. After it closed she breathed out a sigh. Even dressed in jeans and a heavy winter coat, the man was gorgeous! She made a small turn to watch the handsome man leave her deck. She continued to watch until she heard his patio door close and then she let out another sigh. "That man... he will be the most wonderful date ever! How in the world did I ever find Joel Lawson? He's my neighbor, a super man and oh, my! So handsome!" She lifted the little box to her face and inhaled the delicate smell. "An orchid! I've never had an orchid." she mused.

Seconds ago she heard Joel's door close. She looked at the clock over her kitchen sink, set the box on the table and rushed across to her bedroom. "Girl! What are you doing standing here? You have a date to get ready for and you must look good enough to wear that lovely corsage!" She stopped in her bedroom to collect her bathrobe; her patio curtain was still open!

Joel had left by several minutes as she stopped in her bedroom thinking about what she needed in the bathroom before she put on that beautiful gown. Just seeing Joel had sent her heart into arrhythmias. It was no calmer now than when he'd given her that little box! Her neighbor – the guy next door – would soon be back to take her for a star-studded evening. Probably those stars were already in her eyes! She could never remember being so excited about a date!

She rushed in the bathroom with her bathrobe over her arm, hung it on the hook behind the door then stood in the middle of the room looking around. "Nails, *nails*! I need a basin to soak my toes! I'm to paint my toenails! Oh, my, where's Allison when I need her." She went in search of a basin to soak her toenails, but none materialized.

Jenni finished the last few tidbits from her take-out box from the Thanksgiving dinner she and her parents had at the restaurant. Of course, it was too early for her parents to have their supper. There was no reason to eat much she knew refreshments at the reception would be lavish. She needed to leave early to stop by the TV station to collect her battery-pack and the mike. She and Len had agreed to meet there, since he needed his cameras too. They would take a company SUV to the event. There was no sense in both of them driving. Besides, why should they each pay the fee to park when they were going to this gala as an assignment for the station?

They might be working, but they'd also be in evening clothes so they didn't stand out too much. Riding the interurban was out of the question. Everybody in their suburb knew there was a train station downtown, but you had to make a connection in another suburb that was well out of the way. It took longer to ride the train than to drive from here.

She looked at herself in gown and heels and shook her head, was it possible to mingle and not stand out? Len with camera around his neck and movie camera on his shoulder and her with mike in hand and battery-pack strap on her shoulder! Yup! Sure they'd blend right in!

She collected her trash and was about to grab her coat before heading out the door, when her dad said, "Girl, I want to see you all dressed up! That's a rare happening!"

"Dad," Jenni sighed, "It's hard to dress for a gala when I'm to be mixing in the crowd to get interviews, carrying a mike and a battery-pack, but I guess what you see is what you get."

"You look lovely, Jenni," Loretta said.

Pulling on her coat, Jenni said, "Thanks, Mom, I'll stop at the station before heading downtown. Len's meeting me; we'll get our equipment, and go together in a company car."

Marvin raised his eyebrows and said, "Girl, you will knock their socks off! Is that a new addition to your wardrobe?"

She made a face and looked down at the cocktail dress she wore. "Well, yes and no, I bought it last year but I've never worn it."

Jenni pulled in a breath. "About knocking anyone's socks off, probably not, Dad. I'll have that battery-pack strap on my shoulder and a mike in my hand. People don't like to talk to reporters and especially at something like this. They like to come and show off, but not be interviewed. Maybe the mayor won't mind an interview he's good with words and always has something to say, but most everybody'll run the other way when they see a mike coming at them. I've had it happen before. And Len with a camera around his neck and a movie camera on his shoulder? Only a few people like their pictures taken at a thing like this!"

The man continued to look appreciatively at his daughter and said, "With that winsome smile? I have my doubts, Girl."

"Yes, Dad, it happens all the time. People really don't like to have their words recorded. Lots of times they don't think before they speak and that's what goes on the air. And pictures? Mmm, yes, it's at things like this people like to appear, show off, really, but not to broadcast where they are and very often who they're with. I've seen people take one look and scurry the other way. Long gowns, stilettos and an immaculate tux make no difference."

Looking admiringly at her daughter Loretta asked, "Jenni, will Lucy's nephew be there?"

Jenni's heart sped up, thinking about Joel, but she said, "Mom, I have no idea. He's not connected to the hospital in any way, why would he be?"

Scowling she said, "Oh, surely, since he's almost a doctor he'd be there! They'd keep him away because he's not a doctor yet?"

Here was her mom's one-track mind again! Could she ever get her mom to think about something else besides how old her daughter was? Exasperated, Jenni said, "Mom, he's not going to be a *medical* doctor. I'm pretty sure I told you that. He's going to be a PhD and that has nothing to do with hospitals at all."

"Oh," she said, very disappointed. "What's a PhD? You said he'd be a doctor. What do you mean he has nothing to do with the hospital?"

"Mom, there are many kinds of doctors. Someone with a PhD will teach college and university classes or do scientific research, they have nothing to do with medical anything."

Very perplexed, Loretta said, "So why will he be a doctor? I thought doctors took care of people when they're sick or hurt."

"Mom, PhD tells people what kind of doctor he'll be. The Ph means something and the D stands for doctor. He will be a doctor, but not a medical doctor."

Looking sheepish and knowing her daughter knew lots more than she did, she said, "I guess I didn't know that."

"I'm sure I told you that, Mom." *You're so intent on my getting Joel for a husband that you conveniently forget all this!* She sighed, but didn't say those words out loud.

Curly saw Jenni with her coat and came up to her wagging his tail, but she said, "Curly, I'll be back a whole lot later, but for now, you'll have to watch TV with Dad."

The dog slunk away, his tail drooping down to the floor and flopped down with a sigh beside Marvin. Marvin reached down and scratched behind his ears, "Come on, boy, we're in this together. We've got it licked." However, Curly was not impressed. He let Marvin scratch his ears a few times then let out a deep sigh and put his chin on his paws. He closed his eyes even before Jenni left the house.

Jenni went to her car, shivered in the cold and looked at Lucy's inviting house, wondering what Joel was doing tonight. Of course, his car wasn't there; she hadn't expected it to be. She hadn't seen it or him since Thanksgiving Day when the infamous sheriff had made a buffoon of himself. She wondered if Joel had finished his thesis or maybe he would spend tonight at the library getting some research done. She hadn't talked with him since they talked about the memorial service for his parents. That's when she gave him to understand she didn't want to talk about what he thought was *the* most important happening in life. That conversation still bothered her. Her dad's reaction hung heavy over her thoughts, but unless she could talk to Joel, she'd never ask. No, her dad had acted so strangely she thought he might have a stroke!

She let out a long sigh, gathered the edges of her gown and stepped into her car. "He's such a handsome man I wish I was going to this gala with him instead of Len. If I was going with him, it would be fun! Still, why would he be going? Would he go as part of the university staff? But it's not for them. It's the hospital's Chief of Staff they're honoring."

She drove away from home, knowing this was her job. It wasn't to have a good time. Theirs wasn't a huge station, so staff choices were limited. Alex hadn't been helpful in who she should interview. She should interview the new Chief of Staff and the mayor and anyone else she thought would be good. If she knew people at all, her interview with the Chief would be a few sentences, but with the mayor, quite the opposite. The mayor could be long-winded and also a bit full of himself. Maybe that's how people in public office got themselves elected. She wondered who the new Chief of Staff was; she didn't even know if the man was middle-aged or old! What did you have to do to get that spot? Then again, the chief could be a woman. She chuckled, she was sure you wouldn't call the top dog of the hospital staff a Chief-tess!

She pulled into the station parking lot and saw Len's car parked in his usual spot. There was a light on in the hallway of the main entrance. "Len's already getting his stuff," she sighed. Of course, there were other staff here doing their jobs, she knew for sure that her stand-in was getting ready to present the seven o'clock news, but the offices and the newsroom didn't have windows looking out at the parking lot. By this time of day most all the staff had gone home, the usual work-day was over, especially since it was Saturday, even more so because it was the Saturday after Thanksgiving. Only the staff that kept the programming going would still be there. She had to tell herself she was glad about that, at least she was out in the field.

As she parked her car, she realized Len was thoughtful and started a company SUV. He'd pulled it up close to the front door. Since it was Saturday and after hours, she could park close to the building, rush in for her stuff and get into a warm vehicle for their trip downtown without losing the curl in her hair! She hurried into the building, because the wind was blowing fiercely and she wanted to keep her hair nice. She didn't get far before Len met her outside the newsroom with his camera around his neck and her mike and battery-pack in his hands.

He grinned at her as she came towards him. He handed her the mike and the strap for the battery-pack, and said, "Here you go, Jenni, need anything else?"

Jenni held out both hands and took both things at the same time. "Nope, that's it, Len, thanks. Thanks for warming up the SUV it is pretty cold out there! Is your movie camera already out there?"

"Yes, actually, I left it in the SUV the last time out, so that's part of why the thing's running. I know it's a long drive downtown, but the camera needs to be totally warm or it won't work right. So, who's on your agenda?"

Len pushed the door open and followed Jenni out, but the wind was cold and Jenni hurried as fast as her heels would let her. As Len took long strides, Jenni said, "Alex said the Chief of Staff and the mayor. Why, do you know somebody else important who'll be there?"

"Got it on good authority that most of the university faculty'll be there, too. I guess they were all invited to this 'black tie' shindig. Since it's downtown, there could be other important people there, I would think. Was Alex talking about the mayor of our suburb or the mayor of the big city, did he say?"

Jenni nodded. "Good to know." *I wonder if Joel will be there?* "Actually, he didn't say who to talk to, only 'the mayor'."

Len nodded, but said, "By the way, you look sensational! Can't remember ever seeing you so dolled up!"

Jenni smiled and fastened her seatbelt as Len pulled the stick into drive. "Thanks, Len, you don't look half bad yourself."

Len chuckled. "Thanks, Jenni. It's a bit much to dress so fancy when we're toting equipment for reporting stuff to put on the air."

Jenni sighed, "Yes, I was thinking the same thing while I dressed. Alex said we should dress for the occasion, but I think we'll stick out more because we're carrying our equipment."

"Yeah, those are my thoughts exactly, but we'll make the best of it." Len pulled into traffic and Jenni relaxed against the seat for the long ride. At least her stomach was satisfied; there wouldn't be any growls from that department.

Evi finally made it to her bathroom after collecting a few things from her bedroom. She started the water for her shower so she wouldn't turn blue when she stepped behind the curtain. It was a lovely apartment, but there wasn't an in-line water heater. It took several minutes for the warm water to reach the shower head. She took a deep breath before she stepped into the shower that feeling of hyperventilating hadn't gone away. She had yet to remember when she was last on a date!

On normal work days she might spend all of ten minutes covering blemishes on her face. Putting make-up on was something she rarely spent much time on. A Surgical mask didn't work well with make-up. After her shower and brushing her teeth, she spent a lot of time working her hair into the perfect arrangement. She did have a natural wave in her hair, but it needed to be tamed for something as important as a date. She put it up and took it down several times before she finally was satisfied with the results.

As she did her make-up she looked at her fingernails and tried to decide the best shade of polish to use. She hadn't found a basin to soak her feet, so she hoped the shower had softened her toenails. Did she have enough polish for both her fingernails and toenails? She groaned, she hadn't had a pedicure in – well… forever! Had she ever painted her toenails? She couldn't remember that ever happening. Did a woman babble when she was alone in her own place? Maybe it was called dithering!

She sighed and said, "Stop it, girl! Stop acting like a ninny!"

The combination of the lovely gown and the exquisite orchid that Joel had brought made her want to look her very best. She couldn't remember the last time she'd spent so much time with a hair brush, a make-up utensil and a mirror! Getting ready for a date took a lot of time! "And with Joel Lawson? Oh, my, isn't there something else I need to do to be pretty?"

She stepped from the bathroom, looked across the living area and out the patio door to see the bleak November sky. She pulled her eyes back, intent on heading for her closet and her gown and her stomach growled. "Really?" she whispered. "You're going to give me fits?" She looked at the clock beside her bed. "Listen, girl, there isn't time to feed you! Joel will be here in a few minutes and you must be ready." Her stomach growled again, telling her what it thought of that. She might be twenty-nine, but that didn't make her feel much like a mature woman!

Joel stepped inside his comfortable apartment, shed his coat, and dropped it on the arm of the couch. After all, he'd need it again in a short time. He looked at the clock over the sink and decided if he wanted to eat something before they left he should get started on his preparations. The invitation said snacks, not dinner and he was used to eating three squares a day. He shed his clothes and stepped into the shower, letting the cool water raise goose bumps on his skin that made him feel alive. He most certainly was alive! He was about to take a most beautiful lady on a date! Yes, after last night, he really was going on a date! And very excited about it, actually.

After his shower and shampoo he found his razor and did the best job he'd done in many days on the whiskers on his face. He worked very hard not nick his face. A blood spot wouldn't go with a tux! It still felt foolish to wear that outfit. He chuckled, maybe that's why people called them a 'monkey suit'. Finally, he felt satisfied with the job he'd done and hurried to his bedroom to dress. On the dresser was one bottle of aftershave. He hoped it made him smell good enough as he splashed some on.

As he pulled the clothes bag from the closet, and hoped he remembered how to work that thing that went around his waist! He opened the zipper and sighed as the bag fell away. He didn't feel right putting on such dressy clothes, but Fred Winsted was counting on him and his family was expecting him to make them proud. Since Fred said the invitation said this was a 'black tie' event, he must conform.

He pulled the long sleeved shirt on and winced as his fingers got tangled in the fussy lace that hid the button holes. He almost despaired of getting his large fingers around the tiny buttons on the cuffs. Why in the world would you wear something so fussy? However, he chuckled as he pulled out the black strip of fabric that his granddad called a cummerbund and his grampa had described as something to hold in an expanded waistline.

He looked at himself in the mirror on the closet door, he and Granddad had no expansion, but Grampa had plenty for both of them! Grampa's waistline had expanded since he'd retired. Rather than fasten it behind his back as his granddad did, he fastened it in front then moved it around. Of course that meant the shirt and trousers had to be readjusted. He sighed, what a trial to put on fancy clothes! He fitted the bowtie under the collar as he did on Thanksgiving and breathed out a sigh. As he told his gramma, a black suit would be a whole lot easier and he would feel a whole lot more comfortable.

Before he left the room he ran his comb through his damp hair then slid the comb in his pocket. Critically, he examined himself in the mirror and said, "Well, Joel Lawson, you'll have to do. Whoever is at this thing, will see me for who I am. I sure don't know how to put on 'airs'." However, the 'jitters' returned with the thought of his date. She would look beautiful!

He picked up the jacket, hooking his finger under the collar and tossed it over his shoulder. From the bedroom he went to his coat and dropped the jacket, now was the time for a peanut butter and jelly sandwich. There might be refreshments at the gala, but all that might be were caviar and crackers – which he'd never tasted or baby cream puffs or maybe even nuts and mints! None of those things would ever fill him up as a well made western omelet would. Would they even have non-alcoholic drinks? He surely had no way of knowing what happened at a reception for a new Chief of Staff at a city hospital. Did he know how to curl that pinky finger the right way? All he cared about doing was getting his thesis approved and teaching his classes, but this? Was going to 'black tie' events part of what he had to do?

"Granddad said I'd be using the tux more once I'm part of the faculty!" He let out a long sigh, he could do without that!

He glanced at his clock; he'd need to get a move on! He pulled out a few slices of bread, the peanut butter and some jam from the fridge. As he found a knife to spread with, he muttered, "Did Fred Winsted say there would be dancing? Oh, my! I have never danced a step in my life! Will Evi want to dance? Goodness! I'm nervous all over again!" He shook his head. "I'll have to tell her I've never danced. Oh, my! I'd step on her toes for sure. And if she wears those shoes that are mostly straps?" He cleared his throat. "Maybe I'll have to take her to the hospital for casts on her feet!"

He made the sandwich and stood at the counter to eat it, then took a swig from the water bottle he kept in the fridge. He looked at the clock and decided it was time to rap on his neighbor's door. He brushed through the lace on his chest to get any crumbs out and noticed his hands were trembling a little. He pulled in a deep breath, wanting to calm down. After all, he was twenty-six years old! Finally, he slid the tux jacket on and buttoned that single button, pulled in another deep breath and slid his arms into his winter coat. At least his winter coat would cover up the fancy stuff until they got downtown.

"Joel Lawson, get it together!" He said, sternly, pulled in a deep breath, unlocked the patio door and stepped out into the cold late afternoon. Almost immediately a gust of wind found him and messed his hair. However, he remembered he had his trusty comb at the ready. The sun was definitely in the west as he pulled the door closed behind him.

Life as he knew it from only a few weeks ago was behind him. He must remember what his sister had told him – 'Bro, stay the course.' Even that seemed to have changed. He and Leslie were orphans, at least he could live on his own and Leslie had their aunt to live with. He wasn't sure if he knew what 'the course' was any more. It surely had been a rocky one in the last few weeks. Was that better or not? Auntie said you could only live one day at a time.

He walked the few steps from his patio door across two wooden decks to Evi's patio door and put his knuckles on the glass. He looked through the glass and easily saw her grab a cookie from her cookie jar because the light over her table was on. She looked at him and he grinned because the look on her face was that of a child with his hand in the forbidden cookie jar! By the time Evi reached the door Joel was laughing, because as beautiful as she was, she'd stuffed the whole cookie in her mouth and now looked like a chipmunk with a mouthful of nuts. Even through her make-up he saw her blush.

As she opened the door, Joel exclaimed, "Evi! You're nervous! Don't be, I'm Joel, your neighbor. Take your time, swallow your cookie, we have a minute if you need a drink."

Joel stepped inside and closed her door behind him. Her mouth was still so full she couldn't speak, so Joel added, "Evi, you're lovely, your gown, your hair – my, you sparkle all over! I feel honored to take you to this reception."

Evi couldn't speak until she went to the sink, drew water and took a drink. As she put the glass back on the counter Joel noticed the pink on her cheeks and Evi squeaked, "Joel, I'm so embarrassed, I'm sorry you had to see me that way." She cleared her throat. "Really, I'm supposed to be this sophisticated burn specialist and because I'm so nervous I'm acting like a four year old! I'm not sure I've ever been to something like this and because I'm so nervous about it my stomach's been growling for ten minutes!"

Joel chuckled. "Well, grab another cookie or two, I'll help you into your coat and you can take your time eating your cookies while we're on our way." To put actions to his words, he took the few steps to her coat and picked it up. "Every time I see you I admire your coat. It must be warm you never have a hat or gloves on."

She came to him and said, "It is warm, but really, the reason I don't wear hat and gloves is because I spend so much time at the hospital in a sterile outfit. That's a cap that does absolutely horrendous things to a hair-do and once it comes off you never have a comb to take care of the mess. The sterile gloves usually have powder in them and they have to be so tight you can feel a needle through them. Outside the hospital I really want to shed all that."

Joel nodded. "I don't blame you!"

He held her coat by the collar and she turned her back to him. It was then he saw that, although the front of the gown was very demure and had a piece that circled her neck, her back was barely covered. Joel pulled in a silent breath and took a step toward Evi, willing her to quickly slide her hands into the sleeves. With the coat covering her back, Joel carefully placed the shoulders of her coat on hers, but gently laid his hands on top.

"Evi," he said softly, "you look very lovely, your gown is spectacular!"

"Thank you, Joel. I saw it there in that boutique and I knew I had to have it. I think this is the first evening gown I've ever had." She cleared her throat. "I really feel a bit exposed."

Taking his hands from her shoulders, he chuckled and said, "That's when you told your friend about your 'hunky' neighbor?"

"Yes, that's when." She pulled in another breath and added, "I need my purse and my orchid. It was thoughtful of you to get that wrist corsage and it is so beautiful! My parents have given me corsages for my graduations, but I've never had an orchid."

Joel was glad for Lucy's advice. He smiled and said, "I'm glad I got you that, Evi. Let's be on our way, it'll take a good while to get there. It is a ways downtown."

Joel reached for Evi's door and she pulled a set of keys from the hook. Joel pulled her door closed and she handed him her keys. With only a few steps, Joel helped Evi into her car. It was a very nice car, with nice heat and lovely music playing. Joel headed to the circle bypass to the Corridor to take them downtown. He hadn't been downtown often, but he did know how to go. His heart was thudding, not that he was nervous or anything…

Evi sat back, ready to relax, if that were possible while she sat beside the very handsome Joel Lawson. Since she was in a bucket seat, she was close to Joel, but felt butterflies in her stomach. "I have every confidence you'll get us where we're supposed to be, Joel. I took my advance training at the big teaching hospital, but I hardly ventured anywhere else. Actually, between studying and procedures I rarely had time for much else."

Joel chuckled. "Hold judgment on that until we arrive, Evi, it's been a while since I was downtown and driving to get there – I'm not even sure I ever did."

Joel had seen Evi's gown, but she hadn't seen him in his evening clothes, although she saw the shiny stripe down the outside of the trousers. However, because of the heavy winter coat that was closed to his throat, she had no idea what he really looked like. However, she was sure he'd take her breath away when he shed that coat. This man had impressed her from the first time she saw him and now that she knew him better, he was awesome, in so many ways. Maybe he hadn't driven downtown in a long time, but he drove with confidence.

He had told her last night that because of his family he hadn't dated, but he was the perfect date! He helped her into her coat, complimented her gown, and bought her a lovely corsage. He took her arm and helped her into the car. Did he just know those things? She knew she would have the best date ever! In fact, she felt like Cinderella, but she hoped the coach and ten didn't turn back to mice and a pumpkin before they got back to their apartments at some undisclosed time… later!

Joel followed the signs and parked in the short term parking for events at the underground parking lot of the massive Convention Center. Evi had done most of her advanced education in this city, but she had never been to this huge place. She could see that the garage was vast and other cars were in front and following them. Others were already parked. Joel pulled into a slot right next to the car ahead of him, put the stick in Park and turned to grin at Evi. She in turn, pulled in a breath for courage and tried to smile back.

"I guess we're here! Ready, Evi?"

She let out that breath and said, "I guess. I've never been to something like this it's all new territory for me."

"I'm with you in that! Hey, don't get cold feet! You'll be the belle of the ball. Wait right there, I'll be around for you."

Figuring her knees felt like jell-o, she was happy to wait for Joel. "Oh, I will." Here was another bit of evidence of what a fine man he was.

Joel walked around the back of the car, since the nose was almost touching the cement wall. He swallowed; his nerves had taken all the moisture from his mouth. His birthday was two days ago, but he didn't feel much like a twenty-six year old man. This was his first date – his very first date! He'd never touched this lady, even though he came very close last evening. However, it didn't feel right to take her hand to help her from the car then drop it and to walk beside her; did he dare keep her hand? He cleared his throat before he reached her door, then opened it and smiled at her. Again she tried to muster something that resembled a smile for him.

His eyes twinkling, he looked down at her face and said, "Evi, you look a whole lot prettier with a smile."

FIFTEEN

SHE LOOKED UP AND ONE SIDE OF HER MOUTH LIFTED. IN A WHISPER NEARLY OVERpowered by the traffic in the huge cavern, she said, "I'll work on that, Joel, I'm a bit overwhelmed."

He held out his hand and said, "I know the feeling precisely! Keep in mind, though, you're the only burn specialist in the hospital, that'll give you confidence! And besides, you are very lovely tonight."

Clutching her purse and the corsage box in one hand, she held out the other and Joel took it. It was cool and Joel chalked that up to the temperature, but Evi knew, since his hand was so warm, that it was because she was a bundle of nerves. Joel took her hand and as she stepped out, it felt natural to thread it around his other arm. Evi was glad for his strong arm. She felt a lot more steady as they walked to the elevator where they met others going to the gala. Many people had gathered since the last elevator left. Evi looked at every face, but didn't know a soul.

Dr. Winsted was one of those waiting and he smiled at Joel. "Joel! Ah, I see you did find a lovely lady to escort to this affair."

"Dr. Winsted, this is my neighbor who's the burn specialist at the hospital, Dr. Evangelyn Fredrickson. Evi, my department chair, Dr. Fred Winsted and I presume this is Mrs. Winsted."

Fred held out his hand to Evi and said, "I'm so glad to meet you! You have a wonderful young man there. He'll watch over you well."

"Nice to meet you, Sir," Evi murmured.

The elevator came they all boarded and were soon leaving the elevator to look across the narrow corridor into the massive, beautifully decorated ballroom. Fred turned and said, "Come on, the coatroom is down here. We can check our coats for the evening. This place is always climate controlled, no coats are necessary, especially later when there's dancing."

Joel turned Evi to follow and Joel said, "Fred, we'll be glad to follow you, I know I've never been here before and Evi tells me she hasn't either."

"Ah, yes, put a smile on your faces and it'll be fine."

Evi whispered, loud enough Joel could hear, "That's easier said than done." She giggled, as she thought of something. "You know, my mouth's usually hiding behind a mask so it doesn't matter if I smile or not."

Joel chuckled. "I never thought of that. Well, it'll show tonight, Evi!"

"I know! Joel, do you dance?"

Joel shook his head. "Evi, I have never danced a step in my life! I'm afraid I'll send you to the hospital for casts on your feet if I try to dance."

That finally brought a real smile to Evi's face. "Joel, you're being silly! Surely we can get on the dance floor and move our feet on the slow numbers."

Joel chuckled. "Perhaps, if I'm not too clumsy."

As they had planned, there weren't too many in the ballroom when Len and Jenni walked in carrying their equipment. They had decided to come early to get a feel of what they'd encounter. Much to Jenni's surprise, Len left the trusty movie camera in the coatroom, but kept the still camera around his neck. She was convinced for a long time that his motto was, 'never leave the station without it.' and because of that would always have that huge thing glued to his shoulder. With only the strap of his still camera around his neck, Jenni wished she could leave the battery-pack in the coatroom, too.

As he left the camera in the coat clerk's care, Jenni scraped her fingers across her forehead and looked at him strangely enough that he whispered, "I think I'll test the waters first. I think you're right, people like to come to things like this, but it's a whole different ballgame being on candid camera. I may rustle it up later."

Jenni nodded. "That's my feeling, but I must start off with my gear."

Len and Jenni made a tour of the huge ballroom, getting the feel of the place and noticing that several tables had name cards set up, obviously for the celebrities who had been invited. Jenni lingered, it couldn't hurt to see who the special people were who had been invited. Of course, one of those tables had a microphone and even a podium at the center place. Many tables were around the sides of the huge room, but the center was clear, most of the room was cleared for dancing.

"You a dancer, Jenni?" Len asked.

"Oh, a time or two, but never on the 'take lessons' level like some. I really don't think that's something Alex had in mind for either of us, for this evening. He said we're to mingle. How do you do that if people are dancing or if we're dancing, for that matter?"

"I'm not sure how you do that, either. It's okay with me I'm not much of a dancer anyway." He grinned at Jenni. "You know, how do you do that with a movie camera on your shoulder? I haven't been without it on assignment in a long time."

"Len, I have no clue!"

Len sighed, "Me neither."

The media pair had finished their tour of the huge ballroom when Jenni raised her head to look at the entrance. Someone had recently opened the doors and many people were coming into the ballroom. It was much closer to seven o'clock than when they arrived, so of course, people were arriving for the gala. However, her eyes snagged on one person, Joel Lawson was at the door. He took her breath away and she pulled in a gasp. The man was the epitome of male beauty. His dark blond hair was perfectly groomed and his smile was devastating. His tux fit him like it was tailored for him and all Jenni could do was stare.

Joel, the guy she knew starting as a little boy in kindergarten, and then all through twelve grades, was something to behold as a twenty-six year old man! For an instant nothing else registered and the words, "Oh, my!" whispered on her lips. Her heart rate kicked up two notches she coughed to get air in her lungs.

However, only a second later something else registered, Joel was not alone, he had someone on his arm and he was paying her a lot of attention. The lady was a beauty, and she complimented Joel's good looks perfectly. Jenni couldn't help it, her heart plummeted. Remembering back to their late night talks, she couldn't remember him ever saying anything about another woman. Perhaps they met where he now lived. Of course, she hadn't seen him to speak with him in a good long time.

Len looked where Jenni was looking and saw the couple. He remembered

Joel from the explosion site, but he looked nothing like that day. "Jenni, is that the son from that explosion?"

"Yes," she gasped. "Yes, that's Joel Lawson!"

Len shook his head. "Doesn't look much like he did that day! I remember seeing him, he looked nearly devastated! Were he and his parents close?"

"Oh, no! His dad had thrown him out of the house the night before. He and his dad never did get along, not since he started school. That's where I got to know him."

"Well, he sure has recuperated since then! He is one handsome specimen if you ask me. Is he hooked to the hospital somehow?"

"Not that I know of, but he is part of the university in our suburb."

"Good to know. A professor?"

"Oh, no, but almost. At the end of this semester I think he said." She cleared her throat. "He's got a lady on his arm. A beautiful lady!"

"Yeah, I noticed. Gonna interview 'em?" Len asked. He noticed Jenni's discomfort and wondered if knowing him through public school was all.

"Prrrrrobably not," Jenni said, breathlessly. "I… I just decided he's way out of my league and the lady…."

Len raised his camera and focused on the oblivious couple. "Maybe he's got you all stirred up, but I'm okay behind this camera."

"Mmm, you would be!"

Jenni tore her eyes away from Joel. It would not do as a reporter to be tongue-tied because of one man! As she looked away she realized that a few people later the mayor and his wife were coming in. She pulled in a deep breath and decided that later in the evening she might try for a word with Joel, but right now, she was too stirred up, but she could concentrate on that interview with the loquacious mayor. She might embarrass herself trying to interview Joel, but she would only have to raise her mike in front of the mayor and he'd be off and running with words. She knew he gave many interviews.

She could more or less stand there with her mike turned on and he'd do the rest. She shook herself, tonight was not the time to get side-tracked by an absolutely devastating, long-time acquaintance! She was here to do a job and that was to snag people for interviews. If she remembered right Alex planned for a whole segment given over to the gala tonight in tomorrow's newscast. After the mayor, she must find out who the new Chief of Staff was.

Once they were in the hallway leading to the coat room Joel realized it was rather warm for their winter coats, so he turned to Evi and said, "It looks like we'll have to wait a bit to check our coats. Could I take yours so you don't melt before it's our turn?" Already Joel was unzipping his coat and before Evi answered, he had his over his arm.

Evi was looking at him and almost lost her thoughts of what he said, as the man in his evening clothes was revealed. A little pink bloomed on Evi's neck as she cleared her throat before she said, "Umm, that'll be okay, Joel. I can put my corsage on and leave the box with my coat. By the way, you look terrific in that tux!"

It was Joel's turn to feel the warmth on his neck, above his collar. He looked at the lovely lady and simply said, "Thanks, Evi. Surely not as spectacular as you."

In the press at the coat room, Joel and Evi were separated from the Winsted's, but Joel had determined that he would do his best to show Evi an evening to remember, so he didn't let the fact that his mentor had disappeared bother him too much. He checked their coats and Evi's box and received the card with the coat check number, turned and smiled down at the lady. When Joel had shed his coat her heart began to flutter, it didn't stop when he smiled at her.

Joel pushed the card quickly in his pocket because he'd liked the feel of Evi's arm threaded around his elbow. He could tell she seemed a little nervous, so he picked up her hand and again brought it around his elbow. "Do you mind?" he whispered so that only Evi heard.

Wrapping her hand around his elbow, she whispered, "Oh, Joel, no, not at all! Umm, in fact, I feel a bit weak in the knees without your arm."

"No need for that, my lady. When I saw my aunt this morning she had some good advice. She told me to be myself. I'll give you the same recommendation, Evi. Really, it's too hard to try for anything else."

Evi breathed out a long sigh. "I'll work on that, Joel."

They stepped away from the coat check and she added, "Like I said, it's not hard to hide behind all that sterile stuff in the OR or in the Burn Unit, but none of that's allowed here." She sighed, "After all, you would think I'd matured enough to leave childish feelings behind."

"Believe me, Evi, they're not childish feelings. If you're like me, you feel overwhelmed with all this."

"Exactly!"

Joel and Evi were oblivious to anyone looking at them as they walked through the doors into the ballroom. Joel was watching Evi, but after only a few seconds she pulled her eyes away from her date and looked around the spectacularly decorated room. "Oh, my!" she whispered, "Wow! Somebody's really gone all out on this place."

"Yes, they surely have! I guess the hospital doesn't get a new Chief of Staff very often."

"Oh, no, I think the man who's been in that position has been there for years. I got notice in my box soon after I started working there that he planned to retire. I don't think it said on the notice exactly when, but he obviously wanted to be gone from the cold country by now. I think that notice said he'd been Chief of Staff for twenty some years. Of course, I was impressed, but since I didn't know him or know what he looked like, I didn't pay much attention."

"If that's what you want in retirement, this is not the place to be. Cold is something that comes early and stays late around here."

Evi nodded. "Sort of like Maine."

By this time Jenni had pulled her eyes away from Joel and focused on the mayor. Knowing Joel as she had and seeing him at the explosion site and now seeing him tonight, was like seeing two different people. Looking at him and his date, then at the mike she held and feeling the strap of the battery-pack on her shoulder made her feel like a dowdy spinster. She knew she was here for her job, not necessarily to have a good time. The thought of having a date to this thing with Joel Lawson fled her mind as she saw him come through the doors. The lady on his arm didn't help with that dowdy spinster feeling.

She hurried to the mayor, intent on catching him before he got caught up with talking to someone else and she couldn't get a word in. Knowing the man as she did and how soon someone would snag his attention, she smiled, held her mike up and said, "Hi, Mr. Mayor, Jenni Mikles from our local TV station. Have you got some thoughts about this evening? This early in the evening it's sure drawing a crowd!"

The man grinned at her and looked around to take in all the spectacular decorations and the people still coming into the ballroom. "Yes, Ma'am, that is a fact! I'm sure glad we have something like this every once in a while!

It brings beautiful people out of the woodwork, if I do say so myself." He brushed his hand down his well-fitting tux.

Jenni mustered up her best smile and said, "Yes, sir! There seem to be lots of beautiful people here this evening."

"That is a fact! Have you seen the Chief of Staff yet?"

"No sir, I haven't, but it's only been a few minutes that folks have been coming in." *I'm really not sure what he or she looks like to know if I've seen him (or her),* she thought, but didn't say out loud. Surely, they wouldn't wear a white coat and have a stethoscope around their neck!

The mayor nodded. "Yes, that's a fact. I'm sure the hospital staff or perhaps the hospital board has a program planned."

Jenni kept her smile in place and asked, "Isn't that a given?"

The man chuckled. "I'd say it is."

Of course, as soon as the doors opened for the official start of the reception, waiters and waitresses in black and white uniforms started circulating with trays with many delightful snacks for those attending to sample. Also off to one side there was a bar set up with several men also in similar uniforms waiting to take requests. Joel watched carefully as people started taking things from the trays and others headed for the bar. Surely he could do this!

A few minutes later, he stopped a waiter and helped Evi take some of the delicious looking snacks from his tray to a napkin he handed her. After they had their hands full, Evi was happy for Joel to take her to a place at a table and seat her. He put his own napkin full of snacks down beside hers then headed for the bar to see what he could get in the non-alcoholic choices. He was relieved to find that there were several options.

He came back to the chair beside Evi and placed a glass on the table for her, then sat beside her and grinned. "I remembered you said you were so hungry and I'm really very thirsty, so I hope you don't mind I started us right off."

"These little things look really good and I'm glad to get a drink. So they have quite a choice over at the bar?"

"Oh, yes, they have plenty to drink! Not all of them are my choice, but that's fine."

"Oh, Joel, I'm so glad we came together!"

Joel smiled at the lovely lady. "So am I, Evi, I'm thrilled to be here with you."

It was sometime later, after all the speeches were made and the new Chief of Staff had been introduced that Jenni looked around to see where Joel and his date were. People were sitting at the tables, but now the band was playing a song and many were also on the dance floor. When she saw him she hurried over and said, "Hi, Joel, how's life treating you these days?"

Joel took his eyes momentarily from Evi's face to look at the person with the familiar voice. Giving her a smile, Joel said, "Hi, Jenni. I'm doing quite well, thank you. Have you met Dr. Fredrickson of our hospital staff?" Jenni kept her eyes on Joel and shook her head, although she almost looked around to look for the doctor he had just named. "Evi, meet a long time acquaintance, all the way back to kindergarten, I believe, Jenni Mikles. Jenni, this is Evangelyn Fredrickson, the burn specialist from our hospital. Evi, for the few days I lived with Aunt Lucy, Jenni was my neighbor, but now that I have my own apartment, Evi is my neighbor."

Evi and Jenni wondered that Joel seemed at ease speaking with both of them at the same time. They silently sized each other up as Joel spoke. Being the reporter, Jenni spoke first. "Dr. Fredrickson, have you worked long at the hospital? Joel says you're the burn specialist."

"No, I've been there about six months, but it's a challenging position. Still, I love the work and most of the time I get to see the patients I work with get better and go home."

"So that means you sometimes don't?"

Evi shook her head. "Yes, Joel's dad was one we lost, but he was burned so badly no one was surprised. Most of us were surprised he was alive three days later when Joel found him."

"Yes, I knew about that. It was quite a shock to learn that he'd lived at all after what I saw there at the site. There certainly was nothing of the house left when Len and I went out there! Joel, has anyone been able to determine the cause?"

"Yes, only a few days ago I received a very official letter from a state lab saying they had determined the explosion was caused by something faulty in either the furnace or the water heater. Some debris in the hole had traces of propane on it. Of course, there was nothing left of either of them, so other than that, we'll never know."

"I see you're here as Dr. Fredrickson's guest, but I also see some faculty from your university here, too."

"Yes," Joel smiled at Evi, but said to Jenni, "we came because of our official positions, but we're neighbors in our apartment complex. We've gotten acquainted that way and I for one am glad to escort my neighbor to this gala." Jenni didn't let it show, but Joel's words put a spike into her heart. It seems she'd lost her chance with Joel Lawson. Their late night chats hadn't put that kind of smile or spark in his eyes – not ever!

"Yes, I'm sure Lucy's house was very small."

A few seconds after Jenni started interviewing the couple Len came up, his camera rolling. Undoubtedly, Dr. Evangelyn Fredrickson and almost Dr. Joel Lawson would be on local news in a day or two. However, Joel didn't mind being interviewed with Evi, not like he avoided talking to the reporter at the explosion site. This event didn't link him to Thad Lawson.

Jenni and Len had finished their interview with Joel and Evi by a few minutes, long enough that they'd moved a few feet onto the dance floor. The band was playing a slow number, so Joel and Evi decided to take advantage of that and try their skills at a slow dance. Seconds later they were surrounded by several other couples enjoying the dance.

Moments later there was a commotion at the entry doors. There hadn't been any stragglers for quite a while and the doors were shut, so most everyone looked toward the doors to see who was coming in and making such a dramatic entry. Joel looked over Evi's shoulder to see someone he'd hoped never to see again – Sheriff Gibbs. His heart nearly stopped at the sight of him. The words, "Oh, my! Why is he here?" slipped from his mouth. Fortunately, there were several couples between where the sheriff stood and where Joel and Evi were. Even so, Joel tried to maneuver them even further away from the doors as the music continued to play.

The sheriff was dressed in his official uniform, even his hat placed squarely on his head. He had his belt with the holster and his sidearm in place. His hand-cuffs dangled menacingly from his belt. Joel's breath hitched as the officer looked around, obviously looking for someone. Joel was sure he knew who the obnoxious man was looking for. The sheriff had barely started his perusal of the huge room when Joel turned his back on the man and tried making his feet cooperate in the dance he and Evi were sharing so that they could move farther away. At that moment Joel was not happy that he was a tall man.

However, Joel couldn't help the helpless tension that spread quickly throughout his body and Evi immediately picked up on it. "What is it, Joel?" she whispered. "Is it that man who just came in? He's the sheriff? Why on earth would he be here? There's nothing going on, there's no disturbance! Why would he be in full uniform?"

He buried his head in her hair close to her ear and whispered back, "Yes, that's Sheriff Gibbs and he's looking around. He hated Dad and visited the house many times over the years. He tried over and over to get him sentenced to prison, but couldn't pin anything substantial on him. Unfortunately he and I were both at the explosion site at the same time. Since then, he's hounded me several times, trying to pin the explosion on me. The last time was only the other day on Thanksgiving. He made some rather radical accusations that day."

"Oh, my! Why would the man come here? How would he know you're here? Surely he's not looking for you!"

Still keeping his head down, he whispered, "Even if he is, I'm hoping he doesn't see me. I do believe I would be mortified if he tried to single me out!"

"Oh, my! Let's move farther away!"

Joel kept his face turned away from the sheriff, but the man had made enough of a disturbance that the band noticed and stopped playing. This also caught Len and Jenni's attention, so they scurried over to catch whatever the sheriff would say or do now that he'd crashed the reception, and caused everything to stop because he'd made such a grand entrance. As they made their way towards the man, Len started his movie camera, catching not only the sheriff but also many of the guests that now stood petrified in their places. The sheriff looked so out of place in the ballroom with his uniform and sidearm.

The guests at the party looked around and everyone seemed confused to see the sheriff and even more so because he was in full uniform. Most of them continued to stare at the man, perplexed. The man had made such a dramatic entrance that once the band stopped playing, there was silence in the huge ballroom. Most of the guests felt as Evi, wondering why the man had appeared. It made no sense for the sheriff to crash a reception for the hospital's new Chief of Staff. Hospitals usually had no reason to deal with the sheriff in any capacity except to care for people with medical problems. Occasionally they had to patch up a police officer or a victim, but that was not a regular occurrence.

The mayor had been talking to someone and had his back to the doors, but when he became aware that everything had ground to a halt, he whirled around, saw who had come in and wasted no time walking over even before the sheriff moved from the doorway. The look on the mayor's face let everyone in attendance know how he felt about the man with the gun on his belt. Jenni quickly turned on her mike to catch every word both the mayor said and also the sheriff.

Even as he crossed the room, into the stillness the mayor said, "So, Sheriff Gibbs, what brings you to this reception for our hospital's new Chief of Staff? I'm not sure who might have called you to say that we needed police protection at this affair, but as far as I can tell and I'm sure you can see, things are peaceful and folks are having a good time. Was there something you needed that you could only find here at this reception?"

"I'm looking for someone," he growled. "I was told he was here."

Because everything had stopped, everyone heard what the mayor said to the sheriff and his reply. Len was right beside Jenni, his movie camera rolling. Everyone watched the mayor approach the sheriff. Jenni had never liked Sheriff Gibbs and after witnessing what he'd done at Lucy's on Thanksgiving, she wondered if the man was looking for Joel. She had no idea why. If that was his reason, she was mortified for Joel! Since she stood so close to the action, she didn't look for Joel, but she hoped he'd gotten far away from where the sheriff stood looking around.

The words had barely left Sheriff Gibbs's mouth when the mayor reached his side, but didn't lower his voice as he said, "You know, Sheriff, I don't know who you might be looking for and I'm not sure it's relevant, but I hardly think it's in yours or anyone else's best interest to bring your problems to this affair at this time. Perhaps you can catch up with whomever you're wishing to speak with some other time and at some other place!" Just the way the mayor said those words let most everyone know how he felt about the sheriff.

The sheriff was a big man and had his mouth open to reply, but surprising him, the mayor took his arm, even though he outweighed the mayor, turned the man around and forcefully walked him to the doors. With his free hand the mayor reached for the handle on one of the doors and pulled it open. Len's camera kept rolling and captured the totally shocked expression on the sheriff's face as the mayor pulled him over the threshold, stepped back, and pushed the door closed behind him, right in the sheriff's face. The sheriff didn't give any resistance.

Perhaps expecting the sheriff to try to push his way back in, the mayor leaned on the door but raised his voice and said, "Let's resume our activities, folks. There's no need to stop dancing or eating. It's still quite early. We are here to have a good time!" Acting totally at ease, the mayor grinned at the full room. "Come on, band, let's get on with this great evening! It's no where near time to close this great occasion down!"

Even so, Joel let out a long sigh and moved Evi farther away from the big doors.

Sheriff Gibbs quickly stepped back from the door that had nearly smacked him in the face. He balled his fists at his sides and let out a hiss. He never liked the mayor of his suburb and obviously the feeling was mutual. He pulled in a big breath and only moments after being unceremoniously removed from the ballroom and having the door closed in his face, raised his fist as if to pound on the door, but instead, jerked on his hat that had been knocked sideways on his head, pivoted on his heel and stormed back to his car.

When he reached his car, he showed his anger by kicking a tire and grabbed his cell phone from his belt, leaned on the fender and jabbed a finger on one number, then put the phone to his ear. When the voice answered, he yelled, "Thought you said he'd be there!"

"He wasn't?"

"Well, achally, I da know. Didn't get much chance ta look around. The old geezer, the mayor come right over and put me out! Slammed the door in my face!"

The voice was irate, as it said, "Listen Gibbs, you gotta git sompin on that kid pronto! Get 'im hauled in and behind bars or you and me is gonna suffer big time!"

The man whined, "Can't do nothin' looks too illegal, my job'd be on the line, ya know!"

"Listen man, who put you in that office anyhow?"

Much more subdued, Gibbs replied, "Yeah, I'll work on that."

"You do that!" The dial tone echoed in the sheriff's ear.

Sheriff Gibbs said a few choice words into the dead phone, slammed it into his belt carrier, kicked the tire again, yanked open his car door and slouched into the seat, maneuvered his long legs under the steering wheel and slammed a fist on the wheel. He yanked on the door and grumbled, "First of all, I never saw 'im there. If he was, don't know how long he'll stay. Don't know if he drove – I could be settin' here a good long time and never see 'im. The kid's slicker'n oil on a rainy road! Can't seem to catch 'im 'cept there at that Steel woman's place. Wonder who's pad he hangs his hat?"

He sighed, if this had been a perfect time to snag Joel Lawson, like his contact said, he'd lost it. He started the car and made his way to the street from the circle drive in front of the massive building. "Guess I'll save that for another day. Ben kinda watchin' that Steel woman's house, but he ain't there much." He let out another sigh. "Can't go there much, can't let 'em know I'm watchin' – that Mr. Wilson's there some, too. Me and him don't get along!" The car lurched its way onto the city street and left.

Joel was about to ask if Evi was ready to leave when he saw a man with white streaks in his dark hair coming purposefully toward them. He glanced down at Evi and asked, "Know that gentleman coming this way?"

Evi looked away from Joel and a smile burst across her face. "Dr. Morris! It's good to see you. Have any word I can give Allison?"

The doctor smiled broadly at Evi and said, "You know, Evi, you've been hiding in plain sight all evening! I have been looking for you since I came. I never saw you look so lovely and this fine gentleman with you… my, my!"

Evi laughed. "Thanks, doctor. Yes, when I wear scrubs and that sterile outfit so much, anything else seems foreign. Until Joel took my arm there at my apartment I felt way out of my league. My escort this evening is Joel Lawson. He'll soon have his doctorate and will be teaching at our local university. So… any news for Allison?"

The doctor smiled. "Yes, Evi, you don't have to come, but please have Allison call for an interview as soon as she can will you? I got the official word from the board this morning."

"Oh, yes, doctor, I'll call her tomorrow."

The doctor looked at Joel and asked, "So Evi, this fine young man who's been keeping your interest all evening will be a member of our university faculty soon?"

"Yes, Dr. Morris, it'll be next semester. He's been teaching at our hometown university in the science department."

Dr. Morris turned his full attention on Joel and said, "Joel Lawson… Say, I know you're the fella Fred Winsted can't say enough good things about and a week or so ago agreed to join his staff. Isn't that right?"

Joel felt the heat creep up his neck at the doctor's words. He was amazed that a doctor from the hospital knew about him. He smiled and held out his hand and the doctor took it to shake. "Sir, I am a TA under Dr. Winsted and I did accept the position that's been offered to me to join the Science Department – that is as soon as my thesis is accepted by my committee."

Dr. Morris threw his head back and laughed. "Yes, I believe Fred did say you are a bit too humble about your accomplishments. He's told me you will be a feather in the department's cap and they are very excited for you to join them."

"Thank you, sir." Evi looked up at her date and was surprised to see the pink that was spreading up from his neck to his cheeks.

"Well, Evi, have your friend call me as soon as you can reach her. I'll be waiting for her call in the next day or so."

"Thank you, Dr. Morris, I will."

Only a few minutes after Dr. Morris left them Joel looked down at Evi in time to see her cover a yawn. He grinned and said, "Do I get the impression that you're ready to head back to our apartments and call it a night?"

"Joel, I'm sorry, I'm not a night owl and you know I work lots of hours at the hospital. Now that I talked with Dr. Morris, I am ready. But Joel, what if that sheriff is waiting for you?"

Shaking his head, Joel shrugged and said, "Evi, if he is, he is. I have nothing to hide he's the one who continues to harass me."

"I know, but that would be a horrid way to end this super-duper evening!"

Joel sighed and nodded. "Yes, it would be, that's for sure. I surely can't say for you, but this has been a highlight in my life."

"Yes, it has for me too, Joel. Believe me, you've made this evening very special for me. I've never had such a good time!"

Joel's eyes twinkled. "Evi, even when I happened to step on you toes?"

"Oh, Joel, that was only on the edge of my shoe, it was nothing."

Chuckling, Joel said, "You're being kind, Evi."

However, others must have been watching and had the same idea as Evi, because as Joel linked his arm with Evi and headed toward the big doors several men from the Science Department and their wives appeared and the whole group circled around Joel and Evi and escorted them from the ballroom, to the coat check and stayed with them even down the elevator to Evi's car. When they were safely in her car and Joel was headed for the exit, only then the other couples made their way to their own cars.

"Wow!" Joel said, "That was amazing!" As he paid the parking fee at the exit booth he looked around, the street that they exited onto was empty; there wasn't a white car with letters emblazoned on the side waiting.

Evi laid her hand on Joel's arm and said, "I'm glad they did that for you. It shows how much they like you Joel, and I couldn't agree more."

"Thanks," he said, simply.

As they neared the exit on the circle bypass that was closest to their suburb, Evi asked, "Tomorrow's Sunday. Do you go to church, Joel?"

"Oh, yes! It's a highlight of my week, Evi!"

"Could I… could I go with you?"

"Of course, that would be great, Evi!" In the lights of the exit Joel looked over at her and grinned. "Now, of course, you don't have to be all this fancy to go, you know. But probably that sterile outfit you've been telling me about wouldn't be right either."

Evi laughed, as Joel hoped she would. "I promise I have other clothes that fall somewhere between this and that. I'll be ready when you say."

"I usually pick up Auntie and Les, so could you be ready by say, eight-thirty?"

"Sure! Unless I get an early morning call from the hospital, I'll be ready."

"That's great, Evi! I'm looking forward to taking you."

"Believe me, it'll be a new experience."

Monday morning, a week later, it was still dark and Leslie was still in her gable room getting ready for school when she heard a loud crash not too far away. She quickly looked out her little window to see a spectacular collision half a block away at the intersection. With the impact, there was an instantaneous ball of fire that lit up the entire intersection. The sight sent goose bumps down her spine and tears to her eyes.

Soon, even before she left the room, a siren started blaring, making her wonder how that could have called such quick action. The first to arrive was a first responder's truck, moments later a fire truck, an ambulance and several police cars pulled in completely blocking the intersection. Along with the blaze, each of the emergency vehicles had all their lights on the accident immediately. It was amazing how many dark figures she could see rushing around. It made her heart lurch, it brought back thoughts of the horrible explosion that had destroyed the house she'd lived in for sixteen years and took the lives of her parents only a short time before.

Lucy also heard the commotion and rushed from the kitchen to turn on the TV to the local station by the time Leslie came downstairs. Both of them heard the local news anchor break into the national network and frantically said, "Folks, we interrupt this newscast with local coverage of a very serious accident that only happened moments ago."

The man looked over his shoulder, but continued, "Witnesses report, our city's Sheriff Gibbs was crossing an intersection at a high rate of speed without his lights or siren and was struck broadside by an on-coming car, who obviously didn't see him. The civilian's car burst into flames and momentarily engulfed both cars. Both drivers were travelling alone, but at this time the status of either driver is unknown. We will air more details as they are made available."

Shocked, Leslie exclaimed, "Auntie! The sheriff!"

"I know, sweetheart, we must pray for him and also for the other driver."

"I wonder why the sheriff was on our street so early this morning?"

"I can't tell you, Honey, we'll have to wait to hear more." *Although I can make an educated guess that he thought Joel might be here*! She said, silently to herself.

"Oh, wow!"

Jenni was jolted out of a sound sleep by the crash she heard not far away. Without thinking, she scrambled out of bed and grabbed some clothes, not worrying whether they matched or not and threw them on. She didn't even take the time to comb her hair! She'd never threaded her feet into shoes so fast! Only moments later she grabbed pen and paper and her cell phone, since that's all she ever had here at her house. As an after-thought she grabbed her coat. The minute she was outside, since the accident was so close she started snapping pictures with her phone, even as she ran down the block, her adrenalin pumping. The scene was devastating the fire engulfed both cars.

Moments later, the first responder truck appeared, then the fire truck and before the fire fighters could get set up the ambulance arrived and right on their heels two police cars arrived. Jenni kept snapping pictures. It was then she realized that one of the cars involved in the accident was a sheriff's car and Jenni wondered if it was a deputy or the sheriff. A few minutes after the fire truck started spraying water on the cars the fire was controlled and the first responders and the firemen worked feverishly at getting the two victims out of the cars. The EMTs were at the scene with their gurneys ready to load the victims as soon as they were evacuated from the charred vehicles. If it was the sheriff she didn't have to think long to decide why he was on her street at this hour.

Jenni couldn't get close enough to see who the victims were, so she asked a fireman, who told her, "Ma'am, we believe that's the sheriff's car. He was probably driving it."

"Oh, my! Sheriff Gibbs?"

The man nodded. "We believe so."

"Wow! It's really early, isn't it for him to be out?"

"We've heard by a grapevine there's a place close by he's been keeping under surveillance for some time now."

SIXTEEN

Almost positive whose house the man had been watching, she said, "Well, I guess that'll end today. He sure won't be doing anything but lying in a hospital bed!"

The fireman nodded. "Yes, Ma'am, it looks that way. Can't understand why he didn't announce himself, even this early in the morning." Jenni nodded, but didn't add a comment. Since he was on this street, she was pretty sure she knew. Once the two victims were on the gurneys the EMTs ran them the few steps to the ambulance, loaded them and left immediately.

Right after her coffee maker had let out its last wheeze, Evi received a text message – *Doc; just got call – ambulance heading in with two critical patients from car fire.*

Be right there! Hastily filling her large to-go mug and grabbing the bagel she'd already spread with cream cheese, Evi raced for her patio door, threw her coat around her, grabbed up her food again and ran out the door. From the door she hit the door opener on her key fob. The car beeped at her and the lights went on.

Joel sat at his table that was close to his big patio door with the drape wide open. He hadn't put his full mug to his lips when he saw movement outside and looked into the darkness, but only a second later a grin spread across his face. His lovely neighbor was on the move. Evi waved her mug at him and of course, he waved back. He didn't move from his seat before she was in her car and it was moving. Only moments later she backed out of her place and was headed, with her flashers going out of the parking lot.

"Wow! I wonder what happened? She's in a really big hurry! Something awful serious must have happened!" Joel bowed his head immediately. "Lord, be with Evi. Something really bad must have happened this early. Guide her hands and her mind, Father, God." Joel finished his coffee and went for his briefcase to go to the university for his eight o'clock class. Since he always lingered over his coffee, he didn't consult his phone, the TV or any other means of communication before he left. He didn't encounter any problems on his way to campus.

However, Evi sped towards the hospital, her flashers going, only hesitating at the intersections in the early morning's light traffic. She left her car in her spot, but held the key fob behind her to lock the car, then rushed through the doors into the ER. The doors hadn't even closed behind her when one of the night shift ER doctors ran to her. Breathless, he said, "Doc! We got the sheriff and another guy in those two rooms. Sheriff's burned really bad!"

"I'll scrub – have a sterile gown, mask and gloves ready when I'm finished."

"Will do, Doc!"

A very short time later, Evi, wearing sterile gown, mask and gloves, walked into the triage room where a very still, very extensively burned sheriff lay on the gurney. The staff had removed his burned clothing so Evi could see the extent of the injuries better. Evi took one look at the man and said, "Transport him immediately to the OR. I'll have to take a closer look at him in a completely sterile place to know how extensive the surgery will be. I need to check out this other patient also and see what he'll need. Probably taking him upstairs too would be a good idea. I may have to go from one to the other."

As Evi removed her gloves, ready to leave the room, two other men rushed in with a transport gurney. Evi left the room right behind them and went to the sink to scrub and apply another set of sterile gloves before she went to the other room to see the other patient. Moments later she entered the other room and shook her head. "Yes, get this guy immediately upstairs. He'll need surgery, but let's sedate him before he's moved. He's awake and in a lot of pain."

"Yes, Doctor," several people said.

Joel parked in the parking lot of the science building and headed inside to teach his eight o'clock class expecting to have a moment to sort his notes and get a breath before his first student came. Mondays were notorious for half-asleep students. However, his first student stood outside his classroom, wide awake and bursting with information. Excitedly, he exclaimed, "Prof, did you hear the news? Sheriff Gibbs was in a really bad accident only a bit ago! He was racing through an intersection somewhere, but didn't have his lights or siren on! Some guy didn't see him and slammed into him. The two cars burst into flames instantly! I heard about it and some pictures are here on my phone. It looks really serious and nobody knows how they are! The emergency stuff got there really quick, but still!"

"Wow! Thanks for telling me!" *I'm sure that's why Evi was in such a hurry!*

Something in one of the pictures caught his eye. "Say, could I take a better look at your phone? I'd like to see the scene more clearly."

"Sure, here!"

"Thanks."

Joel took the phone and expanded the print to its fullest, then made one spot bigger. There was no mistaking the corner he knew well not far from Aunt Lucy's house. He cleared his throat, let out a sigh and returned the phone. "Thanks, thanks for letting me see that."

"Oh sure not a problem, Prof."

At suppertime, an exhausted Evi drove slowly onto the parking lot. Joel had heard about the accident several times and seen many pictures on students' phones, so he'd been watching for Evi since he'd arrived home. Even before she'd turned off the ignition, he was at her car. With a somber smile he opened her door and helped her out. Instead of helping her to her own patio, he took her several feet away to his and helped her into his apartment. Without a word, he seated her on his couch, where she leaned her head back immediately. She wasn't sure she could have walked another step.

Evi closed her eyes, but finally, she said, "Joel, the sheriff's really bad. I'll have to grab something and then go back so I can be close by. Allison's there, but she has my cell phone number on speed-dial. This first twenty-four hours are critical and at this time it's really touch and go with him. He hasn't responded since he was brought in. The other guy's not quite so bad, but he's no where near out of the woods either. Believe me, it was a horrendous day!"

Joel sat down and circled her shoulders. Tenderly, he kissed her lips. "I'm sorry to hear that, Evi. I'm sure you've been at full capacity all day! I've got supper fixed so as soon as I saw you I could set food on the table. You rest until

I have it set out. I'm sure it's a terrible trauma for you." Evi leaned forward and Joel helped her with her coat then smiled tenderly at her.

She leaned forward but looked askance at Joel and exclaimed, "Joel, it's Sheriff Gibbs! He's been out to get you! He was on your aunt's street! That means he was after you!"

"I know, Evi, I know. I also learned that he was on the street that goes in front of Auntie's house, so I'm sure he thought I'd be there, since it was so early this morning. I can't figure out why he didn't have his lights flashing, at least. But Evi, he's a member of the human race. He's a person made in God's image. God loves him and wants him to turn his sins over to be covered by the blood of Jesus. I have been praying for him and the other man all day."

Evi collapsed back against the comfortable seat of the couch. "Amazing!" she whispered as she closed her eyes. "Truly amazing! Joel, you are one amazing man! I don't know of one other person who would feel like you say!"

Joel only shook his head, as he said, "Evi, I only try to do what God in his Word tells me to do and that's to pray for my enemies. Surely Sheriff Gibbs qualifies for that."

Adamantly, Evi said, "I know that for a fact! Joel, he's accused you of so much, he's harassed you so many times! I don't know the man personally, but because he's after you, I'm having trouble even taking care of the man! Believe me it's only because of the oath I took as I graduated to treat any and all persons that I'm doing it! To think he put so many people in danger to try to put something on you is beyond incredible." She took in another long, slow breath and added, "When I'm looking at that man's burns it's hard to pray for him."

"Yes, I'm sure that's true, but thanks, Evi, thanks for your vote of confidence."

They ate Joel's delicious omelet and Evi chugged two glasses of tea. As she set her empty glass down, she let out a long sigh and said, "Thanks, Joel, that was delicious, but I hardly tasted it. I must get back. Allison's there, but I know with two men it's hard to keep an eye on both of them. We'll probably have to spell each other all night. Except for when he was under anesthesia, Mr. Whiting's been awake, so we must monitor his pain level because his burns are extensive." She shrugged. "The sheriff; who knows if and when he'll wake up, but we must be prepared; he'll be in a lot of pain."

"It does sound like a bad night for you both."

It was only an hour after she arrived that Joel helped Evi back into her coat and walked her to her car. He closed her door as she inserted her key in the ignition and started her car. She was prepared to spend the night in the Burn Unit doing vigil between the sheriff and Mr. Whiting. Both very badly burned. It would be a long night, there would be no sleep for either she or her PA, Allison.

As Joel watched her tail lights leave the parking lot, he murmured, "My Father, be with Evi. She's been there at the hospital all day working on the sheriff and the other man. She's had one horrendous day. She's exhausted, I'm sure. She probably can't sleep tonight but give her a clear mind and if possible rest her body. I pray also for the sheriff and that other man. If it is Your will, heal them. Amen."

EPILOGUE

IT WAS THE NIGHT BEFORE. TOMORROW WAS THE FRIDAY BEFORE CHRISTMAS BREAK and Joel was to present his thesis before his committee. He and Evi ate dinner together again, but Evi had prepared the scrumptious meal for them. With all her many accomplishments, she was also an excellent cook. Joel dined with her and eaten far too much.

Over the last three days he'd spent hours in the copy room at the university library and used reams of paper making copies of his completed thesis. He hoped he hadn't forgotten anyone and had one copy for all those who had asked for one. Each of his committee members had received a copy. He had given a copy to his chairman to deliver to the publisher. He made another copy for his granddad because he'd asked for one.

Tonight, after coming back to his apartment from Evi's he opened his laptop one more time and read through his completed thesis, hoping that there wasn't one wrong letter that he missed in his final revision. He worried that he read through it so many times that he missed one wrong word that would stand out like a wooden nickel in the batch.

It was after midnight, his shoulders sagged, and his eyes were blurry and scratched so much he had to rub them before he pushed down the screen on his laptop. He slowly shed his clothes, wishing he already had and was in his comfortable night sweats so he didn't have to do that chore. Finally, it was done, but before he collapsed onto his bed, he fell to his knees.

As he bowed his head over the edge of the bed, he whispered, "My Father, thank You for being my God, for loving me as only You can. Thank You for bringing me to this place..." He woke up cold, his knees sore. The clock beside the bed showed him it was long after two o'clock. He put his elbows on the mattress, not even sure he had enough oomph to roll onto the bed or pull up his covers before his eyes closed.

The next thing he was aware of was the music playing in his ear from his clock radio set for the time he should get up to teach his last class before Christmas break. He showered, brushed his teeth and did the best job he could with his razor. Back in his bedroom, he splashed on some aftershave around his face, and went to his closet to decide what to wear. He must dress appropriately for both his class and his presentation because he didn't plan to come back to his apartment in-between. He expected his class to only be half full most of his students would probably take a cut to get an early start on the trip home for three weeks' vacation.

He sat at his table with a mug full of coffee thinking about this day that had finally arrived. He had done everything he knew to do, and everything his committee chairman had told him he must do. As far as he knew, he was as ready to defend his thesis as he ever would be. All that stood between him and that presentation was a class of sleepy students.

His committee chairman, Dr. Henry Lambert, had reserved the amphitheater in the science building for his presentation. He had no idea why they needed such a large room. As far as he knew, he and his committee would sit around a table – on the lowest level - for them to ask him questions and him to answer them. Other than that, he knew all four of his grandparents, Auntie and Leslie were coming. If she didn't receive a frantic, urgent call from the hospital, Evi also planned to come. Perhaps some of his science professors and members of the faculty he was joining in a few weeks would come. But a room more than twice the size of a large classroom – why? The number of people he expected could be comfortable in two rows of seats.

He drained his coffee cup, needing the fortifying caffeine, finally left his chair, washed his breakfast dishes, loaded his briefcase again today for his class and also his laptop and one more hardcopy of his dissertation. He pulled in a deep breath, once again shrugged into his uncle's coat, picked up his briefcase and headed out the door. He tried not to be nervous; he'd done these things nearly every day since the semester started. He pulled in a deep breath of the cold, December air and took the few steps to his car. Leslie's words of all those weeks before went through his mind – 'Bro, stay the course'.

"Yes, I will do my best to 'stay the course'."

The light was on in Evi's apartment and he could see her through her patio door. She waved to him, so he waved back, slid behind the wheel, intent on starting the car. For the first time, when he turned the key, nothing happened. He let off on the key, then a moment later he tried again – nothing happened, there wasn't even a click.

Evi watched him through her door. When he still hadn't gotten the car started five minutes later, she opened her door and looked out, expecting him to notice her. Of course he did and opened his car door, knowing she wanted to say something. "Won't it start?" she asked.

"It doesn't even want to turn over!" Joel exclaimed.

Reaching for her coat and her keys, she said, "I'm ready, come on, we'll go in my car."

"Evi, that's silly! You'll waste two hours. I must teach this class at eight o'clock then there's an hour before my defense starts at ten."

She left the door, pulled on her coat and grabbed her purse and her keys again. As she walked out the door, she said, "No matter, your car won't start, you'd be late for your class if you called for help. I'm coming to your defense, so we'll go together now."

"And waste two hours of your time?"

Evi pulled her door closed and immediately slammed her fists on her hips. "Joel Lawson! Your car won't start; I'm going to your defense; Allison's all primed to take on all things in the burn department. The ER staff knows to call her and so does the Burn Unit staff. I am off the hook! So, don't give me any grief, we'll go in my car! *End of discussion!*"

Giving her a broad grin, Joel couldn't help but chuckle. "Yes, Ma'am!" He touched an invisible hat with a two fingered salute.

She huffed as she used her key fob to unlock her doors as Joel grabbed his briefcase and put his feet on the ground. As they settled in Evi's car he asked, "So what'll you do while I teach my half-asleep, half class of students?"

She let out another huff as her car started immediately and said, "I will sit in the back and be the only wide-awake, intelligent person in your class this morning!"

Joel breathed out a resigned sigh and said, "Okay, don't say I didn't warn you."

However, by eight o'clock not only were every one of his students present in his class, they all were much wider awake than he had ever found them all semester. When he asked the class why, they all had the same answer; everyone was coming to his defense at ten. He was also informed by several of the students that everyone from his other classes would also be there. He breathed out a sigh, now he knew why Dr. Lambert had reserved the big amphitheater. Now he had reason to be nervous! If he had it right, over two hundred people would be in the room.

When the last student left he murmured, "God in heaven! Please, give me Your words!"

As he opened his eyes, lowering the lid of his briefcase, Evi came up to the desk. She exclaimed, "Joel! No wonder your classes are full and they must turn students away! You're an awesome teacher. Believe me; I learned so much from this one class. Now I know why Dr. Winsted thinks his department is getting such a catch!"

"Oh, Evi, I do believe you're prejudiced!"

"Maybe so, but you're great! You make the study of old rocks come alive!"

By this time in their relationship, Joel was not questioning himself. He swung his briefcase off the desk with his left hand and grabbed hold of Evi's hand with his other. He had decided to spend what was left of the hour between his class and his defense in the amphitheater so they made their way through the halls to the large room. When they arrived a janitor was ahead of them. He turned on the bank of lights and went to the thermostat.

Joel didn't know the man and obviously he didn't know who Joel was, when he asked, "How do you want the heat in here, Sir?"

Joel grinned and said, "Well, since it's me in the hot seat, probably as low as it'll go."

Immediately, Evi started to grin, but the janitor didn't seem to know how to take what Joel said. He cleared his throat and obviously confused, he said, "Umm, Sir?"

Joel also grinned and answered, "Sir, I'm a bit nervous, so don't mind me. Set the thermostat in the normal comfort zone. Thanks."

Joel wanted to spend some quiet time before his defense, but that wasn't going to happen. Soon after the janitor left and Joel put his briefcase on the table where Dr. Lambert had instructed him a door opened. In walked Steve and Mary, then right behind them the Wilson's came. Only a few seconds behind them came Lucy and Leslie.

Joel looked up at the big clock on the wall and said, "You guys are here really early! You know, of course, you'll have to sit in the back, don't you?"

Steve came up beside his grandson and asked, "And why is that?"

Joel's eyes twinkled as he said, "You'll be a total distraction, of course."

Ed plunked himself down in the last seat on the front row and said, "Too bad. I've claimed my seat and nobody's taking it from me!" Having said that, all the rest of Joel's family took seats across the front row and Evi took the seat closest to Joel on the center aisle.

Only a few minutes later, Fred Winsted came rushing in holding two rolls of white rope. He looked around the room and saw that Joel's family was here, but they were the only ones. As he started stringing the ropes over the rows of seats across the aisle from Evi, he said, "Whew! I was afraid I wouldn't get here in time!"

"In time for what, Fred?" Joel asked.

"I saw people start coming in here and I knew the faculty wanted good seats, so I ran back to my office for this rope. We didn't want to lose out!"

As Joel watched, a tingle went up his spine and he said, "Fred, you know I wasn't nervous when I drank my coffee this morning, then my car wouldn't start. Then I get here and none of my students have left for vacation and they tell me they're coming to this meeting. Then on their way out they tell me that the rest of my students are coming. I knew my family was coming, but now you pile it on by telling me the faculty's coming and you sure are stringing that rope awful far!"

Fred finished with the second rope and came to Joel. As he put his arm around the young man, he smiled and said, "Joel, we're all rooting for you! You'll do fine."

"Yeah, maybe if I had blinders so I couldn't see you all!"

Still with his arm around the young man the doctor looked at the people on the front row and said, "Some of you want to come be a part of this while I pray for Joel?"

Everyone on the front row stood and came around Joel, but Evi hurried to stand beside Joel and put her arm around him. Joel choked up as he slipped his arm around Evi and quickly bowed his head. The rest of his family circled around him and he felt all their hands on his back and shoulders. In his heart he said, "*Thank You, Lord, for these wonderful people!*"

Fred waited a moment, but then he said, "Father, God, You have blessed our school with this young man. His testimony and his dependence on You has inspired many of us. Quiet his heart and give him Your words. Thank You, amen."

As Fred finished praying the doors started opening. The door close by hardly closed as Joel's committee came in, but right along with them other faculty came in filling the seats Fred had roped off. Doors further back and from other floors opened as students began coming in. By ten o'clock, stragglers had to stand against the wall. Long before ten Joel decided that he would keep his eyes on his committee and concentrate on what they had to say. He had no idea the topic of his thesis had drawn so much interest. Was it true what Dr. Lambert had hinted when he handed him the extra copy that his was one of only a few books on his subject?

The clock on the wall registered ten o'clock and Joel felt a trickle of moisture slide down his back. Dr. Lambert stood up with a mike. Looking out at the audience he said, "Folks, we're here to listen to and discuss Joel Lawson's paper that is his doctoral thesis. We will be asking him questions pertaining to this paper. Thank you all for coming, now we'll get started. We plan to be finished right around noon."

As Evi found out when she'd sat in his class earlier, Joel was very knowledgeable and also very interesting as well as convincing. She sat enthralled for the entire time the questions and answers flew back and forth. She realized she knew a lot about the physical body, but she gained a great education and her beliefs that she had been taught during her years of education in the secular world, were challenged. The time flew by; she never once looked at the clock.

She was astonished when Dr. Lambert again stood up and said, "Folks, I think we have exhausted all our questions for Joel. He has chosen a hard topic to address, but has done it with excellence. I believe all of us on his committee agree that this young man has passed every hurdle that we have thrown at him." He held out his hand to Joel and continued, "Welcome to the academic community as Doctor Joel T. Lawson, PhD. Joel, in only a few days you will receive your sheepskin, or a replica. When you walk in the June exercises you will receive the actual sheepskin. Again, congratulations."

Joel also stood up and took the doctor's hand. In a voice not quite what it normally sounded like, he said, "Thank you, Dr. Lambert, thank you, all of you for believing in me."

The words had barely left his mouth when the entire amphitheater erupted in applause. As it continued, first the faculty, and closely after them, the students all stood to give Joel a standing ovation. He looked up to the far reaches of the room and saw that everyone who was in the place was on his feet applauding. Tears came to his eyes and streamed down his cheeks, he couldn't stop them. He pulled a hanky, the same one that had caught the blood from his temple when his dad threw him out of his house, and attempted to quench the flow of tears.

He remembered something he'd said to himself not too many weeks before – he was the son of a man who had forbad him to continue his education beyond high school. It was indeed amazing what God had performed in his life. When his tears finally stopped, he looked at his family on the front row and remembered Leslie's words – "Bro, stay the course."

Moments after the applause stopped people started coming around to shake Joel's hand. Not only had all of his students come to hear his defense but many from his church, including his pastor came to shake his hand. Tom was profuse with his praise and a very hardy handshake. From the back row members of the press also came to offer their congratulations. One of them was Jenni Mikles. However, she had seen Evi on the front row, so she only shook Joel's hand and gave him a tight smile, then quickly joined Len and they left almost before it registered in Joel's mind that she had been there.

Much to Joel's surprise, his committee and others from the Science Department joined Joel's family insisting that they were taking him out for a noon dinner in a local restaurant. When they arrived, Joel was overcome again when the host ushered them into the private dining room for the meal. There were no menus, Joel's committee had made all the arrangements and all Joel could do was shake his head in awe.

He was the product of an abusive home. His parents refused him their love and kept him from the love of his paternal grandparents. They had also tried to keep him from knowing the Creator God, but God had penetrated all of those obstacles and brought Joel to Himself. Joel was overwhelmed by everything. He also felt he had stayed the course.

It had been a day to remember, a day Joel wouldn't soon forget. Finally, he and Evi were in her car and she was driving them back to their apartments.

Joel reached over and took her hand. "Evi, did you know all that was going to happen today?"

"No, I didn't know about all of it, but I did get a call from Dr. Winsted and he told me some of what he thought would be happening. It was enough to know that you would be tied up the whole day and that, if possible, I should be free." She pulled in their apartment parking lot and gave him her smile. "Joel, honey, you deserved every bit of what you got!"

Joel shook his head. "It truly is amazing! I am in awe of God Himself."

Evi pulled into her parking spot and Joel squeezed her hand. "Stay right there and I'll come around for you."

Evi sat still as Joel moved around the back of the car. Out of Evi's sight, he put one hand in his pocket, but as Evi pulled the key from the ignition, Joel opened her door. Before she could move, Joel lowered himself to one knee, looked up into the blue eyes of the lovely lady before him and reached for her hand.

"Evi, love, I truly love you. I know we haven't known each other a long time, but could you in time be able to love me?"

Evi pulled her hand from Joel's, threw her arms around his neck and exclaimed, "Joel, I love you with all my heart! Yes, oh, yes, I love you!"

Pulling his hand from his pocket, Joel held a ring with a lovely emerald stone and many diamond chips around it, up for her to see. Barely above a whisper, Joel said, "I know this isn't a diamond, but Mary Lawson, my dad's mom gave me her mother's engagement ring not long ago, saying she was sure I could use it before she could. Darling, would you wear it for me, lovely Evi? Would you wear it as my pledge to you to love you always?"

Evi gasped. "Joel! It's beautiful! I'd be honored to wear it. Always? Forever!"

Tears ran down Evi's cheeks as Joel slid the beautiful ring on her left hand, but then he stood to his feet and pulled her from the car into his arms. There on the parking lot, in the cold of December, their warm lips met and sealed their pledge.

Joel had stayed the course.

Lightning Source UK Ltd.
Milton Keynes UK
UKHW041829091120
373110UK00001B/2